Praise for the Amanda Doucette Mysteries

A high-adrenaline [   ] aters

— Pu T0155107

A great evocation of the lakes, the beauty and the power ... Amanda Doucette
is somebody I'd like for a friend.
— *Maureen Jennings, author of The Murdoch Mysteries*

Masterly ... it's the wilderness that provides the story's passion.
— *Toronto Star*

Fradkin populates her series with real people whose lives encompass more
than solving the odd crime. Keep 'em coming.
— *Booklist*

A simply riveting read from first page to last by a master of the genre.
— *Midwest Book Review*

Readers of Tana French and Deborah Crombie may want to investigate.
— *Library Journal*

Fradkin's forte is the emotional cost of crime.
— *Ottawa Citizen*

If you want to get a real feel (and fear) of the woods, this is the book for you.
— *Globe and Mail*

A terrific read.
— *Winnipeg Free Press*

THE
ANCIENT
DEAD

Amanda Doucette Mysteries

THE ANCIENT DEAD

An Amanda Doucette Mystery

Barbara Fradkin

DUNDURN
TORONTO

Copyright © Barbara Fradkin, 2021

All rights reserved. No part of this publication may be reproduced, stored in a retrieval system, or transmitted in any form or by any means, electronic, mechanical, photocopying, recording, or otherwise (except for brief passages for purpose of review) without the prior permission of Dundurn Press. Permission to photocopy should be requested from Access Copyright.

All characters in this work are fictitious. Any resemblance to real persons, living or dead, is purely coincidental.

Publisher and acquiring editor: Scott Fraser | Editor: Allister Thompson
Cover designer: Laura Boyle
Cover image credit: shutterstock.com/Pictureguy
Printer: Marquis Book Printing Inc.

Library and Archives Canada Cataloguing in Publication

Title: The ancient dead / Barbara Fradkin.
Names: Fradkin, Barbara, 1947- author.
Description: Series statement: An Amanda Doucette mystery
Identifiers: Canadiana (print) 20200176781 | Canadiana (ebook) 2020017679X | ISBN 9781459743816 (softcover) | ISBN 9781459743823 (PDF) | ISBN 9781459743830 (EPUB)
Classification: LCC PS8561.R233 A53 2020 | DDC C813/.6—dc23

We acknowledge the support of the Canada Council for the Arts and the Ontario Arts Council for our publishing program. We also acknowledge the financial support of the Government of Ontario, through the Ontario Book Publishing Tax Credit and Ontario Creates, and the Government of Canada.

Care has been taken to trace the ownership of copyright material used in this book. The author and the publisher welcome any information enabling them to rectify any references or credits in subsequent editions.

The publisher is not responsible for websites or their content unless they are owned by the publisher.

Printed and bound in Canada.

VISIT US AT

 dundurn.com | @dundurnpress | 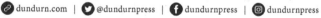 dundurnpress | dundurnpress

Dundurn
3 Church Street, Suite 500
Toronto, Ontario, Canada
M5E 1M2

To my family, and to the ties that bind us close

The rains of ages have laid bare
The ancient dead once buried there,
Far, far below in limestone vault.
— Charles H. Sternberg,
"A Story of the Past," 1911

CHAPTER ONE

Beneath the dry, cracked soil, the tufts of sage and prairie wool, lay the graveyard of the ancient dead. Even after weeks of exploring the open range, Todd Ellison still shivered at the thought, as if ghosts were walking at his side. The sun blazed in the cloudless blue sky and a fitful wind billowed in from the west, swirling dust in its path. After a relentlessly dry summer, the land was parched.

The weather was still hot in late August, but Todd had packed a pullover and windbreaker in his backpack. This was Alberta, after all. Full of surprises.

He tilted his cowboy hat back and turned in place to take stock. The rolling grassland seemed to stretch on forever, broken only by a scattering of Hereford cattle, occasional clumps of trees and farms, and an oil derrick bobbing lazily against the distant horizon. His backpack stuck to his sweaty back as he pulled it around to get at his water bottle and binoculars. He needed shade and rest. According to his GPS, he was not far from a coulee, which carved a deep crevice through the ancient sandstone.

Coulees promised the shade of bushes and outcrops, but more importantly, they were where some of the best secrets lay.

He trained his binoculars toward the eastern horizon, where a smudge of grey humps suggested the edge of the coulee. Nearer still was the slumping shape of an old outbuilding.

Exactly what he'd been looking for! After a quick swig of water, he looped his camera around his neck and slipped his pack into place. With a fresh burst of energy, he started forward, picking his way through the sage and keeping an eye open for the vicious spikes of cactuses.

The wind blew in gusts against his back, tugging at the dry grass and driving fine sand into his eyes. His hiking boot struck something hard. He parted the grass to reveal a smooth stone partially buried in the soil. A quick search revealed other stones arranged in a circle about twelve feet across. Excited, he photographed them, taking care to capture the iridescent oranges and greens of the lichen and the sharp shadows of the sage. Once, the Blackfoot had roamed unhindered across this prairie, hunting buffalo, but now these occasional stone circles were all that remained of their camps and tepees. The stones would make a spectacular photograph for his book.

Closer to the outbuilding, a pair of craggy grey posts poked up out of the grass, and soon he could distinguish bits of rusty barbed wire still clinging to their sides, remnants of a long abandoned fence put up by a farmer or rancher in earlier times. Todd nudged his boot into the soil, which was too dry and sandy even for grazing here. Like the stone circles, the fence posts were testament to long-dead dreams. A title for his photographic history book was beginning to take shape: *Ghosts of the Ancient Dead.*

Snapping photos, he walked around the posts and adjusted settings and filters as he knelt to highlight them against the sun. Subtle hues of lichen glistened in the light. He studied the effects on the screen and smiled. This was going to be good.

As he drew nearer, details of the outbuilding took shape. Barely fifteen feet square, it listed badly as if weary of its battle against the relentless wind. Its sun-bleached walls still propped one another up, but its roof had long since fallen inside. The door hung open, creaking in the wind, its wooden hinges and bolt splintered as if someone had tried to break it down. Holes gaped where the two small windows had been. Todd peered inside. All but a few primitive furnishings had been scavenged, but a willow sapling was flourishing in the relative cool of the shade.

After taking dozens of photos outside, Todd bent his head to squeeze his six-foot frame through the door and adjusted his camera to capture the gloom. He noted the scorch pattern on the wall where the woodstove must have been, the nails in the walls where the few clothes and implements would have hung, and the single shelf on which sat some chipped cups and an empty whisky bottle caked in dust and oddly out of place. A message had been carved into the wall next to the window. He leaned in to photograph it. It was barely legible, and he blew the sand out of the cracks. A horizontal line, and next to it *Snow, March 1907.*

More ghosts. Todd smiled as he photographed it, documenting history. In March 1907, some poor beleaguered pioneer must have been nearly buried in a spring blizzard that had blown in from the Rockies. He had probably been forced to crawl out through the window. Todd wondered whether he'd been alone or whether he'd had to rescue his entire family from the storm. A trip to the local archives or land registry should tell him the identity and fate of the settler who'd once tried to survive on this land.

He retreated back outside to look for more clues about their early life. There was almost nothing left except a nail keg and a broken sleigh runner. He dictated his impressions into his phone. First impressions and a dose of imagination made for powerful reading.

Afterward, he checked his watch, mindful that he had to retrace his steps to the range road before nightfall. In August, the days were already getting shorter and the nights cooler. But it was just past two o'clock, still plenty of time to reach the coulee. The best pictures would be there, amid the old cottonwoods, the ripples of eroded, multilayered rock, and the curving shadows of light. With any luck, maybe even a dinosaur bone or two.

He came upon the coulee quite unexpectedly as the prairie floor fell into a yawning crevice of barren hills and steep slopes down to the ancient riverbed. In the spring, snow melt would tumble down through the gully into the Red Deer River farther east, washing silt and debris with it, but in late August, the riverbed was dry. Willows and gnarled cottonwood trees clustered along the shoreline to sap the last drops of water from the parched soil. The v-shaped valley snaked ahead into the distance, forming an eerie moonscape of colours and shapes.

The wind picked up as it swept through the gully, racing over the barren hills and tearing at the bushes nestled in the crevices. Tufts of sagebrush and prairie grass clung to the desolate southern slopes, but hardy green and gold bushes grew in the lee of the north-facing hills. Todd picked his descent carefully down a crevice through sandstone and popcorn rock that crumbled underfoot, dislodging cascades of debris. Amid the debris, rocks and pebbles glinted in the sunlight. He bent to pick them up, looking for bits of ancient shellfish, seeds, and bones, imprints of leaves and flowers, the ancient dead from a time millions of years ago when this had been a swampy, inland sea teeming with life.

As he walked along the sandy riverbed, he scoured the banks for larger fossils. Dinosaurs had walked these marshy shores seventy million years ago, and these Alberta plains had one of the richest collections of dinosaur bones in the world. Fossil hunters had been excavating bones for over a century, but new finds were still being made. A well-preserved dinosaur bone would be the highlight of his book, and if it were a new species, it might even be named after him. Ellisonsaurus!

THE ANCIENT DEAD

He photographed as he walked, focussing first on the expansive vista of sunlight playing over the striated hills and on the comical silhouettes of hoodoos. Nature's sandstone sculptures loomed like caped sentinels over the valley, their stone caps perched precariously on their heads. Then he switched lenses to capture the tiny fossil fragments that had washed down from the valley walls. The afternoon sun baked the stone, turning the valley into an oven. The wind evaporated the sweat from his face as soon as it formed, and before he noticed, he was parched. A wave of dizziness swept over him. Quickly, he pulled out his thermos and headed for the shade of an ironstone overhang.

He sat on the sand below the overhang, took off his hat, and drank a deep, grateful gulp of water. Then he rubbed his wet hands over his face and poured a little water over his head. The dizziness had passed, but he decided to wait awhile before venturing out into the sun again. He ran his hands through the rough sand and shale, letting it trickle through his fingers.

His fingers struck a hard stone. Curious, he brushed the sand away to uncover a polished round knob bleached grey with time. He tried to pry it loose, thinking it was a rock, but it wouldn't budge. He dug more sand away, revealing a thin grey shaft.

He sucked in his breath. He traced his hands along the hard, pitted shaft, and his heart beat faster. Could it be? The answer to his wildest hope?

Amanda Doucette peered out the side window of the rented Ford SUV. Grey and amber fields stretched to the distant horizon. "Man, it's empty!"

Chris Tymko smiled as he accelerated past a lumbering transport truck. Their SUV was more than two thousand kilograms of steel, muscle, and high-tech gadgetry. Compared to her nimble Kawasaki motorcycle, it was a behemoth, and she had nicknamed it the Hulk. But Chris loved it. He drove it with the casual confidence of a cop, one hand on the wheel and the other propped on the open windowsill. His leather cowboy hat was tilted low against the sun, and behind his large sunglasses, his expression was serene. He'd had that look ever since they'd embarked on their prairie odyssey.

"This is home," he'd simply said.

They were driving west on the Trans-Canada, a divided four-lane highway that angled northwest across the Alberta prairie toward the Rockies. Once they'd left the outskirts of Medicine Hat, the highway was almost empty as it passed through acres and acres of open range. There was nothing to see but cattle and a scattering of oil derricks and grain bins. Amanda chafed.

"Let's get off this highway." She peered at the faint lines on her phone map. "Let's take back country roads up to Drumheller through some of these little towns so we can see what real rural Alberta looks like."

He chuckled. "This is it. At this time of year, with the grain ripening, there's also a patchwork of golds and greens. But it's all fields."

"Still …" They caught up with another transport truck, and Amanda peered inside at the cattle in the trailer. "Headed toward the slaughterhouse?"

He shrugged. "Welcome to real rural Alberta."

"Okay," she muttered, humbled. "But we aren't meeting the people from the Royal Tyrrell Museum until tomorrow, so we've got lots of time to poke around the back roads and see what Alberta's famous farm and ranch country looks like."

He lowered the Hulk's visor against the glare of the late afternoon sun before glancing at her. "Pretty much like the

Saskatchewan farm country we drove through earlier. Fifteen minutes is all you'll need."

"I'll take it. Maybe we can find a place to stretch our legs. Kaylee could use a walk."

The dog had been fast asleep on the console between them, her head resting on her paws as if even she was bored with the monotony. At the word *walk*, her head shot up.

Chris laughed. "Okay, I give up."

"Oh, so you won't listen to me, but you listen to her!"

He shifted his hand to caress her thigh. "I'm just in a hurry to find a place to stay in Drumheller. Four days in the spare bedroom of my parents' tiny condo sure put a damper on our sex life."

She caught his roving hand. "Eyes on the road, Corporal. Behave. Who knows, maybe we can find an old-fashioned road-side motel in one of these little villages."

She turned her attention to her phone GPS and directed him to take the next side road north. After a few hundred metres, the paved road gave way to a flat, straight arrow of gravel flanked on one side by wheat fields that rippled in the afternoon breeze. She studied the rolling vista. Far into the distance, the land shone amber in the sinking sun. Huge sprinkler systems stretched across the fields like giant centipedes, and round bales of hay lay ready for collection. Some homesteads were a cluster of aban doned buildings surrounded by overgrown brush, but most were modern and prosperous, with sheltering clumps of trees, shiny grain bins, and expensive farm equipment.

On the other side of the road, however, the stubby grass and weeds were withered to brown and grey, and only a few dozen head of cattle ranged in the distance.

"Wow, what a difference!" she said.

He nodded. "One side is just used as pasture and maybe some dryland farming. The other side is irrigated. By this time of year, sometimes there hasn't been any rain in three months. Before irrigation, farmers lived on the edge of bankruptcy half the time."

"Where does the water come from?"

"From the Bow River, through a system of canals and pipes."

"What a lot of water they must use to irrigate all this!"

His brow furrowed in faint irritation. "Easy for you to say, coming from Ontario. You have endless lakes and rivers, and it's green everywhere. This is a very different reality, but this prairie feeds a lot of our country."

She fell silent. He was right. Who was she to judge? She was here to explore, to learn, to understand, and ultimately to finalize her next Fun for Families tour: an educational adventure for high school students from a couple of remote Northern Alberta towns. Their area had been hard hit the previous summer by wildfires that had ravaged their lands and wreaked havoc with their livelihood. With the catchy title *Time Travel*, she hoped the weeklong adventure would give the students a glimpse into life in Southern Alberta through the ages, from the dinosaurs to the First Nations to the early ranchers and settlers. But in order to instil some love of this bleak, big sky landscape in their hearts, she first had to find it in hers.

Although Chris had been posted in the north and more recently in Newfoundland, he had grown up on a Southern Saskatchewan farm. This past week had shown her that he loved the vast blue sky and the golden seas of wheat as much as she loved the sparkling lakes and rolling green hills of her own Ontario home. Canada was a jewel with many facets, and every one deserved its share of light.

At the end of a long lane up ahead, she spotted a cluster of gnarled old trees surrounding a small homestead. As they approached, she saw the little saltbox house was long abandoned.

The steep roof had lost half its shingles and the porch across the front had faded to flaking grey. It sat amid dust and dried weeds that passed for a yard. To one side was a collection of equally decrepit sheds and barns, a corral, and a field of rusting tractors, ploughs, and trucks of 1970s vintage. Adjacent to the barn were two round, rusty grain bins.

Behind those, the remnants of a rutted track led out into an empty field.

"This place looks deserted. Maybe we can park in here and take Kaylee for a walk out across that field."

He nodded as he pulled into the lane. A faded *For Sale* sign lay blown over at the entrance. Amanda wondered how long it had been there, forlorn and forgotten like the house.

Chris jackknifed his tall frame out of the Hulk and stretched his back with a groan before tipping his hat back and strolling over to peer through the only window that wasn't boarded up. As she watched him, an old memory stirred. Where had she seen that image before? In a picture frame somewhere. An old orange-tinged photo of a farm like this, set against a barren field as grey and flat as an ocean. The sunlight had cast sharp shadows across the figure of a young man leaning against a fencepost, his cowboy hat tipped back at a saucy angle.

She riffled though her memory. She'd seen the photo in the Laurentian cottage she rented from her Aunt Jean. When her aunt was home from assignment, she used it as her touchstone in Canada, and the tiny, rustic place was stuffed with mementoes from her sojourns in remote lands. The photo had been in a wooden frame on the wall above her bed, among pictures of the Great Wall of China and of candles floating on the Ganges. Amanda had assumed it was taken on some plain she'd passed through, perhaps in Mongolia or Russia. One dry plain could look much like another.

But now she wondered at the similarities. The windswept field, the saltbox cabin, the outbuildings, grain bins, and corral. Even the cowboy hat. Where had that photo been taken? And more important, why had her Aunt Jean kept it framed on her wall among iconic world-class scenes for all these years?

CHAPTER TWO

Amanda spotted the sign for Maeve's B&B almost by chance as they were driving through a tiny village comprised of a handful of streets, an abandoned gas station, a post office, a realtor, and an all-purpose general store. Like the village, the B&B looked as if it had been around since before the First World War and had endured a century of gale-force winds. It had a curling gabled roof and a sagging wraparound veranda cluttered with potted plants and aging wicker chairs. There was little sign of life, but an eighties Chevy truck was parked out front and a *Welcome, Come in!* sign hung on the door, so Chris and Amanda decided to risk it.

Once Amanda's eyes adjusted to the dim interior, she could see the room was stuffed with antique knickknacks and mismatched furniture. Grainy black-and-white photos of farm scenes covered the walls. A little bell had rung when they opened the door, but it was several minutes before Amanda heard footsteps shuffling down the hall. She was expecting a little old lady huddled under crocheted wraps, but although the woman who finally appeared looked at least eighty and had a face like a dried prune, she was dressed in blue jeans and a faded sweatshirt with *John Deere* stencilled on the front. Amanda assumed this was Maeve.

The woman's blue eyes twinkled with amused disbelief. "You're wanting a room?"

Amanda looked around doubtfully. "Are you still open?"

"Sometimes, if I like the looks of you," she said as she rummaged around in the battered antique desk for her record book. "Not too much traffic comes through here these days, but fifty years ago, believe it or not, this village was a beehive of prosperity. We had stores, a dance hall, and a drive-in theatre. It serviced the whole surrounding farming community. Now folks hop in their truck and drive to Calgary, the Hat, or the big-box stores in Drumheller. That where you're headed?"

Amanda nodded. "We're here for a day or two to do some business at the museum." She didn't feel like elaborating. She just wanted a comfortable bed for the night and was beginning to doubt she'd get that here. There was a pervasive smell of old dust that tickled her nose. Maeve was now hunting for her record book in a bookcase overflowing with tattered paperbacks.

"Most of my business now is people visiting the dinosaur museum and the park," she said, pushing her grey hair out of her eyes. She grinned as she pulled out a book. "Ah-ha! I guess I'm a bit of a dinosaur myself. Eighty bucks a night. How many nights did you say?"

"Probably one. It depends how our meetings go." To change the subject, Amanda gestured down the road. "We were just out for a walk on a farm near here. It looked abandoned."

"Yeah, lots of the small homesteads are closed up around here. Damn hard life, broke many a family that settled here in the old days. If the drought and the winters didn't kill you, the grasshoppers and sandstorms did. But nowadays it's big business, eh? You need a big spread and lots of fancy equipment. So lots of folks sold their land to the Hutterites or the big agro companies and moved to the city. That's progress." Maeve peered past them out the front window and spotted Kaylee perched in the driver's seat, watching them intently. She nodded. "Your driver coming in with you?"

"I hope that's all right," Amanda said. "She's very well behaved and will sleep on the floor." A blatant lie, she knew, but she'd packed blankets to protect the beds and sofas.

Maeve hooted. "No dog worth its salt sleeps on the floor when the owner's not looking. I don't mind. Pretty dog. Golden?"

"She's a Nova Scotia Duck Tolling Retriever. A ridiculously long name that no one remembers. Duck Toller for short."

"She good for hunting?"

Amanda sidestepped possible controversy with practiced ease. "They're up for anything."

"And too smart for their own good sometimes," Chris added.

"Well, there are some nice tracks you can walk on, out back. It's leased lands, and the farmers are miles away. As long as she doesn't herd cattle, you'll be fine." Maeve handed an old-fashioned key across the desk. It was attached to a heavy wooden shape that formed a stylized *MW*. "I gave you the room downstairs so you can enjoy the patio. It's at the end of the hall there. The key is stubborn — like pretty much everything around here —" she gave a sharp, barking laugh "— so just fight with it."

Chris parked the SUV at the edge of the gravel lot beside colourful flowerbeds overrun with day lilies and summer phlox. Kaylee bounded through the front door, raced around smelling every corner, and made fast friends with Maeve before scampering down the hall in search of toys.

Once they'd wrestled their door open, they spilled into the darkened interior. Like the main hall, the room was stuffed with furniture from decades ago: a threadbare couch, an old-fashioned poster bed covered in a flowery quilt, an antique chest of drawers and matching dressing table, and a braided rag rug of indeterminate colours on the floor.

The place smelled of must, and Amanda wondered when the last customer had occupied it. She fought open the window to allow the prairie wind to blow through the lace curtains.

Chris sat on the bed and laughed. "Wow."

"That bad?"

"On our first romantic night."

"We won't even notice." She sat beside him. Bounced. "Hmm ..."

Kaylee was busy snuffling in corners, as if checking out all the critters that had passed through. Amanda hoped there were none still in residence. She took the dog bowl and filled it with water.

"We'll have to ask Maeve where we can eat around here," she said.

"We might have to go into Drumheller."

As it turned out, Maeve jumped at the chance to barbeque them some burgers. Amanda suspected she hadn't talked to a soul in days and relished the company. The smell of smoke and seared meat still triggered frightening memories, but her hunger won out. She did give passing thought to how long the burgers had been hiding in her freezer, but the meal was surprisingly tasty. Maeve served it with a couple of craft beers from her fridge and fresh vegetables from her garden.

"I live in the back here," she explained as she served the food in a vintage gazebo behind the house. "This was my family's farm house, and I moved it to town when I sold the farm."

After dinner, Chris and Amanda returned to sit on the patio behind their room. Decades earlier, trees and gardens had been planted to create a lush oasis in the dry, empty landscape. Maeve kept them lovingly tended. Overhead, the violet shimmer of twilight was sprinkled with early stars, and in the distance a lingering smudge of coral marked the western horizon.

The quiet was broken by the symphony of crickets and other creatures that came awake at night. Amanda took a deep breath, feeling small in the vastness. In that moment, the years of hardship slipped away. She was no longer a battle-scarred, thirty-something aid worker but instead a little girl on the brink of new discovery, her freckled face upturned and her blue eyes wide with wonder.

She undid her ponytail and shook her chestnut hair free around her shoulders. Could this moment be any more idyllic? Was it real? Was she truly here, far from the gunfire, acrid smoke, and terrified screams of Nigeria, revelling in the quiet company of a perfect man?

Chris propped his huge feet on the wicker coffee table and caught her fingers in his. "Do you have anything you need to do tonight to get ready for your museum visit tomorrow?"

His tone was hopeful. She smiled and caressed his palm with her thumb. "No, but I think I'll give my Aunt Jean a quick call."

"Why?"

"Just curious."

He knew her well enough not to argue. *Just curious* meant full steam ahead until she had answered the questions on her mind. He was silent as she pulled out her phone, but when she began to dial, he unfolded himself and stood up. He drew his finger down her cheek and bent to whisper in her ear. "I'll meet you in the shower."

Amanda's Aunt Jean was a busy woman who lived alone and answered to no one. She travelled around the world on an obscure job that she had never fully explained. *Consultant*, she'd mutter when pressed, but she was so secretive that Amanda had often wondered if she was a spy. It was an amusing fantasy. Jean would have made a good spy. No family entanglements, a modest cottage in Quebec's Laurentian mountains far from neighbours and prying eyes, a sharp intelligence, and a memory that rivalled an elephant's. She was a woman of few words but had a knack for getting others to babble on foolishly to fill the silence. If Aunt Jean had any opinions, she kept them well hidden.

She couldn't have been more different from her older sister, Amanda's mother, who threw herself into causes with a noisy passion that brooked no opposition. Ever since she'd developed a taste for protest as a young high school student in the dying days of the Vietnam War, she'd drafted petitions, organized rallies, and marched with placards against every evil mankind could perpetrate. Against nuclear weapons, against famine and drought, against corrupt dictators propped up by American corporate interests, and most recently against oil pipelines and the systemic abuse of Indigenous rights.

She was a senior tenured professor at Carleton University in Ottawa, trained in biology but having made a smooth transition into ecology and environmental science. In her view, we were ruining our world and running out of time to fix it. From the safety of her academic ivory tower, she wrote powerful essays and contributed to worthy causes around the world. She was vocal, deeply committed, and judgmental as hell. How the two women could have emerged from the same gene pool was a mystery to Amanda.

Perhaps that was why Aunt Jean kept all her opinions to herself.

Amanda expected her aunt to be off on some clandestine jaunt across the globe and was surprised when she actually answered her phone. Amanda had barely managed a few words of obligatory social preamble before Jean cut her off.

"Nice to hear from you too, Amanda. Why are you calling?"

Amanda dropped the chitchat. "Have you ever been to southern Alberta?"

"No. Why?"

"There's a framed photograph on your bedroom wall of an old house in a field. Now that I'm here, I see a resemblance. The same kind of outbuildings, the same flat land."

When Jean said nothing to help her along, Amanda pressed on. "The similarity is quite striking, so I wondered."

"Wondered what?"

"If the photo was taken out here in Alberta."

More silence.

"Do you know the photo I mean? The one over your bed, along with the Great Wall and the Ganges at sunset."

"Yes, I know the photo you mean. It could have been taken anywhere in the prairies. A friend sent it to me years ago. I liked the moodiness, so I framed it. That's all."

It was an unusually long speech for Jean, which piqued Amanda's curiosity further. As far as Amanda knew, Jean had few friends, at least that the family had ever met. As long as Amanda could remember, she'd always been a dour semi-recluse, but what did Amanda know about what she was like as a young woman? She tried to remember the man in the photo. He'd been smiling at the camera, his cowboy hat tipped back at a saucy angle and his dark hair curling over his open collar. The image stirred a vague memory of playful chase, as if Amanda had met him as a young child.

Had there been a man in Jean's life all those years ago?

"What happened to this friend?" Amanda asked. "Maybe I could look him up."

"I don't know why you would."

"Well …" Amanda cast about. "I'm always on the lookout for local contacts."

Jean grunted. "I have no idea where he is. We lost touch years ago."

"Maybe —"

"And frankly, I don't want to discuss it further."

Aunt Jean's tone conveyed its usual no-nonsense clip, but there was a chill that hinted at more.

"Was it a family friend? Would my parents know him too?"

"Ancient history. And don't go asking your mother about it either."

Jean ended the phone call abruptly after that, leaving Amanda more curious than ever. Her family was a maze of barriers erected between each other to avoid conflict and shut down intimacy. Amanda herself was no different. She talked to her parents a few times a year and saw them only at holiday dinners. She shared little with her father, who'd long learned to keep his head in the clouds, and kept her mother to safe topics. As for her brother, who now ran a business in China, she felt as if they were barely related.

She knew other families had no such walls. The families she met through her work overseas might have lived in huts or shantytowns, but their lives were nonetheless filled with warmth and chatter. Chris's family had shown her more warmth and enthusiasm in the four days she'd spent with them than her own family did in a year.

It irked her that this photo had provided a glimpse into the life of her aunt as a young woman, maybe full of hope and vulnerability, only to have the door to her dreams slammed shut.

Yet the door had clearly been slammed shut, and Amanda had no excuse to pry it back open. No reason to go searching for an old friend who'd possibly broken her aunt's heart years ago. *It's best to get on with taking care of your own life, Amanda*, she told herself as she went back inside to where Chris was waiting.

CHAPTER THREE

The bone kept Todd from sleeping and haunted his dreams once he finally drifted off at three in the morning. He shouldn't have left it where it was. The mounds and hills in the coulee looked so much alike that he wondered how he would ever find it again.

His reasoning had seemed solid the day before when the deep shadows of the sinking sun were creeping across the valley. He hadn't brought the tools to dig it up without damaging it. If it were as fragile and brittle as dinosaur bones usually were, it would crumble in his hands. By the time he'd dug it out, darkness would have fallen. Night on the prairie was blacker than pitch and impossible to navigate without a light. He could get hopelessly lost and stumble down another unseen coulee.

Moreover, although people were allowed to pick up any bone or fossil lying on the ground, it was illegal to excavate them anywhere in Alberta. If he were caught digging it up, he'd face a fine of up to fifty thousand dollars.

But now, at three o'clock in the morning, the voices of dissent were strong. The bone had not felt fragile. It could probably have been pulled out with one good tug, and that wasn't really excavating, was it? In any case, the chances of it being a dinosaur bone were slim. Lots of creatures had died in the Alberta badlands over the millennia. The prairie was littered with the bones of the buffalo driven to their deaths over the edge of cliffs or shot as they charged across the open range. After them, there were cattle that had starved or frozen to death during the unexpectedly brutal winters, horses that had fallen in their tracks from exhaustion. Even settlers themselves who'd been caught in a blizzard or fallen into an unseen abyss. Coyotes, antelope, and deer had all lived and died on the plains as well.

Todd thought of his daughter, Kristy. After her school visit to the Royal Tyrrell Museum, she had chattered endlessly about the huge dinosaur skeletons she saw. About how big their heads were and how scary their teeth. She'd wanted him to take her fossil-hunting so she could find one in the wild.

"The lady said they're everywhere, Daddy!" she'd exclaimed. "I could put it in my room. You could build a special shelf!"

She might be even more eager to visit him if she had a dinosaur bone in the little room he'd set up for her. Hardly more than a closet, really, not nearly as big as the room at her mother's house. But freelance writers and photographers didn't make the money that her stepfather did at the gas company. Todd was proud to own his little house, but seen through the eyes of a nine-year-old used to her own en suite bathroom, it was pretty pathetic.

On the other hand, you moron, said the dark, inner voice of 3:00 a.m., *it might not be a dinosaur bone at all. What do you know about bones?*

The solution came to him in the clarity of morning. He'd taken photos of the bone before he left, improvising with his shoe for scale. He could ask someone else to look at them, someone who'd seen more bones than him and who wouldn't laugh at his ignorance or steal the glory.

Although Todd had grown up in the area, he didn't have many friends left. He'd moved to British Columbia for university without a backward glance twenty years ago, and many of his childhood friends had also left for jobs in the city. They probably couldn't tell a stegosaurus bone from a deer bone any better than him.

But Derek Potter's father still owned a ranch not far away, and Derek had grown up on the range, rounding up cattle, fixing fences, and watching out for coyotes. Rumour had it he'd once shot the cap off a bottle of beer at fifty yards. He'd grown up some since then and now had a wife and three kids, but he lived in Drumheller. More importantly, he was still a hunter. He should know his bones.

Derek sounded a bit surprised to hear from him, especially at eight in the morning, because they hadn't see each other often since their lives had taken different paths. But the hint of mystery and the promise of a case of beer sold him on a meeting that afternoon after work.

Four o'clock couldn't come soon enough, but Todd managed to keep himself busy editing yesterday's photographs, writing some copy to accompany them, and enhancing the pictures of the bone. At three thirty, he tossed his equipment into his truck and set off to Drumheller.

The Town of Drumheller had started its life as a rough and brawling coal mining town, but now, thanks to the world famous museum, it was all things dinosaur. The streets had been renamed for dinosaurs, and comical dinosaur statues greeted visitors on every street corner. Todd drove through town and up the Red Deer River valley to the suburban neighbourhood where Derek had just bought a house. It was nestled on the lush flood plain by the river, but the stark grey hills of the badlands loomed up on either side.

Todd pushed aside a twinge of envy. He could have had the well-paying job and the house in the suburbs, but instead he had his freedom, his camera, and a draughty old bungalow bought in a fire sale. It had been his choice.

Sitting beside Derek in his gleaming, open-concept kitchen, Todd felt like even more of a loser. Derek sported the latest in men's hairstyles — shaved sides and slicked-back top — as well as tattoos covering much of his visible skin. Todd had lank brown hair that stuck out over his collar, badly in need of a trim, and he had only dared to get one tattoo, a modest image of a wild rose on his left shoulder.

Derek scrolled through the photos and only took two minutes before he shook his head. "Not a dinosaur, for sure. Wrong colour. Dinosaur bones look like rocks — reddish brown or black — because they've turned to stone. Sorry to disappoint you, buddy. It would have been a cool find."

Todd's heart sank. "But it looks old. Cracked and eroded."

"Yeah, it's been there a while. But not seventy million years."

Todd sighed. "Okay. So what do you figure it is? It looks like a pretty big animal."

"I'd say it's the top of a femur, where it fits into the hip socket. You'd have to dig out the rest of it to see how long it is. Could be a deer or antelope, could even be a young steer, although it's probably too small." Derek disappeared and returned with his laptop. A moment later he was searching images of large animal femurs. "Hmm. Too big for an antelope. Might be a deer buck."

"What about a buffalo?" Todd asked, thinking maybe he could salvage an interesting story out of this find. The buffalo were legends of the ancient prairie; millions of them had once roamed free across the plains, but they had been hunted almost to extinction a hundred and fifty years ago. A buffalo bone would fit perfectly with his book's theme of the ancient dead.

"Bison," Derek corrected. Todd bit back a retort. "I've never seen a bison skeleton, but they're big-ass bastards. Way bigger than this." Derek clicked through some more links. "Could even be human, you know."

He'd said it lightly, but a chill shot through Todd. He thought about how he had run his hand over it and poked his finger into its eroded end. "Can you tell?"

Derek was reading on his laptop, his expression tense as he shifted his gaze back and forth to study the bone. Eventually, he shook his head. "Not without seeing the rest of the bone. We need an anthropologist or palaeontologist. Cops use them all the time to check out unknown remains."

"That sounds like a lot of trouble for a plain old bone," Todd said. "We'd look pretty dumb if it was just a deer that fell in the coulee." He was already imagining the accusing eyes of the RCMP. "Besides, don't they always suspect the guy who found the body? 'What were you doing here? What made you think it was a human bone?'"

Derek was grinning, his good humour back. He closed his laptop and stood up. "Well, the only way to know for sure is to go dig up some more of it. Or you could leave it there and let someone else find it."

Todd stared at the photo. What were the odds? How many people wandered through the open rangeland or trekked through the barren, inhospitable badlands? How many died and were never found, compared to the thousands of animals who had passed through the coulees over the centuries?

But could he stand not knowing? Would the bone continue to haunt him?

"No, let's dig it up," he said. "Let's see what other bones are there."

The experience at the Royal Tyrrell Museum went beyond Amanda's highest hopes. From the moment they drove up through the surrounding desolate badlands toward the sprawling, modern building, the mood had been set. Although the number of exhibits and the amount of factual detail were overwhelming, the layout and lighting made it feel like a spooky journey back in time. In some rooms, life-sized replicas of ancient marine animals hung from the ceiling, while in another a massive Albertosaurus loomed poised to strike. Hands-on programs, films, and prospecting hikes out into the badlands all offered plenty of variety to keep restless teenagers enthralled.

She spent most of the day with museum staff, touring the facility and hammering out the optimal program. She had planned a seven-day prairie adventure for the students, who came from remote villages in Northern Alberta's Peace River area, home to streams, lakes, and untouched boreal forest. Apart from occasional day trips south to Edmonton for educational or medical purposes, their knowledge of the outside word was limited to the pervasive culture of the Internet and television, both far removed from the future offered in their villages. As they prepared to think beyond high school graduation to jobs or college, Amanda wanted to ground them in their history and offer them a glimpse into some of the magic possibilities just beyond their doorstep.

She was planning a packed, fast-paced itinerary, with some days of trail riding, fossil prospecting, and ranching as well as visits to ancient sites. After speaking to the museum staff, she realized how vast and diverse the province was and what a challenge she had before her.

"I started off just wanting to give them a glimpse of southern Alberta life, but there's so much to see! A week will just skim the surface! I need at least ten days."

Chris had spent the day hiking the surrounding badlands, and now he smiled at her as they drove away. "You know," he said drily. "If they're like most kids from small towns, they'd probably prefer a trip to Disney World."

Amanda rolled her eyes. "Disney World is the ultimate fantasy land. I want these kids to experience the magic in their real world. Give them a glimpse of a life that is actually within their reach."

As they turned into the gravel lane of their B&B, she spotted Maeve playing ball with Kaylee in the garden. The dog raced out to greet them while Maeve hobbled along behind.

"Have you got an extra arm I can borrow?"

Amanda laughed as she ruffled the dog's fur. "Kaylee's motto is there's a sucker born every minute."

Maeve sank into a lawn chair. "I need a drink. Join me for a beer?"

Chris reached behind the seat in the truck for a plastic bag. "I'm already ahead of you, Maeve." He glanced around the empty parking lot. "No other guests today?"

Maeve grabbed the beer and waved the other hand dismissively. "I sent them away. I didn't feel like cleaning today."

Amanda saw Kaylee's bright, hopeful eyes and the golden glow of the sun peeking through the cottonwoods. "I'll just take Kaylee for a quick walk and then join you."

She tucked her phone into her pocket, picked up the leash, and headed out past the gardens into the fields behind the B&B. A pattern of golds and browns stretched out before her like a rumpled quilt. On one side, a distant copse made a shelterbelt around a farm compound, and on the other, cattle clustered around a square slough dug into the pasture. Against the gilded horizon, scattered oil derricks drooped their motionless heads like weary donkeys.

Kaylee trotted ahead, her nose to the ground and her red fur burnished in the setting sun. Amanda took a deep breath. And another. The air was clean and cool, and a persistent breeze tugged at her hair. She walked on, lost in the feeling of vastness.

As the daylight faded, leaving only a coral glow to mark land and sky, the first stars appeared overhead. She felt as if she could reach up to touch them, yet, paradoxically, as if they were infinitely far away. She felt very small. Insignificant. Dwarfed by eternity. She was not a religious person; all her years in the brutal trenches of other people's wars, often religiously inspired, had dispelled all trust in a divine master plan. Out here, however, she could almost sense an awesome power. Not a cosmic plan, not a being, but a power.

As she walked, she revelled in that sense of awe. She was a long way from a god, but she could understand how, through the ages, people had sought and found a sense of the divine in these vast, open places.

The chirp of her phone disrupted her reverie. Was it Chris, wondering whether she'd fallen off the face of the Earth? She was tempted to ignore it, but the magic of the moment was already lost. She pulled out her phone. To her surprise, the text was from Aunt Jean. Short and unembroidered, as always. *Send me a photo of the house you saw.*

She smiled, fully returned to the present, and dialed her aunt's number. After seven rings, as if she'd been fighting with herself, Jean picked up. "You got my text?"

"I did. I don't have a photo but in any case, it wasn't exactly the same house. Just a similar one."

"Similar in what way?"

"The shape of the barn, which had a classic gambrel roof."

"Plenty of barns have those."

"And the old-fashioned house had a porch all across the front ..." Amanda sensed her aunt about to interrupt. "And a row of grain bins and farm equipment."

"I've seen plenty of farms and that describes most of them. Where was it located?"

"Near the village of Duchess."

There was a long pause. Noticing the deepening dusk, Amanda turned back toward the lights of the B&B.

"Does that name ring a bell? It's near Drumheller."

More silence.

"Do you want me to look into this for you? I'm already here. If you scan your photo and email it to me, I can ask around to see if anyone recognizes it. Or him."

"Not necessary."

"What have you got to lose, Aunt Jean? Just a few simple inquiries. Either people around here will know him, or they won't."

"No need to waste your time with nonsense."

Kaylee scampered ahead, and Amanda spotted a lanky figure striding across the darkened field toward her, his flashlight bobbing in the dark. Chris always reminded her of a marionette with elbows and knees flailing in all directions as he moved. Warmth flushed through her. He was not classically handsome, but with his gangly limbs, ski-jump nose, and crinkling blue eyes, he was just quirky enough to be adorable.

"It's not nonsense," she said into the phone. "Do you want me to find this guy or not?"

"No." Aunt Jean's voice firmed up. "He made his choice."

With that parting shot, she hung up. Amanda barely had time to consider that comment before Chris enveloped her in a hug. "I was getting worried."

She slipped her phone into her pocket and stood on tiptoe to give him a teasing kiss. "Thanks for the thought, although it's difficult to get lost in a place where you can see five kilometres in every direction."

"Maeve's got Alberta steaks ready to go on the barbeque."

"Steaks! Oh, boy. This time we have to pay her, though. I don't see how she makes a living out here, especially if she turns people away on a whim."

"She says the place is mostly full in July and August. Sometimes she just takes it easy." He slipped his arm around her. "Nice walk?"

She nestled against him. "Inspirational. It makes me feel so insignificant yet part of something vast."

Kaylee had somehow found a stick of wood among the stalks of grain, and she dropped it hopefully at their feet. Amanda laughed as she threw it. "Kaylee has already found the meaning of her life. I was talking to Aunt Jean. Very curious. She wants to know and doesn't want to know. I think her heart was broken."

He kissed the top of her head. "There could be a lot of reasons she doesn't want to know, some of them not nearly so romantic."

She tilted her head to look up at him. She could see a hint of grimness in the set of his jaw, as if his own imagination had gone to darker places. He was a cop, after all, and had seen as much human depravity as she had, perpetrated not in distant corners of the world but right here on benign home soil, perhaps by the innocuous-looking neighbour next door. She felt a chill. *He made his own choice* did not sound like an act of violence or violation, yet the mere thought of the mystery man was clearly causing her normally sanguine aunt distress.

Perhaps, despite her curiosity, it was best to leave sleeping dogs lie.

Later that night, after a delicious interlude in Chris's arms, Amanda was lying flushed and spread-eagled on the bed, still catching her breath, when her phone chirped.

"Ignore it," Chris murmured, lying at her side. Kaylee had left her perch by the window and had approached the bed, waiting for the invitation to jump up.

Amanda laughed as she leaned over to the night table. "You know me better than that."

THE ANCIENT DEAD

It was a message from her aunt. No words, no name, just a familiar photo of a slim cowboy standing by a farmhouse with his hat shoved back and a sly grin on his lips.

When Amanda called for clarification, no one answered the phone.

CHAPTER FOUR

Todd peered out the window, searching the grey valley wall as they drove along by the Red Deer River. They were using Derek's truck, his own once again in the shop, and towing a trailer with two ATVs.

"I think it should be around here," he said doubtfully. On one side of the highway was the lush green of the river's floodplain, but on the other were the eroded, moon-like hills of the valley wall. Millions of years ago, fierce floodwaters had poured through the valley, carving huge crevices in the soft sand and mud of the ancient seabed and exposing the layers of sediment laid down over millennia.

The grey, hilly landscape all looked the same, like a giant sandbox of castles, moats, turrets, and ramparts. Morning sunlight played off the multicoloured stripes and glistened in the black coal.

Derek scowled. He was driving too slowly for the traffic, which was piling up behind him. An impatient black SUV sat almost on his tailgate. "Didn't you get the GPS coordinates?"

"I didn't think of it," Todd muttered, feeling like an idiot. "And I approached it from up on the mesa, so the view was entirely different."

"Fuck, so this may be a total waste of time!"

"Maybe. It was deeper into the hills. Wait!" He pointed to a side coulee that sliced into the valley wall. "That might be the way in. Pull over!" He studied the distant plateau through his binoculars, trying to identify familiar landmarks on the plain. At first he could only see the tops of a few cattle grazing precariously near the edge, but soon he spotted what could be the top of a broken-down cabin.

Derek pulled the truck onto the gravel shoulder, and together they unloaded the ATVs. Derek had brought some tools from his rock hound days, including a padded bin for transporting their find. They strapped the gear on the backs of the ATVs and set off single file up the rough track into the yawning valley of the coulee. Todd led the way, searching for familiar landmarks. They made slow progress as they navigated over small gullies, around cascades of till, and through clumps of grasses and shrubs that grew in the moist crevices.

The roar of the engines prevented any conversation. After fifteen minutes, Todd stopped as the coulee split into two smaller ones. One had lush grass, suggesting a trickling stream at the base, whereas the other was dry and parched. A hawk soared overhead, but the hoof prints of deer were the only signs of life on the sandy riverbed.

He hesitated. He had lost sight of the cabin perched on the edge of the plain, but he hid his doubt as he pointed to the dry coulee. "I think it's this way."

"Who owns this land?" Derek asked.

"Probably the guy who owns that range up there, but it doesn't matter. No one comes in here but rock hounds and ranchers looking for strays." Todd steered them left along the vague track of the riverbed. All around, the hills pressed in as if the land was swallowing them up. Glacial till streaked the steep hillsides, and the many colours of quartz, granite, and coal sparkled in the sun. Up above, sandstone carved flowing rills down the hillsides.

They drove in silence for a while until Todd felt utterly lost. The sun was heating up the coulee, and he stopped for a drink. "We should have come up on this from the plain. There's a pioneer shed up there that would have been a landmark."

Derek yanked out his own water bottle. "We should have had GPS coordinates," he muttered once again. Now that the engines were turned off, the silence of the coulee was broken only by the rustle of breeze through the dried grasses.

"It's hard to imagine it's a human bone this far from anywhere," Derek said.

Todd scanned the ragged hilltops. "This area used to be hopping with people. I've been researching it. Fossil hunters, for one. Ever since Joseph Tyrrell discovered a brand new dinosaur right near here in 1884, they've been crawling all over these coulees looking for the next great find. And coal prospectors too." He pointed to the shiny ribbon of black that ran across the hills. "That's coal. There used to be over two dozen coal mines around here. Tyrrell was actually looking for coal when he found the bone."

Derek looked at him impatiently. "I do know that. My great-grandfather did some time in the coal mine near Drumheller during the Depression, so the family wouldn't starve like the cattle did."

Todd broke a chocolate bar and offered half to Derek. "Tough years. I've read a lot about them for my book. My great grandfather also had a homestead not far from here back in the 1920s. Not big like your folks'. He tried dryland farming and ranching, everything to make a go of it, but the Depression did him in. He took a job on the railway in Brooks instead. It did in many of the original settlers from around here who were promised cheap land, huge crop yields, and a railway at their fingertips. Instead, they got drought and grasshoppers and blizzards and debt."

He scanned the mesa with his binoculars, and this time he saw the collapsed roof of the abandoned cabin poking up behind a tall hoodoo. He pointed excitedly. "That could even be his cabin up there, you know. Or something like it. Let's aim for the base below it."

Thus energized, it only took them ten minutes before Todd recognized the riverbed, the dead cottonwoods, and the stony outcrop he had sat under to escape the sun. They parked their ATVs a short distance away and approached on foot. Derek eyed the protruding bone dubiously and then the surroundings.

"It looks old, maybe been here decades. Not likely human, though. Why the hell would anyone be down here?"

"Maybe they got lost trying to retrieve a stray steer. Or they fell from the cliff up there in a blizzard or sandstorm." Todd pointed down the riverbed. "Or maybe they used the coulee as a shortcut to the Red Deer River valley. In the early days, people travelled for miles on foot or horseback to get to town or school. They might have camped here in the shelter overnight."

Derek had taken his small pickaxe and had begun to chip away at the sand while Todd readied his camera. "This sand is rock-hard, and the bone's buried pretty deep," Derek said. "It didn't just lie down on the ground and die. Somebody worked hard to bury it."

Todd looked at the pattern of till on the steep hillside and at the dry sand in the riverbed. "Maybe, but nature buries stuff. There's lots of soil erosion from spring and storm run-off, and water could have washed sand and debris over the body." He was starting to feel uneasy. Derek had uncovered the other end of the bone, which formed another knobby joint. The bone was roughly two feet long, too small to be a buffalo, cow, or horse. Too big to be a coyote. He continued photographing while Derek used a small scoop and brushes to uncover a scattering of smaller bones, along with a large, curved plate that looked like a pelvis. Vertebrae were strewn around, and under one piece they found some blackened lumps that neither of them could identify.

"It looks like it was on its side, curled up. Not sure what this is —" Derek stopped as his spoon struck something with a solid clunk. He pried it out, used his brush to wipe it clean, and held it up to the light. A belt buckle, with traces of the leather straps still attached.

Todd sucked in his breath. Recoiled back on his heels. "Maybe we should stop."

But Derek was already digging through the sand, unearthing bones and rocks and shreds of debris that could be cloth, until his brush swept over a smooth, round, mottled grey surface. Two holes, a partial jaw, and an array of teeth. Not like any deer skull Todd had ever seen.

"Fuck."

Kaylee led the way, straining at her leash as the four of them clambered up the steep slope to a high point and stopped to catch their breath. "Whoop!" Amanda cried as she surveyed the moon-like vista of Dinosaur Provincial Park spreading out before them. The midday sun was hot, and she bent over to give Kaylee some water. A mosquito buzzed in her ear and she fanned it away. "The kids are going to love this, Paula! It's like *Star Wars*."

The park guide grinned. "The badlands have been used for lots of sci-fi films. There's one being filmed in Horseshoe Canyon right now. But —" She pointed to a rock shelf visible down below, where a couple of workers were crouched in the rubble. "What's important for us are the secrets hidden in the slopes and in the dry riverbeds. That's a new bone bed we're working on, discovered by a tour group last year. The three-day dig package would be perfect for your kids. You'd camp in the cottonwoods by the Red Deer River, and we'd explore the restricted interior of the park and combine hiking with fossil prospecting and actual hands-on digging in a bone bed with trained palaeontologists. September will be the perfect time too. Not so hot and no bugs!"

The mosquito whined in Amanda's ear again. *I'm not so sure about that*, she thought as she trained her binoculars on the workers down below. They were bent over in the blazing sun, barely moving for minutes at a time as they chipped away tiny bits of ground with what looked like a miniature chisel.

"I know I'd love it," she said doubtfully, "but would it be exciting enough for a bunch of teenagers? Would they actually find any bones?"

"Oh, absolutely! The ground is teeming with bones. Some of them are just lying around pretending to be rocks unless you know what you're looking at." Paula leaned down and plucked a round, reddish stone from the sandy till at their feet. Kaylee danced with excitement, no doubt thinking it was a ball. She wanted to race free over the hills and through the crevices and had been pulling impatiently on the leash. But apart from the fragility of the landscape, there was also the very real danger of rattlesnakes.

"Sorry, girl. It's not on," Paula said with a laugh before turning her attention back to the rock. "This is a vertebrae. See the spongy texture of the inside? That's bone. And this groove is where the spinal cord was. It's a hadrosaur, about the size of a school bus."

She handed it to Amanda, who was surprised at how heavy it was. It felt strange to hold a piece of something that had walked this marshy inland sea seventy million years ago.

"How do you know where to look?"

Paula pointed to the tall hill up ahead, which exposed layers of rock of different textures and colours. "Think of that as a wedge of layer cake. Each layer was deposited in a different time and represents a different type of cake. There's layers of sandstone, mudstone, coal, and ironstone, and each four to five centimetres represents about a thousand years of deposits. The dinosaur era is only a small cross-section of that wedge, in the middle, about seventy million years ago. Bones were exposed by glacial run-off and also by the constant erosion of the hills and valley floors by rain, wind, and spring melt. Bones protruded from the sides of hills or tumbled down the hills onto the flatter surfaces below. So we look in the hillsides and in the debris that has fallen down onto the floor."

Amanda's thoughts drifted to the planning of her trip, while Chris asked questions and Paula expounded with alacrity. Amanda suspected the guide could elaborate for hours, but she knew she had to keep this dinosaur adventure fast-paced and entertaining. Would three days in the dinosaur park be too long, especially when added to the day in the museum and the one-day horseback ride through the coulees and grassland upriver?

But Paula had years of field experience under her belt and knew both her subject and her audience well. By the end of the day's hike, she had knitted together the science, mystique, and entertainment into a perfect adventure. Chris and Amanda were buoyant when they returned to the B&B. This time, reluctant to abuse Maeve's hospitality, they had bought lamb chops to barbeque, along with a bottle of California Merlot. Maeve declined the invitation to share it and returned to her own quarters.

The heat of the day had mellowed to a pleasant glow, and a playful breeze chased the last of the late-season mosquitoes away. Amanda was tempted by the lounge chair under the cottonwoods but instead set off with Kaylee for an off-leash run while Chris tackled the barbeque. Once out on the open field, she pulled out her phone to take another look at the photo her aunt had sent. The landscape was similar: gently rolling fields with a smudge of trees in the distance and a jumble of outbuildings in the foreground.

This time Jean picked up her phone.

"Okay, to be clear, you *do* want me to look up this man."

"No."

"No?"

"Yes. Well, I ... I ... Yes."

Amanda frowned. This was most unlike Aunt Jean. Why the indecision? "Who is he? An old boyfriend?"

Jean snorted with something closer to her normal spirit. "You really think so? Look at the man!"

Amanda shielded the phone from the evening sun. She'd never seen her aunt wear so much as lipstick or a dress. It was difficult to picture her swooning in the arms of this cocksure, sexy young man. "When was this taken?"

"About 1990."

Amanda did a quick calculation. The man looked to be in his mid-twenties to mid-thirties. In 1990, Jean would have been twenty-three years old. Perhaps a more vulnerable, hopeful twenty-three. "He's a good-looking guy," she ventured.

Once again, Jean snorted. "For heaven's sake, Amanda."

Amanda kept her tone light. "It will be hard to identify him from this photo. He'd be in his fifties. Probably bald, pot-bellied, with a wife, three kids, and an addiction to dirt bikes and hockey."

"Not all of us have gone to seed, you know. Anyway, it's doubtful you'll be able to find him. He could be anywhere."

The doubt and hesitation had returned to Jean's voice. Amanda softened her own. "You sure you want to do this?"

A long silence was punctuated only by the hoarse cry of a raven overhead. Jean cleared her throat. "Your going out to Alberta, and finding that farmhouse, seems like an omen. It's time."

Amanda could almost see her squaring her shoulders and shoring up her resolve with a firm hand. "Then I need a name."

A sigh. The resolve melting. A whispered name. "Jonathan."

"Jonathan Who?"

"Lewis."

"Lewis?" Amanda wasn't sure she'd heard correctly. "Jonathan Lewis?"

"Yes, Amanda," Jean snapped, all steel again now that the word was out. "Jonathan Lewis."

Lewis was Aunt Jean's last name. Amanda's mother's maiden name. "Is he a relative? A cousin?"

"He's a brother. *My* brother. Your mother's twin."

Amanda stopped in her tracks. Her world spun as questions tumbled through her. "What? Twin? How come no one ...? What's he doing in Alberta? *What happened*?"

But she found that she was talking to empty air.

CHAPTER FIVE

"I have to call my mother."

Chris topped up their wine glasses and folded his tall frame into the adjacent chaise longue. The remains of dinner still sat on the patio table amid sparkling tea lights. "I don't get it. How can your family just wipe out the existence of one of its members?"

"Not wipe out, exactly," Amanda said. Her world had stopped spinning, and some sense of normal thought had returned. "I remember a Jonathan being mentioned at our infrequent family get-togethers, but I thought he was a cousin of my mother's. I have a few cousins I rarely see because my grandmother had a feud with her brothers when their parents died — a dispute over the will — and so she never saw them."

"It sounds like your family has a habit of cutting people off."

Amanda turned the observation over in her mind. She knew Chris was referring to her own relationship with her mother. It was easy to make that quick conclusion. Her mother was judgmental, brooked no dissenting views, and never suffered fools. Only a select few retained their place in her inner circle.

Chris came from a warm, boisterous Ukrainian farm family. Only last week, she'd felt the enveloping welcome of their arms, so alien and smothering to her that she'd had to take long walks out on the prairie to restore her equilibrium. Luckily, she'd had the excuse of Kaylee.

Chris couldn't begin to understand her own family's chilly, arms' length restraint. Her family lived their lives apart, turning inward instead of to each other for comfort, advice, and strength. Amanda couldn't remember it being any different. She couldn't remember sitting on her mother's lap for storytime or running home for help with a scraped knee. Bedtime had been a peck on the cheek and a quick tuck of the covers. By the time Amanda was four months old, most of the nurturing had been delegated to a succession of daycares and babysitters while her mother returned to graduate studies.

Looking back through adult eyes, she realized her mother had never been taught to nurture. Her own parents had been distant, their marriage and mental health wrecked by the trauma of the Second World War. As a child, her mother had learned to fend for herself and believed she'd managed so admirably that it was a parenting model worth emulating. She should probably never have had children; they posed an inconvenience in her pursuit of her two great passions: her career and her causes. Although no one had ever said so openly, Amanda suspected the pregnancy during her graduate studies had been an unwelcome surprise following an affair with her professor. Nowadays that was a firing offence, but in those days it was almost a rite of passage for young female grad students. Her marriage to the man had been the most passable solution. After all, he was a tenured professor with a respectable intellect and good genes. Good enough, in fact, to permit the conception of Amanda's brother two years later.

That was possibly the last time they ever slept together, Amanda had often thought wryly, for in the intervening thirty-three years, her father had rarely lowered his head out of the clouds. The clouds were familiar and comfortable; they never argued or judged. Her mother seemed happy to have him out of her hair, so in this fashion, the whole family limped along.

Now Chris's veiled criticism touched a nerve. Irritation flashed through her. "My family didn't cut me off. We still talk. Just not about feelings. If anything, I cut *them* off. My mother judges everything I do. Mine is not a career path she can be proud of. Not 'my daughter the world-renowned Harvard researcher or Nobel laureate.' Instead she got a daughter who mucked around in the sordid trenches of failed states and almost got herself killed by thugs in Northern Nigeria."

He slipped his hand through hers. "She's not going to like me, then."

"Maybe not. But even from her rarefied perch at the top of the ivory tower, she's hung on to some of her socialist views. She might view your background as romantic and noble. Son of immigrant parents who came to this country with just the shirts on their backs and all that."

"You make her sound like a terrible snob."

Amanda shook her head. Her mother *was* a terrible snob, but not in the social climbing sense. "She cut her teeth on the Vietnam War and Ban the Bomb protests, and she's been waving placards for great causes ever since, now mostly in the pro-environment and anti-pipeline movements. We never had a lot of material goods — one car and a modest house — but we drowned in books. Every wall in the house was made of bookshelves. No, she didn't want me to get a Harvard Ph.D. so she could brag about it. She wanted me to fulfil my *potential*." Amanda used air quotes. "I was always good in school, so she and Dad figured I'd go all the way. To Mum, education was power. Without it you can't effect change in the world. To Dad, academia was the only world worth knowing. They weren't thrilled when I got my M.A.

in global development — too wishy-washy for them — but at least it was an M.A. Mum was not happy when I stopped there. 'You can't change the world from out there in the trenches,' she said. 'You need to make policy. Use your talent and creativity on the broader canvas.'"

Amanda paused to take a sip of wine and reflect. To her surprise, it felt good to talk about the thoughts she had always kept private. Chris was a good listener. She felt his warm hand in hers, encouraging her to dig deeper. "So now, here I am, back in Canada after an epic failure in the trenches and not sure what to do next. They've started up the mantra again. Mum thinks this Fun for Families project is a waste of my time and talent. Now's the time to go back to school, she says. You've seen the view from the battlefield, now get into the general's chair."

"Maybe she's just afraid of what you went through."

She flashed him a smile. "You're so sweet. You think of this from a mother's perspective."

"But she *is* a mother."

Amanda fell silent, sobered by the insight. Her mother stirred so many confused feelings of hurt, anger, and defensiveness that it was easy to lose track of the basics.

"With a tougher skin than any mother I've met," she replied. "Mum was always right, her causes always the most righteous. No one else's views and causes amounted to a thing. My mother never failed. And yet look at this! How does one lose a brother? A twin! How did my parents fail to mention, in thirty long years, this crucial missing part of their family either to my brother or me?"

"If the photo was taken around 1990, you would have been a little kid. Five or six? Do you remember him at all?"

She studied the photo on the phone then slowly shook her head. "There's something vaguely familiar, but it's more a feeling than a memory. A feeling of fun. And laughter." She glanced at her watch. Nine o'clock, which meant eleven o'clock in Ottawa. Late but not too late. Her mother was a night owl. She belonged to various global think tanks and institutes and often communicated with colleagues in Europe or Asia in the middle of the night.

The phone rang a long time, and Amanda was just wondering if she had indeed called too late when the phone picked up. First, breathing. Then "Amanda," in a voice so low and hesitant that Amanda felt a twinge of alarm before understanding clicked in.

"Aunt Jean told you."

"Yes. I suppose I should have told you years ago."

"What's going on? You make it sound like some deep, dark secret. Like he'd done something terrible."

Silence on the phone. "No. Not really. It's just … we chose different paths. We argued, and we both said things. The longer he was gone, the harder it was to reach out."

"How come you and Aunt Jean never mentioned him? You never showed us pictures? He was your brother!"

"Yes, and how often do you mention your own brother?"

Amanda didn't buy it. Perhaps of her mother, but not of Aunt Jean. "Mum! I may have zero in common with *my* brother and may not talk to him for a year, but at least I know where he is! And if one of us needed the other, we'd be there. What happened?"

"It's in the past. We were young and angry. Now, it seems too late."

"It's never too late! I've seen families separated by war who reunited after half a century. When was the last time you heard from him?"

Her mother's voice firmed, and Amanda could almost see her setting her jaw. "I don't appreciate your tone. He chose to leave. I never heard from him. Jean did, for a while, but the two of them were always closer."

"But he was *your* twin."

"Twins, but as different as night and day."

"Didn't you ever try to find him?"

Silence descended again. Amanda glanced at Chris, who was frowning at her in disapproval. She felt a twinge of guilt. Something had happened to break the family apart, and her mother deserved a gentler approach. Just as she was searching for softer words, her mother sighed.

"Once, when your grandparents died. I mailed a letter to the Norsands office in Fort McMurray, where he was working. It came back addressee unknown. I even phoned them. They said Jonathan had left the oil sands four years earlier, in 1990. They said it's a pretty transient workforce as the oil business goes up and down." Her voice dropped sadly. "Wherever he went, he never thought to inform his family. Ours hadn't been the happiest home when we were growing up, Amanda. I guess he wanted to put it all behind him."

"Maybe he's built a whole new life for himself out in Alberta. We could have a whole family of cousins and in-laws out here."

"Yes." Her mother's voice lost its wistful tone. "One that he clearly didn't want us in. He knew where we were, at least. Don't forget, this was before the Internet. You couldn't just Google someone's name or look them up on Canada 411."

"But now you can. Aunt Jean wants me to look for him. She says it's time."

"I suppose she's right. Well past time." Her mother heaved a deep sigh, sounding every one of her sixty years. "It's been one of the few regrets of my life."

Those words held the weight of a lifetime. Her mother wasn't sentimental or inclined to waste time on past mistakes. For her to sound so old and sad, Amanda knew there must be layers left unsaid.

CHAPTER SIX

"One hundred and seventeen million hits on Google!" Amanda exclaimed as she stared at the list. Actors, soccer players, artists, rappers, and even a racecar driver. If she included John or Jon Lewis, the number reached close to a billion. Adding in the keyword *Alberta* still produced hundreds of hits, and there was no guarantee the man was still in the province.

"Worse than a needle in a haystack! But I can't think how to narrow it down." She was propped up in bed with her laptop on her knees. Beside her, Chris rolled on his side to eye her balefully.

"Amanda, it's midnight. We have a long, tiring trail ride in the morning. That hundred and seventeen million hits will still be there tomorrow."

She scrolled through the list. There were Facebook and LinkedIn profiles, company websites, and random news features. She couldn't even narrow down by year. Jonathan's presence might date to the earliest days of the World Wide Web.

Chris reached over to touch her cheek. "Bedtime, sweetheart. Put that brain to rest."

Reluctantly, she admitted he was right. She shut down her computer, but despite her best efforts at sheep-counting, she lay awake half the night, staring into the darkness and wondering how this could ever have happened. She had only a few memories of her maternal grandparents, who had died when she was eight in a car crash that Amanda had long suspected was no accident. They both suffered from PTSD and struggled for years to keep above the pain and terror. A struggle Amanda had come to know well since Nigeria.

But the two sisters, Jean and Susan, Amanda's mother, had grown up with Jonathan and yet had chosen to erase him from the family story.

She finally dozed off about two o'clock in the morning, only to be jarred awake by her phone alarm at seven. Maeve had prepared them a sumptuous, old-fashioned breakfast of Mennonite sausage, scrambled eggs, toast, and grilled tomatoes. While Amanda ate, she booted up her computer. Chris was right; the one hundred and seventeen million hits were still there.

"You need more information on him," Chris said as he slathered homemade Saskatoon berry jam on his toast. "Middle name, place and date of birth —"

"Presumably the same as my mother's. Sudbury, Ontario, February 2, 1960."

"Okay, that's a start. But more useful to a Google search is where he went to school, his profession, interests, and hobbies. With those we can comb through social media. We just need a toehold to get us started. Your mother should know some of that."

"But it will be out-of-date. Still a needle in a haystack. We should start with the Alberta Provincial Archives. They record all births, marriages, and deaths. He might have married in the nineties, and he's not likely to be dead, but that's worth checking." She Googled the archives and groaned in dismay. "For public access, the marriage record has to be seventy-five years old and the death record fifty." She glanced at him coyly. "But I imagine the cops could have it at their fingertips. Could you ..."

"No."

She prepared to argue but decided against it. The idea was a long shot and not worth getting him into trouble with the RCMP. His record with them already had enough black marks, mostly because of her.

"Get more info," he added as if to soften his refusal.

Amanda glanced at her watch. They were to meet the trail riding guide at ten o'clock up near Drumheller, and time was getting tight. But curiosity drew her on. She phoned Aunt Jean, and after filling her in on the conversation with her mother, asked for more details on her brother and the photo.

"I don't know anything more about the photo, Amanda. He didn't tell me where it was taken. He just sent it to wish me a happy birthday. I'd just turned twenty-three."

"Was there a return address or postmark on the letter?"

"I didn't even notice. I was young. I didn't think I'd never hear from him again."

"What about school? Training, profession?"

"Jonny wasn't much of a student. Not for lack of intelligence but for lack of motivation and patience." Her voice livened at the memory. "He lasted four years in engineering at Laurentian University in Sudbury, with your mother garnering all the As and him failing twice, before he quit in disgust. Never got the degree. He wanted to make money, and he didn't see how learning all these obscure theories was going to help. He got a job in the nickel mine, but Alberta was where the money was in those days, and the maverick spirit. It was still the Wild West, and oil millionaires were a dime a dozen. Or so the legend went."

Amanda jotted some notes in her book. *Search oil companies as well as engineering and technical institutes.* He might have furthered his studies out in Alberta, especially when the oil bust brought his dreams down to earth. Many an impatient but disillusioned thirty-year-old returned to their studies when the sober reality of life hit them.

Jean's voice dropped. "I did try to find him on the web a few years ago, out of curiosity. I probably did much what you're trying to do, but there were too many unknowns."

"Search engines are better these days, so maybe I'll have more luck," said Amanda, although she was doubtful. No one navigated the remote corners of the web better than her mysterious aunt. "What were his interests and hobbies?"

"He was a big kid at heart, at least in those days. He liked toys, the bigger and noisier the better. Fast boats and faster cars. He went out west on a black Harley-Davidson he'd just bought. He used to like hunting too. He'd go duck and deer hunting in the bush every fall. As you can imagine, it drove your mother crazy. He always wanted a gun dog but because of your mother's allergies we couldn't have pets. He did tell me the moment he got to Fort McMurray, he was going to get a hunting dog." She chuckled. "I've often suspected he did half the things he did just to get your mother's goat. Your mother was the original peace activist — no killing of any sort. She and Jonny were like oil and water."

"What did he look like? From the photo, I can't tell how tall he is."

"Not tall, perhaps five-eight. His attitude was always bigger than his size."

"Hair and eye colour?" Chris interjected.

"Blue eyes and light brown hair, much like yours," Jean replied when Amanda repeated the question. "In fact, you look a lot like him. Small but packing a punch."

Amanda jotted the information down. She was beginning to think how much like herself her uncle sounded, and not just in looks. She had a motorcycle and loved the feeling of speed on the open highway. She too had a dog, although certainly not for hunting, and she too preferred action to theory. She too butted heads with her mother at every turn.

Uncle Jonny. What a strange name to roll off her tongue. Yet the sound evoked a flush of warmth. A memory of being wrapped in laughter. In the smell of cigarettes and leather.

Chris tapped his watch. Hastily, she thanked Jean and asked her to send any birth, school, or other records she had in her files. As intriguing as it was, by itself little of the background information went very far toward figuring out where Jonathan had gone next, but it gave her a few places to start the search.

The coulee buzzed with activity. The RCMP had descended on the scene, led by the local constable from the nearest detachment, who had called his supervisor and strung yellow police tape around the perimeter and across the access trail. In this sparsely populated, wide-open land of ranges and massive farms, the RCMP was spread thin on the ground. Each small detachment covered thousands of square kilometres of villages and farms.

As other officers drifted in from farther away, they parked their police Interceptors along the shoulder of the highway by the entrance to the main coulee and hiked in. But later arrivals, on the advice of their commanders, towed ATVs, adding the grinding roar of the engines to the quiet countryside. Police radios crackled in sporadic bursts.

The sun rose high over the hills, baking the scene and the people below. It became a waiting game for a palaeontologist and her team from the nearby Royal Tyrrell Museum to arrive and for the RCMP district commander to take charge. Derek and Todd sweated in the diminishing patch of shade under the rock overhang, ignored but forbidden to leave until the commander had signed off.

Derek was angry at the waste of his day, but Todd was excited at the prospect of witnessing a real-life criminal investigation.

"It's not criminal, you dickhead," Derek said. "Any moron can see those bones have been there for decades."

"That doesn't mean it wasn't murder," Todd said, already spinning a tale for his book. *Ghosts of the Ancient Dead* was taking on a whole new meaning. "Maybe it was part of the frontier justice of the homesteading days. Not a lot of cops back then, so people took to settling their own disputes. A guy kills his neighbour for stealing his wife, or a settler kills a rancher whose cattle ate his grain. Oh, and everyone hated the CPR agents and bankers! In hard years, people risked losing their land and their homes to those pricks."

Derek laughed. "You always did have too much imagination! I'm going to chill out and let these CSI dudes do their jobs."

The growl of an approaching engine broke their focus, and soon another ATV could be seen bobbing and weaving up the trail, towing a trailer filled with tarps, bins, and gear. It stopped fifty feet from the site, and two young women climbed off. They were dressed in heavy work boots, cargo pants, light T-shirts, and broad Tilley hats. After briefly examining the bones, the older one turned to confer with the commander in charge, who gestured to Todd and Derek. Looking angry, she marched over to their sheltered spot.

"Was it you who dug up the bones?" She had an ID card from the museum clipped to her belt, but Todd couldn't see her name.

Bristling at her accusatory tone, he nodded.

"You've destroyed potential evidence, you know, not to mention broken the law. Excavating bones is a delicate science. Their position in the ground, their relationship to each other, their orientation, and the surrounding debris — all this gives us crucial information about how they died and how they ended up here."

"We didn't know it was human," Derek said. "We figured it was a big-ass buck. I wanted the skull for my cabin."

Todd had an apology all ready, but he checked it, admiring Derek's quick thinking. "I took some photos of the leg bone when I first found it, before I touched anything, and a few more while we were digging. I didn't see anything around it besides a couple of deer tracks. The ground and hillsides hadn't been disturbed."

Looking mollified, the woman held out her hand. "Give me your camera and cable. The police and Medical Examiner will want to see the photos." With quick, confident fingers she plugged in the cable and transferred all his bone photos to her phone before deleting them from the camera. "Just a precaution," she said mysteriously as she handed his camera back.

"But that's my work!"

"You can't use any of this. I don't know what you think your work is, but ours is to collect and protect evidence. I'm Dr. Virginia Satov of the museum, by the way. We won't be excavating today. We're waiting for the lead investigator and the forensics team from Calgary."

Todd felt a frisson of excitement. "I'm writing a picture history of these parts. The bones look pretty old. What do you figure? Can you tell how old they are?"

She shook her head. "I could, but that's not my call. I'm just here to excavate the remains, and then they're on their way to the morgue of the chief medical examiner in Calgary. A forensic anthropologist will examine the bones and run tests to determine how old they are, plus age, gender, size. Maybe even race."

"They can tell all that?"

She gave him a smile, which softened her rugged features. "It's not my field — mine is fossils — but yes, an anthropologist can estimate quite a lot."

Todd gestured to the perimeter tape and the half-dozen cops. "All this prep — looks like they suspect something."

"That's standard operating procedure. Finding human remains is not all that uncommon, you know. There are forgotten church cemeteries from the early pioneer days, and some families buried the dead on their own land. First Nations had burial sites all over the prairies in the pre-European era."

"But at the bottom of a coulee?"

"They could have been washed down from somewhere else." She gestured to the cliff top. "Maybe up on that range, for example."

Her phone buzzed. She checked a text and glanced up to see an officer arriving. As she turned to leave, she smiled and handed Todd her card.

"In case you think of anything else," she said and walked back up the trail.

After what seemed an eternity of consultations and phone calls, the new officer climbed up the slope toward them. Todd recognized the staff sergeant chevrons and concluded this must be the boss. The man asked a couple of questions in the usual deadpan tone all officers seemed to practice and then closed his notebook.

"You're free to go. We have your info if we need to contact you again." He narrowed his eyes. "Don't discuss this with anyone or comment on social media. There is already some local press parked out at the highway. We don't want a circus here before we know all the facts."

Todd rose slowly, his muscles stiff from the long wait. "Will you tell us —"

The staff sergeant shook his head. "Once the investigation is concluded, a press statement will be issued."

"When will that be?"

A twitch of a smile crossed the man's face. "Might take months to identify the remains and track down next of kin. That's if identity can be established at all."

CHAPTER SEVEN

As they left the horse ranch to drive down the Red Deer River valley, Amanda draped one arm out the window and gazed out at the valley hills. She felt comfortably sore and tired. It had been a beautiful day exploring some remote badlands on horseback. Conroy, the trail guide, looked as if he'd stepped right out of a Western movie. He was lean, rangy, and well over six feet, with legs that went on forever. He wore a brown leather cowboy hat with a wide, flat brim and a braided band, a long, flowing coat, and hand-tooled cowboy boots complete with spurs. She almost expected him to carry a pump-action rifle beneath the long coat. The kids were going to love him.

"I hope you're planning to wear that outfit on the tour," she said.

Conroy grinned and touched the brim of his hat in a salute. "We aim to please, ma'am," he said in a drawl that would have made Clint Eastwood proud.

She had ended up arranging to take the group on a full day's ride with a possible camp overnight if the weather was co-operative. September could be spectacular in the badlands, but it could also be frigid. The guide had apologized for changing the route at the last minute, saying that the police had closed off part of the trail for some reason. Probably an accident in the interior.

As she and Chris drove back down the highway afterward, Amanda spotted the cluster of RCMP vehicles on the side of the road and the tape across the rough track that snaked into the coulee.

"That's a lot of cops for the middle of nowhere," she said. "Is that usual?"

Chris shrugged. "Depends on the nature of the incident. There's no ambulance, so unless it's left already, there were no injuries. I think if it's a big story, we'll hear about it on the evening news."

She turned her attention back to the road. Soon they were climbing out of the valley onto the flat grassland above. She let her mind wander as they drove by fields and farms, and her thoughts returned to the photo. She glanced at the clock.

"It's early. I'd like to take a little drive."

He cast her a look of dismay. "I'm parched. A beer would go down a treat right about now."

"Maybe we can kill two birds with one stone." She winced. "What an awful expression. We can drive around for a bit and end up at a nice country pub for dinner."

"You may have noticed there aren't a whole lot of country pubs. Many of these little towns have nothing in them except maybe a Chinese restaurant."

She pulled out a wad of papers. "Humour me. Let's drive and I'll search."

"What are we looking for?"

"A farm that looks like the one in this photo."

His eyes widened. "Do you know how many thousands of kilometres of rural roads there are in Alberta? Many of them unpaved."

"I know, but I'm looking for similarities in terrain, the kind of crop grown, the type of house, and maybe even the type of farm implements."

"They'll all be the same. There's only a handful of major farm machinery manufacturers. And all of southeastern Alberta is either flat or rolling prairie, except the coulees, and the same half dozen crops are grown all over." He pulled off the highway. "Let me see that photo."

In Drumheller that morning, Amanda had printed a dozen copies of the photo to carry with her. They were grainy and bleached out, but they were all she had. Chris studied the photo thoughtfully. "There's no sign of sprinklers, so it's probably a dryland farm. That narrows it down a bit. Not all farms are irrigated, even when it's available, but my guess is it's on the fringe of an irrigation district or uphill." He pointed to the cylindrical objects barely visible in the background. "Those are bales of hay."

"Does that mean they have cattle and not crops?"

He shrugged. "Hard to tell from the little bit we can see in the photo. They probably had both, because farmers grow grain for cattle too. This fencing could be part of a stockyard. It doesn't look like a big operation, though, and some of the equipment looks antique."

She grinned. "How handy you are, cowboy! So we're looking for a small farm in a dryland section that's been around for a while."

"That's still hundreds. And it might be abandoned now or sold to a mega company. So this farm might be an empty shell."

"Like the one we saw near Duchess."

He nodded. She turned to look back out the window. After fifteen minutes of driving, the scenery began to blur together: grasslands, golden grain fields, tiny hamlets that were mostly boarded up, and endless unfurling road that sliced arrow straight through the flat land. Reluctantly, she acknowledged that Chris might be right.

"We have to ask some old-timers," she said. "They might have a feel for where this is."

THE ANCIENT DEAD

He brightened. "Beer. Pub. That's the place to find old-timers."

She laughed. They were passing through a village, and she pointed to a general store with an *Open* sign in its window. Made of white clapboard with a peaked roof and an ornate front stoop, it boasted a plaque over the front door: 1913. "There might be an old-timer in there!"

Inside, the store was dark and musty, with uneven floors and a riot of merchandise crammed onto the shelves. Some of it was faded and dusty, as if it had been there for decades, but the girl behind the counter was clearly of this century. She was dressed in the classic outfit of contemporary teens: ripped jeans, tight T-shirt, and pink hair piled into a messy topknot.

Amanda picked up a chocolate bar and approached her with a friendly smile. "This store is marvellous! Just like the general stores I knew as a kid. Is it really from 1913?"

"Yeah. It used to be a railway office, and then, like, a school or something. At least that's what Granddad says. He says he went to school here."

"I'd love to talk to him. Is he around?"

"I guess. Somewhere. I'm just filling in." She paused. Amanda waited and finally the girl blinked. "Oh, you want me to, like, go look for him?"

She disappeared into the back, where she could be heard shouting. As Amanda waited, she browsed the flyers tacked to the bulletin board by the cash. Some looked ancient, promoting country fairs, rodeos, and amateur plays as well as advertising goods and services for sale. Finally, rhythmic thuds sounded on the wooden floor at the back, and an elderly man shuffled out. His hands were gnarled as they gripped his cane, and his skin was the texture and colour of dried mud flats. But he looked thrilled at the prospect of company, not to mention a paying customer.

Amanda had developed an abbreviated explanation of her search; she was trying to track down a distant relative who'd moved here in the late eighties. "We've lost his address," she said as she showed him the photo. "Does this look like around here?"

The old man squinted, held the photo close to his face, and then took it over to the grimy window. "Don't know the fella."

"But the farm. Does it look like any around here?"

The man squinted some more. "Nope. Not much help, I'm afraid. But that house ..." He tapped the gabled roof. "They added a couple of wings on it and raised the roof. Folks did that when they got a little money or the family grew. This type of house was pretty common around here after the Great War and into ... oh, the thirties or so. Porch in front, two bedrooms in the back. My brother tore ours down in the sixties to put up a more modern place. It had no insulation or indoor plumbing, see, and only a gas stove for heating. There was days you could see your breath at the dinner table."

He looked set to launch into a long reminiscence, but when Amanda tried to remove the photo gently from his fingers, he tightened his grip.

"But this one looks to me it might have been a ready-made — a CPR ready-made farm — because those came with a little house like that and a barn like that shed."

"What's a CPR ready-made farm?"

His pale, milky blue eyes twinkled. "Short answer, a big fat con. Long answer? Well, the CPR and the feds were in bed together, eh? The feds wanted the railway built all across the country, so they gave the CPR a whole pile of land and promised them this whole prairie would be settled by farmers who would ship their supplies and goods by rail, right? All of Alberta, Saskatchewan, and Manitoba was supposed to be a farming paradise. But not enough people were crazy enough to try to make a go of it. No towns or services, no decent water, just dust. Those that came, they came with nothing and got dumped off in the middle of a field and got told 'Here's your land, get cracking. Build your house, till your soil, plant your crop, and maybe next year you'll make enough money to buy yourself a horse.' Well, that didn't bring a lot of folks and the railway was running out of money, so they sweetened the pot by building a house and barn on each plot of land. Even tilled and seeded the soil. Plenty of folks took advantage of that." He brandished the paper. "Could be what this is."

"Where are these ready-made farms?"

"Oh, all over, from Calgary to Medicine Hat and down to Lethbridge. Almost eight hundred of them. They were near the railway lines so folks could get their goods to market."

The old man looked as if he could talk all evening, but the sunset was spreading orange shafts of light across the sky. Time to find their pub for dinner. Amanda took his phone number and promised to call if she had more questions.

That evening she sat up in bed and Googled ready-made farms. One link led to another, and after a few sputtering starts, she came across an online essay on ready-made farms by a Ph.D. student at Columbia. On the second page was a map.

"Gold mine!" she crowed, spreading her map of Alberta out on the quilt beside her. "These farms were not scattered helter-skelter but were organized into colonies so farmers could pool their resources and equipment, build schools and churches, and so on. It looks like there were twenty-four colonies, all built between 1909 and 1919, mostly along the railways, like the old man said. Coincidentally, the main railroad runs alongside the Trans-Canada Highway. Two dozen colonies are not too many. Tomorrow we'll start near Calgary in the west and work east."

"Tomorrow we were going to visit that working ranch Matthew lined up, remember? He'll be waiting for your go-ahead."

Matthew Goderich was not only her long-time friend from her time overseas but also the manager of her Fun for Families charity tour, responsible for enrolling the participants, lining up logistical supports, and managing the money. She'd met him twelve years earlier when they were both in Cambodia, and although he'd been assigned to report on war zones, he'd shared her interest in the struggles of ordinary people caught in the crossfire. He'd been the one who'd reported on her harrowing, month-long escape from terrorists in Northern Nigeria. More than anyone, he understood her passion for helping people and her struggle to find a new, less traumatic path. He had given up his career as an international journalist to follow her tour across the country and was now based in Calgary.

She felt a twinge of guilt. As if on cue, her laptop alerted her to an email from Matthew. *The list of potential attendees is nearly complete*, the email said. *I'll need your itinerary and your contact people by Friday. How's it coming?*

To which she replied as vaguely as she could, *Hit some delays. Working on it.* She sighed as she closed her laptop. The ready-made farms would have to wait.

It was two days before she could turn her attention back to the mystery of her uncle. Armed with a printout of the map of the colonies, they set off toward Calgary. The first colony located north of Calgary was now a midsized town with urban streets, businesses, and industry. All traces of its pioneer past had been bulldozed in the twentieth century boom. The next two villages also bore little resemblance to their original roots. Lawns and gardens had replaced barns and corrals, and everything looked tidy and prosperous.

"Hmm," Amanda muttered as she peered out the window. "Maybe we'll have more luck deeper into the country."

Guided by the GPS, they drove east along back roads to the next colony, which was no more than a collection of small farms on a dusty road. Some of the farmhouses looked abandoned, although the fields were planted and cattle grazed on a small rise near a slough.

They picked a farm with a truck parked outside and turned in the lane. A Border Collie raced up, barking and setting up a furious exchange with Kaylee. Chris and Amanda waited until a man emerged from the barn and called off the dog. Ordering Kaylee to stay, Amanda climbed out and approached with the photo in her hand. The man looked in his mid-thirties but already sported a beer belly that strained against the suspenders of his work jeans. He squinted at them from beneath his faded Stampeders ball cap.

"Can I help you folks?"

There was no suspicion in his tone, merely puzzlement. Amanda explained they were trying to track down a long-lost cousin and asked him if he recognized the farm.

The man, who said his name was Isaiah, studied the photo. "Can't say. Photo looks pretty old."

"From 1990. How long have you lived here?"

"My family? From the thirties. But most folks around here are Brethren. Mennonite Brethren. This man isn't."

"Can you tell anything about the farm? Or the surroundings? About where it might be, I mean."

He shrugged. "It's a ready-made. Not too many of those left, although even that one could be torn down by now."

"What villages still have some? Or at least did thirty years ago."

Isaiah chuckled. "I was barely in kindergarten then. You could ask at the Brooks Museum. There's a historian there who knows everything. Part of history herself. Ask for Lillian."

The City of Brooks was a modern regional hub that benefitted from a railway terminal, a huge meat-packing plant, a historic irrigation aqueduct, and the proximity of Dinosaur Provincial Park. Chain hotels had sprouted up along the highway, and even Walmart and Tim Hortons had set up shop. The Brooks Museum, however, felt like stepping into history. Original pioneer buildings, including a tiny home and a schoolhouse, had been relocated onto the grounds.

When Amanda inquired after Lillian inside the main museum, she and Chris were quickly directed to a small back room, where a woman was bent over a desk piled high with documents. Similar piles crammed the bookcases and teetered on the floor. The woman looked up and swung her wheelchair around as they entered.

When Amanda explained her mission, Lillian's eyes sparkled. "You're in luck! I was born and raised in Brooks, and I remember the old days much better than this morning! If it's from around here, I'll know it."

She reached out her hand, trembling and knobby with arthritis, angled the desk lamp, and held the photo inches from her eyes. For a long time the only sound was the rattle of her lungs.

"Rings a bell," she said finally. "It's around here, but I can't say the exact farm."

"I understand it's dryland farming. Does that narrow it down?"

She shook her head. "The ready-mades were all on land irrigated by the CPR; that was the point of them. It promised a decent crop yield. Mind you, that didn't always happen in the old days, and even when it was a good crop year, the farmers were so far behind on their taxes, loans, and water payments, they couldn't keep afloat."

She picked up a magnifying glass and peered at the photo. "I don't see any other farm buildings, so it might be a more remote one, farther from the main irrigation channels. Oh!" The magnifying glass hovered. "There's a windmill over here. Looks like a Monitor, but if you want to know exactly, there's a museum in Etizom that has displays of antique farm machinery and windmills. Their windmill display is the biggest in Canada."

"What was the windmill used for?"

"For power." She winked. "Funny how what's old is new again. You could use it for pumping well or irrigation water, for washing clothes, grinding grain, you name it. They used to be all over the countryside, but they're mostly torn down now. This one is probably long gone. This whole farm may be too. It's not making anyone much money."

Amanda tried one more question. "Do you recognize the man at all?"

"No, but I can tell you he's no farmer. His clothes are for show, more like a tourist."

They thanked the woman and headed out into the sunshine. Amanda groaned when she Googled Etizom. "Almost two hundred kilometres south."

"Food," Chris said. "Before we start driving over hell's half acre."

After a picnic lunch and a quick walk with Kaylee, they set off again. This time Amanda took the wheel while Chris studied the map. "Do we really need to do this?" he asked as they headed into barren land. "It's a pretty shaky lead."

"I know, but I'd like to see the southeastern corner of the province anyway. It's not far from Writing-on-Stone Provincial Park, the amazing badlands of hoodoos and First Nations petroglyphs. It's on my list for the kids to see, so two birds with one stone again. Matthew will be pleased."

The drive southeast led them through some parched, desolate lands where farms were few and villages even fewer. Etizom proved to be a tiny, forgotten crossroads of a hamlet that was being rejuvenated by the building of a massive water pipeline across the county. Although the little museum had a wonderful display of windmills standing tall in the field, it was unfortunately closed. Amanda wandered around the display, comparing windmills to the one in the photo and reading the accompanying explanations, but the sun was relentless, and by the end of half an hour she was hot and frustrated.

She sighed. "Lillian's right, it's a Monitor, but they appear to have been very common back in the early twentieth century, so we're no further ahead."

Chris had retreated under a shade tree with Kaylee. "We have to approach things from a different angle."

"You're the cop. What would you suggest?"

He wiped his forehead and grinned. "Usually it's not a thirty-year-old cold case. We'd start by tracing their last movements. Interview friends, family, and work colleagues to find out their usual routines and hangouts. Also, nowadays we'd look at their social media, credit card, and banking activities."

"None of which we have." She headed back to the Hulk and turned the air conditioning on full blast.

"And on a thirty-year-old case, we'd use age-progression software on a photo."

She shot him an excited glance. "Can you —"

"No," he said as if anticipating her next request. "But there are commercial apps available, if we can get a good photo of Jonathan."

She felt a lift of optimism. Why hadn't she thought of that? "Good. I'll ask my mother tonight. Any other bright ideas, Sherlock?"

"Well, we do have one other lead, along the lines of interviewing friends and colleagues."

She studied him, thinking. "Norsands? The dude my mother talked to? He didn't actually know Jonathan."

"No, but he might be able to give us some names of workers who did."

"Us?" she said hopefully.

"You."

She steered west onto the straight, empty highway toward Writing-on-Stone Provincial Park and drove in silence for a few minutes, feeling slightly miffed at his lack of support. It was true that he had booked two weeks away from his detachment in Deer Lake, Newfoundland, and had cheerfully jumped at the chance to come with her to Alberta, even though it was largely a working trip for her. He'd followed her whims and put up with all these last-minute side detours in search of Jonathan.

He'd been a poster boy for the accommodating boyfriend, and all he'd asked in return was four days to meet his family in Swift Current en route. Even that had not been a hardship. His mother couldn't have been more different from her own: cheerful, down to earth, unflappable, and without a judgmental thought in her head. She'd fed Amanda almost continuously at the scarred wooden farm table that took up most of her condo kitchen.

Amanda had felt welcome the moment she walked in the door. Chris's father was shy and seemed happy to hover on the periphery, presiding over his brood. Chris's six brothers and sisters, along with assorted partners and children, breezed in and out of the condo as if it were their second home, which it probably was. By the end of four days, Amanda's head was spinning. No wonder Chris couldn't understand her family! Maybe she should put off the introductions forever.

Despite his easygoing nature, however, she found herself irritated that he was putting the search for Jonathan firmly in her lap while he sat back and smiled benignly. He was the one with the expertise and the contacts; an inquiry might yield more cooperation if it came from him. Shouldn't he be more intrigued? Shouldn't he care more about how important this discovery was to her?

He was gazing out the window, apparently lost in the barren beauty of the endless fields. She was about to push him further when he broke the silence.

"Us. Sorry."

She wanted to hug him. "I'll ask my mother for the Norsands man's name tonight. And for a better photo of Jonathan so we can age it." She hesitated before going further. She'd already caused him considerable trouble with his superiors in the past, all because he'd been trying to help her. "I can call the Norsands guy, I guess."

"No, I will." He leaned over to squeeze her hand. "I'll tell him I'm RCMP but pursuing a personal matter. It might open more doors."

CHAPTER EIGHT

Now that the curtain of secrecy had been swept aside, Amanda's mother seemed eager to help and to learn the paltry results of her search to date. She'd quickly located the Norsands contact information and promised to hunt for a better photo.

"If Jonathan is running true to form, there was likely a woman involved. I suggest you ask the Norsands manager about female friends as well as male."

A belated thought occurred to Amanda. "Did he leave a girlfriend behind in Ottawa? Someone he might have stayed in touch with?"

There was a beat of hesitation. "No. No, he didn't."

"Any other friends? He sounds like a sociable guy."

"No." Again, her tone was sharp. "I never had anything to do with his friends."

"Do you remember —"

"No, Amanda. That was years ago. Concentrate on Alberta."

After she'd hung up, Amanda puzzled over her mother's reaction. The curtain of secrecy had come crashing down again. Her mother had claimed the estrangement was due to youthful disagreement, but Amanda was beginning to suspect something deeper. Something more wounding.

They had stayed the night at a basic motel in Milk River near Writing-on-Stone Provincial Park and were now enjoying the motel's idea of a self-serve hot breakfast. Armed with a full plate of waffles and scrambled eggs, Chris began a series of phone calls to track down the Norsands HR manager Amanda's mother had spoken to years earlier. Hank Klassen had risen in the company until he reached a senior position at headquarters in Calgary. He was now mostly retired and spent more time on the golf links than in his ceremonial office in the downtown tower. Amanda listened as Chris cajoled some underling into putting him through. He had to lean heavily on his RCMP credentials before the woman reluctantly acquiesced.

Amanda listened with growing admiration as Chris adopted his best cop speak. "This is Corporal Tymko of the RCMP. I appreciate your time, Mr. Klassen. I'm investigating the disappearance of one of your workers in the early 1990s. A Jonathan Lewis. Foul play is not suspected at this time, but information has come to light that makes it imperative that we locate him. I understand you spoke to the individual's sister in 1993 when you were an HR officer at Fort Mac, and at that time you informed her he'd left the job in 1990."

The man finally interrupted. He had such a booming voice that Amanda could hear every word. "What in hell do the cops want with Jonathan Lewis?"

"It's a personal matter. I'm not at liberty to divulge that as yet."

"Not at liberty." Klassen gave a barking laugh. "We're talking ancient history! I barely remember the guy."

"I appreciate it's a long time ago," Chris replied. "I'm not asking you to remember him. Thousands of men have worked for Norsands. What I'm asking for is the contact information of a coworker there at the same time — a site or shift supervisor, for example. Someone who might be able to help us move this inquiry forward."

The man sputtered out a few more objections that Chris patiently deflected. Information way out of date, records not in Calgary office, too old for their digital database, and that old favourite, privacy concerns.

"Can you give me the name of someone who does have access to that information, then?" Chris asked finally. "Or has the authority to release it? In the interests of giving this individual's family closure and peace of mind."

Klassen's voice grew touchy. "I got the authority, Corporal. I just ... oh, for fuck's sake, hold on."

His voice dropped to a mutter and Amanda couldn't make out his words. Soon, Chris thanked him and turned to give Amanda the thumbs up. "He's connecting me to HR with instructions to look up a few workers' names from around 1990."

It was a long wait, during which Chris poked at his congealing eggs and drank his cold coffee, but eventually a sharp-voiced woman came on the line. She spoke all of five seconds before hanging up. Chris grinned at Amanda. "She's texting me info on a few guys."

The text came through just as they finished breakfast. Armed with names, last known addresses, and phone numbers, the two of them began to comb the Internet. One man had died, one had never heard of Jonathan Lewis, and two others had common enough names that multiple possibilities surfaced on Canada 411. Amanda groaned, but Chris laughed.

"Welcome to the nail-biting world of police work."

They left vague messages at the most likely phone numbers, asking whether they had worked at Fort McMurray in 1990 and knew Jonathan Lewis. Afterward, Chris slammed his laptop shut. "There! We've put the fishing lines out; now all we can do is wait for a bite. So let's go look at hoodoos."

After the otherworldly moonscapes of Drumheller and Dinosaur Provincial Park, Amanda was not expecting to be awed by Writing-on-Stone. She had intended to schedule a day trip rafting down the Milk River against the backdrop of lush riverside cottonwoods and the stone hoodoos that soared up behind them. That proved impossible, however. After weeks without a drop of rain, the river was reduced to a lazy trickle meandering between sandbars, not the rushing rapids she'd seen in the promotional videos.

But the medieval turrets of the hoodoos were like nothing she'd seen before. Mindful of signs warning of rattlesnakes, she and Chris leashed Kaylee before they set off on a hike among the hoodoos to enjoy the panoramic views across the river plain. For millennia, the Blackfoot First Nations had revered this valley as a sacred gift, an oasis of beauty and bounty in the parched sands of the prairie. They camped and fished on the shore, buried their dead in crevices between hoodoos, carved their stories in the rock faces, and even waged battles on the flood plain. The hoodoos themselves were believed to house powerful spirits.

Amanda paused in front of a piece of rock art depicting a famous battle between warring groups, complete with flying arrows. *This park deserves more time*, she thought with growing excitement; *it highlights a long human history different from the dinosaur sites. It will complement our days on the ranch and on the Blackfoot reserve.*

Back at the visitors' centre, she met with park staff to hammer out the details of her new plan while Chris sat on a bench to check his phone. When she joined him, he brandished his phone.

"We've got a nibble from Robert Powers in Calgary. He says he was a friend of Jonathan's in Fort McMurray. Do you want me to call him?"

"I'll do it once we're done here. I want to talk to the rafting company in Milk River anyway. The river looks way too low for rafting."

She tried not to get her hopes up, but once they got back on the road, she could no longer resist.

The man who answered the phone had a hearty voice with a faint Newfoundland inflection. "Well, I'll be!" he exclaimed when Amanda told him no one in the family had heard from Jonathan in thirty years. "That doesn't sound like Jonny! Had a heart of gold, life of the party."

"Have you heard from him since?"

"No, but that was the way of things up there. People came, made a few bucks, and went home. Lots of turnover. You had fun together while you were up there, but it was all a bit like another world."

"Did he ever mention his family?"

"N'ar a word. Plenty of us guys, especially from down east, missed home, and flew back for holidays and such, but I don't recall Jonny did." Robert paused, and when he resumed, his tone was more subdued. "Jonny was a lot of fun, loved to play practical jokes, but he did have a temper. He got into a couple of fights. Seems to me one was because some guy asked why he wasn't going home for Christmas. Jonny got mad, said the family didn't want him there."

Amanda remembered her mother's words. *We both said things.* What had she meant? What words had been so damaging that they had opened up a thirty-year chasm?

"I was told he left Fort McMurray in 1990," she said. "Do you know why? Fired? Laid off?"

"Oh no, he quit. I told you he had a temper. He got mad at the boss, punched him in the nose, and took off."

"Did he have any other friends he might have stayed in touch with?"

"Well, there'd be Shelley. She's the reason he quit in the first place. She got fired."

"Who's Shelley?"

"Office girl at the site. Real nice girl. Her and Jonny got into it hot and heavy, and when she was laid off, he quit too. Shelley might know where he went, but then again, he might have moved on. Jonny had a way with the ladies. He wasn't the biggest, strongest, or richest guy on the rig, but he was real smart. He even talked about going back to school. I'm betting wherever he is, he landed on his feet."

"Do you remember what school?"

"No, it was just talk, like we all do when the job gets too boring. He said he was sorry he quit before he got his degree."

"Do you remember Shelley's last name?"

"Everyone just called her Shelley. She was from down south somewhere. Her family had a farm."

Amanda's pulse quickened. She gripped the phone with excitement. "This is super important, Robert. Can you remember anything about where the farm was?"

There was silence on the phone as Robert searched his memory. "Yeah. She talked about dinosaurs. It was near that museum. Drumheller."

"Do you think you could bug that Norsands dude in Calgary one more time?" Amanda asked Chris after she'd hung up. "Ask him about Shelley?"

Chris shook his head. "That would be pushing it. He's pretty high up, and he might decide to complain to some golfing pal in the RCMP. If I thought he actually had any answers, I might risk it, but with only a first name to go on — of a lowly clerk thirty years ago — he's unlikely to have any useful information."

He steered down the main street of Milk River toward their motel. "We'd probably have more luck starting at the other end," he added. "Inquiring of local farmers around Drumheller to see if anyone knows a Shelley who worked up north in the late eighties."

"Maybe we could do that tomorrow before Calgary."

"I thought we were going river rafting."

"The rafting company says the water's too low. It gets diverted for irrigation, and sometimes there's not much left. We could try kayaking if you don't mind pushing us off a few sandbars."

Seeing his disappointed, little-boy face, she smiled. "I'm sorry. You're enjoying this, aren't you?"

"It's great fun! That's what I love about you. Never a dull moment." The word had been tossed out in light-hearted jest, like a trial balloon to test the waters. To drift harmlessly between them, ready to be snatched back at the first hint of rejection. They had known each other almost two years but had spent only a few weeks together. They had kept their feelings light and teasing, dipping and circling in a slow, seductive dance toward intimacy.

She grinned back at him. "Hold on to your hat then, cowboy."

At that moment her phone chirped. A clipped text from Matthew. *When are you coming to Calgary?*

"Matthew!" she exclaimed to Chris. "There's the answer. Mr. Super Sleuth. As soon as we get to Milk River, I'll send him an email."

CHAPTER NINE

Todd Ellison hunched over his large desktop computer, which took up most of the tiny alcove table in his kitchen. He'd been going through the photos he'd taken of the Alberta plains and badlands, supposedly making selections for his book, but in reality he was wasting precious time on news sites and Google searches related to the body in the coulee.

After the first flurry of police activity, the forensics and excavation teams had been more subtle so as not to pique the curiosity of the media. Their equipment and vehicles were parked in the coulee out of sight of the highway, and only the most astute observer would know they'd been there all week. One day, Todd had sent a camera drone over the coulee, only to discover that a tent had been erected over the site, making it impossible to see what they were up to.

Today, the tent was gone. The vehicles had left the mouth of the coulee, and the land had been returned to nature, leaving nothing but a gaping hole and pile of debris to blend in with the landscape. Surely at this point the police would issue a statement, even if only a few sentences about the discovery of remains in the coulee and the next steps in the investigation.

The bones could be an important chapter in his book. On the basis of the story, he'd already made contact with a local publisher who'd expressed tentative enthusiasm for the project. Photography books of the badlands, especially with a hint of history, sold well with tourists. This could be his light at the end of a very dark tunnel.

He already had the photographs and the hint from the palaeontologist that the bones looked old. Knowing the police might take months to release the identity of the victim, Todd had been scouring the Internet for old stories of missing persons in the area. A few reports had surfaced, but the person had usually turned up alive and well hundreds of kilometres away or the body had been recovered. Natural causes most of the time: drownings, snowmobile crashes, or heat stroke.

But without access to police files, his reach was limited. He'd discovered the RCMP had a National Centre for Missing Persons and Unidentified Remains that maintained a database to help investigators to make links. He knew there would be a flurry of investigation behind the scenes, and he chafed with frustration that he had to wait for the official police press release.

He wondered if there had been any local gossip over the years about disappearances that had never made it into the papers or police files. Although he grew up in the area, he'd been gone for nearly twenty years, and his childhood memories were mostly of fishing, playing hockey, and flirting with girls — without much success in any field.

His friend Derek had much deeper roots here, stretching back generations to the settlers, and he might be much better tuned to the gossip channel.

"Hey, man," he said in his most cheery, casual voice when he called Derek up. "How's it going?"

Derek muttered something about being late for a meeting and cut him short. "What's up?"

Todd gave up on the preamble. "Have you heard any more about the body?"

"Nope."

"Did you tell anyone?"

"We were sworn to secrecy, remember?"

"I know, but ..."

"I mentioned it to my old man because he noticed my truck alongside the cop cars that first day, and he figured maybe I was in trouble. I bet half the valley's wondering what that was about."

"Did your father say anything? Like who it might be?"

"Not to me. You heard anything?"

"No, but I'm working on my book —"

"What the fuck's your book got to do with it?"

"If it's an early settler story, it would be gold for the book. I discovered it!"

"Why don't you ask that palaeontologist? What was her name? Virginia? She was kind of cute. Science nerd, just your type, and she was into you. Ask her out."

Todd's cheeks flushed hot. She was attractive, but in truth, he'd found her rather scary. "I can't just phone her up."

"Why not? She gave you her card, didn't she?"

"I hardly know her, and besides, she's way out of my league."

"Says who? You got a university degree, and you're an artist. Chicks love that."

Todd was silent, playing potential date scenarios over in his head.

"Dude!" Derek said. "Get on this. At your age, you gotta be bold to get the good ones. Listen, I have to go. Just do it. It's a drink, not marriage."

Todd turned the woman's card over and over in his hands. When she'd handed it to him, she'd smiled and said it was in case he remembered more details about his discovery. But had it really been an invitation? Had that smile been more that just friendly?

His marriage and divorce had left his confidence and trust in tatters. For more than two years, he'd sworn off women, the root of all pain and betrayal. When he'd finally ventured back into the fray online, he'd done so expecting to fail, and he had. The women were either super messed up or they were after a guy with more than a broken-down truck and a pile of debts.

But Derek was right; this was just a drink to chat about the body and to share his plans for his book. He could even ask her if she had any tidbits on other bone discoveries he could use.

He eyed the card, faced with the next doubt. What should he call her? Dr. Satov sounded too formal. Virginia? It was a pretty name that almost seemed to soften her. How should he contact her? Texting was too abrupt. It gave no chance for pre-amble or context. Phoning was scary. What if he couldn't find his tongue? What if she didn't know how to respond? Email would give him the chance to explain and her the time to get used to the idea and consider her response. It was impersonal, but it protected them both.

He typed up a short email to her, hoping she at least remembered who he was. After a short *Hello Virginia, hope you are well,* blah, blah, he told her he was working on a book called *Ghosts of the Ancient Dead,* and he thought she might have some interesting stories. How about a drink after work sometime? His treat.

He edited and reedited until he thought it hit just the right tone. Casual, friendly, confident, and not at all desperate. Then he pressed *Send.* For the rest of the day he had to resist the urge to check his email every five minutes. Nothing, His confidence began to fade. Then at four o'clock, a response popped up.

Just got in from the field. How about the Last Chance Saloon in Wayne? Five o'clock?

Todd froze. That was way too fast. He needed time to prepare his pitch. Time to psych himself up. Holy fuck, he needed a shower! It was at least a half hour drive to Wayne, which was deep in the coal mining hills near Drumheller.

He loved the Last Chance Saloon, an iconic, old-fashioned bar that had almost single-handedly rescued the former mining village of Wayne from certain death by combining excellent food with live music and a Western saloon atmosphere. There was even a bullet embedded in one of its walls to tell the tale of rougher times when bar brawls were common. It said a lot about her character that she'd chosen it instead of a safe, boring wine bar in Drumheller or a chain restaurant on the outskirts. The choice showed imagination, daring, and a love of things beyond the ordinary.

His fingers hovered over the keyboard as he waffled. Finally, he tried to hit the same tone as hers. *How about 5:30? And maybe add in dinner. Can't pass up their shovelhead burger.*

He hopped in the shower, pleased with himself. He had a few moments of panic as he hunted through his closet for something vaguely clean before finally settling on the Western uniform of jeans, jean jacket, and leather cowboy boots. His height was his best feature, and the outfit showed it off well. He stared at his unruly hair in dismay. No time for a haircut. He tried a man bun but felt ridiculous, so he decided to let it fall where it wanted.

The drive to Wayne was itself a step back in time, past the ugly, modern big-box stores in outer Drumheller, down the Red Deer River valley, and then along a narrow, snaking road into the barren, coal-striped hills. He crossed over the winding Rosebud River nine times on single-lane bridges. The Last Chance Saloon and its adjacent Rosedeer Hotel had a line of cars and pickups out front where once there would have been horses and wagons. The weathered yellow buildings were the only signs of life in the town. Inside, the smells of beer, beef, and grease enveloped him as if they were steeped into the very walls. A skinny old-timer tinkered away at the piano, and a handful of people were clustered around old-fashioned wooden tables.

To Todd's delight, Virginia Satov was already perched on a stool by the window, studying the menu and sipping a beer from a Mason jar. She greeted him with a big smile, and he felt his doubts fade away. She was making this easy.

He ordered a beer, and they exchanged chat about the weather, the picturesque drive, and their last visit to the saloon. Then an awkward silence fell. She twirled her mug.

"I don't usually do this," she began, her eyes on her mug. "I mean, on such short notice. It's just I'm going to Calgary tomorrow, and I figured …"

He spotted his opening. "Oh? Anything to do with the remains?"

"Oh, no." She whipped her head back and forth. "That's in the hands of the forensic anthropologist and the medical examiner now. They took the whole skeleton to the lab in Calgary, so it will take time. We excavated it still encased in sediment, and it will be up to them to separate out the bones, clean, and examine them. The lab has X-ray machines and all the specialized equipment for chemical analysis like radiocarbon dating."

He was disappointed. "So it's all still in one big chunk? They can't tell anything about it like its age, sex, or how long it's been there?"

"We have some preliminary estimates. You did excavate some of the bones, and based on that I recommended they should move it intact to the morgue."

"Why?" When she frowned, he backtracked. "I mean, I'm curious about the process. Would you always dig it up that way?"

"If you want to see exactly how the remains lay in the soil, what position the body was in, I mean, then yes. It helps you determine how it got there and how the various injuries might have been sustained."

"There were injuries? You could see that?"

She hesitated. "The skull had a hairline fracture above the left ear that could have been caused by a fall or post mortem by debris falling, or ..."

He sipped his beer to feign a casual air. "Or it could have been caused by someone hitting him on the head."

She sat back with a nervous laugh. "Possibly. But they're not going to tell me that."

"Because that would mean murder."

She smiled. "We're a long way from that. We use this kind of positional and trace injury evidence all the time to figure out how a dinosaur might have died, but it's still just a theory that we fit with existing knowledge. In this case, obviously, we have to leave it to the experts."

"But can you tell how the skeleton ended up buried? Because if it was deliberately buried and not washed over by sand ..."

She nodded. "That's another reason for removing it intact. If it fell or lay on the surface, the bones would have fallen to the same horizontal plane once the soft tissues dissolved. Furthermore, it's likely some of the remains would have been scattered by water flow and scavengers like coyotes, foxes, even crows. At the lab they will look for signs of tooth marks and eye sockets pecked."

Todd squirmed. The poor man. Or woman. He pictured the scene he and Derek had uncovered. The bones had not been on a horizontal plane. The femur had been sticking up, and the skull and some of the ribs were way above the others.

"But when you saw it, you thought it was deliberately buried, didn't you?"

She looked alarmed but not surprised.

"Is that why you told them to take it out intact?"

"I'm not allowed to comment, Todd. I've already said more than I should. The RCMP want to keep a lid tighter than an oil drum on this whole thing because of all the missing and murdered Indigenous women. They want to manage the information. All they're saying is the investigation is in its early stages."

"So you're saying it's a woman?"

She stared at him. Blinked. "I didn't say that. Please. You're getting way ahead of things."

CHAPTER TEN

Matthew Goderich puffed his way up the five flights of stairs to his one-bedroom sublet. The highrise hadn't been refurbished since the seventies; its toilet required constant jiggling, extension cords crisscrossed the rooms to supplement the inadequate electrical outlets, and gale-force winds whistled off the Rocky Mountains through the windows. But the location in Calgary's lower downtown was perfect. It was a short walk up the hill to the centres of Big Oil power with their fat chequebooks, as well as down to the bustle and eclectic ethnic restaurants of Seventeenth Avenue.

The single elevator did work most of the time, but Matthew was on a fitness campaign, determined to lose thirty pounds and tone up his pudgy, middle-aged body. In his former days as an overseas war correspondent, edible food had sometimes been sparse and motorized transportation sporadic, so it had been easy to keep trim despite an overindulgence in the local homemade booze. But two years of living back in Canada had taken their toll.

One of the drawbacks — or perhaps unexpected perks — of his current furnished sublet was a full-length mirror in the bathroom opposite the shower. Even covered in a haze of steam, it told the brutal truth the instant he stepped out of the shower. He saw himself through Amanda's eyes and pictured the lean, impossibly tall Mountie standing beside him, and he made a vow. It might all be in vain, but he wanted to be ready to offer comfort if things fell apart with the Mountie.

The odds of that were good, if Amanda's past history with committed relationships was anything to go by. Even the most liberated and free-spirited men found it difficult to keep up with her. Chris Tymko was a spit-polished, straight-laced cop. He believed in rules, and they had already had several clashes over her stubborn disregard of them.

Secretly, Matthew didn't think they would last this trip.

When he reached the top of the stairs, he stopped to lean on the wall and catch his breath. Not bad. He'd made it all the way up in one go this time. No more hanging over the rail, gasping for breath. Baby steps. Back in his apartment, he set his bag of Indian take-out on the kitchen counter and woke up the four computers that were propped around the living room. Each was tuned to a different twenty-four-hour news channel: Al Jazeera, BBC, CBC, and CNN. Once a newshound, always a newshound. A fifth was open to his email, and his pulse took a small leap as he spotted one from Amanda.

His hopes faded as he read it. She was postponing her trip to Calgary while she dealt with a personal matter, but she wondered whether he could help her with some research in the interim. He read the email several times before picking up the phone to call her. In spite of himself, he felt a flush of arousal at the sound of her cheerful voice.

"Where are you?" he asked.

"Milk River, south of Lethbridge. We're running a test to see whether it's feasible to kayak down the Milk River."

"We?"

"Chris and I."

His spirits fell. "Oh. Of course."

"We should be all wrapped up soon."

"When are you coming to Calgary? I'd like to go over finances."

"Probably in a couple of days. I've got one more day of work down here. But meanwhile, you can help speed things up at your end. You work miracles with that computer of yours."

He sat down heavily. "I saw your email. You want me to track down someone named Shelley, last name unknown, who might have lived on a farm that might have been near Drumheller?"

She chuckled. "Yes, thirty years ago. Did I mention that?"

"Why?"

"It was too long a story to try to explain in the email. But I'm trying to track down a long-lost uncle."

He listened as she sketched out what she'd uncovered about her uncle to date. "This Shelley is the first solid lead we have tying him to a specific time and place."

"It's hardly what I call a solid lead."

She laughed. "It's better than driving around the countryside looking at farm houses, which is what we've been doing. You're the journalist, Matthew. You know how to dig up information. Bug the HR department at Norsands. Check records, social media, newspaper archives —"

"Jesus, Amanda! That's a needle in a haystack! I'm organizing a trip here. *Your* trip, which starts in two weeks. Time is running out to get it finalized."

"I know, and that's the first priority for all of us, but in our spare time Chris and I will be asking around in person in the Drumheller area. Shelley is not that common a name. If she's still around, you should be able to find her."

He could never stay angry with her, and he could never refuse her either. Even before he hung up, he was already working out a search strategy. He started with a general search with the keywords *Shelley Drumheller*. Scrolling down through the list of hits, he quickly amassed about twenty potential names. He knew that was probably the tip of the iceberg, and after making cold calls to two of the most promising, he realized he needed a more focussed strategy.

"1990?" one Shelley exclaimed. "I wasn't even born then!"

To complicate matters further, he knew that Shelley wasn't actually from Drumheller but from a farm somewhere in the general area. Would she even show up in a search?

In 1990, Jonathan Lewis had been thirty years old. Reasoning that he would have picked a woman about his own age, Matthew estimated Shelley's age as between twenty and thirty in 1990. That meant she'd likely been born between 1960 and 1970 and was now fifty to sixty years old.

He knew she'd spent her childhood in the Drumheller area, but he had no guarantees she'd been there since 1990. He had to focus his search on 1960 to 1990, when there were precious few searchable, digital records. Birth and school records would exist but were not readily accessible to the public.

When he searched for schools that existed in the seventies and eighties, he found dozens of small, local schools had closed, relocated, or amalgamated during the period. Moreover, staff from thirty to fifty years ago would likely be retired now, if not dead.

His breakthrough came when he unearthed a local high school that served as a catchment for the large rural region as well as the Town of Drumheller itself. It was first established in 1963. If Shelley had indeed lived anywhere in the area, there was a good chance she'd gone to Drumheller Composite High School in the 1980s.

On his next search, he struck gold. Eager to connect or reestablish old friendships in the Internet age, thousands of high school and college alumni had registered at sites like classmates.com, and within minutes he had found the lists of Composite School students from the 1980s. The numbers were small, but when he scrolled through the names, he found four Shelleys.

He searched the first name on Google and with ease found out her married name, business, and current town of residence, which was still Drumheller. He hit snags with the next two Shelleys, and after wandering down several rabbit holes, he returned to his one successful hit. Even if she wasn't the right Shelley, perhaps she would know who was.

When he called in the morning, he kept it simple and mostly truthful. "Hello, this is Matthew Goderich from Calgary, and I'm trying to track down a woman who attended Drumheller Composite High School in the 1980s and whose first name is Shelley."

A long pause. "Yes?"

"I understand you attended the school then, along with a couple of other Shelleys. Did you happen to work in Fort McMurray around 1990?"

"Why?"

"Why what? Why did you work there?"

"No. Why are you looking for her?"

"It's a personal matter. I'm helping a friend to trace her relative."

"Are you with the cops?"

Matthew was taken aback. "No, I'm a newspaper reporter."

"Oh! Are you working on a story?"

Matthew was about to deny it, but the hint of excitement in the woman's voice stopped him. Was there something there? "What makes you think that?"

"Well, because of who ..." The woman's voice trailed off. "No, forget it."

"Are you that Shelley?"

"I'm not, but I know who you're looking for. Shelley Oaks. Her brother is Peter Oaks."

The name rang a faint bell, but Matthew couldn't place him. "Who's he?"

Shelley chuckled. "You're obviously not from Alberta. He was a big gun in the premier's office before … well, you can read about it yourself. Does this mean you're not chasing a story on him?"

Matthew Googled Peter Oaks, and to his dismay the Internet spat out nearly two million hits. Among them were some news articles about a financial scandal, which he scanned quickly before sensing the woman on the other end of the line was growing restless.

"No," he said. "I just want to talk to Shelley. Is her name Oaks as well?"

"I can't say. She hasn't been around in years. Came back from Fort Mac, stayed a bit, and took off."

"For good?"

"Yep. It caused a bit of gossip back then, I remember, people wondering why she was in such a hurry to leave. But then the Oakses sold their spread, and Peter and his family moved to Calgary. We pretty much lost touch."

"Do you know anyone who might have kept in touch with her?"

"It's been a long time. Peter and his wife, I suppose. I heard they had a falling out after their father died, but … you know, blood's blood."

After hanging up, Matthew returned to the Internet. A quick search of Shelley Oaks turned up nothing, but by adding Alberta to his search for Peter Oaks, he pared the list down to a more manageable size. Newspaper articles, company reports, and political opinion websites, most reporting on a recent financial scandal but others written by fervent environmentalists who characterized Oaks as an incarnation of Satan.

Browsing through the list, he slowly pieced together a comprehensive picture of the man. Peter Oaks was fifty-six years old, born and raised on a ranch in Newell County in Southeastern Alberta. As a young man, he'd amassed a modest fortune by developing oil wells on his ranch. He ultimately sold his small company to a larger oil interest and went on to become a senior vice-president in that company. He became active in provincial government, first as a lobbyist and later as an adviser to the government on the energy sector, a position he vacated a year ago under a cloud of suspicion. Speculation was rampant about missing funds and possible embezzlement, but the official reason given for his retirement was deteriorating health. He now lived quietly in Calgary with his wife Natalie.

To Matthew's surprise, the man was hiding in plain sight on Canada 411 under N. Oaks. He jotted down the contact information and looked up the address on Google Maps. It was in the exclusive neighbourhood of Eagle Ridge, tucked into a bend in the Elbow River. He phoned Amanda to fill her in on his search efforts and asked her whether she wanted him to give the man a call. No, she said, she wanted to take this crucial step herself.

When Amanda phoned the number Matthew provided, a man picked up. His tremulous voice was barely audible.

"Hello? Is that Peter Oaks?"

"Natalie?"

Matthew had mentioned deteriorating health. Was hearing part of his problem? She spoke slowly and loudly. "No, Mr. Oaks. My name is Amanda Doucette. I'm trying to locate your sister Shelley."

"Who?"

"Shelley. Your sister."

"Oh … I don't know. I don't think … she's not here."

"Can you give me her telephone number?"

"No. You'll have to talk to my wife."

"Is she there?"

"Shelley?"

"No, your wife."

"I don't think so." His voice trailed off.

Amanda gave up. "Okay, I'll call back in an hour or two."

"But you can't talk to Shelley."

"I'll talk to your wife. Don't worry, Mr. Oaks. Thank you for your help."

When she hung up, she glanced across at Chris. He was standing at the water's edge at Poverty Rock on the Milk River. The kayaks and camping equipment were still on the trailer, ready for their kayak attempt down the river to the hoodoo campsite at Writing-on-Stone. Chris was conferring with the guide, who was shaking his head.

"In two weeks when your group will be here, there won't be enough water to float a rubber duckie down this river," he said. "Even now, your paddles will be scraping the bottom. They've even stopped the irrigation diversions to the farms."

She knew how much the kids were looking forward to the rafting, which was to be the thrilling climax to their trip, but it couldn't be helped. This too was the reality of southern Alberta.

"We'll have to make do with hiking and swimming at the park campground," she said. "But for now, let's take the camping gear to the campsite by car, so we can at least enjoy that part. In the morning we have to go to Calgary to see the Oakses."

When she filled him in on her phone conversation, Chris looked at her in dismay. "It's my last weekend. Can't you just phone again?"

"I could, but I think this would be handled much better face to face. Peter Oaks sounds frail, and I think there's also some dementia."

"At fifty-six years old?"

She grimaced. "It happens. Early onset Alzheimer's is brutal."

Early the next morning they left the campsite and drove north. The sprawling city of Calgary emerged slowly, heralded first by heavier traffic and more frequent exit ramps, then by businesses and suburban enclaves scattered in the rolling hills, before exploding in an urban tangle of crisscrossing expressways, oddly named Trails. Amanda was grateful for the Hulk's GPS system, which guided them expertly through the hurtling traffic toward Eagle Ridge.

As they drove slowly up the street, searching the house numbers, she began to have misgivings about an unannounced visit. She was uncertain what she faced and how she would be received. Eagle Ridge, she'd learned, was one of Calgary's wealthiest neighbourhoods, and the sprawling homes, multiple vehicles, and lushly treed yards felt inaccessible.

By comparison, Peter Oaks's turned out to be a modest bungalow with an aging GMC Sierra parked in the drive. After parking in the shade and opening the windows for Kaylee, they approached the house with some trepidation and rang the bell. Amanda saw a curtain flick, but there was no sound from within.

"Maybe he's a bit deaf," she said and rang again.

Chris eyed the truck. "From what you've said, he probably doesn't drive. Do you suppose his wife tools around town in that?"

"I don't know anything about his wife. But I doubt she'd leave him alone for long."

At that moment, she heard fumbling on the other side of the door, and it creaked open. A man stood in the doorway, framed by a collection of cowboy hats behind him on a coat tree. He was tall and imposing, with a square jaw and a full head of white-blond hair, but he blinked at them through bewildered, deep-set eyes the colour of a washed-out sky. Amanda's heart sank.

"Mr. Oaks?" she asked as gently as she could. "I'm Amanda Doucette, and this is my friend Chris. I called yesterday about your sister Shelley."

"What do you want?" He looked behind him as if he'd already forgotten where he was.

She reached out to focus him. "I'm looking for your sister, Shelley. Is your wife Natalie at home?"

"I don't think so." He peered warily out into the drive. "Probably at a board meeting. Are you a friend of Shelley's?"

"Yes." Amanda felt Chris's elbow in her ribs. "Well, not exactly a friend. But I do want to talk to her about my uncle. They were friends long ago in Fort McMurray."

"Oh, my. No, no." Peter shook his head as if to chase away a thought and wandered down the hallway, leaving them standing at the door. Amanda looked at Chris questioningly, then shrugged and followed him into the living room. Windows splashed light into every corner and shone off the hardwood floors and distressed leather furniture. Framed photos of wheat fields, prize cattle, and smiling blond children covered the walls. The side tables were cluttered with photos, dirty dishes, and empty wine glasses. Sweaters and jackets had been tossed over couches, and a half-empty bottle of Aberlour single malt sat on a side table. It was a comfortable, lived-in room, not a showcase.

Peter stood in the middle of the room, looking lost. To help him, Amanda gestured to a La-Z-Boy chair by the window. "That looks like your favourite chair. Beautiful view of your garden."

He nodded. "Natalie's work. I don't know where she is. Shelley, you say?"

"Can you tell me where she is and how I can get in touch with her?"

He shook his head. "She never comes. Not in years. She went away."

"Where did she go?"

He frowned. "Why do you want to speak to her?"

"She knew my uncle back in Fort McMurray. I'm trying to find him, and I hope she knows where he is."

"Fort McMurray was a long time ago. A bad time."

"A bad time?"

"She got into trouble."

"What trouble?"

He pressed his lips tight. "We don't talk about it. It's a secret."

A flash of light caught Amanda's eye through the window. A small red Audi was pulling into the drive. Sensing she had only a few minutes before Peter's wife intervened, Amanda leaned forward. "What's the secret? What did she do?"

"She's happy now," Peter countered. "She's far away."

The front door flung open. "Peter? Peter?" A hint of panic shook the woman's voice. An instant later a tall, lithe woman appeared in the archway, elegantly dressed in designer jeans, high boots, and a white linen shirt. She had short, silver hair with a streak of blue that matched her eyes, which were sharp with alarm and accusation.

"Who are you?"

Amanda rose. "I'm Amanda Doucette, Natalie. I'm trying to track down your sister-in-law, Shelley."

Natalie's eyes widened. "You let them in? Peter, I've told you over and over, do *not* let strangers in."

"They're friends of Shelley."

"Nonsense!" Natalie swung on Amanda. "I want you out of my house."

"We just want her phone number or email. That's all I need, and we'll leave you in peace."

Natalie fumbled in her purse. "I'm calling the police."

Chris unfolded himself to his full six-four height. "I'm Corporal Tymko of the RCMP, Mrs. Oaks. And this is Amanda Doucette, who you may know from the news is organizing a charitable event here in Alberta."

Natalie Oaks sucked in her breath when Chris mentioned the RCMP. Now she blinked. "I still don't understand why you're in my house harassing my husband, who as you can see is not well. And is not responsible for our charitable donations."

"I'm not here about a donation. I'm looking for my uncle," Amanda said. "His name is Jonathan Lewis. The family has lost touch with him, but we know he was with Shelley in Fort McMurray."

Rather than appeasing her, the explanation seemed to alarm her even more. Even Peter's eyes widened. "That — that was years ago!" she snapped, stepping in front of him. "We know nothing of that period."

"But have you ever heard of Jonathan Lewis? Did Shelley ever mention him?"

"No."

Amanda sensed the woman wouldn't budge. She'd lost all chance at cooperation by trying to talk to her husband. "Okay. If you'll just give me her phone number, I can take it up with her."

"No."

"No?" Amanda frowned. "I'm sorry we got off on the wrong foot. I'm just trying to find my uncle."

"Has your family been hiding from him under a rock?" Natalie shot back. "Clearly, your uncle doesn't want to be found, and I can tell you Shelley wants to put that part of her life behind her too. So I won't give you her number."

Amanda took a business card out of her purse. "Then at least tell her —"

"No. Out! Or I will lodge a complaint with the RCMP."

It was an undignified exit, with Natalie crowding them into the front hall and slamming the door so fast, it hit Amanda's heel. But not before she managed to slip the card onto the hall table. It was a Fun for Families card, which listed Matthew's phone number and email as points of contact, but it was a small victory that might bear fruit.

CHAPTER ELEVEN

"That went well," Chris said as he steered the Hulk back down Eagle Ridge Drive. Kaylee perched on the console between them, delighted for the company.

Amanda stroked her silky fur as she turned the scene over in her mind. "That was plain bizarre."

"Something seriously freaked her out."

"Perhaps. But I think there's something else going on. She doesn't want us to talk to Shelley, so she manufactured some outrage."

"She has a point, though. Why hasn't Jonathan contacted your family in all this time?"

"I can't answer that. Our family is stubborn. You may have noticed that."

He chuckled. "Then maybe he doesn't want to be found. Maybe they *both* don't want to be found."

She pondered the question. Did that make any sense? "Peter alluded to trouble in Fort McMurray. Some kind of secret. All we know is that she was laid off, and Jonathan quit in sympathy. Could it have been criminal? Could she be on the lam from the law?"

He leaned over to ruffle her hair. "What an imagination."

"Have you got a better idea?"

"No."

"Okay, then." She glared out the window as the elegant neighbourhood scrolled by. "I'm not holding out much hope that Natalie will reconsider and call me. We need a Plan B."

"Who else might know Shelley?"

"Well, we know her name and where she grew up now. We can go back there and talk to people who might have known her. Old friends or classmates who may have stayed in touch."

He sobered. "You know what day it is, don't you?"

"It's Friday. What difference does that make?" Her eyes narrowed warily. "Why? Have I forgotten something?"

"My flight back to Deer Lake. It's on Sunday. The sergeant has booked me on the seven a.m. shift Monday morning, Newfoundland time."

Her heart sank. She'd been avoiding facing his impending departure for days. She leaned over to twine her fingers through his. "What do you want to do with our last day? See the sights here in Calgary?"

He shook his head. "I'm a country boy at heart. The traffic here is enough to drive me nuts."

"A day trip to the Rockies?"

"Let's save that for another holiday. The Rockies deserve more than a few hours. I'd like to hike, fish, swim in the mountain lakes, and climb a peak or two." He took the ramp going east on the Glenmore Trail. "No, I want to go back to the prairie wheat fields and soak up the feeling of home one more time."

"Maeve's?"

He grinned. "Maeve's."

That evening, Chris fired up the barbeque and invited Maeve to join them for Angus striploins, grilled vegetables, and Big Rock beers. As the evening cooled and the sky deepened to lavender, they wrapped themselves in Maeve's handmade quilts while Amanda recounted their adventures.

THE ANCIENT DEAD

"What do you know about Peter Oaks?"

Maeve reached for another beer. "Plenty. I've known the man since he was born. A local boy who made good. He started off as an ambitious little kid hustling raffle tickets for his mother at five and running bets at the rodeo at ten. Imaginative, fearless. His family had been ranchers on a spread up near Duchess, just east of here, for generations. Like all of us, they earned a decent living in good years, but man, it was back-breaking work, and you never knew when the weather was going to kill the year, even with irrigation. Not enough rain, too much rain, or a freak snowstorm in June or September, and you'd lose half your crop. Some of the ranchers leased a bit of their land to the oil companies to make a few extra bucks a year. Others, like me, weren't sure what the oil and gas would do to the groundwater and to our crops. Besides, once the well ran dry or the price of oil went too low or the company went bankrupt, the oil well would sit there on their property, leaking god knows what kind of poison into the soil while the rancher got zero money on the lease."

Amanda listened as Maeve rambled on about orphaned wells and the bust-and-boom oil economy fuelled by greed, oil fever, and desperation.

"Peter Oaks was one of the lucky ones," Maeve finally said. "But he made his own luck. Did, anyway." A cloud passed across her features. "His father was an old-fashioned cattleman from one of the pioneer families. He loved his cattle and his land, and he took great care of it. He never once overgrazed it, and he wanted no part of oil derricks. He figured they'd pollute the land and poison his cattle, or at least stress them with all the noise and activity. But he got sick, and Peter took over his affairs, and before the old man was even dead, Peter made a deal with a local oil company. They went into it together, made a pile of money, sold out to a bigger company, and Peter moved into one of their fancy offices in Calgary. I had him pegged to be premier someday; he was about to go into politics in the next election when ... wham!"

She paused and rose to her feet on creaky knees. "Gotta keep the old joints moving these days," she said as she hobbled over to the cooler for another beer. Giddy from her own two beers, Amanda wondered how the older woman could put it away with apparent impunity. She swayed only slightly as she fell back into her chair.

"He got sick," Amanda said.

Maeve nodded. "Same thing as his father. Some sort of early dementia. Moves fast. First hint was when a whole pile of money went missing from a project he was running. The audit accused him of embezzlement. Turns out he approved things but forgot to record them. A couple more crazy decisions and he was quietly retired. His wife took over."

No wonder she's protective, Amanda thought. "Yes, we met her. She didn't want us talking to him."

"She's had to handle a lot of crap from the media." Maeve shook her head dolefully. "Goes to show you, you think you have life by the tail, but you can't outrun your destiny. Me? My mother died three weeks before her hundredth birthday, so I figure I can still kick up my heels." She lifted the beer bottle in a mock salute.

Returning the salute, Amanda smiled. "More power to you, Maeve. What about his sister, Shelley? Did you know her too?"

"Sweet girl, cut from a different cloth than her brother. She took after her mother, who was tough as nails in her own quiet way and loved the land as much as her husband did. But she died even earlier when her tractor rolled over on her. Shelley took that hard."

"Is she still in the area?"

Maeve shook her head. "Haven't seen her in years, but the family hasn't lived in the area for a long time. Why all this interest in the Oakses?"

Amanda went inside to get the photo of Jonathan on the farm. "Could this be the Oaks farm?"

Maeve peered at it in the dim lighting of the patio before moving closer to the light. "Could be. I never went there, just drove past it. So you think ..." She tapped the photo. "Your uncle was mixed up with the Oakses?"

"With Shelley Oaks, yes. Supposedly they left Fort Mac together."

"Well, if they did, I don't think they moved back here. That was about the time Peter went into the oil business, and I heard he and Shelley didn't get along. Especially after their mother died. I remember them as kids at the rodeos and fairs, he was pretty mean to her. Big brother stuff, mostly, like locking her in the barn, stealing her shoes and making her walk home barefoot. He and his friends had quite a few laughs at her expense."

It reminded Amanda of her own childhood. Her brother hadn't been truly mean, but he played a lot of juvenile, thoughtless pranks on her, especially when he got together with his friends. Her earliest memory was of them spinning her around and around until she threw up. She'd ruined her new shoes, and they'd laughed.

She'd learned not to cry or show weakness. She'd learned not to turn to her mother, who told her it was preparation for life. *Fight back, Amanda.* And so she had. And she'd taken the fight against bullies to the global stage.

"It sounds like she didn't have much to keep her around here," Amanda said, "or in touch with her brother."

"You're right there." Maeve burped and hauled herself to her feet, leaving her half-empty beer bottle on the ground. "Kids, it's been nice, but I've got to take this old corpse to bed. Tomorrow's around the corner."

———

"Why do we keep hitting dead ends with Shelley?" Amanda asked. She was curled up in the crook of Chris's arm, her head on his naked chest. She felt the rise and fall of his breathing slowly return to normal. For a few moments, she had revelled in the flushed afterglow of sex before her restless worries sneaked back in.

Chris ran his finger down her back and sighed. "Because she moved away. Her parents died when she was young, and she and her brother were not close. There should be other people — friends and relatives — who know more."

She turned her head to kiss his fingers. "You're right. Tomorrow we —"

"Tomorrow's my last day, Amanda."

His voice was soft. She felt a rush of sadness. "I haven't forgotten. How could I forget?"

"I think the visit with my parents went well," he replied.

She tried to follow his train of thought. "Yes. You have awesome parents."

"And they liked you too." He paused. "My mother asked if we could come for Christmas."

Amanda propped herself up on her elbow so she could see his face. "Did you say yes?"

"I said it was up to you."

She shoved him. "And you. You have to invite me!"

"Would you say yes?"

"Of course I'd say yes, you doofus! A Ukrainian country Christmas? I love the idea."

"Won't your family mind?"

"God no. What my family does hardly qualifies as Christmas. I don't think my brother and his family will even come over this year. My mother is already making noises about going to Paris for the holidays."

He smiled. "Okay, then. That's something to look forward to."

"It's almost four months away. What would you like to do tomorrow? It's your day."

He eyed her warily. "Promise?"

She tickled his chest. "I'm not that impossible. I can hunt for Shelley once you've left. She's been gone thirty years. Nothing is going to change in one day."

"What are you planning to do?"

"What Maeve suggested. Ask around at the nearby farms and towns like Drumheller. We know she went to high school there. I'll see if I can find friends and relatives who've stayed in touch with her."

He let the silence lengthen. "Promise me something?"

"What?"

"Promise me you won't do anything ... unwise."

"What do you mean, unwise?"

"I know you, Amanda. When you get on the trail of something, it's no holds barred."

"What kind of trouble can I get into asking questions in some peaceful prairie backwater?"

"If it's there, you'll get into it."

It was her turn to be silent. She knew what he was alluding to. Her dogged, single-minded pursuit of answers had landed her in the middle of trouble in the past. But the implication that she did it on purpose irked her. She took a deep breath.

"I just want to find Jonathan."

He held her tight and kissed her head. "I know. Just be careful. I want you around."

CHAPTER TWELVE

Todd was carrying his few groceries to the cash at Freson Bros. when he spotted the latest edition of the *Drumheller Mail* on the shelf. He snatched it up. For a week he'd been scanning the Internet and the major dailies like the *Calgary Herald* for news on the body in the coulee, to no avail. Maybe the police had not yet released an official statement, or maybe the story was too vague to warrant assigning a big city reporter. Perhaps the quirky, independently owned local weekly would find the story more interesting.

Back at his little house, he pushed aside his notes and spread the paper across the kitchen table. A thorough search turned up nothing, but there was a story on the Royal Tyrrell Museum's planned expansion. He noted the reporter's name and sent her an email identifying himself as the person who found the body in the coulee and asking her whether there was any news.

In less than three minutes, his phone rang. "Livia Cole here. What body?"

He sucked in his breath. The press didn't even know! There had been a couple of media cars hanging around the entrance to the coulee that first day, presumably drawn by the overkill of official vehicles, and he'd assumed they'd uncovered at least the basics.

"Sorry. Not body, bones."

"That find off 564 was human?"

"I … I don't know more that that."

A beat of silence. "Jesus," she breathed. "This could be huge! What did the bones look like? Did you talk to the cops? What did they say?"

"Nothing. That's why I contacted you. I thought maybe you'd learned something. Or you could search your archives or something, for news of people missing."

There was another pause, but this time he could hear the click of computer keys. "I can do that. Can you give me any contact names? The cops on the case? The museum staff involved?"

He hesitated. Her excitement opened up new possibilities. There *was* a story here, but it was *his* story. His scoop. Up until now, he'd only planned to put it in his book, but perhaps he could sell it to the big outlets and make some decent money out of it.

"I was just there the first day, to show them where the site was. The cops didn't tell me anything. They hadn't even started digging the bones out when they sent me away."

"But could you tell whether it was adult or child, male or female?"

"No." That much at least was true.

"Can you show me where you found them? Take me there?"

He thought fast. He could see no harm in agreeing, and perhaps earning her cooperation and help would be worth it. "Sure. But I'd like a favour in return. I'm writing a photo book of the history of the area, and I'd like to include this story. So anything you learn, can you let me in on it?"

Now it was her turn to pause. "My book won't be out for at least a year," he added hastily. "So it won't scoop your own story."

"Maybe we can sweeten the deal. Anything you learn, you tell me."

He doubted she'd tell him everything she discovered, but since he didn't plan to tell her everything he learned either, that was fair. A tidbit here and there would be worth it.

She met him at the entrance to the coulee later that afternoon. She was dressed in sneakers, jeans, T-shirt, and big, floppy hat against the sun. Her face was partially hidden by huge, pink-rimmed sunglasses, but she looked twelve years old. She was probably fresh out of journalism school and trying to chip her way onto the bottom rung of the dwindling newspaper business.

He'd brought his ATV for the long, winding journey deep into the coulee. "Where are you from?" he asked as she swung her camera bag out of the way and clambered on the back.

"Lethbridge," she said.

A small city girl, he thought. "How long have you been with the *Mail*?"

She scowled. "I'm older than I look."

He shrugged. "Just wondering how long you've been in the area and how many contacts you have."

He couldn't see her eyes behind the sunglasses, but her brow furrowed. "Are you a reporter too?"

He shook his head. "I used to be a news photographer out in Vancouver, before the paper laid us off and started using freelancers. I tried freelance, but that doesn't pay the bills in Vancouver. So now ... I'm writing a book. It's always been a dream of mine to capture time. Our modern culture is so fleeting, and our history is being bulldozed under. And the record of it is all being digitalized on clouds or dead hard drives, leaving no physical trace for future generations. I love the look of old photographs and letters stored in attic trunks."

The philosophical rant appeared to be beyond her and of no interest. She was a product of Snapchat and Instagram and smartphone texts. She was the present. Feeling silly and old, he started the engine, allowing its roar to block all further conversation as they set off.

At the site, she stood in the shade of the towering hills and peered at the ground. The land had no story to tell now. It was nothing but a gaping hole surrounded by churned up sand and gravel. Every last evidence marker and grid spike had been removed. She asked a few questions and snapped a few photos. She had a cheap SLR and no real training in photography, but he didn't suppose it mattered. Unknown to the police, he had his own photos, nearly a hundred of them, stored on his external hard drive at home.

Afterward, she turned to him and aimed her camera. "Point at the dig site. I want a few shots of you too."

He backed away. "No. The cops told me not to discuss anything, and the sergeant looked like someone you don't want to mess with. So don't mention my name."

She shrugged as if to say *suit yourself* and raised her gaze to the plains at the top of the coulee, where the faint outline of a building was visible.

"What's up there?"

"It's an abandoned pioneer shack."

She was already focussing her telephoto lens. "Who owns that land?"

With dismay, he realized he'd forgotten to check. That could be a crucial piece of the puzzle, and he'd overlooked it! "No idea," he said. "If you find out, let me know."

"Sure," she muttered as she took a few shots.

There was no conviction in her tone, but it didn't matter. It should be easy enough for him to find out not only the current owner, but also all the previous ones from the land registry office.

His scoop was already taking shape.

Todd hit a snag during the first day of his land registry search. The range up above the coulee was part of a large parcel of public land owned by the irrigation district and leased to a local grazing association for use by the surrounding farmers as a summer pasture. So not only did dozens of local farmers have access to the land, but the membership also changed over time. Finding out who had been a member of the association years or even decades earlier would mean ploughing through endless records. In the end, it would probably tell him nothing. He needed to approach it from another angle.

Just before he closed down his computer, a Google Alert popped up on his computer, directing him to an online update of the *Drumheller Mail*. The brief article was front and centre on the screen, accompanied by a photo of the bone site.

Death in the Coulee, blared the headline. *Bones believed to be human were discovered in a sandy riverbed south of Drumheller by a hiker last week. According to an anonymous source, police and palaeontologists from the Royal Tyrrell Museum were called in to confirm the find and to transport the remains to the medical examiner's morgue in Calgary, where a full team of specialists, including forensic anthropologists, will perform a thorough analysis. Age, gender, size, DNA, and approximate date of death estimated through radiocarbon dating will be determined and compared to all open missing person cases in the hope of establishing the identity. No details have been released by the police, and when contacted, neither the RCMP nor the museum staff would confirm or deny the finding. However, it is assumed that inquiries will be conducted in the area and that all active missing and murdered Indigenous women files will be scrutinized. If any member of the public has relevant information, they are urged to contact the Drumheller RCMP or this reporter.*

No sooner had he finished reading the article than his cellphone rang. Virginia from the museum. "You called the press!"

The fury in her voice took him aback. His thoughts scattered as he tried to backpedal. "I—I only wanted to know if there'd been any press releases. Or any more news on the body."

"I told you those things in confidence!"

"I hardly told her anything. She guessed most of it."

"You told her about the forensic anthropologist, the radiocarbon dating, and the missing and murdered Indigenous women!"

"No, I didn't! Well, about the anthropologist, yes. But she must have researched the rest and guessed about the missing and murdered women."

"You gave her an opening, and she charged right through! No one even knew about the remains, let alone that they were human. My boss is spitting nails."

"Does he know you —"

"Yes, he knows, you fucking moron. He hauled us all on the carpet, and I had to own up. I'll be lucky if I hang on to my job."

"I'm sorry, Virginia. I didn't mean —"

"Not good enough. Go to hell!"

The line went dead. Todd gazed at the phone, his heart pounding with shame. He swore aloud, first at Livia Cole, next at his own gullibility, and finally at his own duplicity. He had been after a story, hoping to score a few moments of fame and money, and instead he'd let himself be bulldozed by a kid reporter with far more street smarts than he'd ever had.

And even worse, he'd betrayed the trust of the first attractive, intelligent woman he'd had a chance with in a long time.

All afternoon, he waited for more fallout from the police, but none came. He scanned the online news sources for any comment from them on the case. Now that the story was out there, surely the police would say something, if only to control speculation. Other reporters would be calling them, smelling something big.

Social media picked up the story and shared it over Twitter and Facebook, along with wild theories. A Missing and Murdered Indigenous Women spokesperson published the stories of women who had disappeared in the area in the past twenty years, with demands for swift action and Indigenous involvement. Through the flurry of excitement, the RCMP and the museum remained silent. Todd expanded his Google Alerts to include Missing and Murdered Indigenous Woman and tried to force his mind back on his own work. It was the next morning before a single alert finally popped up: a brief press release from the RCMP.

The RCMP confirmed today that officers from the Drumheller detachment responded to a call last week concerning the discovery of possible human remains in a rural area south of the town of Drumheller. The investigation is still in its initial stages, but the RCMP would like to reassure the public that early post mortem findings suggest the remains are several decades old. No further details are being released at this time.

Several decades old, thought Todd, his guilt dissipating in a surge of renewed excitement. Perfect for *Ghosts of the Ancient Dead.*

Abandoning his work on the book, he fetched his external hard drive, booted up his desktop computer, and loaded the photos he had taken of the bone site. Then he began searching the Internet for information on how to determine the height, age, and gender of a human skeleton. The Internet was a treasure chest of scientific information, but after ploughing through endless anthropological articles, photos, diagrams, and demonstration videos, he realized it took more expertise than he possessed, as well as more detailed information on the bones.

He had taken lots of photos of the bone site as he and Derek dug it up. But he had not paid particular attention to tiny details like the wear on the teeth and in the major joints, which would have helped him to estimate age. Nor had he placed a ruler alongside the bones to provide scale. Without that, he had no way of knowing the exact length of the femur, which could be used to estimate overall height.

Determining gender might be the only factor within his reach. The pelvic bones of a female were broader and differently shaped, and the skull of a male was usually larger, with more rugged features and a squarer jaw. After studying the videos online, he sorted through his photos. He had taken plenty of close-ups, including the scraps of clothing, rubber soles, and the belt, but he had only taken one of the pelvis. He had stopped digging around it when Derek uncovered the skull, so it was still half buried in the sediment. He studied the photo with dismay. He didn't have nearly the expertise to tell the subtle differences in angles and shape that distinguished the genders. That left only the skull. He remembered vividly the moment they realized they were looking at a human skull and not a deer. The horror. The panic. Derek had dropped it as if it were on fire and had reared back on his haunches. They had stopped all work at that moment and thrown their equipment helter-skelter back into the bins. He had taken only one photo of the skull, just as Derek turned it over.

He scrutinized the photo now, trying to picture the person it belonged to. The jaw had become detached and was still buried, so there was no way to tell how square it was, but he thought the skull seemed small and the cheekbones seemed high. Almost delicate, like a woman's. Yet the forehead was wide and the brow pronounced.

This is pointless, he thought. *It could be a small man or a big woman.* He turned instead to the remnants of clothing. The fabric was blackened, but he could see a few traces of red plaid. He remembered the cloth crumbling in his hands. That was not much help, although it did suggest light clothing worn in the summertime. He couldn't tell foot size from the bits of rubber sole either, but they looked like boots that would be worn by either sex.

He turned to the silver belt buckle, the only piece of clothing that had been preserved intact. It was discoloured green and black, but on close inspection, he could see traces of a pattern. He zeroed in and magnified it, trying to make out the image. A picture? A logo? It was too corroded and pitted to decipher, even after he played with the contrast and saturation settings.

He printed out the clearest image and took the paper over to the diffuse light of his studio. Some shapes were emerging. Was it the Eiffel Tower? A stylized combination of letters? With a pencil, he traced the salient lines of the design. He squinted at them, stepped back to study them from afar, and gradually began to formulate a theory.

It was an antique oil derrick, with a banner underneath. On the banner was a name he could not make out.

CHAPTER THIRTEEN

Sunday morning, Chris and Amanda woke as the sun was peeking over the horizon and flooding the field with gold. They drove to the Calgary airport in near silence as the reality of the separation robbed them of small talk. At the passenger drop-off area, Chris held her tight.

"Remember, Newfoundland is only a short flight away."

She tilted her head up and smiled. "I know."

"And after this Alberta tour, your B.C. trip isn't until next spring."

Her smile turned mischievous. "I know."

"Deer Lake is pretty exciting in the fall."

"I remember. Moose-hunting season." She laughed and gave him a mischievous shove. "You're all the excitement I want. Now go before you miss your flight."

Heading back toward Drumheller across the wide-open prairie, she wished she had her motorcycle. Driving the Hulk was like being encased in a tank. She wanted to feel the road rumbling beneath her and the wind whipping past her. She wanted to be surrounded by the view and feel at one with the land. She glanced over at Kaylee, who had taken over Chris's seat and was curled into a comfortable ball, snoozing. She stroked the dog's silky ears.

"I suppose you like this behemoth better than being strapped into your trailer, don't you, princess? And if we spend much time with Chris, we will either have to buy something like this or persuade him to buy a motorcycle too."

She had marked the coordinates for the Oaks ranch on her GPS and eventually found herself on a series of gravel back roads that passed through rolling mixed fields of hay, barley, and wheat. The area looked prosperous, with sprinklers poised like giant insects on the edges of luxuriant crops, but there were few houses. Some homesteads were scattered in the distance behind tall trees and shrubs. She drove slowly, trying to picture how it had looked thirty years ago.

When the GPS announced that she had arrived, she steered the Hulk up the long, overgrown lane and climbed out. Kaylee leaped down in delight and raced to explore the nearest shed. Amanda looked at the forlorn collection of buildings in front of her, and her heart leaped. This was it! This was the view in the photograph, now overrun with weeds and shrubs.

The windows of the main house were boarded up, and the veranda roof was partially collapsed. One shed had listed onto its side, and another was missing a wall. Broken fence posts poked through the weeds where the corral had been, and the rusted farm machinery was tangled with willow. In the summer drought, everything was parched and yellow.

It hadn't been inhabited in decades, but its essence was still there. Behind it, she could see Black Angus cattle grazing on the open range amid motionless oil derricks silhouetted like forgotten sentinels against the blue sky. The prairie grass had reclaimed the land once the wells were spent, and the cattle were clustered around a watering hole in the middle.

In the distance, an irrigated patch had been planted with a bright green crop and another with tall wheat stalks with plump golden tips almost ready for harvest. Bales of hay dotted another field farther down the road. All this had once been the Oaks ranch. Her uncle had posed in front of this very house, grinning impishly at the photographer, who was probably Shelley.

Amanda climbed down from the Hulk and walked to the fence where her uncle had stood. The grass was flattened, and to her surprise, there were traces of tire tracks in the lane and footprints in the dust by the gate. When had they been made? In this drought, it might have been weeks ago. But this place had been abandoned for decades.

Maybe it was up for sale or had just been sold. Curious, she searched the nearby fields for more prints. The dry prairie wool crackled beneath her feet untouched. Far down the road, she could see another cluster of trees and buildings. Calling Kaylee to her side, she walked toward it. Surely these neighbours would know about recent activities. They should at least have known Shelley. However, she'd forgotten how deceptive distance was in the prairie, and by the time she and Kaylee made the long trek, they were hot and sweaty.

The farm was prosperous and well kept. It sported numerous shiny silver grain bins, equipment and animal barns, and huge, modern machinery. The farmer proudly told her he owned all the land along the range road, including the Oaks land, and had expanded the irrigated area so that he could grow beans and potatoes as well as wheat. He had only lived here twenty years, however. Although he knew Peter Oaks because he used to lease his land for grazing while the oil wells were active, he'd never heard of Shelley.

"Is the place up for sale?" Amanda asked.

"Nope." He grinned. "Why? You interested?"

"No, just trying to find Shelley. But I notice someone's been there recently. There are tire tracks. Did you see anyone around?"

The farmer shrugged. "Well, we get curiosity-seekers every now and again, especially when Oaks was big news. Now it's mostly photography or history buffs. They like those old piles of wood. Supposed to be arty. I noticed one the other day; pickup drove right up the lane and stayed a while. That's probably the tracks you seen."

Amanda frowned. "Did you see what they did?"

"Just stood there, looking out over the range, as far as I could tell. But I got better things to do than watch that old place all day."

"Man or woman?"

He shook his head. "Too far to see. Couldn't even tell you the colour of the truck."

It was a small detail, probably irrelevant, but the puzzle stayed with her as she and Kaylee walked back to the Hulk. Maybe it was just coincidence. Who could be interested in the old place besides her? She was exhausted, thirsty, and not much further ahead in her search for Shelley Oaks. Time for another approach. Since Shelley had attended high school in Drumheller, perhaps she had friends and relatives there. Amanda had already checked Canada 411 for other Oakses in the area, without success, but a more indirect line of inquiry might work.

As she headed for Drumheller, she knew it was a long shot. She had given herself only a day to track down Shelley before returning to Calgary for pretour meetings. Drumheller was bustling with tourists. Excited children wearing dinosaur shirts and clutching stuffed dinosaurs skipped down the streets, following the dinosaur paw prints painted on the sidewalks and shouting about toys and trinkets in store windows. Parents snapped photos and urged caution.

On a quiet side street removed from the tourist hub, Amanda found what she was looking for: a pharmacy that looked as if it had been there forever. A woman of equal vintage sat behind the counter with her feet up, reading a book. Amanda judged her to be too old to be a contemporary of Shelley's, but she might know her.

She'd already decided that a direct approach was best. "I'm trying to locate a relative we lost track of years ago. We know he was with Shelley Oaks, but I'm having trouble finding her. Do you know her?"

The woman's eyebrows shot up. "Peter Oaks, yes. But his sister? Oh my, it's been years."

"Do you know what happened to her? Where she went?"

"The States somewhere. I think Peter said she married down there. Mind you, that was years ago."

Married. Amanda felt a quickening of hope. Was it possible? "Where in the States?"

The pharmacist shook her head, her springy grey curls dancing. "I did know her in school, but we were never close. She was quite a few years younger than me. She was a country girl, loved to ride the open range, and she left the ranch when Peter started his oil wells. She said the sight of those oil donkeys on the land had broken her father's heart." She sighed. "I don't think she's ever been back."

"Is there anyone in town she might have stayed in touch with? Any close friends?"

"Like I said, she was a country girl. Quiet. Loved animals, especially horses. She'd spend hours riding the plains and the coulees. I don't think she had many friends in town here."

Amanda sighed. More dead ends. She paid for some sunscreen and stepped back out into the heat of the afternoon, nearly colliding with a woman hurrying down the street. "Oh! Sorry!" was the first thing she heard. She jerked back in surprise to find herself looking into the startled blue eyes of a woman wearing a large red sunhat over a wide forehead, freckled cheeks, and glossy brown hair.

The woman laughed. "Sorry, I was looking at my phone. Terrible habit."

Amanda stared. Transfixed. Managed a muttered "my fault" before the woman stepped around her and continued down the street to her car. Amanda watched her go. Watched her brisk, purposeful gait with feet turned out slightly like a ballerina.

It's a trick of my imagination, she thought. The product of the hot desert sun and days of thinking and wishing. But it was as if Aunt Jean had stepped back in time onto the streets of Drumheller.

Amanda wanted to chase after the woman to find out who she was, but by the time she'd made the connection to Aunt Jean and recovered from her surprise, the woman had driven off. It could be a complete coincidence. People from the same ethnic pool often shared similar features. Deep-set blue eyes were common among the Scots and Irish, as were freckles. Amanda judged the woman to be anywhere from twenty-five to forty. Was it possible Shelley and Jonathan had married and had children? Was it possible they were still living in the area, almost under her nose?

Sitting in the Hulk, she started a simple Internet search on her phone. Canada 411 revealed two Lewises living in Drumheller, one only a stone's throw from where she was parked. She phoned both, but neither had worked in the oil sands in the 1980s, nor did they have any relatives who had. Searching social media sites proved frustrating and ultimately futile as well. She needed the technical skills of Matthew Goderich.

"Matthew, I've got another sleuthing job for you."

"Are you in Calgary?" he countered.

"Not yet, but —"

"I thought Chris's flight was this morning."

"It was, but I went back to Drumheller."

"Jesus, Amanda! I've lined up two potential corporate sponsors, but they want to meet with you in person. If you want this charity to continue, you have to put your heart into it!"

She thought fast. Forget the Internet searches. The most obvious way to find out whether Shelley and Jonathan had ever had a child was to ask Peter Oaks or his wife. Since they'd denied any knowledge of Jonathan and evaded all questions about Shelley, they were unlikely to divulge that information without a fight. For some reason, this family had a deep secret.

"You're right," she said. "I'm coming in first thing in the morning. Who are they?"

"They're both in oil. One is the president of one of the subsidiaries of Sandstar, and the other is on the board of a research project into carbon capture, which is connected to Norsands. Sandstar owns most of Norsands too, by the way. It's all incestuous."

"Big oil and I are not natural bed partners, Matthew. They must know I'm much more on the habitat protection side. Why are they interested?"

"Probably because of that. It's an optics thing. It makes them look good to be supporting a local charity helping the less fortunate, who in your case are from areas where that habitat is threatened. The oil sands are trying to improve their record. Or at least their image in the rest of the world."

She mulled that over. Usually, money raised by Fun for Families supported an overseas charity in a struggling part of the world, but this year, because her adventure tour was aimed at Indigenous youth from northern Alberta, she had chosen Reconciliation Canada. Matthew was right. Indigenous groups were gaining strength and support in their protests against oil sands expansion and pipeline construction. The big oil companies needed all the goodwill they could muster. Or buy.

But was there something more at play? These were huge corporations, with far bigger fish to fry that her little charity. A thirty-year-old mystery, no matter how scandalous, was unlikely to cause a ripple in their reputation today. Yet was it sheer coincidence that these sponsorship offers had come on the heels of her own inquiries into Shelley and Jonathan? Was there something they did not want coming to light? Why were they insisting on meeting with her personally? Either they wanted to dazzle her with their charm and goodwill, or they wanted to find out what she was digging up.

"I'm not sure I want any part of this," she said. "Next thing, they'll be wanting their corporate logos on our T-shirts. Fun for Families is not for sale."

He sighed. "It's big money. Would it hurt to know what they want?"

Maybe not, she thought. Maybe two could play the digging game, and she could use the meeting to find out more about Jonathan and Shelley's background in the company. And meanwhile, since she was returning to Calgary tomorrow anyway, she'd ask Peter and Natalie Oaks about the Aunt Jean lookalike who'd shown up on the streets of Drumheller.

CHAPTER FOURTEEN

Amanda was prepared to have the door slammed in her face when she rang the bell at the Oaks house, but instead Natalie greeted her with her most charming smile. "I am sorry for my rudeness the other day, Ms. Doucette. I didn't realize who you were until afterward, and I confess I am protective of my husband. He gets so easily upset."

Recovering quickly, Amanda matched her charm. "I understand perfectly, Mrs. Oaks. I don't need to disturb Peter. I'm sure you can answer my questions just as well. I've discovered something new."

Natalie had made no move to invite her in, and a flicker of alarm crossed her face. "What do you mean?"

"Maybe we can talk about it inside?"

"Well ..." Natalie glanced warily down the hall behind her. "I don't want to disturb Peter. I was planning to get a caregiver so I could go downtown."

Amanda continued to smile, but the effort was beginning to wear. "Maybe we can sit in the backyard? I'd like to take my dog out anyway. It's too hot for her to stay in the car."

Natalie's gaze flicked to Amanda's SUV, and a smile softened her tense features. "Your famous Duck Toller. Of course, bring her around to the back. There's shade and a fence. I'll meet you there."

The woman has done her homework about me, Amanda thought. Kaylee had become a popular part of her image. She had time to take the dog on a tour of the spectacular perennial gardens before Natalie emerged through the French doors with a bowl of water, which she set down in front of Kaylee. She moved in a brisk, business-like manner.

"Actually, come into the kitchen while I make coffee. Peter's upstairs, so we won't disturb him."

The kitchen was all marble and stainless steel, but homey touches were evident in the children's art taped to the walls, the hand-crocheted pillows on the breakfast bench, and the array of photos, drawings, and memos stuck to the fridge. Coloured notes of instructions were posted on the walls and cabinets, some of which had locks on them.

Once inside, Natalie bustled around an elaborate espresso machine and spoke with her back turned. "No point in beating about the bush. When I found out who you were, I asked our financial officer to make an appointment with your manager, Mr. Goderich, to discuss a corporate donation. I assume that's why you're here? We were going to meet downtown tomorrow, but this will give us a chance to discuss it on a more personal level first."

Amanda was startled. This was not the direction she'd intended to go at all. Was Natalie involved with Sandstar or Norsands? She cast about to regain her footing. "Why?" she managed.

"Why discuss it personally? Well, if I'm going to commit money —"

"I mean why are you interested in Fun for Families?"

"Well, you're contributing to Reconciliation Canada, for one thing. And I have a strong record of supporting programs for children, both personally and through the company. I'm on the board of a research and development company working on carbon capture. We've sent the material to Mr. Goderich. Children are our future, and the ones you are helping need our support most of all."

It was the perfect segue, and Amanda slipped right through. "Do you have any children of your own?"

"Yes, one. And three grandchildren."

"Does Shelley have children?"

Natalie's back stiffened. She whipped the milk with vigour. "I don't think Shelley's private life is relevant to our discussion."

"I saw a woman in Drumheller who looked the spitting image of my aunt, and less so, my mother. And she'd be the right age. Thirty-ish."

Still, Natalie didn't turn from the counter, but she leaned on it as if her legs could no longer support her. Amanda approached so that she could see her face. Natalie had turned white.

"Oh. My. God," she breathed.

"Did Shelley have a child?"

Natalie took several gulps of air. Shook her head. "Sorry," she murmured. "Minor dizzy spell. No. Lots of people look similar in that part of the country. Same ethnic stock."

"But I don't know what Shelley looks like," Amanda said slowly. "I only know what my Uncle Jonathan and my aunt look like."

The other woman's gaze darted to the fridge and then toward the hallway. Somewhere in the house, a floorboard creaked. Abruptly, Natalie plunked the coffee on a tray and headed toward the French doors. "It's a lovely day. Let's go back outside."

Amanda ignored her and walked over to the fridge. Most of the photos were of children, grinning in school photos, in soccer uniforms, and on horseback. But their parents were in some of them, and there was one smiling photo of a freckled, fresh-faced young girl in a graduation gown. Younger, softer, but undeniably the woman she'd seen in Drumheller.

Amanda tapped her index finger on the photo. "Who is this?"

Natalie appeared ready to fight. "Those are private photos. If you don't want to discuss the sponsorship —"

"Is that Shelley's daughter?"

The woman hovered by the doors, her jaw set. Kaylee stood looking through the glass, tail wagging in anticipation. "I told you, I will not discuss Shelley's private life. Now please come outside."

Amanda took in the smiling children and the Aunt Jean lookalike who stood proudly at their side, arms enveloping them. "This is *your* daughter, not Shelley's," she said, trying to make sense of it. "Did you ... were you and my uncle ...?"

Natalie blinked. She set the coffee tray down on the counter with a crash. Coffee sloshed over the rims, and she snatched up a rag. "No!" she whispered hoarsely. "I barely knew the man."

Expecting to be thrown out at any minute, Amanda pressed forward. "Then talk to me! Is this Shelley's and Jonathan's child that you and Peter raised?"

Natalie flung the soggy rag into the sink. A whimper escaped her tight lips. Finally, she shook her head. "I don't know."

"What do you mean, you don't know? Is it Shelley's or not?"

"Yes, it's Shelley's, but we don't know who the father was."

Amanda felt a huge weight lift. "Obviously my uncle."

"But Shelley didn't know that. There was another man."

"Ah." Amanda thought back to those days thirty years ago. Before DNA tests. Back to the days of blame and shame and secrecy. "So what did she do?"

Natalie crossed the kitchen to shut the hallway door. "What could she do? Some bastard got her pregnant and then your no-good playboy uncle left her high and dry, and she had no way to support the baby. She was just nineteen herself, hoping to go on to college when she had enough money. So Peter and I adopted the baby. She is our child! We couldn't love her more if we'd created her in my own womb."

"I'm sure you do, Natalie. I'm not here to take that away. I'm just thrilled to learn I have a cousin —"

"No!"

"What's wrong?"

"Our daughter doesn't know."

Amanda stared at her. "Oh, Natalie."

"Don't 'Oh, Natalie' me! We never told her. Why complicate her life? Why have her wondering who her mother and father are? Or worse, knowing it's Shelley and wondering why Shelley has no relationship with her." The words poured out of her — the fears, the doubts, the layers and layers of justifications. "She has Oaks blood in her, not Peter's but close enough. We couldn't have children of our own, and it was so very, very important to Peter that he carry on the legacy. The Oaks family is one of the original settler families in Alberta, and he's the end of the line. He wanted this!"

"But what about Shelley? Didn't she want some relationship with her daughter?"

"Shelley knew it was for the best. She knew we could give her baby a good life. More than a good life — the best of everything. That's what Ella got. So please!" Natalie slammed her hand down on the counter, rattling the cups again. "Please don't ruin it."

Amanda took a deep breath. They both had a lot to absorb. She had discovered a cousin and children who could add richness and interest to her calcified family. But Natalie had to face the possible disintegration of her carefully constructed fantasy world as well as the confusion and wrath of her daughter when the deception came to light.

Amanda's family had gone thirty years without this knowledge. There would be time to explore the cousin relationships and time to let Natalie figure out how to reveal it.

For now, Amanda had to concentrate on Jonathan. According to Natalie, he had left Shelley high and dry, but she only had Natalie's word for that.

"Okay," she said carefully, "I don't want to cause your family pain. For now, I just want to talk to Shelley. I need to find out what she knows about my uncle."

The phone number had a 480 area code, which Natalie reluctantly admitted was in Phoenix, Arizona. When Amanda pressed her on why Shelley had moved so far away, Natalie had tightened her lips in a gesture Amanda had come to recognize. It seemed Natalie was practiced at keeping secrets.

"You'll have to ask Shelley."

Amanda could barely wait to phone. She found the nearest Starbucks, bought a latte, and settled herself and Kaylee in a quiet corner of the patio away from the irritating pop music and the tables of laughing teens. Her hands trembled as they hovered over the phone. Was this the moment of truth?

A woman with a soft, breathless voice answered the phone. Amanda had expected Natalie to have alerted her, but judging from the stunned silence that followed when Amanda explained who she was, there had been no warning.

"I'm sorry to call you out of the blue. I only found out about my uncle a couple of weeks ago, and your sister-in-law gave me your number."

Now she heard a sharp intake of breath. "I ... I don't understand. You never knew about Jonathan?"

"Not exactly. It's a long story," Amanda said. "I was only a little girl when he went out west. My mother and aunt lost touch with him, and they never talked about him."

"That's astonishing!"

"I'm hoping you know where he is."

"Thirty years is a long time."

Amanda hesitated. The woman's tone was firming up, as if she was recovering her footing. "I know about the baby. She looks just like my aunt. I know my uncle hurt you badly. I know he may not be a good person. But if you can give me any idea where he is, I don't need to bother you any more."

"What did you say?"

Amanda started to repeat herself.

"What did you say about the baby? About your aunt?"

"That Ella looks like her. Don't worry, I didn't say anything to her. I didn't even speak to her."

Silence. A strangled whimper.

"Shelley?"

"She's ... Ella is Jonny's baby?"

"I'm pretty sure. The resemblance is striking. Not just the face, but the laugh. The ballerina walk."

"I never knew. I thought ... There was another man. And back then, there was no DNA testing." Another whimper. "Oh, Jonny."

Amanda heard the anguish and disbelief in her voice and listened to her struggle with the pain she had kept secret for decades. "What happened?" she asked gently.

"I can't ... I can't talk about it."

"I'm sorry, it isn't really my business."

"It doesn't matter. I loved Jonny. We loved each other, and we were going to marry. When I found out I was pregnant, I was afraid it was the other man. I told Jonny ... what happened, and he was very upset. He promised he'd stand by me no matter what I decided. I told him I could never get rid of it. I could never kill a baby. He told me he was going to take care of things. I thought he meant take care of me, but ..." Her voice clogged with tears. "He never came back. He left like he was going to the corner store. Then —" She stumbled and blew her nose. "A week later I got a letter in the mail at the farm. It said he was sorry but he couldn't accept it, and there was a few hundred dollars to get rid of it."

Amanda was stunned. That was beyond callous. "I'm so sorry."

Shelley took a deep, quavering breath. "Yeah, that was some kick in the teeth, isn't it? I've gone through three marriages believing all men were monsters. Proven right every time." Tears gathered again. "Maybe if I'd been sure the baby was his, Jonny would have treated me different."

"He had no right to treat you that way regardless."

"It always comes down to the woman's fault, right? Like babies happen because we screwed up. Never mind the man's part." Her voice grew harsh as she stoked her anger. "We were raised Baptist. All that talk about sin and evil, it gets under your skin. I didn't know where to turn, and then my brother gave me an offer I couldn't refuse. He and Natalie were trying, but no luck. So I gave the baby to him." She laughed bitterly. "Sold her, in fact. Peter gave me a bunch of shares in his new oil company and plenty of money to start a new life."

"And in return?"

A pause. "In return, I was supposed to move as far away as I could and never have any contact with the baby. After Jonny left, I didn't want the baby anyway, so it seemed like a fair price." She stifled a whimper. "I'm sorry, I can't talk about this anymore. It's all too much. I have to go."

When Amanda hung up, she reached instinctively to run her fingers through Kaylee's soft fur. That poor woman. Amanda felt bad that she'd stirred it all up again. And for what? For a bastard who'd abandoned the woman in her time of greatest need?

As the dog nuzzled her, she felt calm settle back over her. She puzzled over the conflicting impressions of Jonathan that roiled around in her mind. She chased fleeting fragments of memory, of hide-and-seek, swoops in the air, and most vivid of all, big, crushing hugs that smelled of cigarettes, gasoline, and leather. Most of all, she remembered warmth. She remembered laughing.

Could this be the same man Shelley described?

She had only a child's view, and elusive at that. She needed someone else who knew him as an adult.

Her mother's voice was fuzzy. Belatedly, Amanda glanced at her phone. One p.m. in Ottawa. Too late to be in bed but too early for alcohol. She brushed aside her twinge of concern in her headlong rush to bring her mother up to date.

"So the bottom line is," she said when she'd finished, "I know a whole lot more about what Jon was up to but still no idea where he is now. His buddy from back then said Jon would give you the shirt off his back, but he's not coming across as a very nice guy, at least to Shelley. Does that sound like something he'd do? Run out on a pregnant girlfriend? A nineteen-year-old pregnant girlfriend?"

"Jesus," her mother muttered in a rare burst of profanity. "Jesus."

"Mum?"

"Yes. Yes, it sounds exactly like something he'd do. To a woman. He was a man's man. Fast cars, beer, loud music, juvenile pranks. His male friends always thought he was the life of the party, and unfortunately girls were attracted to that. But, well, those were different times, weren't they? Life goes on."

Amanda winced at the casually dismissive tone, but that was her mother's style. Paper over the shit and keep on trucking. It was not Amanda's. "You make him sound like a total jerk. Why? Did he do this before?"

Silence. Then her mother spoke. "I wasn't entirely truthful when I said he dropped out of engineering because he was bored. The truth was, he flunked out. He was in engineering at McGill, living in a fraternity house instead of the residence because he thought it would be more fun. He and his classmates spent their time either getting drunk at a local tavern or doing the rounds of frat parties, where they got equally drunk. Either way, alcohol and young men were not a pretty combination. Those were different times. Well, maybe not so different whenever beer and boys get together, but in those days there was no Me Too movement. Boys could get away with a lot, in fact were *expected* to act up, and universities looked the other way. These were the future cream of our society, after all."

"What happened, Mum?"

"Well, as I said, he failed his final exams. As far as I could see, that last year he never opened a book or turned in a lab report."

"I get that. But what's with the boys will be boys bit?"

"Nothing, Amanda, it was just a sign of his character. A style he carried on when he worked in the nickel mine. The mining culture makes the undergrad engineering culture look like a church picnic. He spent his nights with his friends at the bar and his weekends dirt bike racing. There were a few bar brawls, a couple of arrests for public drinking and rowdiness, but nothing more than high spirits until ..."

"Until what, Mum?"

"I was no longer at home by then, of course. I was already teaching at Carleton, and I had you and Will. But ..." She paused. Coughed to clear her throat. "Jean was still living at home."

Amanda felt a quiver of alarm. "What?"

"It was Christmastime, and we were home for the holidays. He and his friends were down in the basement, watching TV, drinking, and fooling around. They assaulted her." She spat the words out. "Well, not him, but his friends. And he did nothing to stop it."

The flat truth knocked Amanda's breath from her. "Jee-sus. Assaulted? You mean raped?"

"Fortunately, no. But they would have if I hadn't heard her screaming. I came down and found his buddies all over her, her pants torn, their hands over her mouth, and Jonathan half passed out on a chair. They'd plied her with alcohol. She was twenty-one, Amanda."

Amanda tried to catch her breath. A burst of laughter from a nearby table caught her ear. Teenage boys sharing a laugh over their phones. She felt a surge of anger. "Poor Jean."

"The next morning, he was all apologies and tears and claimed he didn't remember. I told my parents, and they kicked him out. He headed off with his tail between his legs."

"Oh, poor Jean."

"Yes. Although Jean was angry I'd told our parents. I think she was humiliated to be in that position and ashamed she'd got drunk. She was a proud and private person even back then, and socially — well, awkward. She'd always looked up to Jonny. Nonetheless, it was done. And as far as I'm concerned he had a lot of growing up to do. It sounds as if he didn't do it."

CHAPTER FIFTEEN

"I'm going to report Jonathan missing."

Amanda had retreated to another table in an even quieter corner of the patio to make her next call. The coffee shop was filling up with workers on their lunch break, smart young millennials in a hurry, dressed in casual chic and chattering in clusters. Her cup was empty, and she knew she had overstayed her welcome, but she needed to hear his voice.

"What happened?"

Chris listened without interrupting while she filled him in on her discoveries. "I've hit a dead end. No one has heard a word from him in thirty years. Not my mother, not Jean, not Shelley. I know he had reason to break off communication with all those people, but the abruptness and finality still seem odd."

"I agree," he said. "But when people want to start a new life, they often drop out of sight completely. Sometimes they even change their names. They're usually running from some major threat."

"Maybe he was afraid Shelley would come after him for money," she said. She spotted a woman holding a tray of food and eyeing her table longingly.

"That seems a bit extreme, especially since he's not likely worth millions."

"I know, but I can't get a handle on him. I can't tell if he's a heartless bastard or just a loser without the guts to face the consequences."

"Either way, it sounds like he doesn't want to be found. And you won't like him when you do find him."

She knew he was right; if Jonathan was as heartless as her mother and Shelley described, she would want nothing to do with him. And yet, why did she remember warmth and laughter, and above all, joy? A feeling she'd never got from her own father.

She raised her eyes to the blue sky as if for inspiration and answers to her vague unease. The tug of danger. "But I want answers. I know it's a process. Do I just walk into any police station?"

"Normally you report to the police station in the area where he disappeared."

"But we don't know where he disappeared. And after thirty years, does it matter?"

"Just procedure. If you hold off until tomorrow, I'll phone around and pave the way for you."

She felt a rush of relief. "I have a meeting with Matthew this afternoon anyway. Some oil baron. Tell me to play nice."

He laughed. "Would it make any difference?"

"Probably not." She pictured his eyes crinkling as he laughed. "I miss you."

"Me too. Love you."

After she hung up, she savoured those last whispered words. She remembered the heat of him cradling her. A flush of desire rose through her.

"Are you finished with that table?"

The sharp words jolted her back to the present. The woman was hovering nearby, tray in hand. Muttering an apology, Amanda jumped up and untied Kaylee. The dog leaped to her feet in delight, as if she'd been in shackles for years. Amanda took her on a long walk along the Elbow River, hoping nature would settle her thoughts. She had a trip to finalize, but the revelations of the past week had crowded out almost all other concerns from her mind.

Watching the birds flit from tree to tree and listening to the quiet rustle of the river, she felt peace steal over her. Until her phone rang. Was there no escape from outside demands? Reluctantly, she glanced at it. Matthew.

"That meeting with the R&D company that was scheduled for tomorrow?" he said. "It's cancelled."

"Oh." Amanda thought fast. "The carbon capture one?"

"Right. They called to withdraw their offer."

Natalie's company. That was quick.

"No reason given," Matthew continued. "The guy who called was very apologetic."

"That's Natalie Oaks's company, and I know the reason. I freaked her out."

"Jesus. What did you say to her?"

"Matthew! You know this is complicated. There are secrets she wants to keep a lid on, and this is probably her way of pressuring me."

In the silence that followed, Amanda watched Kaylee splashing around in the shallow water, snapping at bubbles with glee. The water was low and muddy. *She's going to be a mess*, Amanda thought.

"It would be a shame to lose that money, and the carbon capture research plays well with our commitment to protect the planet," he said eventually. "Would it help if I talked to her personally?"

"You can try. But only if you treat it as a straight business transaction. None of this background stuff comes into it."

Matthew snorted. "Give me some credit."

She was about to sign off when a thought occurred to her. "Speaking of background stuff, that oil exec we're meeting this afternoon, he's with Sandstar, right?"

"Yes. Why?"

"Sandstar owns Norsands, right?"

"It owns just about everything one way or another."

"Can you ask if they can send an exec called Hank Klassen instead? I'll give you his contact info." She thumbed through her phone.

"Why?"

"Killing two birds with one stone."

"Amanda ..." he said warily.

"I just want to meet the guy and maybe ask him a thing or two about the good old days."

"What reason am I supposed to give?"

She laughed. "Matthew, you're the PR genius, you'll think of something. Tell them I want someone with a long history in the company. The big picture."

Matthew muttered a few lame protests before ultimately agreeing to try. He phoned back a few minutes later to say that Klassen was unavailable today, but someone in the company had confirmed they would try to line him up as soon as possible. *Interesting*, Amanda thought. *Sandstar must really want this sponsorship.*

She knew her charity was a tiny blip on the huge company's radar, but it had a personal face, and that meant social media as well as traditional media coverage. Moreover, the Alberta Fun for Families trip involved First Nations youth from the Peace River region, where the impact on health, environment, and wildlife habitat from the oil sands was a hot-button issue. She worried about what the oil giant might want for their generosity.

When she and Matthew had first conceived of Fun for Families, crowdfunding through social media had been the main financial support, small donations by ordinary people who had modest means but believed in what she was doing. Amanda was proud that it was a charity of the little people for the little people. Over time, it had snowballed, and she wasn't sure she liked this shift toward corporate handouts. In the grand scheme of global finance and industry, the little people were usually the biggest losers.

Matthew rolled his eyes when she told him of her concerns later that afternoon. They were sitting on the patio of the River Café in the Prince's Island Park, where they had gone to give Kaylee a run. It was yet another cloudless, sunlit day, and a brisk breeze ruffled the papers Matthew had spread out on the table.

"Sure they want something out of it," he exclaimed. "Welcome to the real world, Amanda."

"I've been in the real world for more than twelve years, Matthew. I know all about the power of corporations."

As a nod to Alberta, he had exchanged his trademark fedora for a white Stetson. He sat back and tipped it apologetically. The prairie sun had given him a deep tan, and his pudgy middle had been pared down. For a short, balding, fifty-something ex-chain smoker, he was looking better than she'd seen him in years. All that hiking up and down the Calgary hills, he'd said with pride.

"I know. I'm just saying. They're a business; their eye will always be on what's good for their bottom line, and at the moment their image as evil, dirty oil polluters is the biggest impediment to their future. The oil industry is in crisis. Prices are tanking, countries around the world are finally waking up to the imminent catastrophe of climate change and are trying to cut carbon emissions. Wind, solar, and other sustainable energies are the new darlings. Pipelines are being blocked east, west, and south, not just by fringe environmentalists but by duly elected governments."

"I happen to be one of those people who think we need to reduce carbon emissions," she replied. "At least Natalie Oaks's company is making some effort to do that."

"Yeah, and I'll work on that. I know green initiatives are sexy right now. There aren't too many people saying, 'Sure, let's pollute the hell out of the planet.' But meanwhile people continue to buy giant SUVs and trucks, they build monster homes, they want their lamb from New Zealand and their blueberries from Peru. And they close their eyes to the fact that their oil is coming from human rights abusers in the Middle East by way of massive tankers."

She held up her hands in surrender. "I know. People are hypocrites. We don't need to argue about the geopolitics of oil. I'm sure we're on the same page."

"My apartment is piled high with a whole lot of shit Sandstar has sent. Flyers, pamphlets, reports on their efforts to address environmental and climate concerns. And on their outreach efforts in the Indigenous communities. They're mentoring Indigenous youth, offering summer work programs, and making an effort to recruit and train them. I'm sure we can find something in there that we can get behind."

She was tempted to retort "propaganda," but she held her tongue. Matthew was right. Sandstar was a business trying to figure out the best way forward in a PR nightmare. "So what do you think we're looking at here? What will they want?"

"Beyond bragging rights and a shiny new pamphlet to add to the others? I think they'll want the chance to talk to our kids and maybe have them spend an interactive afternoon at one of their research facilities."

"The agenda is already overly packed, and we're exploring Southern Alberta, not the oil patch."

Matthew shrugged. "You asked. We can counter-offer. Maybe a talk one evening, with a video and an invitation for a visit later in the year?"

It was a small price to pay, and it was true that the oil industry would offer one of the biggest employment opportunities for these kids once they were out of school. "If they are willing to focus their presentation on their Indigenous job programs and their research into sustainable practices, that would be fine."

She lay awake long into the night, worrying less about whether she was selling out her principles and more about what she was going to ask Klassen when they met. She hoped her offer would break the ice a little and make him more willing to offer information of his own.

The next morning, in preparation for her pitch to the police, she was sitting in the hotel breakfast room with a cup of coffee, scrolling through the photos and documents her mother had sent of Jonathan. Most of the photos were small and faded, but they captured moments that the family had shared. Amanda and Jonathan sitting on the floor under the Christmas tree, Jonathan pulling her and her brother on a toboggan, building a snowman, at the wheel of a speedboat. Always laughing, always happy. A memory flashed before her of barrelling down a hill on a toboggan in Jonathan's arms and shrieking with laughter as they tumbled into the snow.

When had her family ever been happy like this? Had it all died when he left? When he tore the family apart with one reprehensible deed?

The spooky tones of Skype startled her out of her reverie. A familiar face popped up on the screen. When she accepted the call, Chris came on live, his eyes crinkling with mischief.

"I couldn't stand another day without seeing your face," he said. "And I've got some info for you about reporting your uncle. As I said yesterday, procedure is to report him to the detachment where he disappeared, or was last seen."

"But we don't know that. Drumheller? Fort Mac? Someplace else? And I did some digging myself. The Alberta RCMP has a special missing persons and unidentified human remains unit at their Edmonton headquarters. Shouldn't I go directly to them?"

"No, they work with the files sent to them from the local detachments. Someone has to take the initial report. That is still your entry point into the system. And I suggest Drumheller because from what you said, he was more likely at the Oaks farm than at Fort Mac when Shelley last spoke to him. I've already been in touch with them, and they're expecting you."

She groaned. "Drumheller? I'm in Calgary, and I've got a meeting coming up with Matthew and a Sandstar exec, hopefully tomorrow. I feel like a yo-yo bouncing back and forth."

"I know, honey. Luckily, it's not far, and they are flexible about when you come in. So it can wait a couple of days."

The day had dawned steel grey and ten degrees colder, with wind gusting off the Rockies. Along with everyone else in Alberta, Amanda hoped it might mean rain. Crops were withering, and wildfires were raging in neighbouring British Columbia, sending smoke wafting over Calgary. Once she took stock, she realized she had little to do in the city except chafe with impatience, so it was as good a day as any to make the drive out to Drumheller.

The Drumheller RCMP detachment was a modern, sprawling low-rise clad in rich blue with the multicoloured RCMP stripe across its façade. Chris's initial contact had obviously paved the way, for she was ushered quickly through the security doors into the main room, where a Constable Brinwall greeted her, invited her to sit by his desk, and offered her coffee. Even bulked up with all his gear, he looked impossibly young, and he had a stiff, plodding style that did little to put her at ease. He typed in her name, address, contact information, and Jonathan's name before getting to the details of the disappearance.

Here the interview went from bad to worse. To question after question, she had to reply "I don't know." After five minutes, he pushed aside the computer and turned to her with a frown.

"So what you're saying is this man's been gone thirty years. You barely remember him. You aren't sure where he was last seen and by whom, you don't know whether he disappeared voluntarily or had an accident or …?"

"That's all correct," Amanda said. "Because for thirty years, no one put the pieces together. His girlfriend figured he'd ditched her, and his sisters figured … well, they hadn't parted on good terms. There had been an incident back home in Ottawa, and they'd had a falling out."

"What sort of incident?"

"Family dispute. An assault, but it was never reported to the police."

The constable turned back to his computer and typed some notes. "Any further involvement in criminal activities that you know of?"

Amanda shook her head. "But he seemed to get himself into personal messes. He was young and wild."

The constable typed some more. "Do you have any reason to believe his disappearance is anything but voluntary? Do you have reason to fear for his safety?"

Amanda realized then that her mother or aunt should have been the ones to make the report, not her. She knew nothing about Jonathan, and she had no sense of what would be normal for him. She had only this vague feeling that things didn't add up. She could almost hear the constable's dismissal in his tone, and it galvanized her.

"He has dropped off the face of the earth! No one — and I mean not his old friends, his girlfriend, his family — has had even a postcard from him since he sent this photograph taken outside the Oaks homestead thirty years ago. It's time to find out what happened."

"You realize that after thirty years, the trail is very cold. And without reason to suspect foul play or imminent risk ..." He paused and shook his head. "There are thousands of missing persons on the books across Canada, and many of them are people who don't want to be found. Your uncle sounds like one of those. He got himself into some trouble and decided to drop out of sight. Even if we do find him, if he doesn't want us to reveal his whereabouts, that's his right."

"That's fine. We just want to know if something bad has happened to him. So is there any more information that you need?"

Constable Brinwall studied her a moment, deadpan, before returning to his form. Laboriously, he filled in the blanks on Jonathan. Full name, age, date of birth, height, weight, eye and hair colour, build, ethnicity, distinguishing marks, tattoos, last known address, location and date of last known contact, known associates and friends, areas frequented. Amanda did her best to answer. Having made it through his form, the constable sat back with a grunt.

"What next?" Amanda asked.

"This goes up on the Canadian Police Information Centre and the missing persons database —"

"Just in Alberta?"

"No, nationally. This detachment is designated the primary investigative agency, but the information will be available to police services across Canada. Given his ties to Ontario and even Arizona, information could come from anywhere."

"Besides filing the report, what exactly will you do?"

He eyed her thoughtfully, as if debating how candid to be. "We'll check the databases for potential matches. And probably give this Shelley Oaks a call to gather more details on his disappearance. It will be an active case and will remain on the books until it's resolved in one way or another." He paused as if once again choosing his words carefully. "The database also contains all cases of unidentified deceased persons, so I'll crosscheck against that."

"And you'll call me with the results of these searches?"

He nodded, printed off a sheet of paper, and stood up. "Here's a list of resources and fact sheets with more information that you may find helpful. It also has the file number and my contact information if you learn more details or want an update."

Afterward, walking back toward the Hulk under chilly, leaden skies, Amanda felt vaguely disquieted. She suspected the officer had already concluded Jonathan's disappearance was deliberate, and he would make little active effort. But checking the databases would be worth something. At least she might learn whether he was alive or dead. She wondered whether it would be better for her mother and aunt to know that he was dead or to imagine that he had a nice new life without them. What had she unleashed by initiating this search?

Back at the Hulk, Kaylee greeted her with her usual exuberance and leaped out for a walk. As Kaylee bounced from bush to bush, Amanda felt her discouragement slowly fade. No one could stay depressed in the face of such *joie de vivre*. She pulled up the collar of her jacket, and as she walked, she phoned Chris to update him. She revelled in the cheerful confidence of his voice, and afterward she clutched the phone, unwilling to let him go.

THE ANCIENT DEAD

"I miss you," she said.

"Me too. I never felt so empty as when I got on the plane. I can't … can't be apart from you any more. We have to find a way."

"But that way involves me moving to Deer Lake, Newfoundland."

"There are worse things."

She thought about the places she'd called home in the past ten years. Places without safe water and sanitation, places often under threat of violence. Places that were nonetheless filled with joy and warmth. With people she loved.

"Yes, there are," she said.

CHAPTER SIXTEEN

When Livia Cole's name popped up on his call display, Todd wasn't sure he wanted to answer. His feelings of being used were still raw. But he'd spent a few futile days trying to get a lead on the silver belt buckle from the bone site, and he was running out of ideas. Maybe Livia had uncovered something. Maybe she could be useful for once.

He let the call go to voicemail and waited to see whether she'd leave a message. She did not, but two minutes later she called again.

"Ellison, pick up. I hate voicemail. I've been doing some digging, and I thought we could compare notes."

Compare notes, he thought, clutching at the hope. Despite a warning niggle, he phoned her back.

"Can we meet for coffee or a drink?" she asked without preamble. "Vintage Tap?" When he hesitated, she added, "Or are you more a Timmy's kind of guy?"

Stung by the hint of mockery, he had to take her up. "The Tap's fine."

"Half an hour. And bring your photos." Before he could object, she hung up.

She was already seated at a corner table when he arrived, swaying to the rhythm of the Terri Clark country song that crooned in the background. Despite the bar's sultry lighting and the tall glass of amber ale that sat in front of her, she looked younger than ever. She wore no makeup, and her hair was piled in a messy ponytail. She didn't look the least bit dangerous.

Hoping to set the tone, he'd already prepared his opening salvo. "Your treat, right? You're the one getting paid."

"Paid?" She laughed. "Is that what you call it?"

He tucked his laptop under his arm and pretended to leave.

"Fine, Ellison. Ho-lee. Sit down and show me what you've got."

As if she'd been practising all her life, she crooked her finger to signal for a second beer. Amused, he sat beside her and opened his laptop to access his photos. He still wasn't sure he wanted to cooperate, but she was entertaining. "You can't use any of these," he said.

She shrugged. "I'm just looking for leads on the deceased's identity. The cops and the Medical Examiner's office in Calgary are giving me a big, fat zero."

"Welcome to the club." Their heads bent together, they browsed through the photos slowly. "These aren't much help," he said eventually, sitting back to take another sip of his beer. "I've tried, but I can't even tell if they're male or female."

"What about the clothes?"

"No high heels, if that's what you mean. No jewellery either, except ..." He hesitated before clicking to the photo of the silver buckle. The ace up his sleeve. "It's an antique oil derrick."

She peered doubtfully. "If you say so."

"But that doesn't get us far. This symbol is everywhere. It could be from a rig anywhere in the province. It might not even belong to an oil worker. It could be an equipment manufacturer or even a custom job for a fan of the oil business."

Her eyes took on a sparkle of excitement. "But we could start with the oil companies around here. The old ones, since this is an antique and the bones are old. There used to be many active oil fields in the area around Brooks." She stood up abruptly and tossed back the rest of her beer. "This is great. I'll check this stuff out at home."

"But wait —"

"My laptop and notes are there."

Was she trying to blow him off now that she had the lead she'd been after? "Then I'm coming too. We'll check the stuff out together."

She scowled. "My place is a shoebox. And a mess."

He shrugged. "You should see mine."

She snatched up her coat. "Fine," she said, rattling off an address as she slammed some money down on the table and headed for the door. He had intended to follow her, but she took off in her car so fast that he wondered if she was trying to lose him. Had she given him a fake address?

He punched it into his phone as he drove through the quiet downtown streets, scanning ahead to catch sight of her. The address was a modest bungalow on a side street, and he was just drawing his truck to the curb when he heard a crash and a faint cry. Seconds later, a figure appeared from the far side of the house and ducked through the trees toward the street.

"Hey!" Todd yelled, jumping down from his truck.

A door slammed, an engine revved, and tires screamed as a truck shot away into the dark.

Todd raced around the bungalow. At the bottom of some stone steps, the door gaped open into darkness. A faint moan shot chills down his spine.

"Livia?" he cried, plunging down the steps. He groped on the wall for a switch and flooded the tiny space with light, revealing a mattress overturned, cupboards hanging open, and papers strewn on the floor. And in the corner by the door, the crumpled form of Livia.

Todd's fingers shook as he dialed 911. As the dispatcher talked him through the call, he took a close look at Livia for the first time.

"Is she breathing?" the dispatcher asked.

"Yes, but she's bleeding. Hurry!"

"The police and EMS are on their way, sir. Don't move her. I'll update them with this information. Where is she bleeding?"

"From her head. There's so much blood." Todd forced himself to focus and noticed a hall table with sharp corners near by. "She might have hit it on a table."

"Is she conscious?"

He placed his hand on Livia's arm and shook her gently. "Livia?" A flickering of her eyelids, nothing more. "Not really."

The dispatcher took down her name and his. "Are you a relative?"

"No, just a … a friend." He strained to hear sirens. Where the hell were the paramedics? How long did it take to drive three kilometres from the hospital? Even as he was cursing, he heard the wail. He raced upstairs to intercept them, and within seconds, the two paramedics had taken over. They worked quickly and calmly to check out her injuries, put her on a backboard and stabilize her neck and head, but Todd sensed their urgency. Livia had not opened her eyes or made a sound. One of them talked by hands-free radio to the hospital, and although Todd could not understand all the medical shorthand, he understood the request for a neurosurgical consult.

An RCMP officer arrived to lend a hand just as the paramedics were carrying her up the stairs. Once the ambulance had taken off, the officer returned, and Todd found himself face to face with Constable Brinwall. The officer said nothing while he checked out the scene and phoned his supervisor. Only after he'd reported in and requested backup did he turn to Todd, who was leaning on the concrete wall in the basement stairwell.

Brinwall's face was blank but Todd sensed suspicion. "Can you tell me what happened here, Mr. Ellison?"

"I don't know. I didn't see the attack. But —"

"What attack?"

"This! She was attacked. I saw the man running away. He got into a truck parked outside and took off."

Brinwall's expression didn't flicker as he took Todd through the standard questions. Height, weight, clothing, hair colour. Todd shook his head helplessly. "I didn't see. It happened so fast, and there were trees in the way."

"How do you know it was a man?"

"Well ..." Todd stumbled. As the adrenalin of the crisis wore off, he began to shake. The air in the stairwell closed in, and the metallic smell of blood turned his stomach. "I don't. I just assumed. Because ... Livia's a woman." He pictured Livia lying on the floor. Her clothes had not been disturbed. Nothing had been torn. He shrugged. "I don't know if it was a man."

Brinwall nodded, deadpan. "The vehicle. Can you describe it?"

"Yes, that I did see. It was a pickup truck."

"Make, model, license plate?"

Slowly Todd deflated. "It was too dark."

"Colour? Too dark for that too?"

Todd shut his eyes to conjure up the fleeting image he'd seen through the trees. His head spun. "Light-coloured."

"White, silver, beige?"

"I can't say."

Brinwall looked inside the chaotic apartment. "Looks like there was a fight in here. You do this?"

"No! I didn't touch her! I just heard her scream, saw her here, and called 911."

"What were you doing here?"

"I was meeting her. I mean, we'd been out and were going to her place, driving separate cars."

Brinwall allowed himself a smirk. "Are you and Ms. Cole in a relationship?"

"No! I barely know her." Todd flushed. He felt queasy and turned toward the steps. "I need some air."

Brinwall seized his arm and peered at him. "Have you been drinking?"

"One beer. Livia had two. I have to ..." He sagged against the wall and stumbled up the steps to gulp fresh, cold air into his lungs. He sat on the ground with his head between his knees.

Car doors slammed as a second patrol car arrived at the scene. Brinwall conferred with them briefly before returning to Todd. To Todd's surprise, he held out a chocolate bar.

"Eat this, it will help. And go home. We'll take your full statement in the morning."

Todd lay awake half the night, unable to get the memory of Livia's unconscious body out of his mind. She had looked so fragile. So close to death. Would they have reached the hospital in time? If only he'd driven faster. And who would do such a thing?

He replayed the scene endlessly, from the moment they left the restaurant to the moment he found her at the bottom of the stairs. The drive from the bar could not have taken longer than three minutes, and even if she'd driven like a rocket, she could not have arrived home more than a minute ahead of him.

That was not enough time to arrange to meet someone. Not enough time for them to knock her out, trash the apartment, and run away. Which meant the apartment had already been trashed when she got home. The attacker was already there. Lying in wait? Why? Break-ins were rare in Drumheller, especially violent ones, and people often left their doors unlocked. Had a burglar simply been casing out the street and chosen her apartment to rob? Bullshit. It was a quiet side street with modest houses, not likely to hold much worth stealing. And her apartment was on the side, in the basement, not visible from the street.

He stared at the ceiling, his heart racing. It was not a random attack. Livia had been targeted. He knew nothing about her past or about possible enemies. She was nosy, and she might have pissed off a few people with her articles, but she was just a small-town reporter. What could she possibly have done to provoke such rage?

And the attack wasn't just directed at her; her apartment had been ransacked, as if someone had been looking for something and they didn't have much time. What? In his panic the night before, he hadn't noticed whether she had a TV, but he knew she had a laptop. It would have all her notes on her investigation into the body, including his name and his role in it.

Fingers of dread ran down his spine. Was the laptop missing?

By morning, his fears had taken away all chance of sleep. He needed answers. He started by phoning the Drumheller hospital but hit the brick wall of patient confidentiality. Next, he combed through the online news, but there were no reports. Taking a deep breath to steel himself, he phoned the police. To his surprise, Constable Brinwall was still at the station, but he sounded tired and irritated.

"We may need more information on last night, Ellison, so keep yourself available."

"How is she?"

"We have no recent information on her status."

"But is she in the hospital?"

"I'm not at liberty to divulge —"

"Oh, for fuck's sake! Is she still alive?"

Brinwall paused, and his voice softened. "She was airlifted to Calgary Foothills Medical Centre. We've had no further update."

Todd felt a chill. Airlifted! It must be serious. "Do you know what happened?"

Mr. Deadpan was back. "The police investigation is ongoing, and I'm not at liberty to divulge any information at this time."

"But Livia — Ms. Cole — wrote a piece in the *Mail* about the bones —"

"Yes. On an anonymous tip."

Todd ducked the sarcastic undertone. "I'm wondering, do you suspect a connection?"

"Until we know otherwise, it is being investigated as a home invasion. We will be issuing a press statement recommending people lock their doors for now."

"But could I —"

"That's all." Brinwall's voice dropped. "Ellison … a warning. And a suggestion. Stay out of it, and if you get any information to report, call us ASAP." With that, the line went dead.

That ominous warning did nothing to reassure him. A phone call to the Foothills Hospital hit the same brick wall. He wasn't a relative, and patient information was confidential. After a frustrating half-hour runaround, he jumped into his truck and headed to Calgary. He didn't know what he hoped to accomplish. He hadn't even liked the pushy kid. She was too cocky and pig-headed for her own good. The attack could have nothing to do with him.

Yet he felt a floating sense of dread that he couldn't put his finger on.

The Foothills Medical Centre was part of a massive medical compound occupying a huge chunk of land off the Trans-Canada Highway opposite the University of Calgary. Todd thought he'd encountered the worst traffic possible in Vancouver, but nothing prepared him for the chaos surrounding Foothills. Construction, closures, and confusion seemed to be everywhere. He had no idea where Livia was, or if she was even still alive. He was inching around the circular drive, trying to find a parking lot close to the Emergency, when he spotted a red STARS air ambulance swoop down onto the top of a tall tower.

That must be it! he thought. The helicopter would have brought her in there.

He finally squeezed into a parking lot and headed across the complex toward the tower. McCaig Tower, according to the large black letters on its white concrete side.

His vague apprehension had grown to full-blown anxiety by the time he got inside, and he had no trouble convincing the clerk at the main desk that he was a relative of Livia Cole. He sighed with relief when told she was in ICU. "No visitors," the clerk said, "but you're welcome to join the family in the ICU waiting room."

At least she's not dead, he thought as he walked down the wide corridor toward the waiting area, which was packed with people. Some were slumped in their seats, trying to sleep, others were flipping through their phones or talking to each other, and still others were pacing. He studied faces, trying to guess who Livia Cole's family was. She'd had no wedding ring, and she was young, so the family was likely to be siblings of similar age or middle-aged parents.

It turned out to be easy. As he was looking, a bald man crossed the room with two coffees from the vending machines and handed one to a woman who was a rounder, wearier version of Livia. He approached.

"Mr. and Mrs. Cole?"

They looked up, eyes widening with alarm.

"I'm Todd Ellison, a friend of Livia's from Drumheller," he said as a mix of disappointment and relief crossed their faces.

He hesitated, wanting to keep his involvement out of it. "I heard about the attack. How is she?"

"You a reporter too?" The father's face sagged in bitter crags of grief.

"No, I'm a photographer. I'm just worried about her." Todd's voice shook, and it was not an act.

The father stared at him for a few long seconds. His eyes glittered with a rage that simmered beneath his grief. "She's in a coma. They did surgery, and they're keeping her in a coma to stop the brain from swelling. That's what they say, anyway. We won't know how she is until they bring her out of it."

"Do the police know who did it?"

Cole shook his head. "How does this happen in a quiet place like Drumheller? Here in Calgary, or on a remote farm where it takes the cops an hour to arrive while hooligans go —" His wife reached out, lightning fast, to squeeze his arm. He pressed his lips tight as he glared at her. "Well, you know what they're like! No respect for hard work."

"The police think it was a home invasion," Todd said to steer him back.

"She'd only been there three months. She just got out of university. What did she have worth stealing?" The man's eyes filled, and his wife touched his arm again, gently this time.

"Maybe it had something to do with her work. Like a story she was working on."

Cole's eyes narrowed. "You know something? What she was working on?"

Todd backtracked. "No, but she was pretty ambitious. She wasn't afraid to go after a story."

"That's how I raised her."

The mother had been eyeing him intently, and now she intervened. "She was always asking questions. Always pushing.

The police said her apartment was ransacked. They wondered if the guy was looking for something."

"Yeah, drugs," the father muttered.

"Did they say what?"

The mother continued to stare at him. "Do you know?"

"Jewellery? Electronics?"

"If the police know something, they're not telling us," the father said. "And you know what? I don't give a fuck. I just want my little girl to wake up from that coma and be whole again. You want to help? Pray." He stood up and walked away.

The mother, however, remained still. "Who are you? Why are you so interested?"

Sharp like her daughter, Todd thought. "I'm a friend. And yeah, I'm worried. Sometimes she's like a dog with a bone. She might stir up trouble."

The mother offered a grim smile. "She wouldn't even know the dangers. She's just a kid. So if you know something …"

He shook his head and fled as soon as he could after promising them both he would pray for her. A lie, since he'd given up praying a long time ago, but he figured it was what they needed to hear.

It was late afternoon by the time he was back on the open road. As he navigated the torrent of cars in Calgary's rush hour, he agonized over the role he might have played in the attack. It was true that Livia had done a lot of extra research and had published information far beyond what he'd told her, but he'd been the one who'd provided the crucial first tip. Without his fateful phone call, she would not even have known about the body in the coulee.

A brief shred of hope drifted across his mind. Clutching at it, he phoned the editor of the *Drumheller Mail*. The man had just heard about the attack and was preparing a piece for the paper.

Ducking questions about his own involvement, Todd gave a vague story of his friendship with Livia before getting to the point.

"Livia was pretty hungry," he said. "Maybe she pissed someone off. What stories was she working on?"

"The cops asked me that. Nothing dangerous, unless you count the fierce rivalry at the county bake contest. I know folks can get pretty riled up. But other than that? An outdoor rock concert, a special museum event."

"What about that story about the bones?"

There was silence on the phone, and Todd feared he'd gone too far. The last thing he wanted was to rouse the interest of another reporter.

"Yeah, she was doing some digging," the editor said.

"Did she find anything?"

"I'm not comfortable revealing anything."

Todd's phone chirped an alert that there was another caller on the line. The RCMP. "Listen, I've got another call."

"Do you know something about it?" the editor pressed.

"I gotta go."

By the time he connected to the other caller, the call had gone to voicemail. He listened as he drove. The message was brusque and to the point.

"Mr. Ellison, Constable Brinwall of the Drumheller Detachment. Would you come into the station at your earliest convenience, please."

Todd glanced at the clock on his dash. It was nearly five o'clock, and the sun was deep in the western sky behind him. He wondered whether the constable would be on duty by the time he arrived. In the end, he decided to take the chance. Brinwall had been on night duty the evening before.

The man was munching a muffin when Todd arrived. He didn't smile as he ushered him to his desk, and his poker face was unnerving. "You went to see Livia Cole's family in hospital," he said without preamble. "You pretended to be a relative."

Todd bristled. "I wanted to know how she was. Is that a crime?"

"Did you attack her?"

"What? No! I called 911!"

Brinwall shrugged. "Stranger things happen in relationships."

"There is no relationship. I barely know her! We were working on —" He stopped abruptly.

The poker face flickered. "You're the leak."

Todd sighed. He raised his eyes to the ceiling. It was time to cooperate, for Livia's sake. And his. "Yes, I am. I didn't give her all the information she printed. I didn't know most of it. But I did tell her about the bones. I was trying to find out if there was any new information."

"Why?"

"Why? Because eventually, when all the ancient history is uncovered, I want to include it in my book."

"You were instructed not to disclose any of it."

Todd eyed him thoughtfully. He had no reply to that, but he sensed it didn't matter. Something more important was at play. "The attack … You *do* think it was about the body. The attacker figured she was a threat, maybe because of what she knew or the questions she was asking."

"I can't comment on an ongoing investigation. We are considering all possibilities."

"But her place was ransacked. The person was obviously looking for something."

"It could have been anything. Jewellery, for example."

"Under the mattress?"

The poker face closed down. Todd took a deep breath. "Look, I know I made a mistake. I feel terrible. If Livia has been hurt because of what I told her, I'll …" He shook his head to banish the guilt. "But it also makes me worried. What if they found my name in her files? What if they come after me too? I need to know what they took. Her notes? Her laptop?"

"Mr. Ellison, how do I know you're not fishing for information for that book of yours?"

"Because I'm scared! Fuck, man, this guy doesn't fool around! Was her laptop missing?"

Brinwall regarded him in silence before shoving back his chair and going into the office marked *Staff Sergeant*. Todd heard the mumble of voices, but despite all his efforts to decipher them, he could make out nothing but his own name. Brinwall yanked open the door just as Todd was hustling back to his chair. Brinwall glared at him.

"My advice to you — my strong advice — is to stay out of this, Mr. Ellison, and let us do our job."

"But was her laptop missing? You can tell me that much!"

"No electronic devices were found in the apartment. Which could just as easily mean an ordinary burglary."

"But what are the chances? She lived in a little basement rental, not a fancy big house. She was nosing around, asking questions about the body in the coulee. Maybe she spoke to someone; maybe she learned something about its identity."

"None of that information is available yet."

"But you said in the press release that the bones were decades old."

"That was to reassure the public that there was no imminent threat."

"Then it wasn't true?"

Brinwall glared again. "I didn't say that."

Todd sighed with frustration. "But if the body was decades old, why would it matter now? Why would someone bother to cover it up?"

Brinwall stood up to herd him toward the exit. "Usually, the simplest explanation is the correct one. A straightforward burglary. Anything she left on the table would be fair game."

"But she was beaten within an inch of her life!"

"Maybe she surprised the burglar in the act. It looks like he may have knocked her aside trying to get out, and she hit her head on the coffee table."

"So you're telling me I'm not in danger."

Brinwall hesitated a beat. "I didn't say that either. I called you in to tell you two things. First, stay away from the Coles. They have enough on their plate. And second, stay in town. Don't forget, until Ms. Cole wakes up and tells me otherwise, you're my prime suspect."

CHAPTER SEVENTEEN

Because of the huge distances and prohibitive costs of flying to the two schools they were working with up north, Matthew and Amanda had been relying on the miracle of virtual communication to organize the tour. Matthew had set up an interactive website and Facebook page, and through a discussion forum, blog, video, and audio software they had created an itinerary, recruited interested students, exchanged concerns, and provided orientation. One final video conference was planned with all the attendees as well as the teachers and community elders who'd be accompanying the group. In one week the group and their gear would be loaded onto a plane and flown south to Drumheller, where their adventure would begin.

The video conference was scheduled for late afternoon at the larger high school. Amanda had been in Calgary dealing with last-minute inquiries and she was hurtling down Crowchild Trail to the AV room Matthew had rented when her phone rang.

"Ms. Doucette? It's Constable Brinwall from Drumheller Detachment."

Her heart jumped. She narrowly missed a car cutting in.

"There has been a development in the missing persons case of Jonathan Lewis."

"Hold on a minute." Amanda wrestled the Hulk off the highway at the next exit and pulled onto a side street to park. Her hands were slick with excitement. "Sorry. Go ahead, Constable."

"We'd like a DNA sample from a family member who is biologically closest on the maternal side."

"You've found something."

"Having the sample in our database will help match possibilities, that's all."

"But you have a possibility. What — who is it? Is he dead?"

"I'd prefer not to speculate, Ms. Doucette."

"What do you need for the sample?" She did a quick calculation of her commitments. "I can come to Drumheller tomorrow."

"According to your report, there are two sisters, both alive. They would be closer matches."

"But they live out east."

"They can provide the sample at any police station and it will be entered into the database."

Amanda thought fast. She had told her mother about making the missing persons report and assumed her mother had told Jean, but neither of them had called for progress reports since. Which one was likely to be less upset and more cooperative?

"How long does this take?"

"It's a quick swab and a couple of forms."

"No, I mean to match it?"

There was a pause. "Weeks, unfortunately. It gets sent up through channels and our forensics lab in Edmonton does the testing. But there is a backlog and samples are prioritized, so it won't be a fast process."

In which case, who would be more patient? Her mother or Jean? It took her only a moment to answer that. Aunt Jean could stay still for hours, watching a bird, whereas her mother was always on to the next thing. "I'll contact my Aunt Jean. Jean Lewis. She lives in Quebec. Will that be a problem?"

She heard him give a rare chuckle. "No, it's a national database, even includes Quebec. All the samples go to the same place."

"Thank you. Is there any hint, no matter how small or vague, that you can tell me?"

Another pause. "This is an old case. It may take even longer to complete the investigation."

After Amanda hung up, she sat a minute, clutching the steering wheel to stop her hands from trembling. *They know something!* They're sitting on a potential match, and they can't even tell me if the person is dead or alive. Not for weeks! I'll have to go through my entire tour pretending it's life as usual.

She took a deep breath and looked up Jean in her contacts. The phone rang and rang until voicemail came on. Was Jean even in the country? Should she phone her mother instead?

She left Jean a message to phone ASAP and continued on to her video conference. The meeting went so well, and the students were so enthusiastic and full of ideas, she even managed to forget about the DNA test. Thanks to the wonders of the Internet, the students had already done a lot of research about the places they would visit and were thrilled at the prospect of digging up dinosaur bones, climbing hoodoos, and riding horseback over the open range. They lived in a land of forests and lakes, but the endless plains of cowboys and buffalo were the stuff of legend.

Matthew had chosen the students well. Among the group was Kari, the daughter of a band chief, who was already planning to study law, and Michel, a Métis youth who had started a radio show interviewing community elders. There was an equal number of boys and girls, which might prove interesting if hormones took over, Amanda thought wryly. There were high achievers and those struggling to get by. Amanda hoped the strong, supportive bonds between them would last beyond the trip.

The video conference ended with a new to-do list for Amanda to address at Dinosaur Provincial Park before the group arrived the next week.

"I called Natalie Oaks yesterday," Matthew said as he and Amanda settled down for a debriefing afterward at his favourite restaurant on 17th Avenue.

"How was she?"

"Cordial." He paused. "Well, she didn't hang up on me. She agreed to meet me Friday in person. I'll see if I can salvage the donation."

"She's had a couple of days to calm down. Maybe she's realized it might be better not to piss me off."

A faint frown furrowed his brow. "Amanda. She sounds like a nice woman who's juggling a lot."

She sipped her wine, feeling chastened. "You're right. See what you can do. I like the carbon capture angle better than Sandstar, and it would be nice to have enough money left over to give a hefty donation to Reconciliation Canada."

"I'm still working on a time to meet that Klassen dude, the Sandstar sponsor. He seems to spend most of his time on the links. You sure you still want to meet him personally?" He beamed with delight as the server arrived with his soft-shell crab. Kaylee's nose twitched with interest. They were seated at a corner table on the patio with Kaylee at their feet and the chilly shadows of early September already stealing across the street.

Amanda pulled her fleece tighter around her. Jonathan was still a mystery to her. She had Shelley's version of what had happened between her and Jonathan, but Hank Klassen had worked with both Shelley and Jonathan. Perhaps Jonathan had confided in him. If he could shed more light on Jonathan's character or on what exactly had changed his mind about the pregnancy, it would be worth it.

"I'd still like to talk to him," she said, "but I'm not sure there will be time before the tour starts. I've got a ton of things to do down at the park and the museum, so I'll be staying out at Maeve's again until the tour starts. Maybe he can meet us out that way."

Kaylee watched Matthew's every move as he sucked succulent juice off his fingers. He dipped a scrap of bread into the juice and fed it to her. It vanished in an instant, and she was back for more. "Is there any decent place to eat out there?"

She laughed. "Maeve cooks a wicked burger. And Drumheller has some nice places."

He made a face. "I'll run it by him, but I won't hold my breath. This guy likes his luxury."

Jean's return phone call came at seven o'clock the next morning, just as Amanda was fumbling with the coffee pot. "I hope I'm not too early," Jean said without preamble. "Have you news?"

"Yes and no. My mother told you about the missing persons report?"

"And?"

"The police want a DNA sample from the closest female relative."

"Ah."

"That's you. You phone the Sûreté du Québec and make arrangements to go to the station."

"Why me? Your mother is his twin."

"Biologically, that makes no difference."

"There's more to being a twin than biology."

"I know, but ..." Amanda groped for the right words. "You seemed to care more than she did. You kept in touch with him and kept that photo on your wall."

"That doesn't mean she didn't care. She was angrier."

"Less forgiving, you mean."

"It was a protective older sister thing."

Amanda had difficult imagining Jean in need of protection, even as a young woman. "And that's the other reason. Mother would be more argumentative. She'd grill them about where her results would be stored, who would have access to them, and how they'd be disposed of. Everything is a fight with her."

Jean chuckled. "That much is true. But I will ask them the same questions, Amanda. Just perhaps more subtly."

"I'll ask her if you don't want to do it."

"No, I will. I thought of doing it myself when this new humanitarian DNA database was created a couple of years ago. It's time to get on it." Jean paused. "Do you plan to tell your mother, or shall I?"

"No, no. I have to do it. I'll think up some explanation."

"Good luck with that." The last Amanda heard was a soft chuckle as her aunt hung up.

Kaylee greeted Maeve like a long-lost saviour, leaping out of the Hulk and racing over to snatch up the nearest stick. Maeve was on her knees in the garden, weeding around the day lilies. She grunted as she struggled to her feet.

"I should let Mother Nature have her way with them. Let only the strong survive." She tossed the stick. "You look like you've had a busy few days. Lunch? Beer?"

Amanda dragged her bag out of the back seat. "I've done a lot of driving back and forth. Kaylee and I are both sick of it. I'm going to take her for a quick walk, and then a Big Rock would be awesome. I'll help you with lunch."

She headed out across the prairie. Beneath her feet, the soil was parched and cracked from the summer's drought, and on the horizon the abandoned oil derricks and scattered cattle were silhouetted against the relentless blue sky. But on the adjacent irrigated fields, the alfalfa was rich green and the wheat fields were deepening to rich amber. Wind rippled the wheat, creating a golden ocean. Slowly, that cherished prairie peace stole over her.

She returned to find Maeve in her huge, cluttered farm kitchen, grilling up bacon and cheese sandwiches. The smell of bacon filled the room. As always, the radio was on full blast, and Maeve shouted over the chatter of the farmer's report, much of which was about water restrictions and depleted reservoirs. Amanda pushed aside canning jars and boxes of supplies to set two places at the long harvest table. After pouring two beers, she handed one to Maeve and took a grateful sip of her own as she filled Maeve in on the latest news about her uncle.

"My aunt is submitting DNA." She grimaced. "I have to call my mother."

Maeve flipped the sandwiches. "Do you think the Mounties know something?"

"I'm not sure. I can't get past the brick wall. Do you know Constable Brinwall out of Drumheller?"

"He's not from around here. Nova Scotia. But he's trying hard. Been doing some volunteering on kids' sports teams since he came." She grinned. "He gave me a speeding ticket once. Does that count?"

Amanda laughed at the image of Maeve tearing up the back roads in her 1980s pick-up. "Probably won't help my case."

"Well, Canada's a big, empty country. Lots of places to get lost in and never found. Sometimes they make the DNA connection years later." Maeve paused and her eyes lit up. "You know, they found human remains not far from here just a couple of weeks ago. The cops said they'd been there for decades."

"Where?"

"They didn't say exactly. In a coulee somewhere up the river. A hiker found them. Not a big deal. This is a land littered with old bones."

"Was this reported in the newspaper?"

"Just a short article in the local paper." Maeve pointed to a stack of old papers piled by the woodstove. "It'd be in there somewhere. Why? You're not thinking ..."

Amanda was already across the room, rummaging through the newspapers. "I don't know. But something made the cops call me back to get a DNA sample."

"It's the most recent issue, I think. Cover page."

Amanda found it and sat back to read, her heart racing with excitement. A burnt smell wafted across the room, and Maeve turned back to the stove with a curse. She flipped the two sandwiches onto the waiting plates and made a face. "We can just cut off the burnt edges. The middle should be perfect."

Amanda looked up. "I remember this. The day we went trail riding, there were cops on the edge of the highway. But —" She waved the paper. "There's no mention of where the body was found. Just the fact the bones are being examined in Calgary. That could take weeks, but part of it would certainly be DNA extraction. There are so few details! I wonder who this hiker is. Do you know? Has there been any gossip?"

Maeve's head was deep in the fridge, and her "no" was muffled. Amanda peered at the byline and turned to the next page. "Is there anything more by this reporter, Livia Cole? She should know."

Maeve had emerged with a head of lettuce and was beginning to wash it, saving the water in a bowl. She stopped in mid-motion. "Livia Cole? That rings a bell." She scrunched up her face as she riffled through her memory. "Her home was broken into. She was badly hurt."

"When?"

"Just a couple of days ago. It's all over social media. She's in critical condition in Calgary."

Amanda stood up, her thoughts racing. "That's quite a coincidence."

Maeve frowned. "What would connect a decades-old body and a small-time kid reporter? She's barely been on the job three months."

"Her knowledge. Something she knew but didn't report. Or something her attacker thought she knew."

"That's a stretch. Break-ins do happen, especially in tourist season."

I bet Constable Brick Wall knows, Amanda thought. *He must have his ear to the ground about everything that happens around here, including who the anonymous hiker is.*

After lunch, she used the excuse of updating him on the DNA request to phone him, with predictable results. "The Livia Cole case is an ongoing investigation, and no information is being released at this time."

Undeterred, Amanda breezed ahead. "The body she reported on. Do you think that could be my uncle? Is that what the DNA testing is for?"

"That speculation is premature, Ms. Doucette."

"Can you tell me any details about the body? Age, male or female, how long it's been there?"

"It's way too early in the investigation. The remains are undergoing thorough analyses, and once all the results of the post mortem are in, those details will go up on the national missing persons and human remains database. Until then —"

"Can you tell me where the body was found?"

"No, I can't."

"Why not? I assume it's not a crime scene?"

That seemed to stump him. He sputtered, and she thought he was going to fall back on "Because I say so." Instead, he tried for a placating tone. "Ms. Doucette, I know it's frustrating for family members, but these things take time. The scientific analyses are complex. Don't get ahead of yourself. Or us."

"Then can you at least tell me who the anonymous hiker is?"

"No!" His tone was sharp. "For the last time, stay out of it. I will call you!"

The phone went dead. Amanda eyed it in frustration. Was that a hint of alarm? She looked up the number for the Calgary Foothills Medical Centre. The friendly but distracted clerk who manned the main switchboard informed her there was no room number for a Livia Cole. That could mean anything from privacy restrictions to death.

Next she phoned the *Drumheller Mail* and was sent to voicemail. She left her name and number, not holding out much hope for a quick reply, and went back to the urgent meal planning details she'd been neglecting. Unlike some previous tours, which had a dedicated cook, the Time Travel tour was going to be a collaborative effort, with all staff and students sharing meal preparation and clean-up. They were going to have some Indigenous Siksika dishes as well as original settler foods, but teen favourites like barbequed burgers and corn on the cob would also be on offer.

To her surprise, the editor phoned back within half an hour, sounding excited. "We'd love to do a feature on you!" he exclaimed before she could explain the reason for her call. "We're so thrilled you're highlighting the museum and the park, and the demographic you've chosen is perfect! Right now, the needs and prospects of our First Nations, Métis, and Inuit are front and centre across the province. Is it possible for one of our reporters to shadow your group for a day?"

Amanda thought fast. Notoriety and public exposure had not been an issue in her earlier tours, but now that Fun for Families was attracting more mainstream media attention, she needed a protocol. That was something to discuss with her media guru Matthew.

But the editor had unwittingly given her a lead into her real reason for calling. "I will have to talk to the group and their parents first, of course, but that's a possibility. Who would you send? Livia Cole? She's young. They might relate to her."

His voice dropped. "Oh no, she's off the job. Injury."

"Yes, I heard something about that, but I was hoping she was back."

"No. She's in the hospital."

"What happened?"

"Burglary. I guess she caught the guy in the act."

"Do the police know who it was?"

"Nope."

"And what happened to her? Was she badly hurt? Maybe she'll be back soon."

There was a pause on the line, as if the editor were questioning whether to breach privacy. "She's in a medically induced coma, and until she comes around, they won't know."

"I'm so sorry. Poor woman. I hope she will be okay." Amanda was at a loss what to say next. She was running into dead ends with every inquiry. Finally she decided to ask directly, no matter how insensitive it might seem. "I read the article she wrote on the human remains in the coulee. It made me curious to check the area out. Do you know where it is?"

Silence. Amanda winced. That was *too* direct.

"No," he said finally. "She never said."

"She said a hiker found them. A local dude?"

"No idea. Why?"

Amanda groped for a reasonable cover story but could find none. "Sorry, I know it's a weird question. It's a personal story, nothing to do with my tour."

"Oh. Well, Livia played that whole thing real close to her chest. I know she was looking into it more, but that's all."

"Do you know anyone she might have talked to?"

"She was new here. Didn't have many friends here yet. Maybe her mom? I know she called home pretty regularly."

"Do you have a phone number for the mom?"

Another silence. She didn't give him time to refuse. "I'm sorry, I know I'm asking a lot. I don't want to upset anyone, but if I can find out anything at all about this discovery, it would mean a lot."

"Hold on," he said, resignation in his tone. She felt a curious mixture of guilt and triumph when she thanked him and signed off, repeating the number until she could enter it into her phone.

Amanda dreaded making the call and intruding on the family's anguish. Surely there was another way. Maeve had said the coulee was "just up the river." Amanda headed up the road toward Drumheller, staying as close as possible to the Red Deer River and trying to remember where she'd seen the police cars. Maybe something would trigger her memory or give her a clue. A marker off the highway, remnants of police tape. She knew the hiker could give her more information about the body than the burial site alone could, but at least it would be a start. To stand in the place where Jonathan had died, to see where and possibly how he died, might give her some answers.

She crisscrossed the back roads for an hour to no avail, leaving trails of dust in her wake and squinting into the brilliant prairie sun. Everything looked the same. One hill, one coulee, was much like another. *What an insane waste of time! You don't even know if the body is Jonathan.*

She returned to Maeve's B&B, dusty, stiff, and frustrated. Evening was falling, washing the fields in ripples of amber. She took Kaylee for a long walk as she tried to shake off her frustration. Thrilled that there was a ball in play, the dog bounced around like a crazed ping-pong ball as she waited for each toss. Amanda's thoughts were hundreds of kilometres away, with Livia's mother.

"It's a terrible invasion of her privacy," she said to Kaylee, who cocked her head. "This is an awful time for them. They're wrestling with life and death, and I phone to ask about their daughter's news story."

Kaylee barked her impatience, bringing Amanda back to the present. "If only my life was as uncomplicated as yours, princess." She tossed the ball and watched as the dog raced off, her copper fur flashing in the sun. "How can I possibly frame this in a way that won't sound selfish? Because it *is* selfish."

She poked and prodded at the problem, trying to find another solution. Chances were the mother wouldn't know the hiker's name anyway, so the distress caused would be in vain.

Kaylee returned and flung the ball at her feet. Shaking her head, Amanda picked it up. "You and me. One-track minds. No wonder I love you." She threw the ball and watched the dog hurtle after it.

I can't not do this. I can't not know.

With trepidation she phoned the number, half hoping it would go to voicemail so she could explain her request and give the mother time to decide whether to return the call or not.

A woman picked up on the second ring. Tentative, wary, but in control. Quickly, Amanda gathered her wits and introduced herself. "I know this is a terrible time for you, and I'm so sorry to intrude —".

"Who did you say you were?"

Amanda repeated her name, and to add credibility, she tacked on Fun for Families. From the dead silence on the phone, she suspected the woman had never heard of her.

"Why are you calling?"

"I am very sorry to hear about your daughter. How is she?"

"What do you want?"

Amanda watched Kaylee return. She didn't want to simply blurt out her request, but the mother left her no choice. "It's about the bones discovered in the coulee. Livia's been working on a story about it. I … I think it might be my uncle's body, but the police won't tell me anything. I'm wondering if she shared any details about it with you. Whether it was a man or a woman, how old, how big. Any clothes or other clues?"

"It's an old body. Been there decades."

"Yes, I know. My uncle disappeared thirty years ago."

"Oh." Silence. Was the woman wavering?

"Did she talk to you about it at all?"

"Livia is in a coma. We still aren't sure she'll ever wake up."

"I'm so sorry. They do amazing things with brain injuries these days, so don't give up."

"Oh, I won't give up. Neither will my girl. My husband is busy praying, but I'm hounding doctors. Every single twitch and moan, I tell them about, even if they don't think it means anything. She squeezed my hand this afternoon. That was like … the earth moved."

"That's wonderful. Her recovery is the most important thing. Way more important than my uncle."

"A few people have called to ask about that story of hers."

Amanda froze. Kaylee was dancing in circles at her feet, but Amanda barely saw her. The present receded. "You mean reporters?"

"They didn't say. Just asked to talk to her, and then if I knew anything."

"Did you tell them anything?"

"I sent them packing. Like coyotes circling the wounded. Livia had big plans for that story; she'd been asking farm neighbours and such, and I wasn't going to give it away."

"Did you tell the RCMP about the calls?"

"No, why should I?" She sounded surprised. "Why? Is there a problem?"

"I think you should tell the cops. She was working on that story when she was attacked."

Amanda heard a sharp intake of breath, followed by a mumbled exchange of voices as she spoke to someone else. "There was a guy," the mother began, "even came here, acting all concerned, like he was her buddy. He didn't seem dangerous, more freaked out. We told him to buzz off."

"Did he tell you his name?"

"Tall guy. About forty? Todd somebody." Another exchange of voices. "Yeah. Todd Ellison."

CHAPTER EIGHTEEN

Amanda was propped up in bed, just beginning to research Todd Ellison on the Internet, when Skype rang and Chris's mischievous face popped up on her screen.

"What are you doing calling so late?"

His big, crinkly grin vanished. "Why? You don't want to talk to me?"

"Of course I do! I'm over the moon to see you. But it must be midnight in Newfoundland."

"I couldn't sleep. Couldn't stop thinking about you."

The teasing sexuality in his voice set her body humming. She blew him a kiss. "Miss you too. Hold that thought ... and whatever else you want to."

He chuckled.

"What have you been up to?"

"The usual summer stuff. Tourists getting lost in Gros Morne, capsizing in kayaks because they think how hard can sea kayaking be? Speeders, moose collisions. Major criminal stuff."

"That sounds idyllically calm."

He laughed. "It needs you to spice it up. What's new with you?" he added quickly, as if remembering too late that Newfoundland had already beaten her up.

She filled him in on the DNA request. "Do you think it means they have a potential match?"

"No, it means they did some preliminary inquiries and determined you're not a nut case. That the MisPers report is legit."

She was about to tell him about the human remains and the attack on Livia Cole when he spoke again. "Have you told your mother you asked Jean instead?"

"No, I was going to, but …" In truth, the intervening events had driven it from her mind.

"Honey, you have to tell her before she finds out from Jean."

"That might be easier."

"For you. But she needs to hear from you why you chose Jean. She'll be hurt."

"You don't know my mother. She might be angry, but she doesn't do hurt."

"All mothers do hurt."

He was right, of course. Her mother would hide it, as she always did, and she would agree that Amanda's reasons made perfect sense. But beneath the bravado, the affront would sting.

"All right, all right. I will, first thing in the morning. Now, can we talk about something else?" She gave a low chuckle. "Your trouble sleeping?"

After another fifteen minutes, she signed off and curled up in bed, cradled in a warm glow.

As soon as her mother answered the phone the next morning, Amanda knew she was too late. Her mother spoke only one word, "Amanda," and her tone was chilly.

"Jean told you."

"She did."

Amanda was sitting at Maeve's kitchen table, toying with a cup of coffee. She'd found herself unable to eat the pancakes Maeve set in front of her. Now she looked at the ceiling as if guidance would magically appear. When in doubt, deflect.

"Old human remains have been uncovered in a coulee here. I think that's what the DNA is for."

Her mother stayed the course. "I see."

"It will take weeks, but it's a start. I hope it's not Jonathan, but I'll keep you posted."

"Will you?"

Again, Amanda had to dodge the hostility dripping from her mother's voice. "I've got more news about him. His pregnant girlfriend in Fort McMurray had a daughter who was raised by an uncle. She looks just like —" Amanda was about to say Aunt Jean but stopped herself on the brink. "Like you. She has kids of her own now."

Predictably, her mother seized on the suspicious part of the story. "Why was she raised by an uncle?"

"I told you, Jonathan ran out on the woman. It seemed best for the baby."

"Right. Typical."

"It's not clear what happened to Jonathan after that. He ..." She hesitated. Telling her mother about his letter with the abortion money would only cement her mother's contempt. "He and his girlfriend lost touch."

"So he has a daughter he never laid eyes on and never bothered to tell us about."

"Yes."

"I don't know why you're taking the time to look for him, Amanda. He obviously hasn't changed."

That's exactly why I asked Jean instead of you, Amanda thought, but bit back the retort. "That was thirty years ago.

Maybe he has changed. Maybe he's ashamed, or afraid of disrupting his daughter's life. And maybe, Mother, he's dead."

The word hung in the silence. In that silence, in the soft, measured breathing she could hear over the phone, Amanda tried to guess her mother's reaction.

"Yes," her mother said finally. "That wouldn't be a surprise."

"I will keep you posted," Amanda said. "And I'm sorry. I'm sorry I didn't involve you sooner."

"Well, nothing new in that." One parting shot, followed by the beep of a disconnected call.

Maeve had been discreetly washing pots at the kitchen sink throughout the phone call, but now she turned to Amanda with a sympathetic smile. "It sounds like you dug up a lot of old skeletons yourself."

Amanda sighed. "I've never been good at managing my mother."

"Your aunt is easier."

"We're more alike."

"And there's none of those pesky expectations. No big hopes or disappointments."

"She's so prickly!"

"I wasn't talking about her."

A protest was on the tip of Amanda's tongue when Maeve laughed. "Nice thing about getting old? The mouth gets a will of its own."

The man walked into Tim Hortons as if he were entering an ambush in a bad Western movie. He peered through the glass door before opening it and then sidled along the wall to check out each section. Amanda had told him she was wearing a green Fun for Families windbreaker, but instead of approaching her directly, he betrayed no hint of recognition when he saw her. Instead, he continued to scour the restaurant. It could have been comical, but something about his fear was contagious.

She had found him on Facebook and messaged him. The public venue had been his idea. He probably figured she wouldn't stab him in a coffee shop packed with double-double lovers. Eventually, he slipped into the chair opposite her, clutching his own coffee.

"Got any ID?"

As she showed him her driver's license, she studied him. He was tall, slim, and tanned, with a mane of thick, dark hair. He should have carried himself with confidence, but he had a whipped look.

He flashed a weak grin. "Sorry. The attack on Livia Cole has me spooked. I'm even imagining stalkers in dark corners, mystery dudes following me in trucks. I asked her not to tell anyone, but it seems to be all over town."

"She didn't tell me. Her parents told me you'd visited, and I took a guess. Why don't you want people to know? Was there something about the bones that spooked you?"

He shook his head. "No, they were interesting. You could tell they were old. I just wanted to keep the discovery to myself. I'm writing a book, and I'm sure the bones have a story to tell." He leaned forward. "What makes you think it's your uncle?"

"Once again, a guess. I could be way off base. He's fallen off the face of the earth, and the police are suddenly interested in the family's DNA." She didn't elaborate on the sordid details surrounding Jonathan's disappearance. She barely knew the man. "But they're not telling me a thing about the body or the investigation. About what they think happened. Can you take me to the coulee?"

"There's nothing there anymore. Just a hole and a bunch of tire tracks."

"It doesn't matter. I'd like to see the surroundings, to see if they can tell me anything about what happened. How he died."

He played with his coffee cup. "I'd like something in return. We're both interested in what the story is. Maybe we can team up and share what we know."

It wasn't a bad deal, Amanda thought as they stopped by Todd's place to pick up his ATV. The bungalow was little larger than a shed, but it was surprisingly well kept, with a garden out front and a bright sunroom on the side. She could decide later how much to share with him, but meanwhile it would be useful to have the help of a local who had contacts and knew something of the history of the area. Not to mention someone who had an ATV.

They bumped over a well-worn track in the sandy riverbed deep into the maze of hills and hoodoos. The south sides of the hills were parched stripes of barren rock, but tufts of wild grasses and flowers clung to the northern sides, which were protected from the fierce sun. Amanda had left Kaylee with Maeve, thinking she'd have more fun keeping her new friend company, but now she regretted it. Kaylee would have loved every rock and secret cranny.

"Was this track always like this?" she shouted in Todd's ear. "It looks as if a lot of people come down here."

He shook his head. "There was no track. The cops and forensics people made this mess. It used to be pristine rock and sand and grass. The only tracks in the sand were deer and coyotes."

She gazed up at the towering hills. "How did you get down here?"

"From up above. I followed a fissure in the hills that wasn't too steep."

"Why? What made you come here?"

"I was following camera shots. I see light and shadow, silhouettes, colour contrasts … whatever. Sometimes I just want to photograph a tiny flower. I can easily wander for hours."

He steered the quad around a sharp bend, and the dry river-bed opened into a broader plain that looked like a battle scene. The sand was chewed up and pockmarked with holes. A larger, irregular hole scarred the base of the hill near the bend. Amanda caught her breath.

Todd switched off the engine. Together they gazed at the hole. There had been no rain since the excavation, and already the blowing sand had begun to soften the harsh edges of the dig marks. In the stillness, the sun blazed off the rock face. She shrugged off her jacket. Insects buzzed around her head, and high overhead, a hawk swooped against the bleached blue sky. Todd showed her how the bones had been laid out in the grave.

As she pictured the body, sorrow welled through her chest. Had he died here? Not the heartless bastard who had turned his back on his sister and his pregnant girlfriend, but the man with the big, warm hug and the endless love of play. The man who had carried her on his shoulders and played hide-and-seek in the woods. Had he breathed his last, alone and frightened?

"Did the bones seem deliberately buried? I mean, by some-one who wanted to give him a decent burial? Or ..." Her voice trailed off, leaving the alternative unsaid.

He shrugged. "It wasn't laid out on its back, if that's what you mean. It looked more like it was dumped. But I didn't see how it looked when it was all exposed. I was only there the first day."

She looked at the camera, which was slung over his shoulder as if it were part of him. "Did you take pictures?"

He squinted into the distance. "The cops deleted them all."

She sensed he was holding back, as was she. She could have pressed him but decided to postpone that until later when trust was better established. Instead she looked up at the surroundings. At the sweep of riverbed down the valley, the steep cascade of rocks down the hillsides, and the ragged lip of the mesa up above.

"Whoever it is, I wonder how they got here and why."

"Lots of possibilities," he said. "That's why I know there's a story worth telling. In the pioneer days before phones or cars, settlers used to ride or even walk for miles to get to town, to go to the train station, the general store, or the doctor. Sometimes they'd cut across these badlands as the quickest way to get from A to B."

"Maybe they got lost. It all looks the same to me."

"Not to someone who lived on the land. But if there was a blizzard or a sandstorm, yeah, you could get seriously turned around. In the winter you could easily freeze to death."

Sweat trickled into her eyes, and she swatted at the mosquito whining in her ear. "That's hard to imagine right now."

"The temperatures in Central Alberta, and especially in the badlands, are extreme. Freeze in winter, but in summer these gullies act like an oven, and it can reach forty degrees in here at the height of the day. As you can see, there's not much shade, and if you get disoriented and haven't brought enough water, you can die of heatstroke and dehydration real fast."

Amanda had already been warned of that danger and had built in protections for her tour. Even today surprised her. Up on the plains, the cool breeze over the open land had kept the temperature to a pleasant twenty-five degrees, but down here, she was already drenched with sweat.

"But the bones ended up buried," she said. "Not lying there like the person had collapsed."

Todd wandered around the site, pointing to the swirls and lines in the sand. "I'm not an expert, but soil geologists should be able to tell if time alone would bury it in the sand. This landscape is always changing. Sand and till would wash down from the hillsides and from upriver, and it would settle out here at this bend. Even snow melt or heavy rains might bury the bones over time."

She looked dubious. "Wouldn't animals have scattered them all around if they were just lying there?"

He shrugged. "Maybe. It's also possible the person didn't die here, but the body was washed down from higher up. Again, it could have happened bit by bit, until it was stopped by this bend."

"He could also have slid down the steep hill and hit his head." Frustration surged through her. As interesting as the speculation was, it raised more questions than it answered, but at least she had avenues to pursue. She raised her head to the plains up above. "What's that thing up there? A house?"

"A shack. Likely from the pioneer days, abandoned years ago."

"Who owns it?"

"No one. It could have been a shelter used by cowhands back when it was open range."

"What's up there now?"

"Grazing land."

"So who owns that?"

"It's a community pasture. The Irrigation District owns it but allows local ranchers to use it for summer grazing."

"So anyone can use it?"

"Well, no, it's regulated. You have to belong to the grazing association."

"So there would be records of who's been on it?"

"Yeah, and I did look into it," he said. "But over the years, there could be hundreds of people. It's public land, so hunters can go on it in season too, and people like me. You just ask permission."

She sighed. A wild goose chase, especially when she had work to do and no clear evidence the human remains were even Jonathan's. But it was a path forward. A way to satisfy her relentless drive for answers.

CHAPTER NINETEEN

Amanda leashed Kaylee and set off east along a rough track through the grassland. Beneath her feet, the soil was hard baked and rutted with tire tracks, but on either side, the dry, crisp tufts of prairie wool spread as far as the eye could see. In the distance, brown and white Herefords dotted the range, and still farther away was a cluster of trees marking a farm.

She had waited until the next morning to start her expedition, because it would be cooler and give her a whole day to explore leads. Following Todd's directions, she'd parked the Hulk on the shoulder of the gravel range road and set her phone to track her movements. In her backpack were enough snacks and water to last them the whole day, as well as sunscreen and insect repellent.

Streaks of white cloud shot through the sky, and a gusty wind from the west blew sand and debris along the track with her. Mercifully, it also kept the bugs away. The little shack she was heading for was a mere smudge on the horizon, and the flat plain gave no hint of the yawning coulee immediately beyond. It felt like walking toward the edge of the earth.

What might have drawn the dead man here? Why on earth would anyone make this trek into nothingness? Only a real history or photography buff like Todd would find that little shack interesting. What else was around? Nothing but cows and that distant farmhouse.

After frequent pauses to give herself and Kaylee some water, they eventually reached the abandoned shack. It was made of rough boards faded silver by decades of harsh prairie sun. Skirting the small lean-to propped against one side, she creaked open the door to the shack and wrinkled her nose at the faint smell of rodents and decay. Cobwebs hung in the corners. As her eyes adjusted to the gloom, she could make out a single room with a splintered table and a bedframe, both made of rough-hewn wood. One corner was lined with wooden shelves, but they only held a couple of steel bowls and cups and an empty liquor bottle. The label was worn away, but she took a photo of it with her phone in case its bumpy, vintage shape could provide a clue to its age. There was no personal gear left on the wooden pegs except a few loops of rope, a water canteen, and a bucket.

The only hints of its past were the dates carved into the wall over a century ago.

This hasn't been used in decades, she thought. Even thirty years ago, a homestead shack like this one would have been obsolete. Keeping Kaylee on a leash, she returned outside and walked toward the new barbed wire fence that marked the edge of the pasture. The grass crunched underfoot. She stood on the ragged edge of the plain and peered over the fence where the land dropped away unexpectedly into the barren hills and fissures of the badlands.

The bone site was a faint brown smudge at the base of the gully amid the amber, red, and grey that flowed in ribbons through the land. A vague track of sorts sloped down into the gully, which she assumed Todd had taken. Had the dead man travelled the same route?

"Well, princess," she said as she turned back, "this has been a nice walk, but I don't think we learned much. Let's go back to the car and check out that farm over there."

The farm had looked close by, but as she'd learned, distances were deceptive in the prairies. Through many rolling ups and downs, the farm slowly emerged out of the patchwork of golds and greens around it. The modern, two-storey home was surrounded by shiny silver grain bins, corrals and pens, barns, and colourful farm equipment that resembled various large insects. A prosperous place, even to her untrained eye.

She drove down the long entranceway and pulled the Hulk up behind a heavy-duty pick-up. Two mixed-breed dogs rushed out to exchange a barking frenzy with Kaylee, and Amanda waited in the car until a woman emerged from the barn and called them off. She was smiling as she approached.

Leaving an outraged Kaylee inside, Amanda climbed out and shielded her eyes as she took in the sunlit beauty of the place. A couple of horses watched her idly from a field by the barn, twitching their tails against the flies. The air was sharp with the tang of animals, manure, and freshly cut hay. In the distance behind the compound, the patchwork of vegetable gardens gave way to golden fields that rippled out toward the horizon. A machine was crawling across the field in a swirl of dust, leaving round bales of hay dotted in its wake.

Amanda introduced herself and apologized in advance for her bizarre request. Having decided to leave Todd's name out of it, she merely explained that she'd learned about the bones in the coulee from the newspaper article and asked how long she'd lived on the farm.

"Four generations," the woman, who'd introduced herself as Loretta, announced proudly. "My husband's family, that is. Since the thirties, when lots of farmers were losing their farms. It's a cattle operation, always has been."

"Have you heard any stories of people going missing in the area? Probably decades ago."

"That's never been found, you mean? Nope. Before my time here. But you're not the first person to come asking, including the police, so my husband has been trying to recollect."

"That area near the coulee — I understand it's community pasture and lots of local farmers use it?"

"Yeah, but nobody goes into the coulee. No reason to, except maybe tourists and rock hounds. And not even them since they tightened up the fossil rules. Only time any of us would go down there is after stray cattle."

"I found an abandoned shack near the edge of the coulee. Who owns that?"

"No one." Loretta grinned. "You're welcome to stay the night, the price is right. It belonged to a pioneer family, oh … well over a hundred years ago, when this was all open range. That was their original house — can you believe a whole family lived in there? My husband says there used to be a barn too, but it burned down. The family was fresh off the boat from England and didn't know much about the prairies. They quickly learned it wasn't in the best location, so they moved upriver a ways and towed a ready-made to a more sheltered, accessible spot. Since then, till the roof fell in, that little shack was used by cowhands who were out tending the stock or fixing fences, and sometimes as a meet-up place."

"Meet-up?"

She grinned again. "Use your imagination. Folks around here were mostly hard-working and disciplined. They took their religion and their duty seriously. But things could get real lonely."

Amanda remembered the dark, Spartan interior, the cob-webs, and the pervasive stink of rodents. "People must have been pretty desperate."

Loretta laughed. "Better than getting a cactus up your back-side. That was a long time ago. It hasn't been used for that since

I've been here, but it's a piece of history, you know? A reminder of our roots and the struggles of the early days around here, when no one knew how to survive. Winters so cold, summers so dry, and the wind and the bugs enough to drive a man to his death."

Amanda waved away a fly and squinted against the searing sun. "I can imagine."

The woman pointed toward her well-kept, modern house. "You want a cold drink? Ice tea or lemonade? We can get out of the sun."

Amanda was tempted because the woman seemed to be a fount of local knowledge and eager for the company, but she still had work to do that afternoon, and the sun was already beginning to dip toward the west. Regretfully, she declined. "Maybe another time when I have more time. I just wanted to know about the shack and its history. I saw the date 1907 carved in the wall."

"Now that's a story! That was one awful winter, one of the worst on record, and folks still talk about it even though none of us were alive to see it. Snow came in early November and didn't leave until near the end of May. It kept piling up and piling up. Blizzard after blizzard. Cattle couldn't graze, and they starved or froze to death. Some ranchers lost hundreds of cows, and most were kept busy trying to feed their herd and keep them warm. The family in that homestead shack moved into the village of Brooks — if you can call less than a dozen people a village — but the rancher kept hauling hay out to his herd. He was staying out at the shack, watching the snow get higher and higher and trying to stop the cattle from falling into the coulee as they looked for shelter. One day, after a two-day blow, he found himself snowed in up to the eaves. Windows and door buried. He broke a window and dug himself out. But his sleigh was buried, and his two horses had got loose and gone back to town. So he walked all the way back to Brooks through snow up to his waist, so the story goes. Lost a toe and some fingers, but he survived. The Oakses have come a long way since those days."

Amanda had been caught up in the vivid images, and the name snapped her back. "Who?"

"The Oakses. That was the guy's name. They used to have a farm in the area years ago."

Amanda considered phoning but in the end decided to pay a visit in person. She hoped the police would find it more difficult to stonewall face-to-face, and at the very least, she might glean something from their body language.

To her dismay, Constable Brinwall was out on patrol, but when Amanda faced the friendly smile of the female constable behind the desk, she thought maybe Brinwall's absence was serendipity. Constable Kelly had a wedding ring and a photo of a mischievous toddler propped on her desk. A woman and a mother. Things looked even more promising when Constable Kelly's smile broadened in recognition of her name.

Amanda matched her smile. "I know Constable Brinwall is my contact person, but I'm in town today, and thought I would pass on some new information that may help you with the investigation."

"By all means. We all work together." Kelly invited her to sit down while she scanned the missing persons file.

"Some of the information is sensitive, so I trust your discretion. I don't know how all the dots connect, but I'm sure they're relevant." Amanda started to tick points off on her fingers. "First of all, the Shelley Oaks in the report, it turns out she had a daughter who was adopted by her brother Peter and his wife, who are passing her off as their own. The daughter doesn't even know."

A spasm of surprise crossed Kelly's face, but she said nothing.

"I'm ninety percent sure my uncle, Jonathan Lewis, is the child's father. The family resemblance is striking. Secondly, the land just above the coulee where the bones were found used to be owned by the Oaks family. They moved, but they might have continued to use the land until Peter Oaks sold the farm in the early 1990s."

This time Kelly's expression didn't change, but she grew still. Barely blinked.

"Maybe those facts are already on file?" Amanda prodded. Still no reaction. "Third, someone attacked and robbed the newspaper reporter Livia Cole after she wrote about the discovery and mentioned it was made by an anonymous hiker. Her phone and laptop were stolen. And now Todd Ellison, that anonymous hiker, is running scared."

At the mention of Todd's name, Kelly did blink, and her jaw dropped slightly. Amanda pressed her advantage. Brinwall would already have cut her off at the first speculation, but Kelly seemed prepared to listen. Amanda leaned forward. "Put all together, it suggests that, even though the remains are decades old, someone today is very interested in them and prepared to resort to violence to keep information from coming to light. Someone who thought they were home free after all this time, only to have it blow up in their faces when the bones were discovered. And the Oakses are right smack in the middle of it all."

"I can't see how this can be related," Kelly said, finding her voice. "We haven't even identified the remains yet, let alone released the name to the public."

"Yes, but what if someone already knows who it is? Because they put it there. That's the giveaway. The only reason Livia was attacked was because she revealed the discovery and hinted that there was a hiker who might know more."

"There could be plenty of reasons why Livia Cole was attacked. She could have surprised a burglar, for example, and he panicked. Home invasions are not unheard of in Drumheller. We're a nice farm town most of the time, but we do have greedy people, same as anywhere."

Amanda was watching her carefully and could sense the conflict beneath her dispassionate exterior. Constable Kelly was making the same speculative leaps she had, but her role demanded she follow procedure and colour within the lines.

"Fair enough," Amanda replied. "But it's a big coincidence, and I thought you should at least be aware of all the pieces. Have the police put any guard on Livia Cole's room?"

"I have no idea. That would be Calgary's call."

"Okay, but you may want to pass along the suggestion. And if someone is trying to cover their tracks, Todd Ellison may also be in trouble — he certainly thinks he is — and even I may be in danger. Todd uncovered the bones, but it's likely they would never have been identified if I hadn't started nosing around about my uncle. Now the killer's secret is in danger of unravelling."

Kelly recoiled visibly, as if to distance herself from Amanda's wild ideas. "We have no evidence it's a homicide —"

"Then why is someone trying to cover it up? Look, I'm worried, okay? I've given you some clues and some leads to follow. I'll let you know if I discover anything else."

"Don't. I mean, don't do anything else. Leave it to us."

Amanda looked into her eyes. There was a hint of acknowledgement in them. Of understanding and sympathy, as well as concern. "Will do. Thank you for taking the time to listen," she said softly as she rose to leave.

CHAPTER TWENTY

Matthew sized up the property as he walked up the stone path. It didn't scream money. In fact, it was modest by Eagle Ridge standards, and the GMC Sierra parked in the drive was at least five years old. The red Audi was high-end, but it too looked several years old.

Perhaps Peter Oaks had had to pay back the money he'd squandered during his mismanagement of the company, leaving him on a tighter budget than he'd been used to. Matthew felt a twinge of sympathy for Natalie Oaks. Any donation would be made through the R&D company, not her personal account, but nonetheless he was grateful she'd agreed to talk to him.

She must have been watching out the window, because she opened the door before he had a chance to ring the bell. She was tall, willowy, and carried herself with grace and poise as she greeted him. She was wearing a simple white dress with no jewellery beyond pearl studs and a wedding ring. Her only nod to artifice was a blue streak in her hair. Yet she managed to look gorgeous.

"Thank you for coming," she said softly as she led him down the hall. "It can be difficult for me to get away."

"Thank *you* for seeing me," he said, trying to pull himself back on track. "I've looked at the materials your company sent, and I like the —"

"Red or white?" She had set up a tray with wine glasses, two bottles, and a platter of cheeses. "Or would you prefer coffee?"

"Red is fine. Thank you."

She poured them both a generous glass. "How long have you known Amanda?"

"Years. We met in Thailand more than ten years ago. She was an aid worker in Cambodia and I was an overseas correspondent."

"And now you've come back to help run her company."

"Charity. Yes. Ten years is a long time to be doing that kind of work. And there are plenty of ways to help right here in Canada. But financially, yes, we're a registered charity and we have proper financial oversight ..." He was about to launch into his pitch.

"What's she like?"

It wasn't uncommon for big donors to want some background information on the company and on Amanda personally, but in this case, the question was loaded with added meaning. He chewed his lip as he considered the question. In the silence, he could hear the floor creaking overhead, and for an instant, her gaze flicked toward the ceiling.

"She's completely committed to helping people. She's the most genuinely honest and caring person I've ever met, which is why I joined up with her."

"And what does she want out of all this?"

"To give people hope. To show them there's a light at the end of their tunnel."

"No, I mean what's in it for her?"

He met her gaze over the rim of his glass. That too was a question loaded with meaning, the answer far too complex and personal for him to share. What was Natalie after, he wondered?

"What we all want, I imagine," he replied. "A sense of meaning in what we do?"

She broke the gaze and picked at a loose thread on the chair. "That's a luxury for most of us, don't you think? Survival is more common."

"That too," he added. "Only our psychoanalyst knows for sure, right? But whatever her motivation, she does good work. Fun for Families makes a difference, not just to the individuals who participate in the adventures but also to the charities we support. The bulk of the donations this time goes to Reconciliation Canada."

"It's a good cause, and I'm happy to commit some money. I'm just curious about Amanda. Her past, her family, what makes her tick."

"If you like, I can arrange for you to meet her some time," he countered.

"Oh, I have met her. She's … very pushy."

He laughed. "She is that. That's how she gets things done."

"And does she usually get what she wants?"

"Do any of us?"

She flushed. "Sorry," she murmured, "that was too personal." She leaned over to top up his glass. He didn't object, although he didn't intend to drink it all. Keeping one step ahead of her was requiring all his concentration.

"I appreciate you're loyal to her," she began again. "That's a rare thing, loyalty. I hope I can trust her."

He was about to reassure her when the phone shrilled. They both jumped. Upstairs, he heard the thump of footsteps and a moment later a man's voice. Natalie shot to her feet and hurried toward the end table to snatch up the phone. She said hello, listened a few seconds, and hung up. Upstairs, the voice stopped.

Natalie looked at the call display. "They hung up."

"Telemarketers," he said. "They're a scourge."

"This number has called a few times when I'm not home. I hope Peter isn't answering it, because heaven knows what they'd get out of him. All our bank account numbers, probably."

"You should cancel the landline. Who needs it these days?"

"You're probably right. I've been reluctant to go completely mobile, but with all these scammers and fraud artists about, Peter would be an easy mark. And we still get harassing phone calls. People angry with Peter or hostile to the oil and gas industry. It has died down, but people can be cruel." She continued to look at the phone. "Although this doesn't look like a scammer phone number."

"Sophisticated scams can be run through any number." When he rose to go to her side, she showed him the number. "I don't recognize that area code. Do you?"

She shook her head.

"If you're worried about Peter, you could Google the number or try reverse phone look-up on Canada 411. Or —" He shot her a grin, "you can just cancel the landline."

She returned to her chair and sank back. Her second glass of wine was nearly empty, and she looked profoundly weary. "That might be safest. If Peter's been answering, who knows what trouble he could get into?"

Hank Klassen was almost exactly as Amanda had pictured him. His massive, linebacker frame matched his booming voice, and although he had to be at least sixty, only a few glints of silver shot through his bristly hair. He had a deep tan that suggested hours of sun, fresh air, and exercise. From his expensive but casual shirt and slacks, Amanda suspected it was on the golf links.

Hank had proposed a lunch meeting at Caesar's Steak House, an institution in downtown Calgary from the cattle baron days. "I hope he's picking up the tab," Matthew muttered when he told Amanda. The décor at Caesar's was almost worthy of the Palace of Versailles: burgundy leather chairs, white linen, crystal chandeliers, marble pillars, gold accents, and a plush red carpet that muffled all sound. Hank rose to greet them with an extended hand as they approached and took control of the meeting from the moment they sat down.

"It's real nice to meet you in person, Amanda. I been reading up on your work since I spoke to your friend on the phone. I admit I never heard of your outfit before, but I was impressed. You do good work. Not just right here in Canada but in your overseas charities. You know that world over there, you got connections, and there's nothing like eyes on the ground to separate the glossy pamphlet crap from the outfits that make a real difference."

"Thank you. But we seem like an small organization for a company as big as yours to bother with."

Matthew shot her an alarmed look that she ignored. When the waiter arrived with three martinis, Amanda managed to hide her dismay. She'd never seen the appeal of the drink.

"This is just to get us started," Hank explained. "To your point, nothing is too small. Everybody starts off small, myself included. It's quality that counts."

"Yes, you did start off in the trenches. Those must have been interesting days. Were you there in the boom of the seventies?"

He sipped appreciatively. "Just squeaked in at the end, but I've seen plenty of boom and bust. You hitch your wagon to the oil business, you're in for a wild ride."

"Have you always been with Norsands?"

"Started there, moved around a bit, companies came and went, but now here I am back again. And in a position to help out your enterprise."

Matthew smiled and looked ready to make his opening pitch, so Amanda pressed on. "You've certainly done all right for yourself."

Hank grinned and picked up the menu. "Before we get down to brass tacks, let's order. And it's gotta be steak. You don't come to Caesar's to eat rabbit food. You're not one of those vegan types, are you?"

Both she and Matthew demurred and picked up the menus. Hank directed them to the main section and pointed to Matthew's stomach.

"You look like a man who could handle the ribeye. Individually cut to size, with their signature steak spice, and charbroiled on an open flame. And you, young lady, the melt-in-your-mouth filet is made for you. Am I right?"

Amanda had to suppress a laugh at Matthew's red face. Hank summoned the waiter with a quick glance and took over the ordering. Amanda had taken him for a beer kind of guy, but to her surprise and delight, he ordered a well-aged Spanish red. She took a small sip of her martini before sliding it subtly aside.

Once the waiter left, Hank rubbed his hands with glee like a small boy. "Every chance I get, I bring people here. It's not just a great meal — it's an experience. So let's get the business out of the way so we can sink our teeth into it."

This time Amanda let Matthew proceed. Within less than fifteen minutes they had hammered out a reasonable contribution in exchange for a opportunity to do an evening presentation and put the company logo as a proud sponsor on the Fun for Families website. Amanda was surprised at how little Hank had asked for and wondered if he had a hidden agenda, just like her.

The waiter had just whisked away the Caesar salads when they wrapped up the business portion. Amanda wasted no time in plunging back into her own agenda. "I've been busy too. I found the woman my uncle was seeing in Fort Mac. Shelley Oaks. As it turns out, she's the sister of Peter Oaks, whom I'm sure you know."

Hank managed a nod as he took a gulp of his martini. "Everyone knows Peter Oaks, but his sister's been a recluse. Where'd you find her?"

"In the U.S. She's been living there for years. Do you remember her?"

Hank made a show of thinking. "Yeah. Pretty little thing. Did you find your uncle too?"

"Not yet, but I did learn they were an item in Fort McMurray, and they left under a cloud. They came back to the Oaks farm near Drumheller. Do you remember why they left?"

"As I recall, she was fired. At least that was the story."

"Why was she fired?"

"No idea. That was between her and the site boss."

"What was the boss's name?"

"Can't remember. Sean somebody."

Amanda picked her next words carefully, for Hank had abandoned his folksy charm and become wary. "Was there anything between her and this Sean?"

"Not that I heard."

"Hank ..." She leaned forward. "Those were different times, and I'm not trying to judge anyone. I know those work camps were a man's world. A young woman — pretty and straight off the farm — would have been an easy mark."

He shifted in his chair. "Not that easy. She was a playful little thing. There were lots of guys sniffing around her."

"Including the site boss?"

Hank drained his martini. "Could be. So what?"

"I haven't been able to find my uncle. No one has heard from him, or of him, since those days thirty years ago." She considered telling him about the baby but decided to respect the Oakses' privacy. "He quit in sympathy with her, didn't he? What exactly happened?"

Their wine and steaks arrived, providing Hank with the perfect distraction. He had Matthew rhapsodizing over their ribeyes, and even Amanda had to admit her filet mignon was exquisite. She allowed them all a few minutes of ecstasy before retrieving the thread.

"I don't know what happened to him, and frankly, I'm worried. I've reported him missing. So what happened between them all?"

Hank studied her as if weighing his options. "You haven't heard anything in thirty years?"

She shook her head. "Neither has Shelley or Peter Oaks or my family. You know something, don't you?"

Hank sliced through a piece of oozing red meat. "Okay. I don't know much, and most of it was just talk, but I don't suppose it matters now after all these years. I never liked the guy much anyway. Sean O'Regan, I remember his name now. And yeah, he was after her. Not much else to chase up there, and she had that fresh, farm girl beauty. No make-up, no airs, just sweet. Jonny fell head over heels, and so did half the camp. Guys looked for any excuse to drop by the site office just to hear her laugh. But the boss was at the head of the line. He figured he was owed. He didn't take too good to being turned down."

Amanda felt a chill at the thought of a young girl all alone in a work camp miles from nowhere. "What do you mean?"

Hank looked up from his steak. "What do you think? He made advances, she turned him down, the more she turned him down, the more he wanted her. Followed her back to her dorm and hung around outside. Turned up at bars where she and Jonny were."

"You saw all this?"

"Some of it. Heard the rest. Jonny got upset. Jealous. He wanted her to quit, but she was a little firecracker, that one. She wanted to prove to —" He broke off abruptly.

"Prove what?"

"She wanted to make her own money, not depend on her big brother."

"So what happened? Why was she fired?"

"The thing is, she was giving Sean mixed messages. Trying not to piss him off too much, because he was the boss, after all. Lots of guys thought she led him on. I guess it blew up. She had a showdown with him — the boss, that is — and next thing we knew, she was out on her ear. And Jonny right on her heels."

"What was the showdown?"

He shrugged as he chewed. "No idea," he mumbled through a mouthful of steak.

Amanda mulled over what he'd revealed. None of it surprised her. Even today, men's work camps in remote regions were notorious for their caveman attitudes. Alcohol, isolation, and male bonding could turn even decent men into jerks. Nothing Hank had told her was out of the norm.

"Why didn't you want to tell me this?"

"Because of Shelley. Back then, I mean. Guys were spreading all kinds of rumours. That she wanted it, that she teased. You know the drill. Peter Oaks asked me to keep it all under my hat."

Amanda couldn't hide her surprise. "Peter Oaks? Why?"

"To stop the rumour mills. Protect his sister's reputation. Like I said, those were different times. None of this Me Too stuff up there."

"And how did you know Peter Oaks?"

"He came up to the site a couple of months after Shelley left. He was expanding his oil business, putting some more wells on his property. He said he was looking to recruit, but I guess he was looking to make sure things stayed quiet."

"So did he recruit you? What was your reward for helping him?"

Hank shoved aside his empty plate and looked across at her. His eyes flashed. "We made a deal, just like you and me did. That's the way the world turns. You got something I want, I got something you want."

Her gaze drifted over the opulent restaurant at the hushed waiters and the quiet glow of money. "Peter Oaks has been good to you."

Matthew shot her a furious look. Hank's shoulders bunched like a linebacker about to defend the line. "I made my own way. Yeah, Oaks and I have given each other a helping hand, but I got here because I'm good."

She held up her hands. "Sorry, Hank. I didn't mean to offend you. I'm frustrated and worried about my uncle, and sometimes my big mouth gets the better of me. I appreciate everything you've told me."

Hank's shoulders relaxed. "Fair enough. Now maybe we can put all this away and think about dessert?"

"Great idea!" Matthew said, but Amanda wasn't done.

"Only if you can tell me one last thing. What happened to the site boss? Did he face any flak?"

Hank looked genuinely surprised. "Why should he? No, life moved on. So did he. I think he left before Peter Oaks turned up."

"Do you know where he went?"

Hank shook his head. "But the oil business was beginning to tank. Lots of guys were getting laid off."

"Have you heard from him since?"

"No, but like I said, I was never a big fan. He was an east coaster, like half the guys. Guys come, make a pile of money, and leave." He nodded to the waiter, signalling they were all moving on.

CHAPTER TWENTY-ONE

The pick-up was in the driveway, parked slightly crooked, but the little red Audi was gone, and blinds shuttered the windows. Amanda's heart sank. It was late afternoon, and she was still struggling with the effects of her martini, red wine, and rich, glorious steak. She had taken Kaylee on the Elbow River path to try to walk it off, but now all she wanted to do was lie down on a pile of soft pillows and sleep.

But the meeting with Hank had pried loose a whole lot more questions, and she'd dropped in on Natalie in the hope of getting answers. Matthew had told her about his meeting with Natalie and her subsequent donation, which had been substantial. No strings attached, he'd said, but Amanda doubted that. The strings were probably to buy her silence about their daughter, along with a dollop of penitence. But Amanda hoped that meant the woman wouldn't slam the door in her face.

As she contemplated the silent house, she thought she saw a blind twitch upstairs. Encouraged, she rang the doorbell. A piano arpeggio echoed through the house. As it faded away, she heard the whisper of footsteps inside. She rang again. Nothing

Out of curiosity, she tried the door, which was locked. She stepped away to peer up at the upstairs window. The blind didn't move. With a sigh, she turned to go just as an engine roared behind her and Kaylee began to bark. The red Audi shot into the drive, and Natalie leaped out with a look of alarm.

"What do you want?"

"I've learned some more, and I have a couple of questions. Can we talk inside?"

Natalie's gaze flicked to the truck, and her eyes widened. She scanned the house anxiously. "We can talk around back. Peter should be napping, and I don't want him disturbed."

As she led the way around the side path, Natalie chattered as if to cover her nerves. "I try to get someone to stay with him when I go out, for safety's sake, so he doesn't turn on the stove or fall down the stairs. He's very frail. But he doesn't like strangers in the house, and he orders them out. So sometimes it's not worth it."

After freeing Kaylee to roam in the immaculate garden, Amanda settled into a patio chair. Natalie, usually a gracious hostess, did not offer refreshments. The last few days had taken their toll. She looked unkempt and sweaty, and she eyed the sanctuary of her house with yearning.

"I won't keep you long," Amanda said. "Your husband's family used to own the land above the coulee where the body was found."

Natalie turned white as a ghost. "What —" She licked her lips. "What body?"

"A few weeks ago, a hiker found human remains in the coulee. It's being analyzed in Calgary, and the police have asked for DNA from my family."

Natalie was still struggling to find words. "Why?"

"To compare. Because my uncle hasn't been heard from in thirty years. I've reported him missing."

Natalie rose to her feet and wavered unsteadily. "How awful. I hope ... Where was this body found? Where exactly?"

When Amanda described the coulee and the land above it, Natalie seemed to pull herself together. She sat back in the chair and straightened her shoulders. "Oh, that's been open range for nearly a hundred years. The irrigation district owns it."

"But you still had access to it while you owned your ranch."

"Along with everyone else around."

Amanda leaned forward and lowered her voice. "I know it's a long shot, but I am worried the body might be my uncle. I really hope you can help me understand what happened up in Fort McMurray back then."

Natalie's expression didn't flicker, but Amanda pressed on. "I've spoken to an old oil rig buddy of Jonathan's and Shelley's. He told me Shelley was being harassed by their site boss before he fired her."

After a long pause, Natalie shrugged. "Par for the course. In case you haven't heard, the Me Too movement isn't big up there. Peter hadn't wanted her to go there in the first place."

"Why did she?"

Natalie eyed her warily. "Rebellion? Peter could be ... overbearing. There were a lot of pressures at home. Their mother was dead, and in recent years their father's health had been declining."

"Dementia."

A flash of alarm crossed Natalie's face before it settled into resignation. "He'd been a powerful man. Very proud. But he was running the farm into the ground. Peter had to have him declared unfit to manage his affairs so he could put in a few oil wells. His father fought it. It was extremely messy, and Shelley was very upset with her brother."

"That's understandable. I'm sure she loved her father."

Natalie shrugged. "She always loved the open range. She didn't want the oil wells ruining them, but Peter said it was the only way to save the farm. In the boom times, farmers everywhere were leasing parts of their land for oil. It was good money, and it helped with the lean crop years. And it worked." She gestured to their house and garden. "But Shelley ... Well, I guess she wanted to prove she could manage on her own, make her own money to help the farm. She was only eighteen when she went up north. Just out of high school."

"The reality must have been a shock."

"If it was, she never admitted it to us. Not then, anyway."

"Did she mention Jonathan to you?"

"She hardly ever wrote from Fort Mac. Remember, this was before email and such. I think we got one postcard."

"But later, when she came back, she brought Jonathan with her. I have a photo of him in front of your farm."

Natalie hesitated as if trying to sort out her story. "Yes. Briefly."

"Why only briefly?"

"I don't know. It wasn't my business." She twirled her wedding ring, and Amanda let her squirm. "It didn't seem appropriate for him to stay with us. It's a conservative community."

"Do you know where he went?"

"No. I stayed out of it."

Amanda leaned forward. "I appreciate your honesty. You were stuck in the middle of this."

"I was a new wife," she replied as if it explained everything.

Amanda switched topics. "The site boss, Sean O'Regan. Did you think he was the father of Shelley's baby?"

Natalie's eyes widened. She glanced around the garden as if looking for an escape. Finding none, she pressed herself deeper into her chair and said nothing.

"You were surprised when I said Jonathan was the father, because you believed it was someone else. Sean O'Regan?"

"I had no idea."

"You're a woman. Her own mother was dead. Did she not confide in you at all?"

Natalie whipped her head back and forth. "She was a bundle of nerves when she came home. She got angry and tearful whenever we tried to talk about it. She'd tell us to mind our own business, and she'd slam out of the house. That was Shelley. Always taking off when the heat was on. She'd get on her horse, and off she'd go at a full gallop across the range. Wouldn't come back for hours."

A thought struck Amanda. "Where did she go?"

"Who knows? As a kid, she rode all over the range."

"Did she meet Jonathan on these rides?"

"I don't know!" Natalie's breathing grew rapid. "Ask Shelley. Maybe you can get more answers out of her than I ever could. Peter tried. He was worried. You think he wanted his sister heaven knows where at all hours? But she never listened to him, did she?"

Unexpectedly, Kaylee ran toward the house with a sharp bark, and Amanda turned to see a shadow flit past the kitchen window. Natalie sucked in her breath and pushed herself out of her chair. "You have to go. I don't want him upset. He gets so confused, and it takes me hours to calm him down." She hurried to the side gate. "I've told you all I know. Now go. Out this way."

Amanda called to Kaylee and hurried out through the gate, wondering how long Peter had been there and how much he'd been able to overhear.

As Amanda drove away, a sense of foreboding settled on her. Fragments of a picture were beginning to emerge — Jonathan and Shelley arriving back at the farm from up north, Jonathan being sent packing to keep up appearances, Shelley disappearing out on the prairie for hours. Had she gone to meet Jonathan? The homestead shack had been a notorious meet-up spot for local teens and lovers. Amanda remembered the liquor bottle that looked as if it had been there for decades. Would there be fingerprints on it, and what tale would they tell?

Driving up the Crowchild Trail toward her Airbnb, she spotted the Foothills Medical Centre and on impulse steered toward the exit ramp. She had heard no more news about Livia Cole, but perhaps no news was good news.

The sun was sinking below the rooftops by the time she inched through the clogged traffic to an available parking space. A pick-up truck loomed in her rear-view mirror, uncomfortably close. Its tinted windows flashed in the sun's glare, blinding her.

"Back off, idiot," she muttered. "None of us are going anywhere."

When she finally squeezed into a spot, the truck accelerated past with a squeal of tires. Todd had told her what building Livia was in, and the tall tower was easy to spot. Inside, she found Livia had been moved out of ICU onto a regular inpatient floor. Amanda had no difficulty obtaining the room number and directions. To her dismay, there was no security or protection, despite her warning to the police, and she was able to waltz right in.

The room was empty except for a tiny, frail figure propped up in bed. The young woman was dozing but opened her eyes at the sound of footsteps. Her head was swathed in bandages, and she had yellow and purple bruises around her eyes, but otherwise looked far better than Amanda had expected. Amanda had meant to buy flowers to brighten the room, but there were already vases of cheerful flowers overflowing every spare surface. Beside a large vase of red roses, she noticed a card saying *Get well, Todd.*

Livia smiled. "I know. I should open a flower shop." Her voice was weak and sleepy. "My brain is on strike. Am I supposed to know you?"

Amanda laughed and introduced herself.

"Oh, was I doing a story on you?"

"No. Well, yes," Amanda amended quickly. "I hoped you would, but that doesn't matter now. I'm actually here about your other story — the one about the bones in the coulee."

Puzzlement flitted across Livia's face. Amanda filled her in quickly about her search for her uncle, her suspicion about the body, and her trip to the coulee with Todd. "The police are being super coy, but I'm wondering if the attack on you and the robbery were connected to that story. Do you remember anything about the attack?"

Livia reached up to massage her temple. "No. The police came today to ask me about that. I told them I don't remember much. The person was already in my apartment, I'm pretty sure. I remember noticing the door was open and things were a mess, but nothing after that. The doctor says I might remember, but I might never."

"Apparently your phone and laptop were taken. Did you have any material about the story on there? Anything the attacker might be after?"

Livia started to nod but winced. "I had tons of stuff on them, so if the guy can get past my password, he'll access it all."

"Including Todd Ellison's ID?"

Livia looked distressed.

"You said 'he.'"

"That's just a guess. I have no clue."

She shut her eyes, and Amanda sensed she was fading. "I'm sorry. I know how rotten you feel. I've had a concussion, and it's no fun. I'd like to help by picking up the research where you left off. Not to write your story, of course — you'll do that when you're better — but to investigate what happened to the person. If it is my uncle's body, I want to know. Can I ask you ... what have you uncovered so far? Any specifics about the body? Or about the area it was found? There's a homestead shack on the mesa up above."

Livia's eyes were shut, and she took several deep breaths. Then her eyes fluttered open and she licked her lips. Amanda offered her some water, and she stared at her in confusion.

"Livia? Are you too tired?"

"I talked to a few neighbours. I mean, folks on nearby farms who use the pasture. They told me it's been there since 1905, and people sometimes used it as a shelter. Didn't look much like a shelter to me when I checked it out. But in the old days there used to be a couch and mattress."

Amanda pulled out her phone and accessed the photo of the glass bottle. "Did you see this? It looks like an old liquor bottle. Whisky? Rum?"

Livia took the phone and squinted at it as if her vision were blurry. "Yeah, I remember it. I looked it up. It's a whisky bottle from Alberta Distilleries. Big local company. They've been around since 1946, but they've used that bottle shape since the seventies. Alberta Premium. It still looks like that today."

Amanda's heart sank. "So it could be from any time in the past fifty years."

Livia leaned her head back wearily. "Doesn't narrow it down much, does it? Oh. There was a fire."

"What fire?"

"One of the farmers told me. There was an old barn next to the shack. Burned down. He was only a kid, but he remembers flames in the night. Bright orange. See it for miles."

"What was his name? Maybe I can follow up and pinpoint the timeframe."

"Don't remember." She groaned. "It would be on my laptop. And on the cloud."

Amanda brightened. "The cloud? Can I access that?"

"Too complicated." She shut her eyes. "I'm done."

Within seconds, she was breathing deeply. Amanda rose, thanked her, and murmured that she would be in touch. As she slipped out the door, she wasn't sure whether the young woman had even heard her.

CHAPTER TWENTY-TWO

For the eighth time, Amanda peered in her rear-view mirror. The line of cars behind her in the right lane was long, and they all looked similar and harmless in the cheerful morning sunlight. Grey, black, and white, SUVs and pick-ups interspersed with the occasional sedan, all heading east out of Calgary into the prairies. She couldn't tell if the white pick-up was among them. It had been parked down the street from her Airbnb and had pulled out behind her that morning. Was it the same one that had tailgated her at the hospital? There were so many trucks on the road that it could be a complete coincidence, but after it took the same turn as her for the fourth time, she began to feel spooked. It always kept at least two vehicles between them as they navigated the trails and merges, but when she'd left the main highway in favour of a lesser road, she had lost sight of it. She heaved a sigh of relief.

Nothing but her overactive imagination.

She turned her attention back to the road. Once again she was heading out to the badlands. She had spent the night on the Internet trying to find out more about the barn fire the farmer had mentioned to Livia, but after using multiple search words and ploughing through dozens of stories and photos of burning barns, she had given up. Either the fire was too insignificant to warrant a mention, or it had happened before the Internet age.

She wasn't even sure it mattered. Barns burned all the time. The prolonged heat and drought of summer made the grassland tinder-dry, and the smallest spark could ignite an inferno whipped up by relentless wind. Even now, wildfires were burning in the forests of British Columbia and Northern Alberta. Without access to water, farmers usually had no choice but to save the livestock, light backfires to protect their homes, and abandon the barn itself to nature.

She had no objective reason to think the fire had anything to do with the drama that had taken place between Shelley and Jonathan. And yet the question had nagged at her. Could there be a connection between the secret meet-up place and the body in the coulee?

After a restless night, she'd known she couldn't ignore it. It would needle her until she answered the question, or at least determined it was irrelevant. She was due to return to Drumheller for last-minute preparations anyway, so it wouldn't be much out of her way to check it out.

After making some last-minute purchases and packing up equipment, she'd checked out of her Airbnb and hit the road just after ten o'clock. There was still no hope of rain, but the parched heat had been replaced by a crisp breeze off the Rockies that carried the scent of smoke from the wildfires. As she left Calgary behind, the rumpled prairie spread before her beneath hazy skies like a chequered quilt of amber grain and bright green alfalfa. Peace stole over her.

Her eye caught a glint of white in her mirror, gone in an instant. She gripped the wheel and stared. Nothing. Then again, a headlight peeked out from the line as if it were trying to keep her in sight. She pressed her foot to the accelerator and felt the Hulk throb in response. One-twenty. One-thirty. The line of cars fell back, and when no white pick-up tried to pass, she eased up, not eager to get a ticket. The truck reappeared and darted back into line two cars behind her.

What the hell? They were passing through Siksika Territory. and little bungalows painted yellow, red, and blue were scattered through the rolling hills up ahead. She remembered there was a small crossroad that led through their village and connected to the main highway farther north. Almost no one took it unless they had reason to go to the village. It would be the definitive test.

Without signalling, she swerved left onto the crossroad, fought to keep control of the steering wheel, and rocketed north toward the village. When she checked the mirror, the truck was gone. Nonetheless, she kept a wary eye out as she wove north through back roads toward the homestead shack. The incident had unsettled her. She felt vulnerable out on the prairie with only a dog for company. With little place to hide, the Hulk was visible for miles.

She reached over to stroke Kaylee's head. "We're a great pair, aren't we? It's pretty lonely out here. Would you be able to defend me? A nice, tall, intimidating Mountie would come in handy right now." It was then she thought of Todd Ellison. He too was interested in the story and just as spooked.

The sound of his voice on the phone filled her with relief. When she explained her request, he jumped at the chance to help, as if he'd been holed up with his computer for days. They arranged to meet on the range road nearest to the shack. He brought with him a topographical map showing all the surrounding farms. They unfurled it against the dash of the Hulk, and after some searching, Todd put his finger on the small dot near the coulee.

"That's the shack. This is all community grazing."

Amanda traced her finger north along the road. "And that's the farm I visited. Loretta was the wife's name, but she didn't grow up on the farm, so she won't remember the fire."

She broke off. "Wait. She said her husband's family had been there four generations. He might remember." And as a bonus, she thought, he might remember the Oakses and the drama of thirty years ago.

This time as they drove up the long lane, the farm dogs wagged their tails as they barked. Kaylee bounced around the front seat in noisy response. A woman's feet were protruding out from under a mud-caked tractor, and when she scooted out, a broad smile lit her oil-smudged face.

"You again! Back for that cold drink this time?"

Amanda shook her hand, grease stains and all. She introduced Todd and said they were looking for more information on a barn fire that had happened years ago. "Do you think your husband would remember it?"

"Probably. Things like that are a big deal around here. A grass fire can be big trouble. Come on in. I'll get him. He's just on the phone."

Loretta led them into a most unlikely farm kitchen. All shiny, stainless steel appliances, white cabinets, and modern gadgets. But pickling jars were lined up on the stone counter, and the sharp smell of vinegar filled the air. The woman pulled a jug from the fridge, and Amanda barely had time to sit down before a man appeared. He was built like a barrel, with arms like tree trunks and a face like a round melon. His wife introduced him as Bob, and when she explained their request, he enveloped Amanda's hand in a powerful, calloused grip.

"So you want to know about the barn fire?"

Amanda nodded, once again wondering whether her minor celebrity status opened doors for her or whether the locals were always this welcoming. "I don't know if it's connected to my uncle's disappearance or to the bones in the coulee, but I'm trying to piece together possibilities."

"What year did he disappear?"

"Probably 1990."

"Yeah, that'd be about right. The fire was in September of 1990. I was fifteen years old, and we were bringing in the wheat. The land was dry, just like this year, and I remember my folks were real worried. There was no dirt circle around those old buildings. If it got into the grass, it might sweep all the way up to our place. But it burned itself out."

"Did anyone check it out afterwards?"

"Not that I remember. The place was abandoned. By morning all you could see was a bit of smoke."

"Was there any talk about what caused it?"

"Just Mother Nature, reminding us who's boss. Like I said, it was real dry."

Amanda glanced at Loretta, who was pouring ice tea into tall glasses. "You mentioned it had been a meet-up place. Did you mean for lovers?"

Bob grinned. "That was before my time, I could only dream. But yeah, the local kids liked to use the barn for parties."

"I gather the Oakses used to own it."

"That was years ago. It got repossessed in the Great Depression by the CPR. But yeah, that was once their little place. Afterwards, they got a better spread north of here, nearer the river."

"Did your folks know them?"

"Everyone knew the Oakses. Peter was a hustler even back then. He was one of the guys that used the old barn for parties, whenever he could escape his old man and kick up his heels. I remember his father. Not his mother, although I heard the story. Terrible thing. Old Man Oaks was a tough old buzzard. Fair but man, was he strict! Those kids were older than me, but I remember he had them working to the bone on that farm.

Before school, after school, and when they weren't working, they were in church. By the time I remember him, though, he was already getting senile. Maybe it had started years earlier, who knows."

Loretta brought tea to the table, and Amanda smiled her thanks. Todd had said nothing, but she could see him taking in the surroundings with interest, the pickling jars, the pots of herbs on the windowsill, and the colourful hand-painted bowls brimming with tomatoes and peppers. She imagined he was itching to take photos but knew it would be rude.

"When did he die?"

"Oh. I don't know that. Peter had already started the oil company and moved to Calgary, so they put him in a home in Calgary then."

"Did you know Peter personally? Or his sister, Shelley?"

He shook his head. "I was younger, and like I said, the father kept them busy. The only thing I remember about Shelley was her beautiful horse. Man, could that girl ride!"

Loretta piped up. "You told me that was her one escape."

"That's more what my folks said. I just remember the horse — a beautiful sorrel mare that ran like the wind, her mane flying, Shelley's hair flying." He pointed out the window toward the open range, and a dreamy look crept over his face. Then he ducked his head and laughed. "Haven't seen her since. Peter sold the house, picked up stakes, and went to the city. Not many happy memories on the farm, I guess."

Delighted to be loose, Kaylee snuffled through the brittle grass while Amanda and Todd walked around the outside of the homestead shack, peering at its weathered wood.

"No sign of scorching," Amanda said.

With his keen cameraman's eye, however, Todd pointed to a shadow of darker grey in the corner. "Here, but it's very faint. The shack was never in danger."

Amanda inspected the rusty hinge and padlock on the door. "It looks as if someone tried to break in here at some point."

"Probably to take shelter. Sandstorms, blizzards, you name it, you don't want to be caught out in them."

"Maybe." She examined the inside of the door, which was marred by gouges. Almost as if someone was trying to break out rather than in, she thought, dismissing a twinge of alarm. That made no sense. It was the barn that had burned, not the shack.

She watched as Todd aimed his camera for a few close shots of the broken padlock. "You take a lot of photos."

"You never know which will be perfect. And sometimes you see unexpected things. Digital photography is cheap, unlike film."

"You told me the cops deleted all your photos of the bone site." She shielded her eyes to meet his gaze. "Was that true?"

He looked away. "Technically, yes. But I'd already downloaded them."

"Can you pull them up on your phone?"

"They're on an external drive. Just lots of bones, Amanda. Pretty grim, but they won't tell you anything."

She considered pressing him but decided it could wait. The sun was hot, the insects annoying, and they had more important questions to answer right here. But Todd was flipping through his phone, and after a few seconds he held out his phone. "This is the only useful clue. A belt buckle. The cops will be able to tell more when they clean it up."

She shielded the phone and squinted at the image. "What is it?"

"I think it's an antique oil derrick."

She looked up in dismay. "Oil derrick. Like an oil worker would get at his work?"

"Or maybe buy. Lots of people might own them. This is Alberta."

"Can you forward this to me? Maybe I can track it down."

"I tried already, but sure, you can too. There are hundreds of oil derrick logos, and this is a classic antique shape." He took the phone and emailed the photo to her. It was a clue, small but ominous, and Amanda tried to put her worry aside so that she could return to the much more significant issue of the fire. She pointed to the nearby grass.

"If the scorching was on this corner, that means the barn was situated on this side, but not too close or the shack would have caught fire too." She walked a few metres away, spread her arms in a circle, and peered at the ground. "Somewhere in this area."

"I'm not sure what we're looking for," Todd said as he joined her.

"Neither am I. After all these years, probably nothing."

Together they patrolled the area, crunching over the prairie grass and poking it apart with their boots. Nothing but bare dust. Kaylee had been rummaging in the grass, and now she trotted over to them, her tail waving excitedly, and dropped a small chunk of wood at Amanda's foot. When Amanda picked it up, Kaylee bounced around in anticipation of a throw.

"What's that?" Todd asked.

"A piece of board." She turned it over in her hands. "Charred."

He hurried over. "Where did she get it?"

"Over there." Amanda strode farther from the shack and studied the ground. "Here's another, mostly buried in the sand. And another."

After a search, they discovered a few more over an area about fifteen feet square. "There should be more debris. There was a whole barn here, including a roof with shingles. It almost seems … cleaned up." Backing up, she snagged her foot on something and fell, her palms hitting something sharp. She pawed through the grass and uncovered the rusted remains of coiled wire, partially buried in the soil.

"What the hell is this?" she muttered, cradling her injured hand. "Fencing wire?"

He zeroed in for some photos. "Too curly. It looks more like springs, like from a chair."

"I wonder …" She fingered the coils. "There was no mattress on the bed, and even if animals took all the stuffing, the coils at least should have survived."

"It could've been a straw mattress, or even old rags. This was a primitive place." Todd began to tug the wire out of the ground.

"We should leave it," Amanda said.

"Why? It's all thirty years old."

"I know, but … what if something happened here? What if this is a crime scene?"

He stared at her. "You think someone set the fire deliberately?"

"Well, somebody buried the body in the coulee."

"We don't even know the two things are connected!"

"I know," Amanda said, "but I'm getting a bad feeling. Let's check the shack again."

Todd followed her into the gloom. As her eyes adjusted, she studied the bedframe. There were no traces of coils or cloth residue, but the rough-hewn wood was indented with gouges with traces of rust.

"What do you think?" she asked. "Could these be marks from metal coils?"

But Todd was not looking. Instead he was frowning at the shelves on the wall. "That's funny," he said. "The whisky bottle is gone."

CHAPTER TWENTY-THREE

Once again, Amanda parked in front of the RCMP station. Todd hunkered down in the passenger seat and pulled his cowboy hat low. "You go. I'm not Constable Brinwall's favourite person."

She was about to protest, but in the end, she agreed the fewer people who got on the wrong side of Brinwall, the better. As she was climbing out of the Hulk, she spotted a white pick-up truck nosing into the corner of the lot. As she stared at it, it backed out of sight behind a large camper van. Through the tinted window, she'd been able to make out only a vague shape in the driver's seat. The person appeared to be wearing a cowboy hat.

She leaned in the window to talk to Todd. "Have you seen a white pick-up following you at all? Or anyone following you?"

Todd looked around, eyes wide. "Don't freak me out!"

"Just keep an eye out, and if anyone comes near you, blast the horn."

With her phone ready in her hand, she slipped behind the line of parked cars and ducked low as she approached the camper van from behind. Once she reached the van, she peeked around it. The truck was still there, idling throatily, but as she raised her phone to take a photo, the truck accelerated and turned in front of the van.

She ran forward just as it nosed into traffic and headed down the street out of sight. With fumbling hands, she checked the photo. The rear of the truck was blurry but visible, as was the licence plate. The sunlight played off it, blurring it even more, but on a bigger screen, it might be enough.

Her heart was racing with a mixture of fear and excitement as she crossed the parking lot. When she got inside the station, she was relieved to find Brinwall out on patrol but Constable Kelly at her desk. Kelly's friendly smile faded when she saw Amanda's face.

"You look like you could use a coffee," she said.

"Thanks." Amanda sank into the chair and worked to calm her nerves.

Kelly brought them both a cup of coffee and sat down. "How can I help you?"

Amanda decided not to begin her story with the truck. Better to establish some credibility first. She described the fire that had occurred around the time of her uncle's disappearance and the suggestion that an effort had been made to clean it up. She reported the popularity of the shack as a meet-up place in the old days and Shelley's love of riding across the open range. She finished with the missing whisky bottle.

"Someone took that in the last few days, not decades ago. Someone is still actively trying to cover up the old death."

Kelly had been taking notes quietly. "Maybe some tourist just likes vintage whisky bottles."

"Tourists aren't supposed to go on that land. And why now? Why precisely when the old death has been discovered? Whisky is an alcohol. It could have been used to start the fire."

Kelly stopped writing and eyed her obliquely. "Not easily."

"I know it's all speculation, and it hinges on that body being my uncle, but I can't ignore the picture that's emerging. Shelley was being stalked by her boss. He was obsessed with her, and ... I think he raped her. We both know guys like that. They don't take no for an answer and they're insanely jealous. What if he followed her down south, what if he surprised her and Jonathan in the barn and set fire to it with what was at hand? Shelley escaped but Jonathan did not."

"And why wouldn't she go straight to the police?"

Amanda felt a niggle of doubt. If Shelley knew Jonathan had died in the fire, why had she concocted an elaborate lie to explain his disappearance? "I don't know. Maybe she was terrified. Maybe she didn't want her whole sordid story dragged through the mud. She was nineteen years old, pregnant, and in those days, let's face it, this was a pretty strict, judgmental community."

"Okay. I'll pass this up the line, but frankly ..."

"There is one other thing. I think I'm being followed. A white truck followed me from Calgary, and I just saw it again out in the parking lot."

Kelly's expression hardened. She shoved back her chair. "Show me."

"It drove off when I got near."

"All the same, let's check."

Outside in the bright sun, Amanda shielded her eyes as she scanned the parking lot. She saw Todd slide down in his seat as she headed for the camper van. "It was hiding behind this."

The space beside the van was still empty, and there was no white truck anywhere in the parking. "It was here, and it looked like it was trying to hide."

Kelly pulled out her notebook. "Did you get a plate number?"

Amanda dug out her phone and shielded the screen from the sunlight. "It's a bit hard to make out, but you might be able to enhance it."

Kelly studied the phone. "Not much to go on, but it's not an Alberta plate. Probably a tourist."

"I'm pretty sure it's been following me. I've seen it several times, first in Calgary and then on the highway. And now here. It's got tinted windows that hide the driver."

"And screen the sun. Do you know how many white pick-up trucks with tinted windows there are in Alberta?"

"But this one was acting suspicious. And I got the licence plate. Can you at least run a check?"

Kelly had been jotting notes. She paused to wave her hand at Amanda's phone. "Okay, send me the photo." Her expression was skeptical as she snapped her notebook shut.

Amanda had the sinking feeling that she'd just squandered all the credibility she'd built up. "I just want the investigators to know all this. I don't know what you've already found out from the body or when I'll be informed of any results."

"Amanda, it's still too early. Once DNA results are in, you'll be informed. In the meantime, just keep your distance. Believe me when I say we know what we're doing, and if you go bumbling around in the middle of the case, you could mess it up for us."

Bumbling! "You wouldn't even have known about the fire, or Shelley's pregnancy, or the missing whisky bottle unless I told you about it!"

Kelly managed a wry smile. "Thank you for your help. And if any other information comes your way, or you see that white truck again, let us know."

Amanda sighed as she watched the woman stride back across the lot. She was relieved that the police now had more pieces of the puzzle but frustrated that she hadn't been able to pry a single fact out of the woman. She'd settle for knowing the gender and age of the body. She'd be even more satisfied if she knew the cause of death. Surely they knew those things by now!

That evening, back in Maeve's B&B, she and Chris had their nightly Skype call. The sight of his goofy, grinning face filled her with warmth. After a few teasing, sexually charged moments, that goofy face grew serious.

"There's a nice little bungalow for sale on Deer Lake. Waterfront near the top of the lake. Three bedrooms, stone fireplace, nice dock with slips for a boat and canoe. I'm thinking of putting in an offer."

She sat back in surprise. Before she could collect her thoughts, he rushed on. "I–I'd like a place of my own anyway. I'm tired of renting, and this one has a beautiful view down the lake, facing south, close to the station."

"I guess, but ..."

"I know — at least I hope — this decision affects you too. If you come here. I mean ..."

She watched him flounder as he searched for the right words. "Send me the link."

He broke into a broad, crinkly grin. When the link popped up in her messages, they discussed the amenities of the house, as well as the ridiculously low price compared to big mainland cities. She felt a wave of yearning. It truly did look like a welcoming home in a peaceful, restorative setting. She could imagine herself sitting on the dock, sipping wine and watching the sunset. On impulse, she told him to go ahead. His grin became so broad that she was reluctant to break the spell.

"I have a favour to ask." She let the comment float gently between them.

His smile disappeared. "What?"

She told him about the fire and Shelley's stalker, as well as the reaction of the police. "I know it's a big favour, but I'm wondering if they might tell you more than they're telling me. One cop to another."

"Amanda ..."

"I'm trying to stay out of it. At least I'd like to. But I have to know they're taking this seriously. I think Jonathan was murdered." She took a deep breath. "There. I've said it."

Silence, but she could see the shock on his face. At least he didn't tell her she was crazy. "Still a lot of ifs, honey."

"But if I had answers to some of those ifs — like if the body is even male — I could reassure myself. You know me. I need answers. I can't stand not knowing. And if someone got away with murder and whole lives were ruined as a result —"

"If I can get some of the answers for you, will you be satisfied? Will you keep out of it?"

She hesitated. The truth was, maybe. But maybe not. She had contacts the police did not, and she was privy to secrets they might never learn. But now was not the time to argue with him.

"If I know they're taking it seriously, yes."

"I'll see what I can do."

"You're ... you're perfect." She hesitated. "There's one more thing. Can you stand one more request?"

He frowned. "Do I need to be more perfect?"

She told him about the white truck, and to her relief, he did not downplay it as Constable Kelly had. He quizzed her for details on how often she'd seen in and how certain she was that it was the same truck.

"It took off when I approached it. That was the most suspicious of all. I got a photo of the licence plate."

"Good. Give it to Kelly."

"I did. But she thinks it's just a tourist and I surprised him."

"But she has the plate number?"

"Yes. But Chris, can you look it up for me?"

He rolled his eyes. "Amanda, you can't keep asking me these things. I can't abuse my position."

"I know. But I need to know if I'm in danger. A journalist has already been attacked."

"You'll be in less danger if you stay out of it, honey."

She sighed. "I'm going to send you the photo. Do what you like with it."

CHAPTER TWENTY-FOUR

Chris stood in the living room and gazed through the French doors at the stone patio, the flower garden, and the lake beyond. A strong wind had whipped the water into whitecaps that danced in the sun. He pictured himself and Amanda having their morning coffee on the patio on a warm summer day, or their glass of wine at sunset as they watched the sport fishermen motor back toward town.

He turned to look at the living room. A floor-to-ceiling stone fireplace dominated one wall, promising warmth and peace on snowy Newfoundland nights. At the other end, an open-concept kitchen allowed a view of the fireplace and the lake beyond. It was perfect. He didn't know how long he'd be posted in Newfoundland or whether Amanda would ever join him, but he could see her in this house. It felt like a home, and she had had so little of that. He hoped that if she saw it, she'd be as captivated as he was, and she'd be able to put aside the traumatic memories Newfoundland still stirred up.

He'd made the appointment with the realtor for first thing in the morning. He knew there were still a few steps to navigate, but he already knew the ending. He was going to buy this house.

When he arrived at the station afterward, it was still too early to call Constable Brinwall. The day shift at the Drumheller detachment wouldn't start for at least another hour. After he'd waded through the change-of-shift routine of updates and assignments, he still had fifteen minutes to kill. He poured himself a fresh cup of coffee, sat at his desk, and opened the photo Amanda had sent. It was the tailgate of a white pick-up, blurry and mud-spattered, but all except the final few letters were legible.

The first step was to figure out which jurisdiction it belonged to. Licence plates were issued by provinces, territories, and states, each one with its own distinct colours, motifs, and slogans. Alberta had red letters and numbers on a white background. This plate had blue on white, which wasn't much help because about half the provinces had that combination, including British Columbia and Ontario. Although quite a few American licence plates had blue on white too, most were more colourful and elaborate than the one on the truck.

He studied the fuzzy design. There was a slogan at the top and a coloured symbol in the centre. He enlarged the photo and identified the slogan as *Beautiful British Columbia*. He accessed the B.C. database and, armed with the partial plate number, narrowed down the search to five vehicles.

One was a white Ford F-150, registered to a Jack White of Coquitlam, B.C.

Who the hell was Jack White, and what did he want with Amanda? It made no sense. Surely she was imagining things. But before he told her that and risked getting her angry, he did a quick Google search of *Jack White Coquitlam*. As he suspected, the name was too common to give him any clear leads, and adding the phone number and address on the vehicle registration yielded dead ends. Puzzled, and with a twinge of concern, he ran a police information check and criminal records check. Clean as a whistle.

But finally, amid all the clutter and noise of Internet hits, one small tagline caught his eye. *White Investigations, specializing in locating people and property.* The firm had no website and almost no Internet presence beyond a listing in the directory of security firms, but its address was the one listed on Jack White's driver's licence.

A private investigator? What the hell? Did it have to do with Jonathan Lewis? Was someone else looking for him too?

Now he really did have a decent reason to phone Constable Brinwall. Amanda had warned him that Brinwall was a stickler for rules — a brick wall was the phrase she'd used — but he was hoping a man-to-man, cop-to-cop approach, along with this tidbit of intriguing information, would loosen a few chinks in the wall.

It was a long shot. If the situation were reversed, he'd never have discussed a case with another officer from the other end of the country without an official professional reason. But he'd promised Amanda he'd try.

After introducing himself, he came straight to the point. He told Brinwall he was making inquiries on behalf of Amanda and had determined that the white truck following her was registered to Jack White, a PI from the Vancouver area. Brinwall's response was silence.

"Did you already know that?"

"You know I'm not at liberty to discuss the case, Corporal Tymko."

So much for loosening chinks in the wall. "Why would a private eye be tailing Amanda?"

"No idea."

"Did you guys hire him?"

A short, humourless laugh.

"Okay, but you gotta admit it's weird. It looks like someone besides Amanda is looking for Jonathan Lewis."

"That's a stretch. It could be a lot of things. Maybe your girlfriend has secrets you don't know about."

Chris let that slide.

"Or maybe someone just wants to keep tabs on her. She's poking her nose into places she shouldn't."

That was the perfect segue into the next issue he wanted to discuss. "You're right. She wants answers, so I'm trying to help her. Is there anything you can tell me about the investigation that would ease her mind?"

"I've already made my position clear to Ms. Doucette," Brinwall said. "I have nothing to report yet." His voice cracked as if he'd barely passed puberty, and Chris had a funny flash of the man sitting poker-straight in his chair, clutching his rule book like a talisman.

"Yes, and you're absolutely correct. I know what a bind she's put you in. But here's the thing. When Amanda wants to find out something — no, *needs* to find out something — she doesn't give up. If she can't find out from you, she'd going to investigate on her own. I know her. I've seen her in action. Full steam ahead, straight through the mountain." He felt a twinge of guilt that he was painting Amanda as just shy of crazy.

"It won't help her," Brinwall said.

"She's already found out a lot, hasn't she? She's been asking questions, putting pieces together, confronting people. She's fearless. And I'm afraid she's going to get herself hurt."

"That's your problem. I don't know what you expect me to do about it."

Brick wall doesn't cover it, Chris thought. *Self-righteous little prick comes closer.* He reined himself in with an effort. "She doesn't believe you are taking this seriously enough."

There was a long pause. "I can assure you we are taking it seriously, Corporal. We're just not at liberty to discuss it with Ms. Doucette."

"Is there anything you can tell me, anything that might satisfy her and make her patient enough to wait for the results of your investigation? Anything about the body?"

"No. The DNA results are not in yet. The tests have not yet been completed on the human remains."

"I get that it's early days. But the Medical Examiner must know some details about the body by now!"

There was silence. Chris made one last try. "Is it a man?"

More silence. Chris persevered. "Adult, twenty to thirty years old? Any signs of trauma? Cause of death?"

Still silence. Finally Brinwall spoke. "It's not likely cause of death can be determined from the remains, but the lab has confirmed minute traces of burnt cloth at the site."

"The guy tailing you is a private eye from B.C.," Chris said. He had phoned just as Amanda was finishing her coffee at Maeve's and about to leave for the Time Travel tour. The big day had finally arrived.

Words failed her. "What the hell?"

"Yeah, I know."

"Why?"

"Who knows? Maybe to keep tabs on you? Maybe he's looking for Jonathan too?"

"But who hired him? And why now?"

"I don't know. But it's quite a coincidence that it's happening just when you're stirring things up."

"Can't you just phone and ask him?"

"He'd never divulge that confidential information. And maybe we don't want to tip him off that we're on to him yet. But I did pass the info on to your buddy Brinwall to add to his file. And at least we know you're probably not in danger from the guy."

Amanda's thoughts were still reeling. "Did you ask Brinwall about the case?"

He chuckled. "I did. And I didn't get much. Like you said, Brinwall is by-the-book. Not that I blame him."

Amanda was about to protest but bit her tongue. Chris himself was straight as an arrow, so this could not have been a comfortable move for him. He had tried, and that's what counted. "Did you at least find out when the DNA will be in?"

"Brinwall wouldn't know that. They have to extract the DNA from the bones and profile it, and then it wends its way through the lab bureaucracy. They'll know when they know. I've had cases take six weeks."

She forced a smile. "Okay, I'll try to be patient. But did he give you any details? Age? Sex?"

"One detail, but it's significant. Traces of burnt cloth at the bone site."

She sucked in her breath. "Fuck! I'm right!" To her surprise, her breath quickened and a lump rose in her throat. She had not expected to feel grief. Over the years, she'd all but forgotten the Jonathan of her childhood, but in her quest to trace him, he had once again become part of her.

"We don't know that," Chris cautioned. "These are pieces of the puzzle, but we don't know how they fit together."

"You're right. At least now I know the police are working on it." She softened. "You're the best." A whisper. "Love you."

"I'm buying that house."

Her tongue was tied. "It's beautiful."

"I've got an appointment at the bank this afternoon."

"Good." She searched for words. She wanted to be supportive. Enthusiastic. "Keep me posted."

After she disconnected, she stared into space. Maeve, who was bent over her harvest table elbow-deep in bread flour, looked over questioningly. "They found something?"

"Lots. Wow. Someone hired a PI to tail me. But damnit, I'm about to start my tour, and I've got no time to make sense of all this. There are so many unknowns, so many secrets and cover-ups. Is the PI looking for Jonathan too, or does he want to know what I'm up to? Chris thinks I'm not in danger. Maybe not from the PI, but what about from the person who hired him? Is it one of the Oaks family? Or is it someone from the Fort McMurray days? I've talked to a lot of people and turned over a lot of rocks. It could be someone who thought he'd gotten away with murder thirty years ago and is now afraid it will all come to light." A chill stole over her. *Someone like Sean O'Regan.*

"The stalker holds the key," she said. "That's the guy I have to find."

"You have a name?"

"Sean O'Regan."

"Doesn't ring a bell."

"He's not from around here. But I'm on my way to Drumheller to meet the group's plane. I can't do anything more until the tour is over. Damn!"

She was back in her room doing last-minute packing when the answer came to her. She picked up her phone to call.

"Matthew! Buddy!"

"Problems?" he asked. How well he knew her and how easily he recognized a hidden agenda in her tone.

"No. Everything is on track, but I've got a favour to ask. Well, two favours, actually."

"Of course you do."

"I need your amazing sleuthing skills again. Can you try to track down this guy Sean O'Regan that Hank Klassen mentioned? I'm not sure how it's spelled. Hank said he was the site manager in Fort McMurray when Jonathan and Shelley were there."

"What's he got to do with anything?"

"Maybe lots. I don't have much time to explain, but remember, he was harassing Shelley, there was a huge blowout, and

Jonathan and Shelley were fired? I think more happened between them all, and I need to talk to this guy."

"Amanda ..."

She heard the lecture in his tone, and her temper flared. "I'm not going to do anything stupid. So far, every single thing I've learned, I've turned over to the police. They wouldn't know anything if it weren't for me."

"Do they have Sean O'Regan's name?"

"Yes."

"Then maybe let them run with it."

"What's the harm in a little poking around on the Internet? Maybe making a few phone calls? I promise, I'm not going to do anything stupid. I'll be out in the boonies with the group. I just want to know where he is and what he's up to."

"And what makes you think he's up to something?"

"Because that's the second favour. A private eye from B.C. is tailing me. Name of Jack White." She filled him in on the white truck and Chris's license plate search. "Can you find out who he is and who hired him?"

Matthew had been surprisingly quiet throughout her explanation. "That's not going to be public, Amanda."

"I know, but maybe you can find out if he has any connection to oil companies or to the Oaks family. Or to this guy Sean O'Regan. I can't think of anyone else it could be."

Matthew was hurt and angry. He adored Amanda and believed in what she was doing, but sometimes he felt like nothing more than an errand boy, always there to fulfill her every whim, asking nothing in return and getting precious little. He'd barely seen her since he came out to Calgary to work on the tour. She'd spent two weeks shacked up with her Mountie and only a couple of afternoons with him. Yet she thought nothing of phoning him up to dump more tasks in his lap.

He'd been reluctant to agree. He wasn't a wuss. Ten years chasing stories in violent hellholes had taught him to be as tough and unbending as steel when he needed to be. But he'd never been able to say no to her. Never been able to hold her in check when she got caught up in a mission. Not when they were both overseas, him as a foreign correspondent and her as an aid worker trying to expose a tragedy or right a wrong, and not now that he'd joined her charitable crusade. As with all other times, he decided to go along with it. He told himself that keeping track of her was better than letting her sail into dangerous waters on her own.

But if he were honest, he'd do whatever she needed to keep her close to him.

In his spare time over the course of the next two days, he dug around on the web. He started with a general Google search of Sean O'Regan that proved too broad, even when he used qualifiers like Alberta, Fort McMurray, Norsands, and oil. He tried social media with the same results. Who knew there were so many Sean/Shawn/Shaun O'Regan/O'Reagans? He figured the man had to be at least fifty-five years old, which eliminated many who seemed too young, but the remaining profiles were too vague and numerous to show promise.

He tried a search on the Norsands site itself but turned up nothing. But a lot could have happened in thirty years in an industry famous for mergers, partnerships, and subsidiaries. Norsands was owned by Sandstar, itself owned by a tangled web of other mega-companies, both foreign and domestic. With his expertise in site management, Sean O'Regan could have moved around from project to project.

He checked a couple of databases, including Canada 411, and noted down a few promising candidates, but cold calls to each yielded nothing. Phone calls to Norsands, Sandstar, and a couple of other major oil interests also yielded nothing. A lot of people had lost their jobs during the downturns in the eighties and nineties, but if Sean O'Regan had been employed anywhere more recently, there was no record.

He phoned Hank Klassen to ask what he remembered about Sean O'Regan. Family, hometown, club memberships? Hank said he could hardly remember the guy, especially since he quit shortly after Shelley Oaks's firing. Hank didn't remember him talking about family and friends and remembered no pictures of wife and kids tacked above his site desk.

"But he was an east coaster. He hung around with all the other east coasters. They were always talking about home. Maybe he went back there."

"Where on the east coast?"

"No clue. We had guys from all over."

Matthew dropped his head in his hands with a groan. There were four east coast provinces, all of them full of Irishmen. The man could be anywhere!

He turned instead to the private investigator Jack White. The name was too common for an easy search, so after scrolling through dozens of Jack Whites on Facebook and Twitter, he tried LinkedIn. No Vancouver-area PIs named Jack White. For a businessman, he sure kept a low profile!

He looked up the address on Google Maps and discovered it was a modest house in a mixed residential-commercial area. He tracked down a telephone number, tempted to make a cold call, but something about the number rang a bell. The area code was 778. It took him a moment to remember where he'd seen it before.

CHAPTER TWENTY-FIVE

Matthew stood on the doorstep revising his pitch once again. He had not told her why he was coming because he wanted some element of surprise. He didn't want her to have time to cover her tracks or concoct an explanation, if in fact she had any tracks to cover.

He had instead offered a vague excuse of wanting to discuss a potential follow-up mentorship project with her company. Now, however, as her heels clicked in the hall, he realized how feeble that excuse was. He had not yet run the mentorship idea by Amanda, and the early conversations could easily be done by phone.

When she opened the door and greeted him with a huge smile, his apprehension vanished. The woman was hungry for company and desperate to maintain links and purpose in the broader world. She had spiked her short silver and blue hair, put on dangly silver earrings, and highlighted her blue eyes with smoky liner. A hint of pink glossed her lips. For his benefit? he wondered with a quiver of interest.

Now she placed her index finger to those glossy lips. "Peter's asleep," she murmured. "Finally. He's so restless and he wakes multiple times at night, confused and anxious. Anything new — a change of routine, a new place — sets him off. The doctor is trying a new drug, so fingers crossed."

She led the way into the living room, where once again a tray with two wine glasses and a platter of cheese and crackers sat on the coffee table. Without even asking, she began to pour. "I'm so excited about this project. I think a personal mentor is so much more effective than a big corporate entity."

As they sipped their wine and discussed ideas, he steered her carefully into her own personal experiences in the oil industry. She had been a cowgirl, not an oil girl, she said, and it was at rodeos that she'd first met Peter.

"He was a very handsome man. Still is, of course, but …" She shook her head and nibbled on a piece of cheddar. "Very charismatic. Power is sexy, you know, and I found myself wanting everything he wanted. I left the ranch, left my family, followed him here to Calgary, and played the oilman's wife perfectly. I sat on boards, worked on charities, entertained, wheeled and dealed, and raised a wonderful daughter. I had a good life. I'm not complaining, Matthew. I chose it. Peter's life has brought me tremendous rewards."

She topped up his wine glass and poured herself another. "This is the worst tragedy that ever could have happened to him. It was what he feared most, having lived though his father's illness. When the first memory lapses occurred and the first irrational moods, he denied them and wouldn't let me help. He wouldn't accept suggestions and got defensive if I tried. I knew he was mismanaging the finances, but he refused to let me intervene. And so …"

A thump upstairs startled them both. Alarm flitted across her face. She listened intently, but there was no further sound.

"I imagine it's very hard on you."

"And on him. It's been devastating for him. Oh, Matthew, you have no idea how I covered up for him! With his friends and associates, at parties. I rescued him when he forgot who people were. I explained his moods, coped with his rages. Sometimes now I have to lock him in his room if I go out." She took a long gulp of wine, and her eyes filled with tears. "Look at me. I'm fifty-four years old, and what am I? What have I accomplished? Sometimes I look ahead and think of all the things I'd like to do. That's why I'm involved in this carbon capture project, and now this mentorship program. Life after Peter." She shook her head. "Do I sound awful?"

"Not at all. It's good you're looking ahead," he muttered, thinking things had just become much more complicated. He was going to have to speak to Amanda about the mentorship for real.

She smiled and leaned toward him. "I'll tell you a little secret. I think Alberta has to get off fossil fuel and into renewable energy. We've built our fortune in the oil and gas industry, and now we have our heads stuck so far into the oil sands that we don't see the rest of the world is moving on. We've got the expertise and the innovative spirit to be leaders in the new forms of energy, but in some of my circles, it's almost heresy to say the words." Her smile broadened. "I'll tell you another little secret. I voted NDP in the last two Alberta elections. Peter doesn't even know. But frankly, forty-four years of Conservative rule was enough. There's more than one way to build our future."

"Good for you. That gives us common ground to work on. Amanda will be happy."

She poured her third glass of wine and looked dismayed when she saw his was still full. *It's now or never*, Matthew thought, *before she can no longer think straight.*

"Speaking of Amanda," he said, "Something weird is happening. She's being followed. Have you ever heard of a guy called Jack White?"

She frowned in concentration for a moment before shaking her head. "Who is he?"

"The phone calls you've been having — the hang-ups with the 778 area code? Do you think I could have another look at the number?" He had already risen and was moving toward the phone on the end table. She struggled to her feet. While he scrolled through the call display, she came to stand beside him, placing her hand on his shoulder as she peered at the phone.

"What is it?" she asked, breathing in his ear.

The area code popped up, and he knew immediately that it was the same number. He showed it to her. "This number. Do you remember it?"

She nodded. "Telemarketer."

"No, this is Jack White's number, and Jack White is a private investigator who's been following Amanda."

She swayed backward, blinking in confusion. "Why?"

"She has no idea. She thinks it probably has to do with her search for her Uncle Jonathan. So you've never heard of Jack White?"

"No."

"He's never spoken to you? No stranger has phoned to ask you questions about Amanda?"

She whipped her head back and forth. He hesitated before asking his next question. He was confident that Natalie had not hired the PI, because otherwise she would not have called attention to the strange phone calls earlier.

"We're wondering who he's working for. Do you think Peter could have hired him?"

She recoiled. She had set her wine glass down and seemed to be trying hard to sober up. "Why would he do that?"

"To keep tabs on her, to see what she learns about her uncle's whereabouts."

"Impossible. Most days Peter hardly remembers how to use the telephone."

"Most days. But he has more lucid days too, right? Dementia is like that."

"Yes, but to hire a PI? Even if he wanted to, even if he thought it was a good idea, that's far too complicated for him. He'd have to find one, arrange a meeting, tell him what he wanted, negotiate a contract, pay a retainer … No, that's far too many steps for him."

"But you said he's on a new drug. Maybe it's helping. The other day, when this phone call came in, he answered it upstairs. We heard him talking."

"Only for a few seconds."

"Can we just ask him if he's ever talked to Jack White, Natalie? So I can put Amanda's mind at ease?"

"He'll get upset. He always gets upset when he's confronted."

She balked and made excuses, but finally she led him into the hall with the careful, deliberate steps of someone trying to act sober. They found Peter in his room watching a game show on a massive wall TV. The room was large and airy, with a sitting area and a rumpled king-sized bed. Despite the sunny blue and yellow colour scheme, it felt like a prison.

Natalie had brought along the platter of cheese and picked up the cordless phone in the hall. She introduced Matthew as someone she was working with on a charitable project. Peter was gracious and friendly, giving a hint of the polished man he'd once been. After a short conversation about the game show, she steered him around to the phone number.

"This number has phoned a few times, darling, but I always miss the call. I'm wondering if you know who it is."

Peter stared at the number and shook his head. Matthew thought he detected alarm in the man's eyes, but it could have been because he'd been put on the spot. Life with a failing memory must be full of alarm.

"You spoke to him a few days ago. Do you remember what he wanted?"

"I didn't speak to him."

"You didn't talk long. Do you remember what he said?"

"I didn't talk."

"His name is Jack White," Matthew interjected. "Does the name ring a bell?"

"I don't know him. I didn't talk to him."

Peter's voice had risen, and his alarm was palpable now. Natalie laid a hand on Matthew's arm and drew him away. Her voice was calm and cheery. "Okay, darling, my mistake. Sorry we interrupted your game show. We'll finish our business downstairs, and I'll call you in a bit for dinner."

She backed out of the room, pushing Matthew ahead of her, and didn't speak until they were downstairs. "He was one step away from throwing a fit. Let's hope he gets back into his show, but I'd better get up there soon." She turned to look at him. "I think you have your answer. He doesn't even remember the phone call. He certainly isn't capable of hiring a private eye."

As he drove away, he played the scene over in his head. The grim reality of Natalie's life saddened him. She was an attractive, dynamic woman still in her prime, but she was trapped in a life circumscribed by her husband's needs. He was certain she had no hand in hiring Jack White, and after meeting Peter, he doubted the man was capable of it either. Unless there was a side of him that even his wife didn't see.

But if neither Natalie nor Peter had hired the private investigator, who had? And what was he going to tell Amanda? She was less favourably disposed toward the Oakses because of their treatment of Jonathan and Shelley, so she was unlikely to be as sympathetic toward Natalie as he was. Or as willing to believe she was innocent.

When Todd peeked into Livia's room, he thought she was asleep. Because of her concussion, the lights were dim, and she was lounging in the visitor's chair by the window with her head back and her eyes closed. He hesitated, unsure what to do. He knew she needed her sleep above all else, but he'd driven all the way from Drumheller and had spent a fortune on a box of exquisitely hand-crafted chocolates from renowned Calgary chocolatier Bernard Callebaut.

He tiptoed into the room to put the box on her bed tray, figuring he'd go for coffee and try again in a few minutes. As he was studying her, so young and fragile in the shadowy light, she opened her eyes and squinted at him.

A smile spread across her face. "Todd," she murmured.

"I brought you chocolates," he said, carrying the box across the room. "I figured you'd be sick of hospital food."

"Bernard Callebaut. Oooo." She set it down as if it were too heavy for her.

He perched on the windowsill. "How are you doing?"

She managed a careful shrug. "My excitement for the day? I walked halfway down the hall. It turned me into a puddle."

"What do the doctors say?"

"That it takes time. Your brain is working really hard trying to sort itself out, they say, so give it a break." She sighed and shut her eyes.

He shifted awkwardly in the silence. "Do you want a chocolate? Or a glass of water?"

"Not yet." She opened her eyes again. "How exciting am I? I need something to think about besides these hospital walls and my scrambled eggs brain. Can you bring me my phone?"

He glanced around the room. "Where is it?"

"It's at my apartment. I mean next time you come. Maybe by that time my brain will be an omelette. Then I can access the Internet and the notes I took on our case, try to remember what I was doing. What's happened since I've been in La La Land?"

When he hesitated, she scowled. "I'm not a complete scrambled egg! We had a deal, remember?"

"I don't want to tire you out."

"Staying upright tires me out. Let's make it worth my while. Have they identified the body yet?"

He laughed. In truth, he wasn't sure how much he wanted to tell her. She was an ambitious, impetuous kid, and the last time he'd confided in her, he'd ended up burnt and she'd ended up in the hospital. At first, he'd visited her out of guilt and concern, but he found he enjoyed her peculiar mix of fragility and tough-girl sass. Deep down, he had a niggling feeling he was being played again, but he brushed it off. In broad strokes, he filled her in on the discoveries he and Amanda had made about Jonathan, the fire, and the Oaks.

When her eyes drifted shut with fatigue, he stopped.

"Wow," she breathed, her eyes still closed. "This is a story!"

"It can wait." In the silence, he stood up. "I should go. Can I get you anything first?"

She licked her lips. "That tea. It's cold and tastes like paint stripper, but it's wet."

He brought her the tea from her bedside and watched as she gripped the cup in shaky hands. After one sip, she pulled a face and handed it back.

"A cop came to talk to me. That tight-ass dude from Drumheller. He wanted to know what I remembered. I hope you enjoyed the drive, I told him, because that'll be the highlight of your day."

"You don't remember anything?"

She breathed deeply. Fading. "He told me they couldn't get any useful prints. The guy picked the lock — must have been a pro — but there weren't any prints on the knob except mine. Which means ..."

"He wore gloves. If he'd wiped the knob, yours would be gone too."

"I guess. But there was a truck."

Todd stiffened. "What truck?"

"Neighbour across the street saw a white truck. Parked by my place. Took off like its tail was on fire."

"He's sure it was white?"

"I know that neighbour. Bored old man, spends his whole day pretending he's working in his garden. He watches everything that goes on." Her eyes flickered. "Oh. Another neighbour, the end of the block, says there was a truck outside his place half the afternoon. He couldn't see, but he thought there was someone in it."

"And he said it was a white truck too?"

Livia frowned and seemed to be gathering her thoughts. "Don't know. But if Boris said it was white, it was white."

CHAPTER TWENTY-SIX

Time Travel, now in its sixth day, was galloping along at a thrilling pace. The students, initially shy and diffident, had been awed by the Mars-like landscape of the badlands and by the discovery of a dinosaur femur on their first day in the museum park. By the time they were settled in their prospector tents at the camp, they'd been chattering together like a bunch of magpies. Their high spirits were so infectious that Amanda almost managed to forget her worries about Jonathan and the mystery of Jack White.

Almost.

After the museum events, they had spent two days on horseback, exploring the coulees and grasslands north of Drumheller and camping overnight around a campfire under the stars. Conroy the trail guide did not disappoint. Besides striking the perfect cowboy pose for selfies, he also brought along his guitar to lead a campfire singalong.

They had emerged from that adventure flying high, despite pain in every muscle. Amanda was grateful for the horse liniment that Conroy had brought and for his endless repertoire of corny cowboy songs, all of which Michel the radio host recorded on his phone while the girls hung on his every word.

The sixth morning, the group piled onto the bus and headed to Dinosaur Provincial Park for two days of fossil prospecting and excavating an active bone bed in the remote interior. When Amanda left Drumheller early in order to supervise the set-up at the park, she had her first chance in days to let her mind wander back to the case. She had heard from Chris, who was now the ecstatic owner of a little waterfront bungalow. Matthew had been in frequent touch with her by email and texts about minor logistical issues, but not a peep about his search for Sean O'Regan or Jack White. Her one query on the topic had been met with a terse "Working on it. Keep your eye on the ball."

To her relief, the white truck was nowhere to be seen.

As she drove south through flat, empty grassland dotted with cattle, occasional trees, and a line of hydro towers, she passed the gravel range road that led past the homestead shack. Out of habit, she scanned the horizon, expecting to see more cattle and trees. Instead, silhouetted far in the distance, was a cluster of irregular shapes. She parked and pulled out her binoculars. The shapes became vehicles: vans, trailers, and SUVs.

Her heart beating faster, she set her binoculars on the console and steered the Hulk onto the gravel road. As she approached over the dips and rises of the rolling terrain, the line of vehicles gradually took on more detail. By the time she was close enough to see them clearly, she knew what they were.

The little homestead shack was a familiar smudge of grey in the distance when she pulled up behind the last RCMP vehicle. There was no one around. A thin trail of dust hung over the dry prairie to mark the passage of the quads that had carried the Mounties out to the site.

She leashed Kaylee and set off along the track left by the quads. The morning sun was already heating up, and the flies buzzed relentlessly. She had not prepared for this and could feel the sun burning her bare shoulders. She was barely halfway there when a figure detached itself from the cluster of investigators and strode toward her. She picked up her pace, anxious to see what they were up to before she was blocked. She broke into a sweat, and Kaylee was panting along at her side. She'd forgotten to bring water. *Smart move, Amanda.*

Soon she could distinguish half a dozen officers in white bunny suits bent over the section of grass where she knew the barn had been. They had placed markers on the ground, and a stack of evidence bins sat on an ATV trailer nearby.

"Ms. Doucette!" Brinwall shouted as he approached. She recognized his cracking voice before his baby face beneath his cap visor. "This is a restricted area!"

She kept going until they reached each other. By now she could see a fluttering cordon of yellow police tape around the perimeter and the grid lines in the soil inside. "Have you found anything?" she asked.

"This is a police investigation."

"I can see that! I'm the one who told you about it."

He looked down at her. Both were breathing heavily, and sweat trickled down his face below his cap. "Yes, and your tip was very useful. But we'll take it from here. Let us do our job."

"Will you be able to tell, after all these years, how the fire started?"

"Probably not. Too much has been removed."

"Then what are you looking for? Besides the obvious — burnt bits of wood and wire."

He studied her. "Have you spoken to your aunt?"

Amanda was startled. "No, why?"

"Speak to your aunt."

"Why —"

He turned. "Go. Before you and the dog get heatstroke. Call your aunt."

He seemed almost sympathetic, she thought as she watched him walk back toward the crime scene without a backward glance.

Back in the Hulk, she turned the air conditioning on full, gave Kaylee and herself a generous drink of water, and called Aunt Jean. Something monumental had just occurred. The DNA, surely.

"I was about to call you," Jean said. "I just got off the phone with your mother."

"Is it Jonathan?" Amanda blurted out. Her heart was racing, and her phone was slick in her hand. Now, at the final moment, she wasn't sure she wanted to know. She didn't want to think —

"No, it's not."

Amanda wasn't sure she'd heard properly. "What?"

"The DNA doesn't match."

"Oh."

"I'm so relieved," Jean said. "I've spent weeks thinking about his last moments, wondering if he suffered and regretting that I'd never have a chance to put things right."

"Then who is it? Did the police say?"

"I have no idea. And no, they didn't say. So we're back to square one, which is to say — nowhere."

Amanda gazed out the window at the busy crime scene investigation in the distance. Her pulse slowed as her shock subsided and reason returned. "No, hardly square one. I've learned a lot about Jonathan's actions in the last couple of months before he disappeared. I know he came down to central Alberta with his girlfriend to her farm near where the bones were discovered. I know his girlfriend was pregnant, but I believe she was also raped by her boss up in Fort McMurray, so she was afraid the child might be his. I believe she and Jonathan argued about it. He was not allowed to stay at her house, but he may have been staying at an old homestead that had once been in the family.

That homestead was partly destroyed by fire at exactly the same time period, and I know the police found burnt cloth among the bones in the coulee. I believe someone died in that fire. I was afraid it was Jonathan."

"Dear God," Jean said.

Amanda drew a deep breath. She had tried to summarize the evidence as logically as possible, but now new fears crowded in. Fears produced by the logic itself. "Yes," she said simply. "It's not Jonathan. For that we can be grateful. But the obvious next question is, who was it?"

"And more importantly," Jean said quietly, "how was Jonathan involved?"

The question hung in the air. As much as she hated to consider it, it had to be answered. She had only a small child's memory of her uncle, a memory easily moulded by the young man's playful charm. Jean and her mother would have a more nuanced view.

"Do you think — I mean, from what you know of Jonathan — do you think he'd be capable of killing someone?"

"We both need time to digest this, Amanda."

Cautious reflection was her aunt's way, but it was not Amanda's. "But in your gut, first impression, is he?"

There was a pause. "Jonathan was impulsive. Reckless, even. He didn't always think things through, and he did have a temper. In that respect he was like your mother. I remember some dreadful fights between them where toys were smashed and furniture thrown. And Jonathan could get himself in trouble in the schoolyard too. But killing someone? Even for Jonathan at his wildest, that's a stretch."

Through the window Amanda watched the distant figures with dread. "But as a man, thirty years old, under huge emotional stress, could he …?"

"Who knows what any of us are capable of under huge emotional stress, Amanda?"

Amanda was silent, remembering her own moment of reckoning in the Newfoundland wilderness. The feel of the rifle in her hands, the trigger beneath her finger ... that split second that could have changed her life.

Through her own memory, Jean was talking. "You said there was a fire. Maybe it was an accident? I could see that, especially if they were under the influence of alcohol or drugs. Jonathan did a lot of stupid things when he was drunk. If they lit a campfire and were smoking something, things could get out of hand fast."

Like her aunt, Amanda wanted to hang on to that explanation. Jonathan had been stupid but innocent. But she knew that whatever had happened in that barn, it had not been a party. "Then why didn't he go to the cops? I know there were no cellphones back then, but if the fire and the death were accidental, why not report it? Because he was afraid of getting into trouble? Trespassing, criminal negligence, maybe even drug charges? Would he cover up a person's *death* just to save his own skin?"

"Jonny was not always the best at taking responsibility. Having got himself into this mess and with a dead man on his hands, I could see him running away."

"But he didn't just run away, Aunt Jean! He dragged the body at least half a kilometre down into the coulee and buried it. And he tried to clean up all traces of the fire. That's way more than a reckless accident. That's deliberate and calculating."

Aunt Jean had no answer for that, and Amanda felt worse than ever when she hung up. Tracing it through step by step, the scenario was even more chilling than she'd first thought. For if Jonathan had killed someone and gone to great lengths to get rid of the evidence, he had a good reason to disappear. For thirty years his secret had stayed safely buried, and he'd had a chance to build a new life wherever he'd chosen to go.

But now her own actions might have led the police straight to him. Without her missing persons report, without her discovery of the homestead shack and the fire, the police would never have thought to connect him to the bones in the coulee. Whoever the dead man was, chances were the police would never have put all the players and their roles together as neatly as she had.

She glanced at the clock on her dash. She was running out of time. If she hoped to get to the dinosaur park ahead of the tour bus, she had to move fast. Putting the Hulk in gear, she spun out onto the gravel road and headed for the highway. As she drove, she told Siri to phone Matthew.

"Any luck tracking down Sean O'Regan?" she said when she heard his voice.

"And hello to you too. How's it going?"

"Matthew, it's a mess. The body is not my uncle. So now I have to find out who it is."

"Why?"

"Because …" She cast about. Why indeed? Had she not done enough damage? "I want to be prepared. So I can figure out what to do."

"But that's good news, isn't it? Maybe your uncle has nothing to do with any of this. Maybe it's some other random case from another time entirely."

"Except we know the fire was in September 1990."

"It's a big country. Lots of fires. There could be a dozen other scenarios. Why don't you just step out of the picture and let the police figure it out?"

"Because I may have given them all the pieces. Matthew, I may have totally messed things up."

"All the more reason to step away now."

She was racing up toward the main highway intersection. At the last moment, she slammed on the brakes and slewed around the turn. Kaylee slid across the seat, and the Hulk screeched and rocked. She needed all her strength to protect Kaylee and wrestle the machine back under control. Finally it settled and she slowed her breathing. "There's also Jack White. Something's going on, Matthew, and like it or not, I'm at the centre of it. Any luck finding out what he's up to?"

There was a beat of hesitation. "Nothing solid. Who knows if it's even Jack White? Maybe some guy borrowed his truck to go on vacation. Could be total coincidence."

"That's ridiculous."

"About as ridiculous as some two-bit PI from Vancouver being hired by oil companies to follow you."

Put like that, it did seem ridiculous. "If I get a photo of him, would that help confirm his ID?"

"You get a photo, you give it to the cops."

She sighed. "So what about Sean O'Regan? Did you find him?"

"No, I did not."

"Did you even look?"

"For fuck's sake, Amanda! Listen to yourself!"

She pulled back, ashamed. Of all the people in her life, Matthew had always had her back. Even more than Chris. Matthew understood the need to pursue answers and the need to bend, even break the rules to get them. Their bond had been forged in desperate, at times life-threatening corners of the world run by thugs, dictators, and greed. Where people were expendable and rules were for suckers.

"I'm sorry. I never should have said that."

"Okay." His voice softened. "I checked all the usual channels and databases. I did try. I don't think he's in Alberta. Since he's from the east coast, it's likely he's gone back there. There are a lot of Sean O'Regans on the east coast." He hesitated. "I could plug away, if you really want to find this guy."

She could hear the reluctance in his voice. The road ahead was clear, straight, and fast, giving her a chance to collect her wits. "Let me try something else first," she replied. "Talk soon. And ... thanks, my friend."

He grunted. As she hung up, she felt a wash of affection. What would she do without the grumpy, middle-aged journalist in her corner? *Try not to take him for granted, Amanda,* she thought even as she gave Siri her next instruction.

Chris answered on the second ring, sounding excited but concerned. "What's up, love?"

To her surprise, tears prickled her eyes. "The body is not Jonathan," she blurted out.

"That's great news!"

"Not necessarily. I mean, what happened? If he wasn't the victim, he may have been the ..."

"Ah." Chris's voice dropped. "That's a serious leap, honey."

"But it's where the signs are pointing."

"Even so, don't get ahead of yourself. What do the police say?"

"That it's no longer my concern. But they're investigating the fire."

"Do you want me to call Brinwall again? See if I can get any information out of him?"

"No, not yet. I have another idea. I want you to see if you can find any information down east on a man named Sean O'Regan. He's the Fort McMurray boss who raped Shelley. Matthew can't find him, and he may be back home on the east coast. Can you ... I don't know, check databases, do whatever it is you cops do to track down people?"

"You know I can't use official records for personal searches, Amanda."

"I know, I didn't mean that. Just see if his name crops up locally … I don't know. I've made such a mess of this."

There was silence. She focussed on navigating around a large tractor hauling hay. When he spoke, his voice was gentler. "I'll see what I can do. Not promising, but yeah, sometimes an informal phone call between detachments turns up things."

She felt a flood of relief. "I'm going to be out of touch on a prospecting tour for a couple of days, so no rush. I'm just worried about what I might have stirred up."

It was late the next afternoon before she heard back from Chris. The group had spent the day deep within the park on an archaeological site tucked in between soaring hills, hoodoos, and rocky ledges. The students had worked hard for hours in the blazing sun, using fine chisels and brushes to scrape away the overburden from the edges of a recent Albertosaurus find. Despite the sunhats and frequent water breaks, everyone slouched listlessly back onto the bus. Tempers were frayed and conversation minimal until they spotted the shady cottonwoods and refreshing river of the campground.

Cellphone reception had been nonexistent in the sheltered bone bed, but Amanda's phone chirped to life as the bus neared the campsite.

Chris had left a simple message. "Call me."

Dinner was still half an hour away, so Amanda took the opportunity to let Kaylee roam along the shore of the Red Deer River while she sat on a rock by the campsite and phoned him back.

"I've found Sean O'Regan," he said.

Relief flooded over her, and she cheered aloud.

"Closing date on the house is October seventh. Just before the Thanksgiving weekend."

She heard the longing in his voice — the promise of peace and comfort. Could she silence all the voices in her head, forget the unanswered questions and the old fears of Newfoundland enough to find that peace? She forced the internal clamour aside and focussed on matching her tone to his.

"A perfect time."

CHAPTER TWENTY-SEVEN

Amanda lay awake listening to the soft murmurs and snores from the nearby tents. The students were housed in groups of four with an elder or teacher in each tent to keep the hormones in check. She and Kaylee had a small tent to themselves near the river, and the sibilant hiss of the water helped to muffle the sounds, but still Amanda couldn't sleep. Her thoughts were racing. Sean O'Regan was almost certainly the body in the coulee, but the new DNA testing would once again take weeks. A long time to wait for answers.

What exactly had happened on that fateful night? How had Sean ended up dead? Why had Shelley and Jonathan dropped out of sight almost immediately afterward? Shelley's whereabouts were known, but no one seemed to know where Jonathan was. Was his body also buried somewhere, perhaps never to be discovered?

Something dramatic and violent had happened that September night. Amanda played with the scenario and its aftermath. Jonathan had disappeared, and Shelley had been effectively banished, but not before handing her baby over to Peter and Natalie, who had emerged the biggest winners. What hold did they have over her to persuade her to give up all claim? What did they know? And who had hired the private investigator? If not Sean O'Regan, who else had a stake in what happened thirty years ago?

Only four other people might know the truth: Shelley, Jonathan, Peter, and Natalie. Jonathan was unreachable, and Peter and Natalie risked losing their daughter and grandchildren if the truth were revealed. Of all of them, only Shelley might be willing to talk.

The next morning, as the group slowly woke and staggered out to breakfast, Amanda took her coffee and slipped away to her favourite rock by the river. A delighted Kaylee snatched up her ball and followed while Amanda looked up Shelley's number. She had no idea what she was going to say. In the dark hour of 3:00 a.m., it had seemed like the next logical step, but how do you ask a near stranger whether the man she loved had killed her rapist, and who was involved in the burial and the cover-up? Shelley's outrage and hurt over Jonathan's cold letter had seemed genuine. Was it possible she knew nothing about the killing?

Start slowly, she cautioned herself as she listened to the phone ring. She was just taking a third calming breath when, to her surprise, a man answered. She'd forgotten Shelley was married.

"Hello, can I speak to Shelley, please?"

"She's not here." Amanda was no expert on American accents, but his was an unmistakeable southern drawl.

"Oh. When will she be back?"

"Who's this? Y'all from Canada?"

"Yes, my name is Amanda Doucette. I spoke to her a couple of weeks ago about … uh, a mutual family matter." She knew that sounded cryptic, but it was the best she could think up on the spur of the moment. With this family's penchant for secrets, who knows what Shelley had told the man? "I have a couple more questions."

"Well, you likely know more than me. She's gone."

"Gone?"

"Yes, ma'am. Made a bunch of phone calls a while back, lots of screaming and carrying on, booked a flight, and went to Canada."

Amanda gasped. "You mean to Alberta?"

"Yep. To visit her family. Said it was time."

Amanda could barely wait for a free moment to phone Natalie. She had to stay calm to supervise the bus's departure, and for what seemed an eternity, the students chattered, took last-minute selfies for Instagram, and jostled for the best seats on the bus. She noticed with interest that the Métis radio host had wrangled a seat next to the chief's daughter, and she didn't seem to mind. Something to keep an eye on.

The group was driving south to their cattle ranch homestay, and after Amanda had reviewed the itinerary with the other leaders, she told them she had a couple of errands to do and would meet up with them at the ranch later. She felt guilty for running out on them, but they knew the group far better than she did, and were more than capable of keeping them in line. Her mind was in overdrive, and she knew she needed answers. Was the shit about to hit the fan in the Oaks household? Or had it already hit?

Kaylee had become a much-loved mascot of the group, and the students begged Amanda to let her ride on the bus with them. She hesitated, unsure whether a dozen excitable teens would remember to keep track of the dog and give her water, but in the end she gave in. Kaylee would have much more fun with a dozen eager playmates than she would snoozing on the console of the Hulk.

Afterward, she navigated the steep, winding climb out of the park onto the mesa above before she pulled out her phone and looked up the Oakses' number. It was another clear, parched day, and the vista stretched for miles. The phone rang seven times before Natalie snatched it up, breathless and impatient.

"Natalie, it's Amanda. Has Shelley been to see you?"

"*What?*"

"I've just spoken to her husband. He said she's gone up to see you."

"Omigod! When?"

"He didn't say." Amanda kicked herself. In her surprise, she'd forgotten to ask him. "So she hasn't been in touch?"

"I've been out. Omigod! Peter! Peter!" Amanda heard high heels clattering and doors slamming as if Natalie were racing through the house, leaving a trail of curses in her wake. "He's not here! I hid the keys to his truck in a drawer, but he still got out! If he spoke to Shelley ... Omigod, if she told him she's going to see Ella —"

"What's your daughter's address?"

"Fuck you! You have no idea what you've done."

The line went dead. Amanda took a sharp breath to quell her alarm. What was that all about? Clearly, the family's carefully constructed house of lies was about to collapse, and the result would be messy, but on the face of it, what was the harm in Ella knowing the truth? She would be angry, bewildered, and hurt, but surely a new equilibrium would eventually be reached. One that was healthier in the long run and allowed Shelley, who had suffered the worst through this deception, to build a relationship with her daughter. Natalie and Peter would have to endure some rough times and would have to share Ella, but they weren't likely to lose her forever.

Natalie's panic seemed more visceral than that, as if more was at stake than a daughter's outrage. What was she afraid of? Shelley? Or Peter? What did she think was going to happen?

So many questions that filled Amanda with apprehension. Should she stay out of it or try to help? Were Shelley and Peter together in his truck, on their way to see Ella? Or had Peter set out on his own, perhaps hoping to stop her? Was he capable of driving? Was he capable of finding his way?

Natalie was no doubt already in her car, driving hell-bent for Drumheller to intercept them, to stop them entirely or at least to manage the crisis. Even breaking every speed limit, however, she was an hour and a half away. If Amanda moved fast, she might beat her.

She forced the accelerator closer to the floor, and as the Hulk hurtled forward, she phoned Matthew. "I'll explain later, but can you do me a huge favour and find the address for Ella Oaks in Drumheller. She's married, and I don't know if she uses her married name, but you should be able to find it by searching weddings or something. Please call me ASAP."

"What are you doing?"

"I have to talk to her, or at least talk to Shelley before —"

"I mean what the fuck are you doing? You're supposed to be on a group tour. Right now, on your way to Rolling Hills for the homestay."

"And I'll get there! Matthew, please don't argue. Just help me control this mess."

Matthew swore, promised nothing, and hung up without saying goodbye. She gripped the wheel and shot up the narrow highway, praying he would cooperate and get back to her with the address before she reached Drumheller. She was nearly on the outskirts, passing a comical cluster of sandstone hoodoos on the edge of the highway, when he called back. His voice was cold and angry, but he delivered. "I will explain," she promised him as she thanked him, hung up, and summoned Siri.

THE ANCIENT DEAD

A moment later, Siri began to dictate the route to Ella's house on the outskirts of Drumheller. The town wasn't big, and she soon found herself on a grid of short residential streets tucked in between the highway and the river park. Ella's house was a modest bungalow with a neatly trimmed lawn, curved gardens, and a front drive cluttered with tricycles, strollers, and toys. Either Peter and Natalie had chosen not to lavish their riches upon her, or Ella and her husband had decided to make their own way. Whichever the reason, Amanda warmed to the young woman immediately.

She studied the street. There was a scattering of SUVs and pick-ups parked in driveways, but the street itself was empty except for a small, shiny Kia parked outside Ella's house. A classic economy rental car, not even off the lot long enough to collect country dust.

She was about to ring the doorbell when she heard voices from the backyard. She followed the path around and stopped short at the back gate. Two women sat on patio chairs on the grass. One was holding a baby in her lap, and Amanda recognized her as Ella. The other was wearing a large, floppy-brimmed hat that partly obscured her features, but from the dreamy smile on her face as she looked at the baby, Amanda assumed this was Shelley.

"My two girls are at school. Tyler's the youngest, so far." Ella laughed. "I wanted a houseful of children! I love babies."

"He's beautiful."

"Do you want to hold him?"

Through the branches of a lilac bush, Amanda watched transfixed as Shelley propped her grandson on her lap and cradled him as if he were made of crystal. As she crooned, Ella smiled.

"It's so nice to meet you. Dad mentioned you a few times while I was growing up, but he always said you weren't close. You moved away and got married and were an American now."

"Dual. I never stopped being a Canadian. And I often thought of coming for a visit." She stroked the baby's head. "He's so precious."

"Do you have children of your own?"

Amanda held her breath. Now was the perfect opening if Shelley intended to blow up the lies. But the woman shook her head, the large brim bobbing. "I always dreamed ..."

"I never had any relatives growing up. I'm an only child, and my mother was too. All my friends had cousins and lots of family to get together with at the holidays. It made me sad. It would have been nice to have an aunt."

"I know. I often thought of you and wished I could visit." Shelley lifted her shoulders in a resigned shrug.

"Why didn't you?"

"All this ..." Shelley gestured in a broad sweep to encompass the sky and the distant grey hillsides. "It seemed so far away, and the longer we were estranged, the harder it seemed."

Ella cocked her head. The baby was leaning against Shelley's chest, half asleep, and Shelley rocked him gently. "You're so different from my dad. He never sits still. He'd be all over the yard telling me this needs watering or that needs pruning."

"How is he?"

"Bad. I don't know how Mom handles him. She says he wants to stay at home, because that's what the family does. They kept his father at home too until it nearly killed them. It's heart-breaking to see him disappear, bit by bit." A darkness passed over her face. "Is it in our genes?"

"Lots of things are in our genes." Shelley turned her head. Her eyes locked with Amanda's for a split second before Amanda ducked back behind the bush. Shelley froze in shock, and Amanda muttered a silent curse. She had no business barging into this poignant moment.

"What the …? Someone's there." Shelley handed the baby to his mother and approached the gate. Amanda considered fleeing, but in the end she stepped forward into view. Shelley searched her face, and gradually her alarm was replaced by recognition. "Are you Amanda?"

Amanda nodded. "I'm sorry, Shelley, I didn't mean to intrude."

Shelley stood rooted to the spot. "You are Amanda. I can see that."

Ella came up behind, scowling. "What's going on? Who are you?"

Amanda thought fast. Now was not the time to reveal the truth, but her mind didn't seem to work. "That's not for me to say," she said lamely.

"Aunt Shelley, do you know this person?"

Shelley shook her head. Sadness showed in her eyes but also resignation.

"Then please leave." Ella pressed her baby protectively to her chest. "Now!"

"I would," Amanda said, "except … Shelley, you should know that Natalie is on her way. Maybe Peter too."

"What? Why?"

"Because I phoned her, looking for you, and she said Peter was missing."

"I should go." Shelley spun around and hurried to retrieve her jacket.

"What!" Ella cried. "What's going on?"

"It's … too complicated."

"Maybe it's time to uncomplicate it! Wait for Mom. She's reasonable. And honestly, she could use some help with Dad. He's starting to wander. Talk to her!"

"Maybe. Maybe. But not here."

"Why not here?"

"There are things that happened, things that never should have happened ..." Tears brimmed in Shelley's eyes. She leaned forward to kiss the baby, and her gaze lingered longingly on Ella's face for an instant before she yanked open the gate and strode toward the street.

Amanda hurried after her. "Shelley, let's grab a coffee. We need to talk."

"Not now!"

Ella was following them down to the curb. Shelley jumped into her little car and cast her a final glance. "I'll be back," she said as she started the engine, "but I have things to settle first."

The little Kia's tires screeched as she shot away from the curb. Amanda ran to her own vehicle and took off after her, leaving Ella gaping at the curb. She followed the Kia around the corner to the main highway, where Shelley turned right toward town. As Amanda followed, she honked once in case Shelley wasn't aware of her, but in response, Shelley sped up and slewed left onto the highway toward Calgary. What the hell was Shelley trying to do? Intercept Natalie en route? As they rocketed toward the hill out of town, Amanda leaned on the horn again.

As a Tim Hortons loomed up on the right, Shelley swerved abruptly into the parking lot. By the time Amanda came alongside, she was standing by the car, glaring.

"What in hell do you think you were doing?" Shelley snapped.

"I'm sorry, I wasn't sure what was going to happen, and with Natalie about to barge in —"

"It's none of your damn business! We would have handled it. Things need to be said, and what's between me and my family is not your affair!"

"Then why didn't you want to see Natalie?"

"Because she would have created a scene and upset Ella. And my grandson. *My* grandson."

Standing toe-to-toe with her, Amanda had a chance to truly study Shelley. Her skin was tanned and her short hair bleached platinum by the Arizona sun, but at fifty years old, she still had hints of the wide, blue-eyed innocence that had so captivated men decades ago. She was flushed with emotion, both anger and joy.

Amanda reached out gently. "Of course. I understand. Can we talk?"

It took a few moments before Shelley reluctantly agreed. Once they were settled in a Tim Hortons booth over coffee and doughnuts, Amanda wondered how to begin. There was so much to reveal, so much to ask. "Do you think Natalie will tell Ella now, if she goes to see her?"

Shelley shrugged. "I don't know. I don't know my sister-in-law all that well. She's older than me, and to be honest, when I was a kid, I was a bit frightened of her. She and Peter thought I was nothing but a silly little girl. And now it's been a secret so long." She paused, twirling her coffee cup. "But it was mostly Peter's secret. He was always so strong about not telling Ella, and what Peter wanted, Peter got. He could be real nasty if he was riled. But now that he's getting senile, and Natalie has to make the decisions, I don't know what she'll do. She's protective of him, but she has her own mind."

Amanda chose her words carefully as she edged toward the core of the drama. "Now that she knows Ella is Jonathan's daughter and not Sean O'Regan's —"

Shelley gasped. Her jaw dropped but no words came out.

"He's the man you thought was the father, isn't he? The man who ... forced himself on you?"

"What ...? How ...? Did you talk to him?"

Amanda processed the meaning of that simple question. Did Shelley know nothing about what had happened, or was she a clever actress? Amanda almost mentioned the body in the coulee but stopped herself. *Careful*, she cautioned herself. *Let her tell her version of the story.* "I know he was stalking you. Did he follow you and Jonathan down from Fort McMurray?"

Shelley picked up her coffee cup in two hands and took a shaky gulp. "He was sure the baby was his. I even told him it was Jonathan's, just to get rid of him. Peter tried to get rid of him too. They had a huge fight. My father ..." She faltered, and tears glistened in her blue eyes. "My father was furious. He wanted us all gone. Jonathan, Sean, and even me. Called me a Jezebel." She gave a bitter laugh. "Who uses that word these days?"

"Because you didn't know who the father was?"

"That, and because I got pregnant in the first place. Said I went up into the den of iniquity against his wishes and prostituted myself." She shook her head sadly. "I used to be his little angel. He could be the kindest man if you were good. The Bible's idea of good. But by this time he wasn't all there, you know? Peter was running the show. He persuaded Dad I'd been corrupted by the big, bad world and deserved a second chance."

"What about Jonathan and Sean?"

"Dad hated them both, no distinction. Jonathan was ten years older than me, and even Peter blamed him for my trouble. Turns out he was right after all."

Amanda sidestepped the bitterness. "I imagine Sean and Jonathan hated each other too."

"They sure did. I don't blame Jonny for that. He and Peter both tried to scare him off."

"How?"

She shrugged. "Threats? Bribery? They kept me out of it."

Amanda tried to sound casual. "Where were Jonathan and Sean staying? In town?"

Shelley frowned at her as if startled by the question.

"I found an old homestead shack up on the range not too far from your farm," Amanda explained. "I'm told people stayed there sometimes in the old days."

Shelley flushed and dropped her gaze. "I'm not a Jezebel, you know. All I was was a fool, a young woman in love, and I didn't care that he was ten years older."

"You went to meet him out at the shack?"

She nodded. "But not like you're thinking. We were trying to figure things out between us. Jonathan was upset about the baby. He pretended he didn't mind — that it might not be his, I mean — but I know it bothered him. And I couldn't forget what Sean did to me. I still loved Jonathan, but all I could think of was that bastard. His hands all over me, his ..."

"Did you have anyone to talk to? Natalie, maybe?"

"I hardly knew Natalie. And she would have told Peter."

"What happened in the end? To Sean? To you and Jonathan?"

"Sean just up and left one day, and I never heard from him again. And Jonathan sent me that money, to ... you know." She took a deep breath. "I always figured Peter handled it all. I don't know how. One day Peter came home and said Jonathan was gone."

"Shelley ..." Amanda began, "I don't know what this means, but no one has heard from either Sean or Jonathan for thirty years. I've reported Jonathan missing, and Sean's family has too."

Shelley stared at her, her blue eyes huge with dawning horror. "But that doesn't mean anything. Maybe they just moved on."

"And about the time they disappeared, that old homestead barn burned down."

"It was old. Barns burn all the time."

"There's more." Amanda took a deep breath. "Recently, a body was discovered in the coulee near that old homestead. Police have not yet identified it, but we've had DNA testing, and it's not Jonathan. They're testing Sean O'Regan's family now."

Shelley had turned white. Amanda took out her phone and searched it for Todd's photo of the belt buckle. "Do you recognize this? Does it mean anything to you?"

Shelley held the phone in shaking hands. She stared at it a long time. "Where did this come from?"

"A belt buckle was found with the body."

Her chin quivered. "It looks like the kind they sold at this western outfitter shop in Fort Mac. I forget the name of the place, but you could get your name engraved under the derrick." She traced her finger over the banner at the bottom. "In here. Lots of oil patch workers bought them."

"Did Sean have one?"

She nodded. "So did Jonathan." She handed back the phone. "Oh god, if it's not Jonathan's DNA, does that mean he's still alive?"

"Possibly." Seeing the shimmer of hope in Shelley's eyes, she pressed on. "We don't know that. I just know one man is dead and another has disappeared. And Peter seems to be the only one who knows."

Shelley rested her head in her hands as if it were too heavy for her to hold up. She sucked deep gulps of air into her lungs. "Peter. Oh Peter."

"What are you thinking? That Peter did it?"

Shelley sat in silence, her face hidden as she struggled to pull her thoughts together. Finally, she wagged her head in disbelief. "It was a terrible time. There were so many fights in the house between Natalie and Peter, between Peter and our dad. Natalie would get upset because Peter was always off somewhere, wheeling and dealing, and she was stuck taking care of Dad. Dad was hard to handle. He thought he was running the farm; he thought he could still do the chores. He'd wander off and start the combine in the middle of the night, or go herd the cows on his ATV that he wasn't supposed to drive. And I was no help. I'd go off for hours, trying to get the awful memories out of my head." She looked up at Amanda, her chin quivering. "I brought this upon them. Is it any wonder, with all of that, somebody cracked?"

CHAPTER TWENTY-EIGHT

Todd parked his truck directly in front of her apartment and scampered around to open the door. He held her hand as if she were a fragile bird as he helped her down.

"I'm not broken," Livia said, pulling her hand away. "I'm just concussed. I would've driven myself home if the doctors had let me." She paused to give him a sheepish smile. "Sorry. Irritability goes with the territory. Thanks for driving me. I couldn't stand Mom and Dad for one more moment!"

"I'm glad to help." He flushed, looking for a flippant answer. "Besides, I had an ulterior motive, you know."

She wavered down the walk. Instinctively, he reached out to steady her, but stopped himself. "I know," she said. "Maybe we can help each other."

"I can be your eyes, if you tell me what to look for."

"You can be my wheels. I'll look for myself."

"Livia, you know what the doctor said. Your brain needs a rest."

She laughed, but he could see pain on her pinched features. "My brain never rests."

"Okay, but this is probably enough for your first day. Can we at least dial it back until tomorrow?"

She leaned against the doorframe to catch her breath. "Deal. Pick me up at eight o'clock."

"Where are we going? The homestead shack?"

"Nope. The abandoned Oaks farm."

When he'd brought her phone to the hospital, he had hoped she would share what she'd learned before the attack, but she'd remained maddeningly vague. He knew she'd checked out the homestead shack and spoken to some of the nearby farmers. But what could she possibly learn from the abandoned Oaks farm?

"The Oakses hold the key," she said when they were en route the next morning. "It was near their old homestead shack that the body was found, and Shelley Oaks is ground zero of the mystery. I was just starting to look into their history when I was attacked. Someone must have been watching me. Maybe the same dude with the white truck."

He was silent. He had not mentioned the white truck also following Amanda. Her brain did not need the added worry. Instead, he shifted the focus. "But the place might not even be there any more. I looked it up. The Oakses sold it decades ago. Right after the barn fire, actually."

"Oh, it's there. Just left to fall down because the new owners were too lazy to demolish it. I'm hoping the Oakses left a bit of history behind."

The gravel range road cut through a patchwork of irrigated grain fields and open grassland scattered with cattle. Todd's ancient truck rattled over the rough surface, and Livia propped her head in her hand, trying to hide her pain. Several times he was on the brink of turning back. Concussions were nothing to mess with.

He was relieved when she pointed to a cluster of buildings taking shape on the horizon. As they drew closer, he studied the wooden buildings that had withstood the relentless elements for nearly a century.

"I love photographing these old relics," he said. "It's like capturing time. This looks like it was once a ready-made. They must have towed it here."

She raised her head from her hand to squint at him. "Towed it?"

"Happened all the time. Lumber was scarce, so when a farm foreclosed or the farmer gave up and moved on, someone else towed his house over to their place. Why waste a perfectly good house?"

When they turned into the long dirt lane, he was mildly curious to see traces of multiple tire tracks etched in the dust. Had the cops been here as part of their investigation of the body in the coulee?

They bumped through the ruts and pulled in next to the main building. Livia clambered stiffly down and paused to lean on the hood of the truck. She was wearing huge dark glasses, but despite those, she kept her head bowed against the sun's glare. He let her rest while he took photos. The dusty yard was crisscrossed with tire tracks, but there was no sign of a functioning vehicle. One rusty pick-up and two tractors were encased in weeds and scrub. He walked over to take a few close-ups of them. When he turned, Livia was on the front step, pushing at the door.

"Locked," she said.

Todd picked his way through the weeds to the one window that wasn't boarded up and peered through the gaping hole. The room inside was empty, its wooden floors covered with the fine sand of decades.

"Wait here," he said as he vaulted into what appeared to be the living room. The air was dense and stale, with a faint tang of mouse. His boots echoed as he crossed the floor. Beneath the sand, the wood still glistened with traces of old polish, and faded floral wallpaper graced the walls. This had once been a proud home, he thought. Not a rough shack like the one near the coulee, but a beloved family home.

"Hey!" Livia rattled the front door. "Let me in!"

Todd hit the stiff dead bolt and opened the door, letting a shaft of sunlight into the room. Turning, he froze.

Livia pushed past him. "What?"

He pointed to the floor. "Footprints. Someone's been here recently. I wonder if the cops searched this place."

She pulled off her sunglasses and squinted around the room. "Could be looters."

"After all this time? There's nothing here. I'm going to look around." He started to move and then stopped, causing her to collide with him. "Try not to walk in the prints or disturb the sand. If it's not the cops, it may be important."

He changed lenses and began to photograph the room, crouching to take photos of the clearest footprint. It had the thick, heavy tread of a hiking boot about the same size as his own. Not too many men with size 13 feet.

Afterward, he explored the kitchen, pantry, and bathroom at the back, all of which were stripped bare. The toilet and bathtub had been removed, leaving only rust and water stains, but the sink and vanity were turquoise, a popular sixties colour, and the chequered tiles were black and white. He found no further sign of the intruders, but as he started up the steep, narrow staircase, he spotted more footprints in the dust. Cobwebs wove intricate patterns through the carved railing.

He heard Livia's footsteps on the stairs behind him. "I don't think you should come up. It's steep."

"I'm not a cripple," she snapped. "There's a railing."

Nonetheless, she paused at the top of the stairs, pale and wavering. "Fucking concussion," she muttered, pushing aside his steadying hand. She leaned on the wall and peered into the first bedroom, which was small and empty, given over to sand and tiny critters. The second bedroom at the front of the house was likewise untouched. Judging by its size and the gabled windows affording a view east toward the distant river, Todd assumed it was the master bedroom.

The third bedroom gave him a surprise, however. The plywood had been knocked away from part of the window, letting sunlight into the room and revealing a glimpse of the quilted prairie fields to the south. The cobwebs had been cleared away and the floor swept. A broom was propped against the wall. In one corner were two neatly folded blankets piled on top of a pillow and a vintage suitcase. Livia was about to open it when he caught her arm.

"This is not the cops. It might be evidence."

"Of what? It's probably a squatter. A super neat squatter."

"But why? There's nothing around here for miles."

She shrugged. "Why do people squat? Because they like the freedom, or they've got no money. It could be somebody visiting the dinosaur park. Who knows?"

"That doesn't make any sense. There are campsites in the park, and lots of cheap places to stay. The person owns a vehicle, so they're not completely broke."

She frowned at him, her fuzzy brain slowly churning over. "What do you think? That this is something criminal?"

"Think about it! This was the Oaks place. Someone attacked you when you started looking into the body, and Amanda Doucette thinks she's being followed."

She eyed the suitcase. "We have to open it. There could be a big story here."

"Fine. But let's do it carefully, and I'll take photos of everything that we do."

They knelt on the floor, and she reached for the snaps of the suitcase. "No fingerprints!" he cried and pulled a crumpled tissue from his pocket. She rolled her eyes and accepted it between two fingers. The snaps opened with ease, old but not rusty. Inside was a neatly folded stack of clothes — shirts, sweater, jeans, boots, and underwear — along with some food. A bottle of whisky, chocolate bars, potato chips, and a bottle of olives. Todd photographed each item as Livia unpacked it.

"Men's clothing." She stroked the tooled leather cowboy boots. "Nice."

He held up the boot, which appeared to be the same size as the footprints but not the same tread. The sweater was likewise large. They inspected the pieces, but although the clothes were all good-quality brands, there were no names or clues to the owner. There was no wallet, receipts, or personal papers in the pockets.

But at the bottom of the case, coiled in a circle, lay a hand-tooled leather belt, broken, blackened, and brittle with age. He picked it up.

Livia leaned over to finger the brittle edge. "This looks burned."

When Todd turned it over, he couldn't suppress a gasp. The oval buckle was so black and corroded that he was barely able to make out the details, but in the centre was an antique oil derrick, and engraved below it, too scratched and stained to decipher, was a name.

At sunset on their last day, the group gathered around the campfire at Writing-on-Stone Provincial Park, sharing their favourite moments and greatest discoveries of the tour. The flames crackled, and in the background, the Milk River gurgled as it meandered past the beach. A strong breeze was blowing down the river valley, and even in the shelter of the cottonwoods, the chill of the September evening crept in. The students pulled up their hoodies and clustered around the fire.

They laughed, sang, and talked about the world that had opened up ahead of them. For some, college and scientific research, for others creative arts and journalism, for still others the thrill of ranching and rodeo shows. Friendships had been cemented, and Kari and Michel were now inseparable. Kari was still committed to law, but Michel had expanded his future dreams to include documentary filmmaking.

Amanda was glad she'd been able to set aside all her personal drama to focus on the rest of the tour. The students would fly home out of Lethbridge the next day, and that would be the time to check with Shelley and Natalie to find out what had happened since Shelley's return.

In the morning, after they had taken down the camp and packed everything onto the bus, the students used their final minutes to take group photos under the cottonwoods and selfies on top of the hoodoos. Then they piled into the bus for the climb back up the escarpment to the prairie. Amanda let Kaylee have one last ride with her new fan club while she followed alone in the Hulk.

When she came into range of a signal, her cellphone signalled an alert. To her surprise it was a missed call from Todd yesterday. He had left no message. She hesitated, her finger hovering over the call button. Curiosity nearly got the better of her, but she conceded she would have plenty of time to follow up on the body and her uncle once the students were on their way up north.

She followed the bus back onto the main highway toward Lethbridge, a journey of less than an hour and a half. Although it was another dry, cloudless, Southern Alberta day, there was finally an autumn tang in the air. In another two weeks, it might have been too cold for camping.

The Lethbridge airport was in fertile farmland south of the city. Turning west onto the airport road, she glimpsed a white truck in her side mirror. It didn't signal as it followed her across the lanes at a discreet distance. She gripped the steering wheel more tightly and tried to ignore it. When she reached the airport, it hung back and became almost indistinguishable from the other dusty, light-coloured pickups in the lot. She tried to avoid staring at it as she parked, retrieved Kaylee, and followed the students inside.

At the security gate, the final goodbyes were emotional and full of promises to stay in touch. Amanda accepted an offer to come north to Kari's village to see the beauty and cultural richness of her home. Afterward, Amanda stood watching as the students clambered onto the plane. After one last wave, she turned from the window, feeling that peculiar mix of sadness and fulfillment that always followed the end of her trips.

Only then did she remember the truck in the parking lot. She sneaked back to the front of the terminal and peered out through the glass. The truck was still there, partially visible behind an RV in the corner of the lot. She marched out in full view, gave Kaylee a quick tour of a nearby strip of grass, and then led her to the Hulk, all without a glance in the truck's direction.

She drove rapidly back toward the highway, hoping to put some distance between her and the truck before she whipped the Hulk onto a side road and spun it around to hide behind a nearby warehouse. Her heart pounded as she waited. Should she drive in front and block it? Should she drive in the other direction? *Jack White, who are you and what are you up to?*

In the end, she hid behind the warehouse as close as possible to the road and aimed her phone through her front windshield. After an apparent eternity, the truck crawled past as if it were searching for her. For two seconds, the driver was visible through the driver's side window. He turned his head, and his jaw dropped as his eyes met hers. He slammed on the accelerator and shot forward, but half a second too late. She had no time to block his exit, but at least she had got her photo.

He took off in a squeal of tires and a swirl of dust, his truck rocking as he wrestled it back onto the road. She chased him a short distance up the highway, but her skills and recklessness were no match for his. Gradually, he disappeared among the lines of traffic ahead. She pulled onto the shoulder so that she could look at the photo. Despite using the zoom on her phone, the picture was too small and blurry for her to make out any facial detail. She could see it was a clean-shaven man wearing a cowboy hat and what looked like a dark windbreaker. He looked shocked, but he could be anyone.

It was not until late that afternoon in her Calgary Airbnb that she had time to open the photo on her laptop. The first glimpse was the most powerful. Despite the blurriness, poor lighting, and partial reflection from the window glass, he looked familiar. Something in the set of the eyes and the slant of the brows. She pulled up a series of photos on the screen and flipped between them. She squinted. Was it possible? Thirty years was a long time. Yet the overall impression had not changed.

Could this be Jonathan?

CHAPTER TWENTY-NINE

Her heart was racing, her thoughts in turmoil. If it really was Jonathan, what was he doing in Alberta? Had he changed his name and become a private investigator? Or had he, as Matthew had suggested, borrowed Jack White's truck? Either way, what was he doing here? And why was he following her?

He must know who she was. Perhaps he'd kept tabs on the family and on her all her life and followed her career overseas, her highly publicized escape from Nigeria, and her charity tours back home in Canada. Perhaps it had begun as simple fondness for the little girl he'd always loved, but had become more serious when she had uncovered his connection to the Oakses and started investigating the body in the coulee.

When exactly had she first spotted the white truck following her? Was it when she visited Livia in the hospital? Had he been drawn back to Alberta by Livia's report on the body in the coulee, and had he stumbled upon Amanda's identity quite by chance?

It was possible he didn't even know who she was. Perhaps he was just trying to keep tabs on the person who was poking her nose into his long-undiscovered crime. That seemed far too big a coincidence. But if he did know who she was, why was he following her? Why not identify himself? What was his motive for hiding?

A shiver passed through her. None of the answers were benign. Quickly, she shifted her focus. She couldn't even be sure the man was Jonathan, let alone why he was following her. One step at a time. First, get a few answers about the mysterious Jack White.

"You should report your suspicion to Brinwall ASAP," Chris said. Sensible and straight-up as always. She was sitting cross-legged on the bed, the photo of the mystery man still open on her laptop. The more she stared at it, the more she doubted her own eyes.

"It's so little to go on, and Brinwall already thinks I'm a nosy nutbar."

He chuckled. "Since when has that stopped you?"

She was silent, fighting a spike of anger.

"I'm sorry, honey, I shouldn't have said that. I mean … you've always done what you believed in, even if others thought it was off the wall."

"And I was usually right."

"So why the doubts? This is an active police case. You yourself made the missing persons report. If you have information that could assist the police … Well, you know the drill."

"Brinwall has the license plate," she said. "So if he's on the ball, he already knows about Jack White."

"But not that he's really Jonathan."

"Might be. That's just a theory."

"Even so, it's an important lead. Amanda, you have to tell Brinwall."

"I don't want to make this official yet."

"You already did!"

"I know." She braced herself. "But that was before I knew Jonathan might be implicated in a man's murder and his disappearance was his own choice. I've already put the police on his trail. I don't want to make things worse for him."

"That's not your call, honey. You don't owe this man anything. He's blood, but he's done nothing to deserve your loyalty."

It must be nice to see things so black-and-white, she thought with a flash of annoyance. "Not nothing. I remember him as a loveable goof who made me laugh and played games with me when no one else did. Whatever happened out here in Alberta, whatever he did, I can't ignore that bond."

"But what about this poor family in Cape Breton? They've gone thirty years without knowing. They're waiting for answers too, and justice for their brother who will never come home."

She grasped at flimsy straws. "But even they said he was a bastard."

"He didn't deserve to die."

After she hung up, she was swept by irrational anger. She knew he was right; even if Sean O'Regan deserved to be run out of town on a rail, he didn't deserve to be burned to death. But she hated that Chris was right. Hated that she couldn't make the world go the way she wanted it to.

She flounced off the bed, leashed Kaylee, and took her for a long sunset walk along the Elbow River. Nature always soothed her. The flutter of breeze through the trees and the murmur of water slowed her heart rate and restored order to her thoughts.

She decided it was too late in the day to phone Brinwall. Tomorrow morning would be soon enough to make the official report. This brief hiatus gave her time to figure out who else might have answers. Besides Jonathan, three people might know what happened that fateful night thirty years ago: Natalie, Peter, and Shelley. Peter's knowledge was locked in his confused and fuzzy brain, and Amanda had doubts that Shelley knew all the details. She had seemed genuinely bewildered and hurt by

Jonathan's abrupt disappearance and his letter providing money for an abortion.

That left only Natalie. As Amanda strolled along the river path, watching Kaylee snuffle the grass along the edge, she considered what approach to Natalie would be most likely to yield cooperation. Natalie was in full defence mode, not just to protect her ailing husband but also to maintain the secret of her daughter's birth. She would not give up information easily.

The next morning, while she was still wrestling with the conundrum, her phone rang. It was Shelley, her voice shrill with hurt and outrage.

"I've had it! I'm done with all the lies and cover-ups! She's had days to tell Ella the truth like she promised, but she's done nothing! Worried about Peter, she says. Horsefeathers!"

"Shelley, where are you? In Calgary?"

"Just leaving it. I'm on my way back to Drumheller. I warned her and warned her if she didn't tell Ella, I would. I don't want to dump this news on Ella. It's a big deal to tell a woman her parents have been lying to her her whole life, and they aren't who she thought they were, so I wanted Natalie to be the one to break the news. Ella doesn't know me from Adam. But I have rights! She's my daughter, the only one I've ever had. Do you know how many times I've wished I never agreed to give her up? I thought Peter and Natalie would at least tell her the truth and let me have some relationship with her. But no!"

Amanda kept a sympathetic ear tuned to the tirade as she started to brew coffee, but now she wondered why Shelley had never tried to contact Ella before. Thirty years was a long time to keep such a painful secret, and Ella was no longer a vulnerable child. She was a competent young woman capable of handling the truth. What did Natalie and Peter hold over Shelley?

But she kept her thoughts to herself. Shelley was agitated enough, and Amanda had other priorities. When Shelley paused for breath, Amanda jumped in. "Does Natalie know you're on your way to Drumheller?"

There was a pause. "No. She went out and left me in charge of Peter. She thinks he's a helpless child, but he has his own little secrets. He's not as helpless as she thinks. Last time he disappeared, we found him a block from home, sitting by the river. He just needed to get back into nature. But she's so worried he's like his father that she's scared to let him out of her sight. But if she thinks I'm going to pin my big brother to the floor to stop him from escaping, she's dead wrong."

Amanda was measuring dog food into Kaylee's bowl, and the phrase nearly slipped by her. "Shelley, what little secrets?"

"What?"

"What secrets does Peter have?"

"She took away the keys to his truck, but he has a spare set. He's not so senile he's forgotten where he hid them. But all that doesn't matter. The hell with both of them. I'm on my way to see Ella, and I don't care what they do."

"Are you planning to tell Ella about her real father too?"

"Yes, of course, now that I know it's Jonathan. Ours was a beautiful love affair before that bastard ruined it all."

Amanda picked her way forward carefully. "Have you heard from Jonathan at all? I mean in the last thirty years?"

"No, but he wouldn't know how to reach me. Not after the baby was born and Peter sent me away. He would've had to go through Peter, and Peter hated him."

"What about since you've been back? Any anonymous little gifts? Flowers? Phone hang-ups?"

Silence. Amanda poured her coffee and leaned against the counter to take a sip.

Eventually, Shelley spoke. "What are you talking about?"

"I don't know. I have a feeling Jonathan may be keeping an eye on us."

"What are you *talking* about?"

Amanda shook her head sharply. Shelley sounded dangerously close to another eruption. "Never mind. I'm imagining things. I just wondered if there had been any unusual attempts at contact."

Another long silence. Amanda wished she could see her face. But when Shelley spoke, her voice was calm. Reflective. "There were a couple of phone calls while Natalie was out. I don't know who. Peter answered. I heard him talking upstairs, even though he isn't supposed to answer the phone. That's another of his little secrets."

Kaylee had wolfed down her breakfast and now stood at the front door, ready for her morning walk. "What do you want me to do, Shelley? Talk to Natalie?"

"No! I want you to meet me at Ella's. I want to tell her about Jonathan, and you're the closest I have to him."

After the shortest walk possible, Amanda piled Kaylee and herself into the Hulk for yet another trip east to Drumheller. She drove with some trepidation, unsure why Shelley wanted her there. They barely knew each other. But perhaps she just wanted a sympathetic third party to buffer the emotion of the moment.

Shelley's little Kia was already parked outside the house when she arrived, but a survey of the street revealed no other stray vehicles. Amanda eyed the silent house warily. No sparks, no screaming or slamming of doors. When she rang the doorbell, Shelley herself answered the door and gave her a broad smile.

"Ella is putting the little one down," she said, loudly enough for Ella to hear. "Come on into the kitchen, we're having coffee."

Amanda followed her into the cheerfully lit kitchen, weaving through the plastic toys and baby equipment. "What have you told her?" she whispered.

"I just got here," Shelley said, once again out loud. "I wanted her to meet an old friend."

Footsteps sounded down the hall. "Aunt Shelley is being very mysterious," Ella said gaily as she entered the kitchen, holding out her hand. "I'm sorry I was rude last time. Any friend of hers is welcome here."

She placed an emphasis on the word *friend*, as if it were loaded with other meaning. Amanda flushed but murmured only a vague thank you. Shelley turned her back and busied herself pouring three cups of coffee.

Ella kept her cheerful smile pasted on her face as the silence lengthened. "I guess we have a lot of years to catch up on."

Shelley finally turned and handed them cups with trembling hands. "Yes, we do. More than you can ever imagine." She sat down, clutching her cup as if it were a lifeline. "Now that I'm here, I don't know where to begin."

Ella's smile began to fade at the edges. Her brow furrowed. "How about why you had such a big falling-out with Mum and Dad?"

Shelley fixed her eyes on her cup and shook her head slowly. "No, it started before then. It started with a young Alberta farm girl who went up to the oil patch and met a handsome young man from Ontario. The farm girl thought they were in love but ..." She broke off, gulping air. "When she discovered she was pregnant, the young man turned tail and ran. Oldest story in the world, isn't it?"

Ella's smile had vanished. She had grown as still as a statue, her eyes locked on Shelley's face.

"The girl had a big brother. He and his wife couldn't have children. It was an answer from heaven, wasn't it? A baby in need of a good home and a couple in need of a baby." Her breathing grew ragged. She struggled to form words, but they failed her.

"What are you saying?"

Shelley stared at the table. "You know what I'm saying."

Loud hammering jolted them all from their seats. Before they could react, the front door slammed open against the wall, and Natalie burst into the kitchen, wild-eyed.

"Is he here? Is he here?"

"Mother!" Ella's voice was a whip, as if she'd poured all her shock into one word. "What's going on?"

"Your father! He's gone." Natalie swung on Shelley. "What have you done? I told you to watch him!"

Shelley was blinking rapidly, as if trying to refocus herself. She looked about to burst into tears but instead took several deep breaths. "He was home when I left. Have you checked the backyard? The neighbourhood?"

"His truck is gone!" When Shelley said nothing, her eyes narrowed. "You knew that, didn't you?"

Amanda stepped into the fray, concerned that things could get ugly. Ella looked about to burst. She didn't need to witness this venting of old bitterness. "The important thing is, where would he go? What's he been thinking about? Worrying about?"

"*You!*" Natalie shoved Shelley hard in the chest. "For god's sake, you! I've tried to hide the keys, but he always seems to get away. He's been disappearing for weeks! And now *you've* come back and stirred it all up again."

"Mother!" Ella shouted again. "Will someone tell me what the goddamn hell is going on? Now!"

Natalie blinked and looked at her daughter as if for the first time. She shook her head. "I will, but not now. Not like this." She grabbed Amanda's arm in a surprisingly strong grip and shoved both her and Shelley toward the front door. "We'll talk about this outside."

Shelley tried to shake her off, but Amanda was anxious to avoid further fighting in front of Ella. She hated leaving the poor woman in such turmoil, but she had more immediate worries on her mind. She didn't know how all the disparate pieces fit together, but the emerging picture was ominous. Jonathan was back, and Peter was on the loose.

Once they were outside, Amanda suggested they sit in the Hulk to talk in private. In case fists flew, she put Natalie in the front and Shelley in the back. As a precaution, she drove around the corner and parked out of sight of the house.

Twisting around, Natalie glared at her sister-in-law. "What did you tell her?"

"I just got started. But enough that she suspects."

"*Goddamn!* Don't you realize this will kill Peter? This will send him right off the rails?"

"Peter! *Peter!* I don't give a damn about Peter, Natalie. He made his own bed! Now it's my turn for justice!"

"Justice for who? He did what he thought was right. Ella has had a wonderful life, and you're going to blow all that up, hurt her, and ruin your brother's last years, for your justice?"

Amanda laid a hand on Natalie's arm. "There will be time for all this later, but for now, let's focus on finding him and getting him home safe. Think where he'd go."

"What about the river park?" Shelley said. "Where we found him last time."

"I checked that. Nothing!" Natalie whipped her head back and forth. "It's happening all over again. Just like his father! His father used to wander off, living in the past, still doing the things he used to do. But Peter will get lost. He'll suddenly look around and not know where he is, or where he lives, or ..." She glowered and shook off Amanda's hand. "What are you even doing here anyway? This has nothing to do with you!"

"Actually, it does," Amanda said quietly. "There may be something else at play. I believe Jonathan may have come back."

"*What?*" both Shelley and Natalie shrieked. Natalie's panic shot off the scale. "Where? How?"

"I can't be sure, but I think he's been following me. And he may have been in touch with Peter."

"What makes you think that?" Natalie asked.

"Because Peter got some phone calls. Shelley heard him talking to someone."

That news seemed to jolt Natalie out of her shock. She frowned. "No, that doesn't make sense."

"Why not?"

"Because those calls were from —" Natalie broke off. "Never mind. Shelley, you should have told me."

"I didn't know who it was. The important thing is what do we do now?"

As reluctant as Amanda was to take the next step, she had put it off long enough. "I think we should call the police and report Peter missing."

"I agree," Shelley said. "Let them deal with it."

"No!" Natalie's voice rose. "No police. We'll find him. We must find him before ..." She faltered. "Before he finds Jonathan."

A chill crept through Amanda. "Why?"

"Because ... because he'll be no match for Jonathan."

"You think Jonathan would *hurt* him?"

"No. No." Natalie shrugged. "I just don't know what Jonathan is up to, and I'm afraid of what might happen. Peter's not in his right mind."

The chill crept further. Was she suggesting Peter would hurt Jonathan? "Where would Peter be likely to go?"

"Anywhere. Someplace familiar, maybe? Someplace he knew the way to?"

"The homestead shack!" Shelley exclaimed. "He used to love that old barn."

"No, it burned down," Natalie said.

Shelley frowned. "But would he remember that?"

"I'm sure he would. He was —" Natalie stopped abruptly.

Shelley stared at her, her eyes widening. "He was there that night, wasn't he? Of course he was. You told me he'd gone looking for Dad. You said they came back early in the morning, filthy and exhausted. You knew!" Horror drove her back. "You knew about Sean O'Regan!"

"Knew what?"

"You knew he died in that fire! All these years you've let his body rot in the coulee. Why? To protect Peter? To —"

Natalie was clutching her head. "I don't know anything, Shelley! He said there'd been an accident! They tried to put out the fire, but with all the hay and the straw stuffing, it was too late. I didn't know anything about Sean. Or a body."

Amanda had her suspicions that Natalie knew more than she was admitting, but she doubted that she'd get anything more out of her, at least for now. Natalie's sole goal seemed to be to shield her husband.

"Let's put that aside for now. The most important thing is finding them. If we aren't going to call the police, we need a plan. I'd like to check out the shack."

"I'm going with you," Shelley said.

It was getting claustrophobic in the car with three agitated woman all fighting their own fears. "We should split up. Natalie, you should go back to Calgary. Check out the house in case he's returned, and then check the neighbourhood."

Natalie whipped her head back and forth. "He was coming out here. I know it! He was freaked out about Ella. About Shelley."

"Then tell Ella to call us if he shows up here. But you know him better than anyone. You know his friends, the restaurants and places he liked to go. Even his favourite drives."

Natalie straightened as if an idea had struck her. She was already halfway out the door as she spoke. "You're right. But if you learn anything, let me know."

Amanda watched her scurry back to her own car, leaving relief and silence in her wake. Shelley sighed and shook her head. "What a mess. And it's all my fault. Again."

"No, it's not. All you wanted was to see your daughter and grandchildren. Let's concentrate on finding Peter, a man with dementia who could get himself seriously hurt."

"I know you said we should split up, but I'd like to see the shack too. I haven't been there since before the fire. Too many memories."

CHAPTER THIRTY

Shelley stood on the trampled ground where the barn had once been and gazed out over the browning grassland. They had checked out the homestead shack, and there was no trace of Peter or Jonathan, but Shelley seemed reluctant to leave.

"The last time I saw Jonathan, it was here."

"Do you want to talk about it?"

Shelley didn't move. She seemed to be fascinated by a group of laconic Herefords grazing in the distance. The afternoon sun blazed overhead, baking the ground, and she squinted against it. "Jonathan and I had been trying to work things out. About the baby, I mean, and about the assault. Then Sean showed up at the farmhouse. He'd followed me from Fort Mac. Peter and my father kicked him off the farm, but he kept turning up places, like he was following me."

"Stalking you?"

She pulled her wide-brimmed hat lower over her eyes and nodded. "He'd show up on the street or in a restaurant where I was eating with Jonathan or Peter. He kept saying the baby was his, so he had rights. I told him it wasn't his, but he wouldn't believe me. He said ..." She faltered and dropped her gaze. "I was like a bitch in heat, ready to go, and I'd been begging for it. It was awful. He scared me. Peter was furious. Jonathan was furious. Everyone was on my case."

"Did Sean and Jonathan fight?" Amanda pointed to the shack. "Here, I mean."

"I don't know. I don't know what happened. I'd gone to stay with a girlfriend in Drumheller to hide from Sean, and honestly from Peter and Dad too. I was fed up with them blaming me. My dad called me a whore, and Peter called me a fool. Why didn't I just keep my legs shut, he said." Her chin trembled and she shook her head sharply. "Imagine. Why didn't I just keep my legs shut?"

"You couldn't have stopped him. And you were only nineteen."

She raised her gaze to the distant cattle once again, as if their stillness were a balm. She seemed oblivious to the heat and the dust whipping across the prairie. Even Kaylee had given up rummaging for sticks and had collapsed in the shade of the shack, her tongue lolling.

Reluctant to break the spell, Amanda waited.

"Sean was staying in Drumheller, and Jonathan was staying in the barn here. I went to see him. Jonathan, I mean. It was a day like today, I remember. September tenth. Hot, dry, the grassland parched. Big, beautiful, blue sky. I wanted us to talk. I loved Jonathan, and I thought he loved me. He said he did. He said the assault didn't matter and the baby didn't matter, but I know it did. I could see it in his eyes. That doubt, that ... disgust. He couldn't look at me. He couldn't touch me. And finally, when he tried, I felt that animal's hands on me, and I couldn't ..." Despite the heat, she shuddered. "I pushed him away. I didn't mean to, it just happened. He was hurt. He asked if I'd pushed Sean away that way, or if Sean was better than him. Physically, he meant. What a thing to say. I got on my horse and took off. That's the last time I saw him. That little action, that one push ... and it all unravelled."

"That wasn't your fault. Your reaction was normal. You'd been raped."

Shelley flinched at the word, and Amanda cursed her own clumsiness. She knew from her Nigerian ordeal that the terror and horror of trauma were never far away. She looked for a way to redirect her. "Do you know anything about the fire? About what happened here?"

"I didn't know about the fire until two weeks later. Peter came around to my girlfriend's house. He told me both men were gone and Jonathan had sent me this letter. Money for ..." — she quivered and forced the word out — "for an abortion. Peter said I was well rid of him. Any man who would kill an innocent baby had no place in our family. He was right. But I was so hurt and confused. I went to check the barn for myself, to see if Jonathan had left me anything inside, like a private note. But the barn was gone. There was nothing left, not even a few pieces of wood. It was Natalie who told me it burned down in the drought."

Shelley finally turned away from the cattle to look at her. Her eyes were heavy with sadness and resignation. "That letter did me in. It was the final straw. It took me years to get over it. My world was black. I hated everything. Me, Jonathan, Sean, even ..." She faltered. "Even the baby at first. When Peter and Natalie offered to adopt her, I didn't hesitate. Natalie and I moved to Calgary for the pregnancy, and soon Peter sold the farm and joined us."

She shook her head and wet her lips. "It was an awful time. Natalie was a tyrant. She hardly let me out of the house. It was to stop the gossip and nosy neighbours, she said, but now I know it was so she could claim the baby was hers. I was beyond caring. I hated that baby inside me. It was a demon seed that despicable man had placed inside me violently, frighteningly, and it grew and grew. It took away everything that I was. I didn't want it. I was convinced it was a boy and it would look just like Sean, with his bent nose and his big, slimy lips. There was a point when I would even have had the abortion if Peter had let me."

She broke off, as if she'd heard herself, and shot Amanda a sharp look. "Don't ever tell Ella that. She was an innocent child who, no thanks to me, has become a lovely young woman. I gave her to Peter willingly and took his money to move far, far away. To start a new life. To erase this awful past. It took me a long time and three failed marriages to men I hoped would replace the memories before I wanted to see her. My marriages had given me no other children, God's punishment, I believed." She shook her head angrily. "What torment we women do to ourselves. I finally decided I wanted to see my child, to share in her life, even if just as an aunt, but Peter and Natalie wouldn't let me see her. They said I'd sold her fair and square. I wasn't even on the birth certificate." She shrugged. "Home birth and money under the table fixed all that. They erased my existence from Ella's life, and I was too ashamed of what I'd done to fight. How could I ever face Ella and admit I'd sold her?"

Amanda felt a crushing sorrow for Shelley's unfair fate. She wanted to hug her but knew the touch might be unwelcome. "But once you learned Jonathan was the father, you decided to fight."

Shelley nodded. "It actually started with the Me Too movement. All those women coming forward with stories just like mine, talking about the blame and guilt they'd felt and how many years it took to find the courage to speak up. It was like a huge black cloud began to lift off me. I'd been the victim here, and yet I'd paid the price. Then when you called to say Ella looked like your family, I realized I'd made a terrible mistake. No one can change that. No one is going to pay the way they should. My father is dead. Sean O'Regan is probably dead. Peter is a shell wandering around lost in the past, just like our father."

She waved her hand to gesture vaguely across the prairie, and that gesture seemed to bring her back. "Where is he? Is he meeting Jonathan? Would he even know where he was going?"

Amanda checked her phone to see if there was any message from Natalie and instead saw that she had missed another call from Todd. She'd forgotten all about his earlier call. This time he'd left a message: *Amanda, Livia and I have found something important at the old Oaks farm. Call me!*

He came on the line before the second ring, loud and breathless, breaking the spell of the prairie past that had gripped her and Shelley. "Something weird is going on. Livia and I went out to the old Oaks place a couple of days ago. Her idea. Just a day out of the hospital, and she's hot on this story. Anyway, it's still standing, and someone's been staying there."

Amanda remembered the tracks she'd seen in the yard. She sucked in her breath. "Who?"

"I don't know. A big dude from the looks of it. The place is empty. No furniture, no supplies. Judging from the dust, empty for years. But there are footprints all over. And in one of the small bedrooms upstairs, there's a suitcase of clothes and some bedding on the floor."

That's it! Amanda stared out across the prairie, where far in the distance beyond sight, the farmhouse sat. A place from Peter's past. Of course he would go there! Why had no one thought of it? "Todd, you're a genius! I've got to go."

"Wait! There's more. In the suitcase I found an old broken leather belt with a buckle just like the one at the bone site. Oil derrick and all. There's a name engraved at the bottom. I know we have to report this to the police, even though Livia doesn't want to, so I cleaned it just enough to read the name —"

Amanda's mind was racing. That made no sense! "Peter?"

"No. Jonathan."

———

Amanda and Shelley were racing across the prairie, leaving a plume of dust from the gravel road in their wake. Kaylee perched on the console between them, sensing their excitement.

"We should have thought of your old farm," Amanda said.

"I didn't even know it was still standing. The new owner said he'd tear it down."

"I knew it was still there," Amanda said. She dodged a large rock on the road, and the Hulk slithered on the loose gravel. "But I don't know why Jonathan would stay there. I don't get why he'd be back here at all." She fought the dread rising in her stomach. "I wonder if we should call the police."

Shelley was clinging to the overhead strap. She glanced across at her in alarm. "Why?"

"I've got a bad feeling. Something happened thirty years ago. One man died and another man disappeared for thirty years." *And took on a false identity*, she thought but didn't say. "Now he's back and in contact with the only person besides himself who knows what happened. And that person has dementia. He's weakened, bewildered, and ..." Amanda took a deep breath, stopping short of her last thought.

"I can't picture Peter as a weak man. Our father, even in his dementia at the end, was a powerful man. Not just physically, but in his opinions. If anything, he became even fiercer."

Amanda thought about the Peter she'd met. Uncertain, even paranoid, lurking behind curtains. "What do they want with each other? And also, why would Jonathan have his broken old belt with him after all this time?"

"He loved that belt. He wore it all the time. Ontario wasn't a popular place to be from, and he said that belt made him feel like a real Albertan. That and his cowboy boots. But lots of guys up in Fort Mac had that belt, because it was from a local western outfitter and you could personalize it."

"I still don't get why he hung on to it."

"Maybe because I gave it to him on our two-month anniversary," Shelley said, almost shyly. Pink tinged her cheeks.

Amanda smiled, touched. "Sean had the same belt. Did you give —"

Shelley's sweetness vanished. "No! My Lord, no. He bought it himself, after I gave Jonathan one. Pure jealousy. He told everyone I gave it to him."

The road was straight and clear. Shelley's tone dripped with contempt, so Amanda risked a glance at her. Her gaze was fixed straight ahead. "Did he tell Jonathan that?"

"He sure did. Anything to rub it in."

Amanda was silent. It was one more small piece of evidence tipping the scales against Jonathan. Sean had provoked him, not just by bragging about how much Shelley had wanted him, but also by showing off the gift she had given him. The same gift she had given Jonathan. Amanda wondered whether Shelley was drawing the same conclusion.

A stop sign loomed ahead. Amanda stopped at the crossroads. "Which way?"

Shelley pointed to the right. Amanda turned onto the wider, paved highway and hit the accelerator. The beauty of the prairie roads was that they were straight and flat. Unlike in Eastern Canada, where you couldn't see around the next bend or spruce tree, you could see trouble, and cops, from miles away. She watched the needle climb as the Hulk responded.

"Should we call the police?" she ventured.

"I don't know what we'd say," Shelley said. "We don't even know if they're there."

"Call Natalie then. Ask her what she thinks."

"She won't want the police."

"I know. She's been coy all along. But I think she knows way more about what happened that day than she's admitted, and she knows Peter's current state of mind."

Shelley took out her phone and dialed, leaving Amanda to focus on the road. The prairie whipped by. Hydro lines, golden fields, cattle clustered around sloughs. After almost a minute, voicemail kicked in and Shelley left a curt message.

Amanda looked at her speedometer: 130 km/h. Already way too fast. "Call her cell."

Shelley dialed again and listened. When voicemail came on, she glanced across at Amanda with new alarm. "Still no answer. She's never without her cellphone because of Peter, especially now that he's missing."

"She knows where he is," Amanda said. "She probably realized it the moment I asked about familiar places he might go. And she obviously wants to find him before we do. She's covering up to the very end. The question is what is she covering up?" She puzzled over the fragments of fact that floated disconnected through her mind. How did they fit together? Natalie, Jonathan, Peter. The fire, the death and burial of Sean O'Regan, the stolen whisky bottle and the attack on Livia Cole.

She caught her breath as those two fragments snagged. The whisky bottle had stayed untouched for thirty years and had only disappeared after the attack on Livia Cole and the inquiries she'd made about the farm fire a couple of weeks ago.

Livia's recollection of the attack was fuzzy, little more than a couple of vague impressions. First, that the attacker was already in the apartment when she walked in, and secondly, that the attacker had seemed small. Not likely Peter, who was well over six feet. But Natalie and Jonathan were both smaller. Either one of them would have been desperate to find out what Livia knew.

Her thoughts had just begun down that ugly path when Shelley broke the silence. "That's good, I suppose. She'll stop anything bad that Peter might get up to."

"She doesn't know Jonathan's staying there. He's the wild card in all this. Nobody knows what he's up to."

Shelley shrugged. "She's a smart woman, my sister-in-law. Always has been the brains in that marriage. She managed their investments and foundations for years before his dementia got real obvious. Now she sits on all the boards he used to. Don't underestimate her. She was raised a country girl, tough as any man beneath those manicured nails." There was a bitter edge to Shelley's voice. For a moment it looked as if she'd slipped deep into the past.

But the country reference brought another chilling thought to Amanda's mind. "Do either she or Peter have a gun?"

Shelley's eyes widened. "They used to, for sure. We all did. Peter's had hunting rifles and shotguns all his life — every farmer has — and Natalie loved target shooting. She used to compete at the fairs. They probably still have those guns somewhere."

"Damn. I really think we should call Constable Brinwall."

"They wouldn't use them, Amanda. We were all raised to be responsible around firearms."

In the distance, a cluster of darker shadows emerged from the dust haze on the horizon and slowly evolved into buildings and scrub. As they drew closer, details of the weathered buildings and corrals took shape, and still closer, the glint of vehicles in the front yard. A white truck and a dusty black truck, but no red Audi.

One less complication to worry about, Amanda thought as she turned in the long lane. Her eyes scoured the scene, which looked deceptively serene. No people scurrying about, no shouts or slamming doors. No gunshots. She relaxed her grip on the wheel.

Beside her, Kaylee shot to her feet, her nose quivering. Shelley gasped. Pointed. By the corner of the main house, a smudge of grey drifted into the air. A lick of orange. "It's on fire!" Shelley cried. "Call 911!"

Shelley grabbed her phone while Amanda stamped on the accelerator and rocketed up the lane. By the time they skidded to a stop beside the trucks, flames were shooting up one side of the house. Kaylee barked with alarm. Both women jumped out and raced toward the house. The fire leaped and snapped as the old wooden siding caught.

From inside the house, a mighty howl. "Die! You die!"

The heat was a wall that seared Amanda's lungs and took her breath away. She staggered back. "Around the other side!" she shouted as she raced around the house to the windows on the other side. The front door gaped open, and inside, silhouetted against orange and black, a figure staggered as it tried to reach the stairway. "Die!"

"Peter!" Shelley shrieked from behind her.

Amanda's lungs were on fire, and she pulled her jacket over her head. Shelley pushed past her to go inside, and Amanda grabbed her belt. "You can't go in there!" she screamed over the thunder of the flames.

Shelley leaned in the doorway. "Peter! Peter! It's Shelley. Please come out."

Peter turned toward the sound, a blackened, swaying form clutching a bottle. Fury and panic distorted his face. He turned to look up the stairs and took a step toward them. Jonathan was upstairs, Amanda realized in a flash of brutal clarity. Seconds away from death, unless she did something.

Her rage cut into Shelley's wailing. "Peter!" she shouted. "Come out. He's dead. It's over!"

Peter turned back, wavered a half step toward them, and collapsed on the floor in a fit of coughing. Time slowed. In the chaos of the roaring flames and swirling smoke, Amanda heard staccato gunfire, screaming, the guttural grunts of the dying. The wail of children cut short by a single stroke.

She froze.

A hand on her shoulder, someone shoving past her, screaming. "Amanda, help me!"

In the smoke, Shelley was grappling with her brother's arms and trying to drag him toward the door. "Help me! Goddamn, help me!"

Amanda looked at the stairs. Over the din, she heard hammering and pounding. Jonathan was up there, with mere seconds to live. Even as she watched, flames poured up the open stairs, cutting off all access.

Yet Shelley was struggling to help the man who had taken her child, deprived her of motherhood, and now, in his helpless dementia, had probably killed the father of that child. Through the staccato crack of imagined guns and the wail of villagers, the screaming filled Amanda's ears.

Not this time. Never again.

She plunged inside, grabbed Peter's legs, and together they hauled the unconscious man out the door and across the yard to safety.

As Amanda sank into the grass, coughing and gasping, she caught sight of a red Audi parked out of sight of the house behind a shed. Standing beside it, with one hand on the hood of the car, was a willowy figure in jeans and red leather jacket. Their eyes met. While Amanda's confused brain was still trying to make sense of that, Natalie sprang to life. Shouting in panic, she rushed across the yard and flung herself down at her prostrate husband's side.

"Where the hell were you?" Amanda demanded.

Natalie was flushed in the orange-tinged light. "I just … I just got here."

Amanda started to say, "Bullshit, you hid your car and you were watching —" but a loud crack cut her off. Plywood from an upstairs window splintered and flew across the yard. An instant later, a figure shrouded in a blanket hurtled out the window and landed in the flaming grass below. It erupted into screams.

Amanda rushed over, sensing Shelley close on her heels. Together they dragged the body clear of the fire and rolled it over and over in the dirt to douse the flames. Amanda yanked off her jacket and wrapped it around the man's head.

In the distance, blue and red lights flashed up the road, and bursts of a siren rose above the roar of the fire. In a few minutes, the yard would be filled with firefighters and paramedics who would take charge, beating back the terror of memory and the panic of near death.

Amanda drew a cautious breath of the hot, smoky air. She carefully unwrapped her jacket to look at the man she had tried to save. His face was scrunched tight with pain, his eyes were streaming, and his dark curls, now shot through with grey, were crisp with soot. But somewhere in there she could still see the mischief maker her five-year-old self remembered.

"Hello, Uncle Jonny."

CHAPTER THIRTY-ONE

When Amanda opened her eyes, the pale, subdued light of a hospital room was the first thing she saw. Then the tall vase of red and yellow gladioli on her bedside table, and finally the slumped figure of Matthew dozing in the chair by the bed. His eyes opened as she reached toward the flowers.

"From Chris?" she murmured, more a croak than a voice. She swallowed past the desert-dry needles in her throat.

He scowled. "From me."

She smiled and reached to touch his hand, noticing with surprise that her left arm was swathed in bandages and trailing an IV. "Where am I?"

"Calgary Foothills Hospital."

She flexed her legs, raised her other hand, similarly bandaged, and peered under the sheet. "Am I ... all here?"

"You are. Some second-degree burns to your hands and arms." He tried to smile, but she could see the strain in his hollow eyes. "You got those trying to play hero. As usual."

She struggled to sit upright as the memories washed in. "What about the others? Shelley? Jonathan?"

"Shelley was treated at the scene. Smoke inhalation and minor burns. But she wanted to go with Natalie so they released her. Jonathan is down the hall."

She sank back. "So he's alive?"

"Broken arm and leg, some serious burns, but he was incredibly lucky you put the fire out so fast."

She felt a rush of relief, yet through it, a tug of uneasiness. She tried to wade through the fog of painkillers. Something Matthew had said. Or not said. "And Peter?"

His gaze slid away, and he reached over to rearrange the flowers. "Red and yellow, the colours of passion. That's so you."

"And Peter?"

"Peter wasn't so lucky." He shook his head. "I'm sorry."

She remembered the chaos of smoke and flame, the searing heat and Shelley's screams. She took deep breaths to fight back the hovering threat of panic at the memory of the screams. "We did try to save him, Shelley and I."

He squeezed her shoulder. "I know. There will be an autopsy, of course, but it was probably the smoke. He was an older man, in weakened health."

Amanda forced herself to push past her fear and recall the details of that frantic moment. Peter shouting *Die, die!* Heading not toward the door but back upstairs toward Jonathan, despite the wall of flame in his path. Not understanding, or perhaps not caring, that he was heading toward certain death. Had he been lucid enough to choose that as his final act on this earth? Or had he just wanted to kill Jonathan at all costs?

And on the sidelines, a shadowy figure.

"Natalie! She was there too."

"Yes, so Shelley said. Shelley's been calling every half hour for updates and driving the staff crazy until they put her on to me. She's gone with Natalie to break the news of Peter's death to the daughter."

Amanda winced as she imagined the turmoil of that scene. Natalie frantic, Shelley exhausted, and Ella's neatly ordered, suburban world blown apart in a single day. "Shelley tried so hard to save Peter, despite all he'd done to her, whereas Natalie … I don't know what she was doing there. It seemed when Peter was dying, she didn't try to help at all."

"Some people just freeze."

"Her car was out of sight. *She* was out of sight, watching."

He frowned at her. "What are you saying?"

"I don't know what I'm saying. Maybe that it was a relief for her? That now the ordeal of his dementia is over?"

"That's a pretty strong accusation to make, Amanda. You're saying she's glad he's dead?"

"Possibly. At least part of her? He wasn't going to get any better. She could only watch him slip away, bit by bit losing the man he once had been. And if he himself chose that end …"

"He was her husband. You don't throw all those years away so easily."

"She'd already given him most of her life. Perhaps she wanted …" She let her thought trail off. Who was she to judge?

He hauled himself to his feet, huffing. "Let's not get ahead of ourselves. The police and the arson unit will be investigating. They'll interview everyone, including Natalie, and they'll look at how the fire started. Let's see what the investigation concludes before you dream up reckless and groundless suspicions about the poor woman who just lost her husband."

She sank back into the pillows, feeling chastened and trying to rally her thoughts. She felt as if her brain were ploughing through sludge. "What day is it?"

"Tuesday morning." He touched her arm gingerly. "They brought you in last night."

"What the hell did they knock me out with?"

"Just stuff for the pain and to help you sleep, which is what you need. Your burns are going to hurt like hell."

Her eyes flew open. "Kaylee!"

"Shelley and Natalie have her. They said they'll take care of her until you're discharged, probably later today, provided you can get your dressings changed as an outpatient. But —" He nodded to her bandaged hands. "You'll need to stay with someone. No driving, not much of anything for a couple of weeks. So you can have my bedroom, and I'll sleep on the couch."

She reached out to touch his arm. "Thank you. First I have to get Kaylee. And I have to call my parents and my aunt. They should be told about Jonathan."

He paused. "I called last night. I think your aunt is planning to fly out."

"Not my mother?"

He shrugged.

"Chris?"

"I called him too."

"Of course you did. Matthew the Fixer. What would I do without you?"

He was saved from the maudlin moment by a commotion in the hall. An instant later, the door flew open and Natalie burst in. The woman had just lost her husband and she was dishevelled and distraught, but she was carrying an enormous bouquet of white roses. She flitted about the room, looking for the best place to put the vase down before setting it on the windowsill with an exaggerated flourish. It was on the tip of Amanda's tongue to say *Thank you, sorry for your loss*, when Natalie finally turned to her.

"I-I don't know what to say, Amanda. Thank you? You tried. You couldn't save him, but I like to think he knew you and Shelley tried." She picked up the vase and moved it to join the gladioli. "The police will be coming to talk to you. Because of the death ..." she faltered, "there will be an investigation. The grass was tinder-dry, and the walls were nothing but kindling.

It would take very little to ignite. In the prairie we see this kind of thing all the time."

"Why did you hide your car, Natalie?"

Natalie was fussing with stems. Her hands stopped in midair. "Hide it?"

"Yes. I saw it behind the shed."

"Oh. I ... I ..." Her fingers returned to work with the flowers. "When I arrived, I saw Peter was there. I didn't want him to see me. I wanted to know what he was up to first."

"What did you think he was up to?"

She eyed the bouquet and pursed her lips in dissatisfaction. "You have to understand. Peter had to be handled with kid gloves. Anything could set him off, and he was a strong man, not easy to contain. I knew someone else was there, so I wanted to assess the situation first."

"Did you know it was Jonathan?"

"That was my fear. I didn't know what either man would do."

"Why would Jonathan harm Peter?"

Natalie raised her thin shoulders in a weary shrug. "Why did he come back? What was he after? I'm afraid he's very angry at us."

"Because you kept his baby? Or because you took her away from Shelley?"

From the corner of her eye, she saw Matthew shift in discomfort. She tried to rein in the anger welling up. Natalie picked up the vase and gave a weak laugh. "I guess these are way too extravagant for this tiny room."

"Did you know Peter was going to kill him?"

Natalie nearly dropped the vase. "No! God, no!"

"But you were okay with it, weren't you? If Jonathan died, that would solve a huge complication for you."

Matthew leaned forward, about to head her off, but she shot him a glare. Her uncle had nearly died — *she* had nearly died — and it deserved an explanation. The moment's respite was enough for Natalie to parry with some outrage.

"Amanda, I know you've had a shock. We all have. But I've lost my husband —"

"I saw you standing there when we brought Peter outside. Not helping. Not trying to save him."

"I was in shock! I froze."

"Okay."

"Haven't you ever frozen? Nothing works. Not your brain, not your legs."

Amanda wondered if the outrage was contrived. It was obvious Peter was a source of constant worry and distress for her. But she would get no closer to the truth by a frontal assault.

"Yes, I have," she said and meant it. "I'm sorry. You have a lot to contend with now. Your daughter, your sister-in-law, the police investigation. If I can help in any way …"

"You know how you can help? I'll tell you how. You can tell the police it was an accident. And then you can go back east and take your uncle with you. Let Shelley, Ella, and me put our lives back together." She plunked the vase back on the windowsill and swung on Amanda. Her eyes burned. "And you can say I looked in shock."

That small request, tossed off as if in afterthought, was all Amanda needed. She was certain that, in that split second, Natalie had chosen to let Peter die. But had she gone even further? Amanda clearly remembered Peter shouting *Die, die!* as he headed for the staircase. Peter had wanted Jonathan dead, but had he set the fire? Or had he been helped by someone else who wanted both him and Jonathan out of the way? The sequence of events was complicated for someone with Peter's level of dementia; he had to drive to the farm, locate Jonathan, bring the accelerant to start the fire, and then spread it around. The fire had caught on quickly. One moment it was smouldering in a corner, and barely two minutes later the whole place was engulfed. Even with tinder-dry wood, that required some help.

Was there an invisible master puppeteer behind the scenes?

Natalie was staring at her with grim determination. More than determination. A steely resolve that sent a chill through Amanda's bones.

I don't have to solve this, she told herself. She would tell the police what she'd seen and heard and leave the theorizing out of it. Let the police draw their own conclusions and muster the supporting evidence. Natalie was a well-respected, well-connected philanthropist who had led an exemplary life, even while burdened with a private tragedy. How far would the police push her?

Probably not far at all.

"I'll just tell them what I saw and heard, Natalie. What they conclude is up to them."

She didn't add that it didn't stop with her anyway. There was still Jonathan's testimony to contend with.

After her discharge, Amanda and Matthew found Jonathan in a private isolation room on the third floor in the Calgary Firefighter's Burn Unit. She fought a sense of dread as they put on gowns and masks before entering the warm, humid room. The figure on the bed was barely recognizable. Much of his body was beneath a tented sheet, his head was swathed in dressings, and tubes snaked to various machines and IV poles.

He was snoring softly, drool trickling down his slackened jaw. Amanda studied the parts of him that were visible. A paunchy, middle-aged man who looked beaten down by life, not the mischievous man-child she remembered.

"Do you know what name he was admitted under?" she whispered to Matthew.

"Jack White," Matthew muttered. "He seems to have all the proper ID under that name."

"I wonder if he really is a PI."

"From what I can tell, yeah. I checked out the reviews and testimonials on the security listings website. He does small-town stuff, stays under the radar."

"No wonder," she said. "He probably figured he could stay under the radar, until I filed a missing persons report. And they found the body, of course."

Jonathan stirred in his sleep and moaned as if in pain. His eyes flickered open, and he blinked groggily at the ceiling before Amanda moved into his line of vision. He focussed on her and gave a crooked smile.

"Hello, Squeak."

It was a nickname she hadn't heard in thirty years, a nickname only Jonny used because her mother considered it an insult. Squeak, short for pipsqueak in reference to Amanda's size. Her mother was sure Amanda was destined for greater things.

"Hello, Uncle Jonny."

"Do I look as beaten up as you do?"

"Worse." Words clogged in her throat. "How are you? Are you up to talking?"

"They say most of this is a precaution," he said. His voice was full of gravel but gained strength as he talked. "To prevent infection and bigger complications. They're optimistic I avoided the worst thanks to your help."

"Do you remember what happened?"

"Most of it. Not much after I went flying out the window. Definitely a Hail Mary move, but I didn't have much choice."

"Why were you staying there in the first place?"

"I wasn't. Peter wanted to meet me there. Said he had something to show me."

"What?"

"My old belt buckle from Fort Mac, which I lost in the —"
He broke off as if realizing he'd gone too far.

"In the barn fire? I'm told the belt was broken and scorched."
His face remained closed. "I don't remember much."

She bent closer urgently. "Jonathan, the police are going to
want to talk to you. They know your real identity, and they know
about Sean O'Regan and the body in the coulee."

"What do they know?"

"What do *you* know?"

He looked away. "It doesn't matter. Peter is the only other
person who knows, and since he has dementia, his evidence
won't be reliable."

Her heart sank. "Did you kill Sean O'Regan?"

"Do you want me to answer that?"

"Yes, I do. I don't care about the police. We never had this
conversation. But I need to know."

His gaze returned to her face. His eyes drooped, and he
looked impossibly weary, like a man who'd been carrying a bur-
den for a long time. "Peter said I did. I don't remember. I was
staying in the barn, and I remember us arguing. O'Regan came
to taunt me. Rub it in about his relationship with Shelley —"

"His rape."

"He didn't call it that. He said she liked it rough, even
begged for it. I lost my temper and started throwing punches.
One of them connected with his head, and he went down like
a stone. Then the fire started. I don't remember how. Suddenly
the walls were on fire and the straw flooring caught. I must
have passed out. The last I remember was choking, coughing,
someone screaming *Die.*" He shuddered. "Jesus, last night it
happened all over again."

"Who shouted *Die*?"

"I don't know. The next thing I remember, I was lying on the grass and Peter was shaking me. The air was full of smoke, but I could see the full moon overhead. The fire was mostly out, just smoke and smouldering coals, and Peter said Sean was dead — that I'd killed him — and if I wanted to save my skin, we had to bury him. That's what we did, later that night, and then he told me the price of his silence." Jonathan's voice weakened, and he shut his eyes briefly. Amanda knew she should let him rest, but she had to know. After a moment, Jonathan picked up the thread. "Give up Shelley, give up the baby, and disappear from their lives forever."

"And you believed him? It sounds like an accident to me."

"Peter said I set the fire with a bottle of whisky and nearly killed myself in the process. I think he kept that belt — and the whisky bottle — all these years to prove I was the one there."

The penny dropped. "The Alberta Premium? Was it you who took it from the shack?"

He nodded. "I saw it there when I went out to check the place a couple of weeks ago, and I figured …"

It was one small link that tied him to the tragedy, Amanda thought. She wondered whose prints would have been on it. "So you just … disappeared. Never told your sisters, never told me."

His chin trembled. "I wasn't much of a prize to them anyway. They made that clear. Was it worth it to drag the family name through the mud? And you? Squeak, I always hoped if you remembered me at all, it would be as that uncle who gave you piggybacks. Not as a killer growing old in prison."

His arguments had a certain logic. Maybe in his own way, he'd given himself a life sentence. "Is that why you sent Shelley the letter? To drive her away for good?"

"What letter?"

"The one with the abortion money. That was unbelievably cruel, Jonathan."

His jaw dropped. "I never sent her a letter. That was the deal — never contact her again."

Amanda frowned. "You're sure?"

"Of course I'm sure. I know how much she was against abortion. We talked about it, and she was determined to have the baby, even if it was Sean's."

Amanda's mind raced as she absorbed the implications. "Then someone who really wanted you to disappear sent it. It couldn't have been Sean. Peter? Natalie?"

"Their beliefs were all anti-abortion. Strongly."

"But that was the point. The point was to turn Shelley against you, and it worked! She gave up the baby to them."

He was silent as his weary mind grappled with the enormity of that act. "Just after I got to B.C., Peter sent me a letter telling me Shelley hated me and not to break her heart by contacting her. He enclosed two thousand dollars. 'To help you start over,' he said. There would be more if I kept my word."

"Did you know they adopted the baby?"

He nodded. "I kept track of them, just like I kept track of you and your mother and Jean. It's amazing the tricks you learn as a PI. It looked like everyone's life was going great without me, so after a while I got used to it. I built a decent new life as a PI."

"Then why did you come back? Why were you following me?"

"The body in the coulee. When they discovered it, I had to find out if they'd identify it, and if they'd connect it to me. My new ID is good, but it won't hold up to a serious police investigation. And once you made that missing persons report, I thought, wow, the cops will be coming at me from both directions."

"Did you break into that reporter's apartment?"

His head drooped in shame. "I didn't mean to hurt her. She came home in the middle, and I shoved her trying to escape. Man, I felt bad. I'll be paying for that."

"It was you phoning her parents to ask how she was?"

He nodded. "After Sean, I made a vow never, ever to lose my temper or hurt anyone again. It's been a lot to live with." His head lolled weakly, and he shut his eyes.

Amanda stood up, knowing she should leave. She stared down at the weary figure. Soon the police would be arriving. They might already know his identity, and thanks to Aunt Jean's DNA, it would be easy enough to confirm. He'd be facing quite a slew of charges, but she needed to give him a fighting chance against the worst. Sean O'Regan.

"You only have Peter's word that you killed Sean."

He opened his eyes. Said nothing.

"He lied to you about the letter."

"But ... why?" He whispered. "I mean, Peter could be ruthless, but to make me believe ...?"

"It was perfect leverage to get you out of town."

He shook his head. "Peter's been very good to me all these years. He sent me money when times were lean. It's hard to believe he'd lie about that."

"Unless he set the fire."

Jonathan grew still. He stared into space as if searching for answers in his distant memories. He wet his dry lips. "Last night, when Peter was shouting *Die*, it reminded me. I heard the same thing during the barn fire. I heard screaming. Mine, Sean's, and another voice. *Die, die!* Something about evil. That's all I remember. But later, when Peter and I were dragging Sean's body toward the coulee, I heard pounding from inside the shack. I asked Peter, and he said my ears must be damaged from the fire. He said there was no one there. But there was. Holy fuck! His father! Peter locked his father in the shack."

CHAPTER THIRTY-TWO

"I have to talk to Natalie again," Amanda said. They had left Jonathan wrestling with emotion and exhaustion and promised they'd be back. On the way to the car, her phone chirped in her purse, and her hopes surged. Matthew balanced the flower vases on the car and dug her phone out.

"Chris?"

Matthew read the text. "Your mother. At the Calgary Airport with Jean."

Fuck, she thought, draping herself over the hood as pain and disappointment washed over her. Chris hadn't phoned, he hadn't sent flowers. She knew he hated her reckless side. Was he so angry about her plunging headlong into danger again that he was freezing her out? "Just what I need."

He shot her a disapproving look. "She's your mother, Amanda. And Jonathan's sister."

"You're right. Does she say what their plans are?"

He shook his head. "Do you think she wants us to pick them up?"

"Probably not." She leaned against the car. "I'm done in."

"It might be a nice gesture if I went. This whole thing must be a shock for her too."

"You don't know my mother." She pictured the scene: her mother striding off the plane with her efficient carry-on in tow, knowing exactly where she was going and how she would get there. Thank heavens Aunt Jean would be with her.

"Tell them to come out to Maeve's. I just want to pick up Kaylee and talk to Natalie first. I want to know how much she knows about all this."

Matthew looked up from texting a reply. "Does it matter? It's one colossal fuck-up, but let the police get to the bottom of it. Peter is dead. His father is dead."

"It matters if she knew her father-in-law set that fire in his demented state, thinking he was eradicating evil. When she was freaking out about Peter, she said a few times that it was happening all over again. Did she mean that her husband was losing his mind like his father, or did she mean he was obsessed enough to kill? And going one step further, did she set him on that path?"

He rolled his eyes as he guided her gingerly into his car. "Not that again. You'll never get her to admit that. And if you want any kind of relationship with your newly discovered cousin, you might want to let it go."

Amanda scowled. "And give in to yet another form of blackmail from that family?"

"Amanda, before you do anything, you need to rest. I'm taking you to Maeve's."

She knew he was right. She could hardly think, let alone mount an effective argument. Right now she just wanted to snuggle up with the soothing warmth of her beloved dog and sleep for a hundred years. "Okay. Let the chips fall where they will for now. But that family owes my uncle big-time."

Matthew had climbed into the driver's seat. He nodded out the window. "And maybe that repayment is about to happen."

She followed his gaze across the parking lot to see Shelley locking the door of her little Kia and heading toward the hospital. She struggled to open her window and called out. Shelley detoured toward them. She too was singed and bandaged, but she had a smile on her face.

"I'm glad to see you're out. Will you be staying in town for a few days?"

"I'm staying at Maeve's B&B near Drumheller, so I won't be far. We've got lots to catch up on, but I don't want to be in the way." She nodded toward the hospital. "I've just had a long, long talk with Jonathan, and he's worn out, but he has a lot to tell you. Make sure he tells you everything."

Shelley looked alarmed. "It's all good," Amanda added hastily. "Well, mostly good for you two anyway. Come see me at Maeve's when you can, and bring Ella."

Even before they turned into Maeve's laneway, Amanda spotted a familiar black Ford Explorer parked in the corner. Kaylee began to bounce around and wag her tail.

"What the hell?" Amanda muttered. "That's the Hulk. How did it get here?"

She had left it at the site of the fire and had not given it a single thought since. She assumed either Shelley or Ella had moved it when they picked up Kaylee. She glanced at Matthew, who was grinning broadly as he parked his car.

"Did you …?" Her question trailed off as Maeve's door opened and a tall, gangly figure stepped out. A rush of joy took her voice away. "Oh," was all she managed before he had her out of the car and into his arms.

Maeve hustled her into their old room, where Chris had already opened up his duffel bag, and fussed over her to make sure she had everything she needed. "My best steaks tonight if you're up to it," she said. "And a bottle of decent Okanagan red from my cellar." She winked. "Don't tell anyone. Can you manage that?"

"The wine any time," Amanda said. "And the steak if someone cuts it up for me." She held up her bandaged hands. "I can handle a spoon. Maybe a fork."

"Which is why I picked up the Hulk at the police lot," Chris said. "I'll be driving us back to Regina."

"What did you do? Wheedle more time out of Sergeant Tight Ass?"

"All in the line of duty," he said. "Well, mostly. I volunteered to pick up some sensitive evidence in Regina and bring it back to Corner Brook. I just asked for a small detour out here to get you." He grinned. "You know, I think Sergeant Tight Ass is actually beginning to like you, or at least admire you. Your exploits liven up the cop shop on the long, boring nights. Everyone wants to meet you."

She pulled back from his arms and eyed him balefully. "I'm the talk of the station?"

"Not from me! At least not only from me. You're in the news all the time, and believe me, in Deer Lake that makes you a celebrity."

She sobered as she sank down on the bed. Maeve had left to prepare dinner, and Chris was now unpacking her suitcase. Over time, she'd grown used to the sporadic media attention, but she hadn't realized that her attempts to save two men from a fire had generated national headlines. Again. She just wanted to retreat, to heal her wounds, regroup, and be plain Amanda. She was not Superwoman.

As if he sensed her discomfort, he came to sit beside her and carefully put his arm around her. "I know how scary this was for you. I know what fire does to you. That's why I came. You were so brave. Maybe you don't ask to be, but you can't help it. I finally get that. I can't stop myself from wishing you wouldn't charge into burning buildings, but I get why you do. I get that it's who you are."

Tears rose in her eyes, the first genuine emotion she'd allowed herself to feel since the fire. Tears for her own fear, tears for Jonathan's rescue and for Peter's death. She couldn't speak. She could only nestle in the warmth of his arms.

"I want you to come back to Newfoundland with me," he said. "My house won't be ready for a few weeks, but in the meantime we can rent a little cabin." He pressed his lips to her ear. "I don't want to let you out of my sight ever again."

She got through half a glass of Maeve's wine and most of her steak before crushing fatigue overtook her. Chris volunteered to take Kaylee for a walk, and by the time he returned, she was fast asleep.

Despite the pain pills, her sleep was restless, plagued once more by nightmares of violence and flames. When she awoke the next morning, sunlight was streaming in the window, and the bed next to her was empty. She hurt all over. She peered at her phone: 9:26 a.m. No wonder! Kaylee too was gone. She clambered stiffly out of bed and, after staring helplessly at her pill bottle, she picked it up and went into the main room. She found Maeve sitting at her huge harvest table, nursing a cup of coffee and reading the *Drumheller Mail*. As always, the radio news murmured crop prices and water restrictions in the background, ignored.

"Can you open this and get me one?" Amanda asked.

Maeve opened the bottle and poured a glass of water. "Sore?"

Amanda nodded. "Everything is screaming."

"It's always worst the third day."

"I have to go to the hospital in Drumheller to change the dressing, so I'll get Chris to take me. Where is he?"

"Out taking your wild child for a walk." She chuckled. "Matthew's having some breakfast out on the back terrace. Do you want me to make you some?"

Amanda shook her head. "Just coffee for now, thanks. I'll go out to join him."

Matthew was hunched over a platter of scrambled eggs and toast, and he looked up with a big grin. She eased into a chair, wincing as every nerve in her limbs complained. Maeve brought her a coffee, and she eyed it with longing, unsure whether she could pick up the cup. Finally, two-handed, she managed.

A whirlwind of red caught her eye as Kaylee rushed up to her, her tail wagging, and entwined herself through Amanda's legs. Amanda looked up to see Chris strolling across the field toward them. He raised his hand in silent greeting, but he was deep in conversation on his phone. Just before he reached them, he signed off and slipped the phone in his pocket.

After checking on her and pouring some coffee, he sat down and studied her. "Are you ready for some news?"

"Good or bad?"

His lips twitched. "Not good or bad. Just news."

"Spill it, Corporal."

"Constable Brinwall just phoned me."

"Really? You two best buddies now?"

"Well, I called him first, to find out what they knew about the fire. I left him a message reminding him that since you could have died in it and if not for your quick action, Jonathan would have died, I thought you were entitled to know what they'd found out."

"Wow! And he returned your call?"

"He did. He was almost cooperative. I guess the press have been hounding him because of you. The CBC even sent a crew to the scene."

"And? What did he tell you?"

"The investigation is still ongoing —"

"Yeah, yeah, yeah."

"And the information is preliminary —"

She waved her hand impatiently, prompting him to laugh. "But it appears the fire was deliberately set. There were at least four points of origin around the outside of the building. Several empty bottles of whisky and rum were found near the sites, as well as a barbeque lighter." He chuckled. "Not the greatest arson plan. The booze was high-quality — a waste of good Alberta Premium Dark Horse and J.P. Wiser — but booze is usually not high enough alcohol to get a good fire going. Thanks to the powerful lighter and the dry grass, it did the job."

"Just as it did in the barn fire," Amanda said excitedly. "It was dry then too."

"Possibly. The fire wiped out the entire compound plus quite a lot of the field before they got it under control. The old Oaks farm is no more."

"Do they know who set the fire?"

"The crime scene guys have been able to lift a couple of usable prints off the bottles." When he paused, she held her breath. "Peter's. Only Peter's. Nothing else. Not even some unknown partials. They also got prints from the house, and the Medical Examiner managed to lift some decent quality prints from his fingers."

Amanda sat back. "So, not Natalie."

He shook his head. "Peter set that fire. The bottles were from his extensive cellar. The cops said he had been quite a whisky connoisseur."

"There are easier ways to set a fire than to bring a case of expensive booze from home. Surely he knew that."

"In his right mind, yeah. But it looks like he was following his father."

Amanda reluctantly relinquished her theory. She had been angry with Natalie for her part in their treatment of Shelley and Jonathan years ago. Natalie had wanted a baby and had shoved aside the rights and feelings of innocent people to get it.

Had she known that Peter's father had indeed set the barn fire, and had she remained silent while Jonathan took the blame for Sean O'Regan's death? Or had she merely suspected but hadn't wanted to know? Peter was not only a physically intimidating man, but he was also her ticket to a life of wealth and family. Wilful blindness was a powerful tool.

"Brinwall will be coming out here later today to take a full statement from you," Chris said.

Matthew shot her a sharp look. "No wacky theories."

She balanced her coffee cup in her two hands, took a long sip, and gazed into the distance at the golden wheat fields playing in the sun. "I'll behave."

Constable Brinwall had just left when Aunt Jean texted to say they were on their way. They had stayed the night in a hotel near the Calgary Airport and had set off in a rental car early in the morning for the drive down. Maeve had already aired out the last two rooms, including a closet-like space up in the gables. Amanda smiled as she watched her shove more sheets into the wash.

"I wish I could help. I'm sorry you're having to use so much water. I bet you never expected such a full house when you're technically closed for the season."

Maeve dumped some soap into the ancient tub. "This is the most excitement I've had in years, my dear."

A car door slammed, and Kaylee barked. "That was fast," Amanda said as she headed outside. She hadn't seen either her mother or her aunt in almost a year and wondered if either of them had slowed down.

A white SUV was parked in the laneway, and Ella was leaning into the back seat to check on her baby. Shelley was walking toward the door, laden with bags.

"Sorry we didn't phone, but your mother asked us to meet them here. We brought food for a barbeque." She set down the bags and to Amanda's surprise enveloped her in a cautious hug. "I know we're both kind of sore, but ..."

Ella returned to the driver's seat. "He's asleep, so I'm going to park in the shade and leave him there. Believe me, we'll all be happier."

They were soon settled in lounge chairs on the front patio, with cold beers at their sides and a bowl of potato chips in the centre. Amanda studied Ella. She was smiling bravely, but redness around her eyes hinted at an emotional night. Amanda wondered how much Shelley had told her.

"Ella, I'm sorry about Peter. Your father, I mean."

Ella's eyes shimmered. "I don't even know how to make sense of it all."

Shelley reached out to touch her but drew back, as if recognizing that she was part of the confusion. "It will take time, sugar."

"I haven't told the girls anything. I don't even know how to explain. I wish Scott was here. I'm going to wait until he's back."

"I can be Aunt Shelley for as long as you need. I'm just happy to be in your life. Jonathan feels the same."

"Have you met Jonathan yet?" Amanda asked Ella.

Ella shook her head. "I will. I will. He has a lot to deal with."

"The cops were there," Shelley explained. "And his sisters. And a constant parade of doctors. There will be time when he's ready."

"I thought I'd start with you and my ... my aunts," Ella said. "Everyone has a lot of ground to catch up on."

Amanda winced. Her mother and Aunt Jean were not the warmest, most welcoming place to start. Ella had just lost her father and learned not only that she was not who she thought she was, but instead that her whole identity was based on betrayal and lies, perpetrated by the very people she loved.

Shelley acted as if she understood that shock, but Amanda wasn't sure Jean or her mother would.

And she wasn't sure she herself had the strength to play middleman.

She had little time to worry, however, before she spotted a small blue sedan crawling up the street as if the driver were searching for an address. The car stopped at the lane, and Amanda's mother peered out the passenger window. Recognizing the crowd, she waved, and Jean steered in behind the line of cars.

As always, Aunt Jean looked as if she'd just strode off the Yorkshire dales. She wore corduroy pants, a lightweight beige jacket with half a dozen pockets, and a sturdy Tilley hat that hid most of her short-cropped, iron-grey hair. Her face had a few more lines, but her eyes were as blue and watchful as ever. She stopped in front of Amanda, put her hands on her shoulders, and smiled.

"Don't ever stop getting into trouble, girl. You make the world spin on its axis."

Amanda laughed. She wanted to hug her, but that wasn't done. "You too, Aunt Jean," she said and turned to her mother. To her surprise, Susan looked far more rattled. Her silver hair, normally a perfectly tailored bob, was lank and dishevelled, and her blue eyes were bloodshot. She was dressed in black pants, a brown shirt, and a blue sweater. Nothing matched.

"Hi, Mum," Amanda said softly.

"I disagree with Jean," her mother said, turning away to preclude any chance of a hug. "I think the world has had quite enough of spinning for now. As have you."

Amanda knew that was her mother's oblique way of expressing concern, but it irked her nonetheless. Always the veil of criticism. She felt Chris's gentle squeeze on her shoulder, and she leaned into him. "Mum, Aunt Jean, let me introduce you to everyone."

THE ANCIENT DEAD

Both women knew how to be gracious, fortunately, and soon more chairs were brought to the circle and more beer produced. Amanda discreetly sent Chris to find some wine. Aunt Jean and her mother were not Big Rock people.

Once the greetings and pleasantries had been dealt with, Amanda addressed the elephant in the room. "Have you been to see Jonathan?"

"We have," said Aunt Jean. "He's seen better days. but the doctors assure us most of the burns should heal without too much scarring."

"He'll need some surgeries," her mother said, "and there may be some nerve damage to his hands and feet, but considering it all, he's extraordinarily lucky."

"It was odd," Aunt Jean said. "It felt like meeting a stranger, but then I guess we've all changed. I'm sure the old Jonny is in there somewhere."

"He's tired," Amanda said. "He's been through a lot, and don't forget, for years he's been looking over his shoulder, believing he killed a man. He'll need time to heal in more ways than one."

Her mother picked up her wine and studied the colour critically. "We wanted him to come east with us. There's plenty of room in the house and perfectly good specialists at the Ottawa Hospital for all his needs. But it seems he's got some legal issues to sort out here."

Amanda looked at her in dismay. "I hope not Sean O'Regan's death."

Her mother shook her head. "The police took his statement, but I got the impression that even if O'Regan's identity is confirmed by DNA, there's not enough evidence after all this time to make a credible case. No, this relates to his more recent shenanigans. False identity, break and enter, assault." Her lips pursed. "Good old Jonny."

"Susan …" Aunt Jean ventured.

Amanda's mother held up her hands. "I apologize. Suffice it to say, he'll be tied up for a while when he's better. And after that …" She glanced at Shelley, who was preoccupied with her beer. "It seems he wants to stay out west."

"He has a whole family to get to know here," Amanda interjected before her mother could compound her disapproval. "A daughter, grandchildren … They have a lot of living to catch up on."

"But I'm sure he'll want you to come visit," Shelley said. "I'm going to be buying a little house in Drumheller, so there will be lots of extra rooms."

"A great idea!" Ella chimed in. "Will your husband be coming too?"

Shelley flushed. She gave a faint shake of her head. "We've known for a while that it was over. I just didn't know how to come home."

Ella blinked. "We can have a big family reunion once everyone is better. Maybe at Christmas!"

There were general mutterings of agreement until Amanda's mother said, "Oh. Well. We don't actually do —"

"I think that's an excellent idea!" Aunt Jean said.

"Perfect." Shelley rubbed her hands together. "Let's plan on it."

Amanda glanced at Chris in dismay, but he too was smiling. For Chris, the more the merrier. She ventured to mention the other elephant in the room. "Natalie too?"

The words fell like a stone. Shelley glanced questioningly at Ella.

"I don't know," Ella said. "I feel …"

"I suppose the girls do think of her as their nana," Shelley said. "But it's up to you."

"No, it's not. Not just me. What she did to you and Jonathan, it's … It's beyond …"

"We don't have to decide now," Aunt Jean said briskly. "It can all wait until the dust settles."

As if on cue, the baby woke with a lusty scream, and with relief everyone turned their attention to dinner preparation. It wasn't until late that evening, when everyone else had left or gone to bed, that Amanda had a chance to corner Chris alone. She was nearly comatose, the combination of beer and painkillers being an unwise one, and she slumped wearily into his arms.

"I'm sorry this has screwed up our plans."

"What plans?"

"Christmas. We were going to go to your parents' for a big Ukrainian family feast."

"No worries."

"But won't they be disappointed?" She nestled deeper into his arms. "This feels so weird. One moment I had no real family celebrations, and now I'm drowning in them. How are we going to juggle them?"

He kissed the top of her head and chuckled. "Luckily, Ukrainian Christmas is celebrated on January seventh. I guess I forgot to mention that."

Amanda woke to the soft murmur of voices outside her window. Chris was quietly but firmly saying she was not to be disturbed. She stumbled to the open window and peered out. Soft morning sunlight washed over the fields, and Todd was standing at the edge of the patio, holding a file folder.

He'd cut his hair, she noticed when she got outside, and he seemed to stand taller. Chris went in search of coffee for them while she eased herself into her favourite lounge chair with a view of the far-off horizon.

"I'm sorry," Todd said after the initial greetings. "If I hadn't told you about the farmhouse, you would never have gone there, and you wouldn't have got hurt."

"And I wouldn't have saved Jonathan, so thank you."

He acknowledged that with a bleak nod. "I won't stay long. I just wanted to tell you, Livia Cole is hell-bent on exposing this whole story. She's going to try to weasel as much information as she can out of people — you, Shelley, Ella, Natalie, and Jonathan — so be prepared to be hounded."

"We're pretty good at keeping secrets," Amanda replied with a grin.

"She's a good kid, I like her, but she's a kid. She doesn't know yet that life can hurt. But she can only concentrate for an hour or two at a time right now, so it will be slow going. That gives you time to figure out what to tell her." He fingered the file folder in his lap. "I'm not going to write your story. This has reminded me why I rejected journalism. I don't like invading people's lives. I like photographs. They tell stories without words. They capture emotions, thoughts, moments in time, but leave much more to mystery."

He handed her the file folder. "I brought you a few photos to show you what I mean. This is what my book will be about."

Inside was a glossy eight by ten of the prairie, painted in blurs of green, ochre, and rust. She could almost feel the heat radiating off the ground. She leafed through the others. Barbed wire clinging to a crooked fence post, stark words etched on the homestead wall, a single grey shaft of bone in the sand. All exquisitely evocative. He was right; she could think of no words.

"They're stunning," she said, handing the file back.

"They're yours to keep. If you want."

"Thank you. I'm really looking forward to your book."

"We may never know for sure who the dead man was," he said. "We may never know his whole story. I'm glad it's not Jonathan, but it was once someone's Jonathan. That's how I've decided to tell the story. I'm the one who started this whole process. I found the bone. But it's just one of millions of undiscovered bones out there, claimed by the ruthless wilderness of the Alberta prairie. Many more Jonathans: settlers, explorers, First Nations, buffalo, deer, all the way back seventy million years to the dinosaurs. I'm going to let that bone be the stories of all those ancient dead. It could be a Blackfoot warrior, a frozen settler, a murdered wife, or just a wanderer who lost his way. Victims of the badlands. Of cruel fate, or random misfortune, or a fatal misstep." He smiled, caught up in his poetry, as if he were writing the book even now. He gave a self-conscious laugh. "Or even justice meted out by the gods."

She didn't laugh but instead gazed out toward infinity, where land blurred with sky. Thinking of the demented man who'd thought himself an instrument of God.

"Justice meted out by the gods," she said. "I like that."

ACKNOWLEDGEMENTS

One of the joys of writing this series is meeting new people and getting to know other parts of this vast, varied, beautiful land of Canada. While researching the Alberta badlands, I read many books, visited all the venues Amanda would visit, and picked the brains of my Alberta friends and family. Many of them shared their homes and their knowledge about various topics, from Indigenous issues to farming, ranching, irrigation, and settlement. I would like to thank my Calgary writer friends Randy McCharles and Val King, my cousin Deborah Gregorash for her hospitality and wisdom on our trip to Writing-on-Stone Provincial Park, her friend Theresa Mavis Kearney in Milk River, who shared her home and her Indigenous insights, and Flo Robinson, who shared not only her wonderful Victorian B&B in Linden, but also her own experiences as a Citizen on Patrol captain in rural Alberta. My friend Rick Mofina also provided valuable background.

I also had knowledgeable guides, such as David Lloyd, who answered my many odd questions on the various tours I took in Dinosaur, Midlands, and Writing-on-Stone Provincial Parks. A special thanks to Conway Vidal of Willow Creek Adventures, who took me on a beautiful trail ride through the remote coulees of the badlands, despite the frigid, snowy weather, and cheerfully volunteered information on the vegetation, weather patterns, and potential hiding places for bodies.

I am indebted as always to the people who volunteered to read and critique the manuscript along the way, including my cousin Deb and my long-time friends from the Ladies Killing Circle: Mary Jane Maffini, Sue Pike, and Linda Wiken. As always, a big thank you to my editor, Allister Thompson, for his support, tactful suggestions, and eagle eye; to Laura Boyle of Dundurn Press for designing yet another stunning cover; and to Scott Fraser and all the staff at Dundurn Press for their continued support of my work and the work of all Canadian writers.

MYSTERY AND CRIME FICTION
FROM DUNDURN PRESS

Victor Lessard Thrillers
by Martin Michaud
(QUEBEC THRILLER, POLICE
PROCEDURAL)
Never Forget
Without Blood

The Day She Died
by S.M. Freedman
(DOMESTIC THRILLER, PSYCHOLOGICAL)

Amanda Doucette Mysteries
by Barbara Fradkin
(FEMALE SLEUTH, WILDERNESS)
Fire in the Stars
The Trickster's Lullaby
Prisoners of Hope
The Ancient Dead

The Candace Starr Series
by C.S. O'Cinneide
(NOIR, HITWOMAN, DARK HUMOUR)
The Starr Sting Scale
Starr Sign

Stonechild & Rouleau Mysteries
by Brenda Chapman
(INDIGENOUS SLEUTH, KINGSTON,
POLICE PROCEDURAL)
Cold Mourning
Butterfly Kills
Tumbled Graves
Shallow End
Bleeding Darkness
Turning Secrets
Closing Time

Tell Me My Name
by Erin Ruddy
(DOMESTIC THRILLER, DARK SECRETS)

The Walking Shadows
by Brenden Carlson
(ALTERNATE HISTORY, ROBOTS)
Night Call
Coming soon: *Midnight*

Creature X Mysteries
by J.J. Dupuis
(CRYPTOZOOLOGY, FEMALE SLEUTH)
Roanoke Ridge
Coming soon: *Lake Crescent*

Birder Murder Mysteries
by Steve Burrows
(BIRDING, BRITISH COASTAL TOWN)
A Siege of Bitterns
A Pitying of Doves
A Cast of Falcons
A Shimmer of Hummingbirds
A Tiding of Magpies
A Dance of Cranes

B.C. Blues Crime
by R.M. Greenaway
(BRITISH COLUMBIA, POLICE
PROCEDURAL)
Cold Girl
Undertow
Creep
Flights and Falls
River of Lies
Five Ways to Disappear

Jenny Willson Mysteries
by Dave Butler
(NATIONAL PARKS, ANIMAL PROTECTION)
Full Curl
No Place for Wolverines
In Rhino We Trust

Jack Palace Series
by A.G. Pasquella
(NOIR, TORONTO, MOB)
Yard Dog
Carve the Heart
Season of Smoke

The Falls Mysteries
by J.E. Barnard
(RURAL ALBERTA, FEMALE SLEUTH)
When the Flood Falls
Where the Ice Falls
Why the Rock Falls

True Patriots
by Russell Fralich
(Political Thriller, Military)

Dan Sharp Mysteries
by Jeffrey Round
(LGBTQ, Toronto)
Lake on the Mountain
Pumpkin Eater
The Jade Butterfly
After the Horses
The God Game
Shadow Puppet
Lion's Head Revisited

Max O'Brien Mysteries
by Mario Bolduc
(Political Thriller, Con Man)
The Kashmir Trap
The Roma Plot
The Tanzania Conspiracy

Cullen and Cobb Mysteries
by David A. Poulsen
(Calgary, Private Investigators,
Organized Crime)
Serpents Rising
Dead Air
Last Song Sung
None So Deadly

Jack Taggart Mysteries
by Don Easton
(Undercover Operations)
Loose Ends
Above Ground
Angel in the Full Moon
Samurai Code
Dead Ends
Birds of a Feather

Corporate Asset
The Benefactor
Art and Murder
A Delicate Matter
Subverting Justice
An Element of Risk
The Grey Zone

Border City Blues
by Michael Januska
(Prohibition-Era Windsor)
Maiden Lane
Riverside Drive
Prospect Avenue

Foreign Affairs Mysteries
by Nick Wilkshire
(Global Crime Fiction, Humour)
Escape to Havana
The Moscow Code
Remember Tokyo

Inspector Green Mysteries
by Barbara Fradkin
(Ottawa, Police Procedural)
Do or Die
Once Upon a Time
Mist Walker
Fifth Son
Honour Among Men
Dream Chasers
This Thing of Darkness
Beautiful Lie the Dead
The Whisper of Legends
None So Blind

Lies That Bind
by Penelope Williams
(Rural Ontario, Amateur Sleuth)